EXIGENCY

Michael Siemsen

FANTOME

This book is a work of fiction. Any references to historical events, real people, or real locations are used factitiously. Other names, characters, incidents, and places are the products of the author's imagination, and any resemblance to actual events, locales, or persons, living or dead, is entirely coincidental.

Editing services provided by Red Road Editing/Kristina Circelli
Front cover art by Andreas Raninger
Back cover art by Matthias de Muylder

ISBN 978-1-940757-23-0 (Trade Paperback, 2nd Ed.)
ISBN 978-1-940757-21-6 (epub)
ISBN 978-1-940757-20-9 (Kindle)

Connect with the author:
facebook.com/mcsiemsen * *michaelsiemsen.com*
twitter: @michaelsiemsen * *mail@michaelsiemsen.com*

Also by Michael Siemsen:
A Warm Place to Call Home (a demon's story)
The Many Lives of Samuel Beauchamp (a demon's story)
The Dig (Book 1 of the Matt Turner series)
The Opal (Book 2 of the Matt Turner series)
Return (Book 3 of the Matt Turner Series)

"In nature, chaos leads to order, order leads to chaos,
again and forever in this way, and at all scales,
infinite and infinitesimal."

Foster Dill Norte
UNIVERSAL, 2066

1.0

The cursor bobbed in the air before her: deep purple_ foliage. She opened her bio eye and unblurred the background in her prosthetic *fone* eye. Paragraphs of text floated with Minnie's gaze as she studied the view from her cabin's patio. Blue salvia shrubs flanked the shaded cobblestone path from the bottom of the patio stairs, all the way down to the lake. Just above the distant hillside vineyards, the sun shone at late afternoon, its rays bouncing from the lake's mellow ripples to the blossoming flowers.

Among all the pristine scenery, the salvia stood out to her. Blue flowers—*blaue Blume*—symbols of hope and beauty, of love and desire, of the infinite and unreachable. Yes, blue would work much better than purple. A smidge transcendental, but screw it. If Minnie's readers caught it, great. If they interpreted the color as arbitrary, so be it. The rest of her essay should prove explicit enough for its intended audience.

Minnie rested her head against the lounge chair back and closed both eyes. The doc re-sharpened before her, cursor still bouncing: deep purple_ foliage. She selected purple and recursed for each instance.

Behind Minnie, beyond the wide-open threshold leading into her cabin's living room, wee nails *tik-tik-tik'd* across the hardwood floor. She turned just as her pet ferret, Noodle, skittered onto the patio's decking, and leapt up onto Minnie's lap.

Noodle wriggled his pointy face into her neck and said, "Are you still working?"

Too ticklish, she pulled him back down to her legs and stroked his back. "Yeah, I have to get this essay done before group. At least the first draft."

"What's it about?"

"Context, perspective, and scale. I think it's pretty solid so far, but who knows if anyone will actually read it."

Uncharacteristic silence from Noodle. He rested his chin on his fist. Curious, Minnie glanced at the clock in her fone and waited while rubbing his ears. His anthropomorphized face conveyed deep contemplation.

He finally broke the silence. "So you're feeling *down* about that?" He nodded encouragement, brow furrowed: *This is a safe place for sharing.*

Minnie smiled and went along with it. "Well, *Doctor* … I wouldn't say *down.* Just, I don't know, more wondering than anything else, I guess. I'm supposed to produce these things bimonthly."

"And you came *here* to work," Noodle went on, a flit of his tiny paw toward the lake and mountains. "Not so *confined* as the station?"

Minnie's amusement hiccupped. What the hell was Noodle going on about? Since when did he give two licks about the station? Confined? And then she realized exactly what was happening.

She rolled him onto his back and glowered. "*Et tu,* ferret?"

"I'm sorry!" He pleaded. "I couldn't help it! It wasn't me! Some trigger … You must've said something flagged!"

"I'm going to go work in peace." She pulled up the game's main menu. "You know, what I came *here* for."

Noodle attempted a final apology as he, and the rest of the game app, dissolved before Minnie.

She opened her eyes. The lights in her quarters undimmed.

Sliding out of bed, she growl-sighed. Was nothing sacred? With all the assessments and measures in place, did the station's psych monitors really need to be invading her personal game? Hijack one of her pets? She was the *last* person on the station to consider at-risk.

Plopping down at her desk, she pulled on her headphones.

She wondered, had it been an *automated* psych probe talking through Noodle, or had John set it up? If it was automated, fine. At least it wouldn't show up on some report. More likely the case. Though she could see John sitting in his command office with nothing better to do than setup new monitors: Minerva Sotiras - monitor for signs of depression, cleithrophobia, and full-blown eye-twitch spacewack.

Poor Nood, she thought. He thinks I'm pissed at him.

Later. Noodle would have to wait. The essay was almost done, and just north of fifteen minutes remained before her weekly group session.

She grabbed the stereo lens from her desk and popped it over her bio eye. The doc opened before her, floating in the recessed nook above her desk, flanked by her preferred editing tools. Movement caught her eye and she shifted focus past a patch of text in her second paragraph. Beyond her desk window's frame, starry black space gave way to the browns, teals, and pinks of Epsilon C's dominant landmass. Within seconds, the planet eclipsed Minnie's view of open space.

"No thank you, Northern Hemisphere," she said, and blurred out everything in the doc's background.

Revision mode enabled, Minnie picked up where she'd left off back on her patio.

Where was I? Ah, right ... blue flowers.

"Edit all. Purple to blue."

She reread the passage.

> Pointing downward from low orbit, a scope provides a bird's-eye view of a gently sloped hill, its surface blanketed with deep blue foliage half-lit by a setting sun. A tranquil scene.
> The scope zooms out, revealing the blue hill is the last of its kind. The surrounding area is blackened by fire, dense smoke billows westward, and orange flames rapidly converge on the lone blue circle. A scene of destruction and potentially imminent extinction.

The scope zooms back in, beyond the bird's-eye view, to a microscopic level, exposing a deadly toxin hidden in the lovely blue flowers' pollen. Pulling out again, this time to a few miles overhead, a group of intelligent beings is revealed to the east, torches at their feet as they stand upwind, watching the last of the deadly blue flowers blow away as distant smoke. A scene of survival, of controlling one's destiny, of tragedy aversion.

Focus shifts west, to another people, dead and dying from the poisonous smoke unleashed by their enemies. A war scene.

And finally, zooming out once more, out beyond even the scope, a vast planet is seen teeming with life, two moons circling, along with a looming space station full of scientists from a distant solar system. A scene of learning—of discovery.

Scale. This is what Foster Dill Norte referred to when he coined the term scientific depth-of-field. What we now call simply dof. As a mental footnote, you may wish to commit one of my favorite FDN quotes to memory: "Context is everything, context can be nothing, scale is infinite."

Minnie saved her work, set the stereo lens on the desk, and then navigated to the playback options in her fone. She selected the Sindy voice to read it back to her. Minnie had always wished she could pull off Sindy's smooth, authoritative-yet-dispassionate tone. Instead, she thought her exhilaration always made her sound like a looner.

Minnie selected her desk speakers for playback.

Like all of the synthetic voices, Sindy's Modern English was impeccable. "It can be challenging for observers to fully see the cosms, both micro- and macro-, and so one must always predefine the *scale* of a particular research set—the focal length of the scope, the depth of the optics, the time period with hard-start and hard-end, etset. And they must always account for *themselves*, the observers. It's all too common for the researcher to exclude herself from a cosm, as if she's but an intangible set of eyes absorbing information, identifying patterns, performing measurements, recording statistics. In example two-point-seven, a hypothetical researcher attempted to pluck individual factors from the chaos and arrange them into an order that she understands. This very act marries the observer to the recorded cosm."

"Pause," Minnie said and brought the text back up on her fone. "Edit. Marries to married. Commit."

She set the cursor at the beginning of the last sentence and told Sindy to start again.

"This very act married the observer to the recorded cosm. This isn't necessarily a problem, nor should one attempt to avoid it. We must simply be *aware* of ourselves during review and later stages of research. Unlike the heavily starched foundational research papers of the past, today's scientists shouldn't strive for invisibility, papers appearing as if nature herself spewed them out: 'Here's a bunch of data about ME: Nature!' No, the observer should be represented nearly as much as the observation. Further, we mustn't spend too much time at a single scale, prioritizing macro levels, as if this would allow one to fully grasp essential context. *All* levels are equally critical to capture.

"Case in point: Pointing downward from low orbit, a scope provides a bird's-eye view of a gently sloped hill, its surface blanketed with deep blue foliage half-lit by a setting sun. A tranq-"

The Sindy voice paused dictation as a schedule reminder popped up in front of the essay text.

ALERTS: Group - 5 MIN

The alert faded to a countdown clock: 4:59, 4:58, before Minnie selected DISMISS. She saved her work, copied it to two of her lockers, and slid her feet into her slips. Walking to the hatch, she opened a new message to Aether.

MINNIE: Yay group. Let the healing begin.

She received a near-instant reply:

AETHER: See you in a few.

Minnie exited her quarters into the hall, then scaled the ladder to the main tube. Gravity released her body, and she glided down to the hygiene sub-bay. Even after eight months, there was still something about her relationship with Aether that sent her backsliding into schoolgirl giddiness. And interacting with Aether around everyone else, in a supposedly professional setting, recalled the days when the pair harbored a thrilling secret.

Everyone knew now, of course—Aether had months ago moved out of her shared quarters with John Li and into Minnie's unit—and more than one horribly uncomfortable group session had been dedicated to the relationship transition.

These conversations had been by far the most awkward of the entire mission, and not only for the three individuals directly involved, but for the rest of the crew, as well. As the current mission commander, John was in charge of the weekly group sessions. He could've recused himself, but the backup group moderator was the assistant commander: his *wife*, Aether.

Fortunately for the station's nine inhabitants, John and Aether were the most mature, reasonable, and qualified—if such a thing were possible—to handle a divorce. They'd agreed some time before launch that if anything happened between them, the break-up's initiator would move into the unused tenth personal quarters.

But to Minnie's gratification, the tenth personal quarters had been repurposed as a storage unit, and John allowed Aether to move in with Minnie. There was no third person in line for such decisions. John and Aether's divorce pretty much exemplified why the mission commander shouldn't be in a relationship with a crewmember, let alone their second-in-command. Not that they'd acquired their positions by choice. Both were elected by crew vote and each had voted for the other as mission commander during the past two elections.

"Minerva," John said as Minnie entered the common room.

"Yes?" Minnie snapped, not intending to come off rude, but he'd surprised her. When uttered by him, exasperating things tended to follow her name.

"*Welcome,*" he said, letting her know it's all he'd meant. Disappointment soured his face.

Minnie offered an apologetic smile and sat down at the round, bamboo table. She hated how she came off around him lately, and Aether knew it was an insecurity thing. She'd told Minnie numerous times how transparent Minnie was in John's presence.

"Sometimes you act like he's going to snatch me back at any second," Aether had said one night. *"As if I'd have no say in it."*

"Maybe sometimes I'm afraid you'll want to," Minnie had replied. *"That one day you'll wake up and think 'What have I done?' and run screaming back to him."*

"Maybe I will," Aether had said. *"But no time soon."* She'd grinned a clever grin.

"Oh, it's safe for me to feel settled for at least a few days?"

"Maybe even a week."

Qin brushed by Minnie and plopped into the stool next to her.

Minnie elbowed him. "Sup, Chinstrap?"

His eyes bulged, staring at, yet not through, the dark, panoramic window across the room. "Hang on … this guy's almost dead…"

Minnie waved a hand in front of him. "Does this mess you up? Am I messing you up? Watch out!"

Flustered, Qin swatted her arm away, shut his eyes, and scooted to the edge of his seat. "Aw, what? Come on! I … Oh, how you suck, Minnie."

She grinned, wide-eyed. "No way, did you die? Did I really gank it? *Tell* me I got you killed."

He glared at her. "No, I got him. But *zero* bonus."

"Good enough," she said, cozing back into her seat. "I'll take it. Send me a screencap?"

Qin deadpanned his decline.

All two meters of Tom's lanky stature ambled around the table.

"Sup, Blondie?" Minnie said.

Tom had evidently witnessed the successful ganking of Qin's game and gave Minnie a congratulatory nod as he sat. She dipped her head in return.

"Good afternoon, my pretties," Aether said from the doorway.

1.1

Minnie descended the ladder from Wheel A to the lab pods. One of her probes had M'd her a proximity alert. She had more than three hundred of them distributed across Threck Country, but she recognized this probe's unique identifier the moment it appeared in her fone:

ALERTS: MIN1311 – 1m PROXIMITY – IL

Under different circumstances—those occurring more than two weeks ago—Minnie would have been concerned that an intelligent lifeform had come within one meter of an observation unit. But this particular OU, originally intended for a much less precarious position outside the densely populated Threck City, happened to lose a sail during its early-morning descent, landing just off a stone walkway outside the main wall. Panicked, Minnie had prepared to send an incident report to John and Aether (protocol required the mission commander and assistant commander be notified of much lessor predicaments. But she'd paused mid-compose.

Minnie had waited for the station's next flyover and proceeded to reposition one of the optical arrays, zooming in to estimate the probe's visibility to passers-by. She'd seen in the display that the remaining sails had dissolved upon landing, and the porous, camouflaged outer shell blended well with the surrounding mulch and soil. What if she gave it a day to see what it could gather? The team had never had eyes and ears in so busy an area.

Two weeks and no less than 1,000 IL proximity alerts later, MIN1311 had provided a windfall of data—data that would've taken months, possibly years, to gather with more discreetly placed probes.

Minnie had been able to fill in thousands of gaps in the City dialect, capturing slang, idioms, and much more casual conversation than the very formal language she'd been able to record during public assemblies.

Ever watchful, John had inquired about MIN1311 the day after it landed.

Minnie had lied. "It's nowhere of concern right now, but I'm going to have its internals destruct after nightfall." She hadn't said *that* nightfall.

Two days later, she received an M:

JOHN: Is MIN1311 taken care of?

She'd replied, taking advantage of the ambiguous wording: Yes, it is.

She didn't know how long she planned to keep it there observing. Indefinitely? She'd be caught for sure. But she'd performed multiple risk assessments! If a Threck noticed the probe and picked it up, the internals would instantly self-destruct, leaving only a hollow, charred core within the shell. The Threck might keep it as an interesting find, show it to acquaintances. Worst case, the object would be given to a Threck with geological knowledge. Recognizing the shell's foreign material, they'd tool it open, revealing the burnt core and minute fragments of internals. Their most likely final analysis: some sort of meteorite.

So what was the big deal? After all, the probes were designed with the assumption that an IL would eventually discover one and crack it open.

Minnie stepped from the ladder's last rung to the lab floor, and noticed Ish sitting in her own lab area across from Minnie's, her hands in a combox, manipulating some object on the planet surface. A workaholic even more obsessive than Minnie, Ish had apparently rushed straight here after group.

Ishtab Soleymani was the mission's lead specialist on the primitive Hynka race that dominated the northern hemisphere of Epsilon C, or *Epsy*, as it had come to be known. Though the Hynka were brutal predators, Ish was extremely protective of them. She even refused to call them *Hynka*.

The Threck, for whom Minnie was lead specialist, had recently begun dabbling in transoceanic exploration, and at some point encountered these terrifying behemoths. They branded the creatures "savages": *Hynka*. At the time, as Ish had yet to determine a single name by which the team could refer to her ILs, the Threck word became the default. Once Ish finally ascertained what her darling predators called themselves, *Hynka* had already become ingrained in the team's heads. And besides, the hissing, guttural *Oss-Khoss* just didn't roll well off the human tongue. Minnie didn't think the bloodthirsty beasts would be all that offended.

She'd once told Ish, "Go down and stand in front of one of those things and see if *Oss-Khoss* gets you devoured any slower, or with more compassion, than *Hynka*."

Petite, doe-eyed Ish had merely stared at Minnie with a thoughtful air, seemingly perplexed by the notion that standing before a towering, chest-heaving, wheezing, drooling Hynka would be anything other than a dream come true. In that species, Minnie surmised, Ish saw only a brilliant hunting machine—the highly successful top of the food chain in a land the size of Eurasia.

Minnie (and everyone else) observed a hulking, too-fast, energy-squandering, gorillagator beast that owed its survival to the rapid breeding and bounteous litters of a few of its surviving prey species. And that balance wouldn't last. The Hynka population continued to maintain steady growth and dispersion. Within 200 years they'd eat their way to their own extinction, leaving behind a vast, fertile land for Threck expansion. It was inevitable. There simply weren't enough huntable calories to sustain the population once its size doubled, and the beasts didn't appear to be within a thousand years of agriculture.

Minnie approached Ishtab's combox and peered over her shoulder at the screen. "Whatcha got there?"

Ish was surprised, but thrilled to answer. "It's actually a discarded tool. I've got vids of a female using it to pry roots away from a burrow, and then as an extension to spear the hiding rodent inside."

"Aww. Poor bunny."

Ish glared. "Is it more humane how your people consume living worms or suffocate their fish?"

Minnie shrugged. "Just saying poor bunny. Got a soft spot for fur. Find me a fuzzy Hynka and I'll 'awww' right there with you as it devours its own brother's guts." She turned to go, ignoring Ish's stammered protest.

"Siblings would never ... Conspecific cannibalism isn't..."

At her main console, Minnie accessed her alerting system and cleared the queued probe events. She pulled up the language database and looked at the breakdowns. 114 new words or usages. Reviewing them in their recorded context, she felt that same elated ear buzz she'd enjoyed over the past two weeks. As usual, a few of the definition suggestions were a little off, but she listened to the audio, watched the Threcks' body language in the vids, and input her corrections. The computer always had difficulty pairing gestures with audibles to form single words. Not only were the Threck dependent upon head and arm movements to convey meaning and inflection, the identical word could have two entirely different meanings if spoken during inhale or exhale.

After six playbacks, Minnie discovered a new modifier: a sort of doubletake head gesture with a subtle shrug. "I miss those days" became "I mourn [that person]."

As she had yesterday and the day before, Minnie decided she'd kill the probe *tomorrow.*

* * *

Minnie gnawed a chewstick while watching from their bed as Aether sponged her face in the mirror. Her eyes perused Aether's long body in the dim light.

"You have a bruise on your butt," Minnie said.

Aether twisted and observed it in the mirror. "Ooh, that's an ugly one. That stupid workbench in Engineering. On the left when you enter."

"It's crazy how high your butt is. That corner always gets me on the waist. Hurry up."

Aether leaned into the refresher nook, the soft hiss of microjets as it dried her face.

Minnie rolled onto her back and stared at the perforated ceiling. "How about that drama in group today? Pablo and Zisa."

"They worked it out well." Getting Aether to engage in petty gossip always proved challenging. She tossed back a swig of mouthwash and swished it around in her mouth.

"Yeah, eventually, but *sexual harassment*? Really? He complimented her. I was there when it happened." Minnie deepened her voice. "'Oh, hey Zees. Been putting in extra time on the legger?'"

Aether spat the mouthwash in the sink. "Well, it does imply he's just looked over her body, and she's always been sensitive to that sort of thing. *We* all know he was only talking about her legs, but he should know better with her. It's over though. What matters is they're still friends, and he'll be more conscious in the future."

Minnie's gaze had lost its focus at some point, the ceiling holes blending and merging with the glazed metal's faux wood coating. What time was it in Threck City?

Aether crawled into bed.

Minnie rolled on her side to face Aether and engage, but additional language advancements could be happening right that second. Her mislaid observation unit was down there, hard at work, like some tireless assistant working for her day and night. Joy mingled, in equal portion, with her fear of being caught. She wanted so badly to tell Aether about the OU, but it'd put Aether in a bad spot having to either betray Minnie or lie to John. Better she didn't know.

"Pensive face," Aether said, and tried to mirror Minnie's expression. "You're worried about what to do for my birthday, aren't you?"

Uh-oh, is it this week?

Minnie pulled up the calendar app. "Yeah … exactly. You psychs just see right through a person, don't you?" Two days away. She'd have to make her something. Something physical.

Aether squinted at her. "You just opened your calendar."

"Yeah, busted. But wow! You're fifty-five!"

Aether's speechless face rapidly morphed to a quivering stink-eye. "*Chron-age?* How … *dare* … you!" She pushed Minnie's shoulder back and climbed atop her, pinning Minnie's wrists into the mattress. "You just violated rule number one, m'lady."

"Well hello there, Ms. Sensitivity," Minnie beamed, relishing the moment. "Shall we hack into the system and edit this inconsiderate birth year entry?"

"Not a bad idea, actually. Nineteen years in a metabed equates to around two years of physical aging, so … just subtract seventeen years from both of us." Aether sat back, releasing Minnie's wrists.

"Nah, I'm okay being forty-five. So much *wisdom* tied to that number. But man, oh, man, *fifty*-five*!* Talk about wisdom." Minnie sighed with mock reverence. "Verily, thine eyes hath beheld such wonders."

Their gazes locked—a battle of penetrating stares that gradually devolved into juvenile face-making.

Aether finally gave in and flopped back down beside her. "So, what were you *really* stewing on?"

Can't tell her about the probe…

"Oh, just wondering how many other teams were actually reading my research guides. I know I won't receive feedback from the first installment for another couple years."

"Well, *we* all think it's brilliant. Everything you've published so far. And you know I'm not just saying that. Tom and Pablo, even as backups, absolutely incorporate your methods. I'm sure Ish, too."

Minnie popped her eyebrows. "Ish? Seriously? You think she'd read a word of something *I* wrote?"

A note of disappointment in Aether's face. "She looks up to you; it's just hard for you to see past the wall she's built up. But you can change that. I've always said you can change that."

"You say the same thing about John."

"And I mean it!" Aether said, sitting up. "You were thinking about him again, weren't you?"

Oh jeez. Come on.

"I was so not … Can we not—"

Aether stroked Minnie's arm. "I really think you need to get it out more. Talk to *me* more. Tell me what you dislike about him. Tell me what frustrates you. I'd rather do it here, with you, then have it rear up in the middle of group or assembly."

Minnie sat up and faced her. "Listen. Really hear me right now. You see me thinking, or I'm frowning or something—chances are, I'm down there." Minnie nodded out the window to the violet planet as it rolled by. "I'm not like I was eight months ago. I don't think about him anymore. Honestly. Do you believe me?"

"Of course I believe you."

"Thank you."

They sat quietly, sharing a smile. Aether tilted her head a little. She was waiting. She was doing that psych thing where you just wait for the patient to say more. But it wasn't going to work on Minnie. She was immune to such transparent tactics. Minnie would simply stare at all that exposed olive skin and wait it out, thinking other thoughts.

Minnie broke the silence. "You *know* he has thoughts, though—that he misses you." Aether raised her eyebrows. "And I *guarantee* he has vids of you in his fone. Gross stuff. He could be watching them *any* time, you standing there right in front of him, and you'd have no idea he was overlaying the real you with some … some—"

Aether blinked, stunned. "He's not like that."

"Of course not."

The soft monotone of an impending announcement sounded in Minnie's ear. She could see Aether got it too.

Qin's voice spoke in their ears. "Supply pod on final approach."

Minnie frowned. "Has it been six months? What day is it?"

Aether smirked and crawled out of bed, grabbing clothes from the closet. "It's the fourth. Two days from my birthday, *ahem, ahem.* Time flies, right?" She dressed and pulled on her runners. "I'm just going to check on them; make sure everything's good, okay? He's showing Ish how to run final approach. We'll resume this vid business when I get back."

"No, please, I'm done talking. Disregard everything I just said. Seriously. Just hurry back, you."

Aether stroked Minnie's sandy hair, the way Minnie liked, the way her father used to, and then left the room.

Lying back, Minnie scolded herself once more for letting the crap in her head come out of her mouth. Even if asked directly, she needed to lie. And why couldn't Aether ask about something else? Ask her about the Threck and Minnie would blab her ear off for hours! Ask her more about Ish! That was actually kind of eye-opening for a second. Maybe Ish's standoffishness was a direct result of Minnie's reactions to Ish's standoffishness. Maybe if Minnie was nicer, Ish would relax and act somewhat normal. Hell, violate policy and ask her about *food*.

Minnie felt a sudden wave of ghost hunger and clutched her belly skin. She felt around the sheets and under her pillow, finding the chewstick beneath. Back in her mouth it went. She considered opening her game to sneak a virtual snack. It was strictly forbidden, of course, but Qin had showed her how to trick the system into presenting food. It even activated scent receptors.

But no good would come of it. She had to think like a recovering alcoholic. The just-a-little-sip mentality was highly destructive.

Like the eight other individuals on the station and the dozens of others sent to distant planets on similar missions, she hadn't consumed a solid for almost 27 years. Meds in the water shut down the majority of the digestive process, nutrients and calories supplied by supplements also infused in the water. It was the most extreme part of training and transition on Earth, and it wasn't optional. Quite simply, there existed no practical way to feed a team of 8-12 people on an orbiter, light years from home, for the rest of their lives.

Even though the meds blocked the processes and signals that led to hunger sensations, it was difficult to comprehend the psychological impacts of food, the social importance of eating. The teams still gathered twice daily for this very reason. "Assembly" remained one of the few mandatory entries in everyone's calendars, despite the fact that they drank from their canteens throughout the day. You sat around a table, drank your water, socialized. Many of them munched on chewsticks. There was nothing to swallow, but they kept the teeth and gums healthy, and satisfied latent oral fixations. Some avoided chewsticks as they only reminded them of what they couldn't have, preferring to utilize them as any other hygiene tool before bed.

In training, everyone had been put on the meds right away, meals tapered and cut off two weeks in. Many brilliant, high-potential candidates dropped out at that stage, dreams shattered over food. Others washed out for the sudden stark reality of a one-way trip. They'd thought they could handle leaving home forever: sever ties, say good-bye. But when it came down to it, a truly unique psyche was required to accept that daunting future and consistently remain on task.

Even though she was close with her father, Minnie had always been fine with leaving him, and likewise, he with her. He'd said he wished they could both go off to different ends of the Orion Spur, each knowing the other was fulfilling their greatest dreams. But he was too old for the program, and so they'd spoken their tearless, ecstatic goodbyes when he dropped her off at the training center. She was 16. As the weeks passed, she found herself only vaguely troubled by the realization of what she missed most about her father: the way he'd stroke her hair until she fell asleep.

How fortunate was she, Minnie thought, having found *love* on a journey she expected to live out alone? And how sad was it for John Li, who came with his wife—the person he believed he'd share the rest of his life with—to end up alone, and with no way home? Perhaps Minnie could forgive him a yank or two as he watched those vids of him and Aether.

"He's not like that!"

BS. He's got vids.

Minnie's dulling thoughts shifted to the surface, to Threck City, the stirring architecture, the grand harbor, their Thinkers and artists, their theories about the stars and mathematics, the Fishers out at sea riding on behemoth *afvriks* trained as fishing boats. She imagined life in the city, and, despite Aether's absence, eventually fell asleep.

1.2

John Li reclined in his office chair, perusing the incoming pod's inventory. Scrolling past the usuals—supplements, meds, power cells—to the extras section, he quickly scanned for the object of his interest: fone upgrades.

John's fone had been giving him persistent pain for months. Pablo had pulled it out and run diagnostics but found nothing wrong. John remembered the look on Angela's face when she entered sick bay and saw John's hollow right eye socket. He'd watched with his left eye, the real one, as she blinked and rubbed her own fone eye. It seemed that despite their complete dependence on the technology, not many liked to be reminded of their implants, or the amputated bio eye they'd replaced.

"I think it's in your housing," Pablo had said. "Not the fone itself. Don't see any physio problems. Maybe a firmware upgrade will alleviate though … whenever they come …"

John had nodded and thanked him. Pablo didn't think it a critical issue because John didn't convey it as such. "Some occasional pulsing behind the cavity," John had described.

"How bad? Would you consider it debilitating? When it's at its worst?"

John had forced a convincing laugh. "Not remotely. Just something I thought I'd put on your radar." Would it have helped to describe the pain as that of a thumb pressing in on the fone, harder and deeper? The sensation of building pressure, ever threatening to burst?

John had had to live with the consequences of downplaying his pain, not the least of which was a lack of meds. Without a reportable override, Pablo was the only one who could program adjustments to crewmembers' water.

The throbbing behind John's fone continued as he used the source of his pain to drill down into the pod's tech manifest. He held his breath as it popped into view before him, virtually hovering in the air a dozen centimeters away.

> Brand: LEN Model: LEFONE 8.5 SW: 5.366
> FW: 5.30
> Image: NS23-9 QTY: 12

Their current software and firmware were in the 3s, so he looked forward to whatever improvements two generations had to offer.

He switched back to the medical supplies in search of ocular housings, but found none. The chances had been slim, anyway. Adult housings were considered permanent, and new fones were expected to be backwards compatible all the way to the original 21st Century housings. Not many people were willing to take the risk, or invest in the surgery required. Once your housing was installed, replacing a fone could technically be done by yourself in a mirror, albeit unsanitary.

On Earth, while the vast majority preferred a perfect color match (rendering an implanted fone indistinguishable from a bio eye), others opted for bold-colored irises, wearing matched contact lenses over their bio eye. Kids used them as fashion accessories, choosing fones not for quality or functionality, but for the special gimmicks the off-brands used to entice them, such as animated color-shifting irises, or shocking, full coloration such as all black or all red. Before entering training, John remembered seeing a teenager at the airport with a repeating message scrolling across his fone eye: JAX, MEDZ, SONDZ—a possibly ironic update to "sex, drugs, and rock n' roll."

27 years later, he couldn't imagine what gimmicks the manufacturers and modders had come up with since. He was excited, however, to learn what functional enhancements had been achieved 20 years ago, back when the incoming pod launched from Earth.

Upgrades brought not only augmented software, but also typically included higher resolution pic and vid capability, greater magnification in binoc mode, occasionally new visual spectrums beyond the standard thermo, infra, kinetic, and mag. New versions of ear modules were rarely released, as they too required a surgical installation.

John flicked through his contacts to Qin and selected VOICE. The receiver in his ear activated.

"Hey, what's your best guess on when the pod will be ready for unloading?"

Qin replied, "We don't even have visual yet, but Ish has established control. Ish? … She says it's still decelerating … maybe a few hours before docking."

"Great, thanks. How's she doing with those controls? Comfortable?"

"Totally."

John flipped to his calendar and sent an open appointment request to Pablo, flagging "asap" for the time.

Less than a minute later, John received an acceptance M for tomorrow, 0900. Pablo had included a note:

PABLO: That housing still bothering you?

JOHN: Often enough to make me cut in line like a jerk. But anytime in the next week is fine, really.

Why? John rebuked himself. *Why is it fine? Why can't you just say "I need this."?*

Aether had put up with it as long as she could, among other issues. How many times had he told her "whatever you want" after she specifically asked him to never utter those words again? When it came to the mission, or to a task at hand, he led without hesitation. But if it had to do with him—something personal—there was a sort of block there.

PABLO: We'll do it tomorrow. My first open slot. You will be the guinea pig. I just read the upgrades are 2 generations newer!

Thank you, thank you, thank you! John shouted in his head, but replied with a nonchalant:

JOHN: Whatever works…Thanks!

John shut off his fone and Optical Pass-Through engaged. Everyone was required to shut down into OPT for at least 4 hours a day, but John knew that many slept with their fones still on. It wasn't healthy. He wished he could force a settings change in everybody's devices, but that would only further outrage those with whom his relationship was often precarious. With the amount of complaints Aether received from disgruntled crewmembers, it was a wonder how John managed reelection to a second term as mission commander. He supposed that, when it came to elections, he was the known quantity, or the most desirable of the undesirables.

The least undesirable?

With his fone off, the pain had subsided a small amount. These reprieves were his primary source of optimism when it came to the upgrade. Likewise, when Pablo had removed the fone, John's discomfort vanished entirely.

He leaned the recliner farther back and closed his eyelids. Somehow the pain felt more bearable knowing this could be the last time he'd have to sleep with it.

* * *

The piercing blare of the emergency alarm plucked Minnie from her dream.

A drill at this hour? What a hole!

The room lurched beneath her, followed by a violent vibration. Yellow and green lights strobed above her bed. She clung to a handhold and tried to open the hatch, but the actuator didn't respond. Rotation shift. The personal quarters cylinder was slowing down. They'd lose gravity soon.

A synth voice announced through the PA: "This is not a drill. This is not a drill. Exigency procedures. Exigency procedures. This is not a drill ..."

Minnie hurriedly dressed as she activated her fone to call Aether.

ALERTS: Wireless unavailable.

Crap! Crap! Crap! It's real!

She leapt to the window shade and pulled it open. Bits of debris, small and large, streamed by. Planet Epsy streaked by the window at an arcing diagonal. Something had exploded or impacted the sta—

The supply pod!

Minnie accessed her fone's settings and requested a direct connection to Aether. She accepted a few seconds later and an undelivered M from one minute earlier popped up.

AETHER: Minnie, we are in full exigency. Go to Wheel A and your assigned EV. I'll see you on the surface. I love you.

MINNIE: What happened?!

AETHER: Supply pod impact, hull breach, fire's out but envr + cooling are inop. We have 8 mins.

MINNIE: Backups? BH?

AETHER: Minerva, go to your EV NOW.

Minnie's mind raced. What if it was something she could fix? What about the Backup Habitat? Why were they jumping straight to Evacuation Vehicles? Surface evac was last on the list of exigency measures. Aether didn't want to hear any of it, but she was as susceptible as anyone to groupthink. Someone probably said "We have no other options!" and everyone listened. It was surely John, and no one would think to challenge him in an emergency. People listened for anyone with an authoritative tone, and complied without question.

Minnie slid open one of the emergency panels and grabbed a breather, pulling it over her head, and pressing it to seal.

Back to the hatch.

The mechanism override clicked into place and Minnie forced the door into the bulkhead. The tube was still pressurized. She climbed the ladder, her weight shifting right and then left as the station's irregular rotation toyed with gravity. At the top of the tube, she peered out the window in the hatch to the long duct that led to the Backup Habitat. One entire side of its solar array had been disintegrated, and the escape duct had clearly been breached.

That doesn't mean we can't use it! Minnie yelled in her head. *We only need suits!*

She opened a new M to Aether.

MINNIE: BH intact. Escape duct breached but passable.

AETHER: 3 mins Minerva.

MINNIE: Why EVs?! This is not protocol!

AETHER: Listen in 10 seconds. Sound of EV containing Qin and ME.

Aether severed their fone link.

"No!"

Aether knew exactly how to force her compliance. Epsy's surface was a permanent refuge. Once Aether's EV launched, the only way Minnie would see her again would be to do the same: abandon ship in one of the pre-programmed EVs, all the way down to the rally point in Threck Country. And Minnie was the one responsible for first contact—the only one with a real handle on the language. Even Tom, her backup, had hardly bothered to learn the spoken language. If the duty fell to him, he'd have to fumble his way around the Livetrans app.

The ladder began to vibrate with a new frequency, followed by the loud *clang* of retracting anchors as inverted electromagnets blasted an EV from its bay. Aether was off. And despite the screaming in her head, Minnie knew she had no choice but to follow. She descended the ladder, fighting intense gravity shifts, until she dropped into the hygiene pod. Loose articles filled the zero-grav air, drifting around like a slomo insect swarm.

Minnie bounced from floor to ceiling to bulkhead, swatting away water droplets, razors and combs, washcloths, until she reached the tube to Wheel A. As she grabbed the first rung, another telling vibration began. She pulled herself into the tube and looked out the window.

Clang!

To her horror, she watched an escape vehicle launch not toward Epsy's atmosphere, but straight out into the black of space.

She screamed "NO!" and her breather fogged.

Aether! No no no … Are they all *ejecting wrong?*

Clamoring through the tube to Wheel A, Minnie emerged just as EV4 began its launch.

Who's assigned to 4? Ish and Tom?

Minnie floated across the common area. Chess pieces, a well-gnawed chewstick, and a paintbrush bounced off her visor as she approached the open hatch of EV6, and the person she very much wished to strangle. She was surprised he'd waited for her.

Clang! EV4 launched.

Minnie glanced back to the panoramic window at the far side of the common area. Another doomed launch. The EV's silhouette in front of the Epsilon star shrank to a tiny, heartrending dot. The occupants would already realize the mistake. They'd know they were as good as dead.

Minnie felt something impact her chest. An instant later, her head flew backward as she was yanked forward into the EV. She slammed into the seat just as John came into view through her breather mask. He was already in his orange survival suit, fuming, shouts muffled behind his visor. Sensing her presence, Minnie's suit activated, detaching from the seat around her and wrapping over her head, legs, and arms. Automated clutches stretched out and joined to each other at the seams.

John popped his visor open and shouted again. "Hands, feet, head!"

She remembered and leaned forward, spotting her boots still clamped in their charging docks. She kicked off her slips, pointed her toes, and shoved in both feet. Eager ankle clutches joined to the boots as she stuffed her hands into the awaiting gloves on her armrests. Overhead, she found her helmet, tugged it from its dock, and pulled it on, sealing it to the receiver at her neck, then synced her fone to the suit. System checks confirmed all seals as John turned to the hatch, slapped the ejection button, waited for the three-second safety count, then struck it again. He disappeared out of sight beside her. Restraints sprang out from the seat, binding her shoulders, waist, legs, and head.

He didn't time it! We're screwed!

Minnie regained her senses and struggled to turn toward John. The EV seats were positioned in a V, two passengers facing slightly away from each other. She could only see the edge of his arm.

The EV began to quake. Minnie pressed her head to the front of her helmet, grasped the grips beneath her hands, clenched her eyelids shut.

Clang!

Her body thrust forward from the launch, her restraints a little loose. *g*-force fighting against her, she pulled a hand to her chest, found the adjuster knob, and twisted it until her body pressed snug into the seat.

He didn't override and launch manual. We could be drifting into open space!

Minnie opened her eyes, peered out the little porthole above her. Among the black of open space, she imagined a tiny white dot, a mislaunched EV, drifting away.

Aether…

She tried to calm herself, unmuddle her brain. The EV's intercomms hadn't automatically connected their suits.

Direct Connect!

She sent a DC request to John. He accepted a few seconds later. She had the M primed the second they linked.

MINNIE: Our trajectory is screwed. Other EVs
launched into space.

JOHN: I know.

MINNIE: If you knew then why didn't you launch manual?

JOHN: I know now. Not when I activated.

MINNIE: Well, we're heading for entry, but no way we're on course.

JOHN: The station just went up. It's gone.

The EV rattled briefly from the destroyed station's shockwave, then returned to unnerving stillness. Minnie closed her eyes, inhaled a breath, and held it. She needed to ask the question.

A series of thruster bursts slowly rotated the EV to entry orientation, followed by a new wave of tremors.

JOHN: We are definitely entering the atmosphere.

Brilliant effing observation. Ask him the question.

MINNIE: Do you know if Aether's EV launched on mark?

No response. Violent shaking. An orange glow brightened outside Minnie's porthole. Entry friction.

MINNIE: John? Please answer.

JOHN: I don't know.
JOHN: I don't think so.

Minnie shut her eyes, felt her chest compress from the inside, like hooks over her ribs, winching inward. Her gut twisted. He didn't know. What *did* he know? He didn't know anything. He knew more than her. At least *saw* more than her. What did he see? He must've seen. He knew. He saw. It's why he said he didn't think so. He wouldn't have said that otherwise.

Aether was gone.

Vibrations subsided, but she could feel them decelerating.

She hoped the chute would fail—a 20 km/s impact on land, instant vaporization—done.

She opened her stinging eyes, tried to squeeze away the blurring tears to see out the porthole. They were in the shadow of the planet—nighttime wherever they were headed. And where might that be? She hoped not an ocean. What time was it when she awoke? Her fone indicated it was 0840 station time. She tried to recall her last visuals from the window, the last landmass in view. She remembered thinking EVs on the flagging side would launch roughly correct, could head close enough to Threck Country to make it, but now she wasn't so sure. Had she seen land out there? Could it have been clouds?

She could simply play it back. Her fone was set to queue up 30 minutes.

The chute popped from the EV, expanded, and she felt her spine and legs depress against the seat bottom.

As the EV descended toward an unknown surface below, Minnie retrieved her earlier view outside the common room window and closed her bio eye to see it clearly. Beneath scattered altostratus clouds, she recognized at once the jagged eastern coast of Threck Country, the typical cloud pattern above the inert volcano. Which meant that her EV, launched out the opposite side of the station, was either headed to an ocean, one of the major islands, or Hynka Country.

MINNIE: We're def not on course.

JOHN: I know. I just finished calculations. It's not good.

MINNIE: You have an LZ?

JOHN: Yes. And we're touching down in 10 … 9 … 8 …

The EV landed with a surprisingly soft thud, nothing like the overzealous simulators on Earth. John seemed intent, however, on matching the training drills, right down to the scripted verbals.

Minnie's ear module ticked to life with John's voice breaking up, and annoying crackles accompanying every consonant.

"—aps off ... Full spec—weep ... —ival kit."

Audio was still trying to go through the EV's inop wireless.

Minnie found herself running on autopilot, her restraints flying off, fone shifting through optical spectrums, as she extracted the surface survival kit from the console beside her.

Thermal optics were useless—the EV outer shell was still blazing from entry, displaying only a wall of white in all directions. Kinetic and infra only worked for line of sight. She paused at the mag setting, picking up a muddle of hazy electromagnetic waves, then enabled the bio filter. The world beyond the EV cabin materialized before her in dreamlike color—a black and white vid after colorization, but with transparency and overlapping objects, like a 3D comic book. She closed her real eye and surveyed the area. Focusing past the dim ghosts of foliage revealed a disturbing sight.

"Switch to mag," she said.

"I am," he replied.

"Bio filter?"

A brief silence. "Uhh ..."

"See them now?"

"Yes. We must ... clo— ... a village." It could be one of their helmets screwing up. Both of them needed to disconnect and DC their suits. "... got at le—wenty within two— ... —s'side. You?"

Was that "twenty" he sees?

Minnie slowly panned across her swath of visibility. "I'd say more than a hundred on my side. And they're *all* coming."

1.3

The chute was still burning when the gossamer hoard of approaching Hynka began to spread into a circle around the EV. Once a wall had formed, John couldn't tell how many of the creatures stood beyond the first line, their mag waves merging and blending, obscuring the view. Worse, he didn't think it particularly mattered. 50 Hynka or 300 meant pretty much the same thing. The beasts simply didn't lose interest in things, and a strange, shiny sphere with a flaming cloth waving overhead had certainly made a considerable impression. Retracting the chute on touchdown probably would've been wise.

A tapping on his helmet.

John turned and saw Minerva, perched on her seat, helmet off. Beset with rage, her pointy pixie face appeared poised for attack. She motioned for him to remove his helmet. He found the release and pulled it off.

"Everyone! Dead! *You've* killed us all." She waved her hand around at the sketchy waves of tentative yet eager Hynka, inching ever closer to the EV. "Some of us more *horrifically* than others."

"We *had* to evac. There was no choice. Anyone left on the station would be dead now. Everyone escaped."

Minerva's chin stiffened into pits and lumps, quivering as her eyes fell to her knees. She tried to say "Aether," but faltered.

But perhaps there remained some glimmer of hope. "I didn't *see* her launch. I don't know for sure."

"She was EV-one, storage side. They were *all* faced out after the stabilizers died."

John reached out to her. "I'm just as scared for her as you are right now." She looked at his hand like poison. "What makes me feel better is that she's with *Qin*, they have thrusters and axis controls, and if there's *any* way whatsoever to turn an EV around and guide it in, Qin will figure it out."

He watched her eyes—desperate, glassy eyes that so wanted to believe him.

Something heavy crashed against the hull. John and Minerva refocused their fones on the biomag view through the EV shell.

Minerva said, "I think they're throwing rocks. Think we should dim the lights?"

"Good idea." He shut off the main lights, leaving only the blues. "There's one over here gathering the nerve to touch the hull."

"It should've cooled enough to touch by now. That reminds me ..."

"Thermal?" John swiped his optics setting. Indeed, he could see through the hull now, though the massive blob of red didn't render the scene much clearer. He increased the sensitivity and reestablished the baseline temp higher. He flinched at the new view. "Oh crap. Turn up your sens—"

"Already on it ... oh crap!" she echoed.

The enhanced picture picked up the minutest detail—eyes, mouths, skin lines, and just how far back the horde went. He could see Hynka pushing and shoving, clawing and biting at each other.

"Hang on!" Minerva shouted, and John grabbed a handhold just as the EV was slammed from her side.

A few seconds later, another smash, and the EV rolled completely over, loose objects raining down, Minerva's back crashing into John's chest.

"There went the stabilizer legs! We need to strap back in!" John shouted. "They're going to bowl us all over the damned continent!"

Minerva rolled off of him. "Not going to happen just yet."

John reclaimed his bearings and peered around. The seats now hung upside down above them.

"Just hold on," John said. "I have a feeling they'll help us out any second."

Sure enough, a crash from behind, instantly followed by another. Handholds yanked from tight grips and they crashed once more into each other, John's head banging into Minerva's cheek. She released a small peep of pain, but quickly jumped into her seat as it rolled beneath her. John followed suit and fastened his waist restraint.

"Grab your helmet!" Minerva yelled. "And hang onto your SSK. Nothing loose. And open your visor. My audio went inop."

"Right." John pulled on the helmet, raised the visor, then used his feet to lift the battered survival kit into his hands.

But the EV didn't move.

"What are they waiting for?" Minerva looked at him, her shadow-filled face lit only in blue.

"I don't—whoa!" He thrust a finger toward his porthole, a large, bronze eye staring in, surveying the cabin. A nictitating membrane slid over the eye from one side, then retracted. "Don't move."

"It's looking right at you."

The dark, leathery face shifted side to side beyond the porthole, the creature aiming its jutting snout downward and alternating between eyes for the best view. John glanced at the other porthole and saw two more faces fighting to see in.

"You've got some over there, too."

Minerva turned to her porthole to see the two pairs of large eyes looking her over. A sound began outside the hatch. A scratching, like a large saw taken to a metal pipe. The noise was joined by a rhythmic thud—something striking the other side of the hatch.

Minerva whispered, "Do you think they can get in? If they work at it enough?"

"I've seen Ish's vids. Seen a sciuromorph chased into a tree the Hynka couldn't climb. Three of them spent two days taking turns chipping away at the trunk with claws and sharp-edged rocks until the tree fell. These pods aren't made to keep determined things out." John reactivated the thermal view and took a sweeping look around. "I don't think any have left. There're more, if anything."

"That's great."

John chewed his lip. "If only the skimmers were stored *inside* the EVs. We'd wait for the hatch to roll on top, then blow it out and fly away."

"Skimmers are way wider than the hatch and 'if only' statements are the opposite of helpful."

"I know. We just need to figure something out. I don't know … maybe some way to detonate the EV."

"Really?"

"Well, not with us in it. We have to get away somehow, but use it as a distraction. I don't know."

Minerva fished around in the surface survival kit as she spoke. "Your out-loud thinking doesn't offer me much confidence. I was just imagining if they accidentally rolled us into a lake or something. We could float away …" Minerva extracted the standard multiweapon from the container and inserted a 40-round pack.

"Hynka swim."

"Are you serious? We're screwed! Maybe detonating us in here isn't such a bad idea."

"No. There's a way." John felt confident in his words, and continued to search around the cabin. There was *always* a way. He'd kept this conviction as a sort of mantra for as far back as he could remember. It was why people always thought him arrogant.

Aether had frequently advised him, *"Fake doubt. Say 'there* might *be a better approach, but who knows?' Like, we're all in this together, you know? We're all just* trying*."* But she also had to remind him that he was on a station full of brilliant people, each with different strengths, and many stronger than his. *"Don't let their accomplishments escape you,"* she'd said. *"Don't attribute breakthroughs to luck."* He insisted that he didn't, but knew that he'd been guilty of it, at least once. And here he was with Minerva, widely considered the best thinker of the lot. Where were *her* inspired suggestions?

"She's trying," Aether's voice corrected in his head. *"Ask her."*

He turned to her. She was staring at the multiweapon in her hand. "Minerva?" Her despair-heavy face moved to look at him. "Do you *want* to survive this?"

She swallowed. It looked like she hadn't actually considered it a choice. The sounds of prying and cutting and banging outside the hatch grew more pronounced. Her shoulders tightened, forehead compressed.

He went on, louder, "Because I *want* to survive. But I can't do it without you. You probably wouldn't agree, but I feel fortunate to have been assigned this EV with *you* rather than anyone else. Can you save us? Tell me what to do ... *if* you want to live. If not, let's agree now on an optimal suicide."

She blinked at him for a beat and swallowed again. He could see the screws turning in her head. Her tense expression began to shift and change to one of determination. Her sad eyes reverted to the intense scowl to which he'd grown accustomed.

She cocked her head. "You'll listen to me?"

"Of course."

"First, we need to start at the end. Our goal. Where is it we're trying to go?"

"Somewhere safe."

"Right. Brilliant. No, I mean, our real goal is to make it off this continent, and somehow to the other side of the planet, right?"

John suddenly felt stupid. Of course she was right. They were thousands of miles from their real destination, and escaping the mob around them was only the immediate concern. He nodded for her to go on.

"To make it there without some kind of vehicle, in a place as dangerous as this, is unlikely. And to blow up the EV, our strongest power source, with two skimmers stowed in the chassis, and full of other materials and resources, wouldn't make a lot of sense, right?"

"Right."

"Our first and most pressing concern is leaving the vehicle and reaching a location without being followed—ideally in such a way that they lose interest in the EV. Either way, we need to get out of their crosshairs. We can do that by distracting them, killing them, or negotiation."

"Negotiation?"

"Yes. We know they have a rudimentary language." Her speech was speeding up. He motioned for her to keep it steady. "Sorry, we don't have a lot of time. Keep up. Communication should be our first approach. Not because it's moral, but because I'm pessimistic of our chances with options one and two. We have two weapons, three packs each. If we somehow got out of the EV into a position to fire at them, we'd have two hundred and forty shots in total. I'm also dubious of the multirounds' effectiveness on animals that size."

Multirounds had two settings, activated by the weapon upon firing. The MW measured range for each shot and programmed the projectile to either expand prior to impact or just after. Lethal versus nonlethal, supposedly, depending upon the target.

"I'd say two shots'll do the trick," John said as he readied his own MW. "Then again, nonlethal *could* prove more effective against them … maybe as a deterrent. I don't think we'd be thinning any herds out there, even if we killed everyone currently present."

Minerva scanned around the area again. "It looks like they're doing a pretty good job of that themselves, actually."

John's therm showed him what she meant. The throngs of restless Hynka had taken to infighting. Numerous bodies lay cooling on the ground, each surrounded by ravenous others, tearing their slaughtered brethren limb from limb.

"Listen," Minerva said. "First things first. We've no idea how long we have before they breach the cabin—speaking of, you haven't equalized the pod yet." She gestured to a panel in front of him. "If they *do* breach, we open fire, one shot in each, yes? Mind you, we'll very quickly have a wall of dead bodies out there. Next, we need to know where we're going. There should be detailed terrain maps in the station backups. We know they only live aboveground, so you're looking for anything subterranean."

"You're right. They avoid those due to the floods. If we can—"

"Yeah, if you can pull that up, I'll access Ish's language DB and see if I can't find something we can tell these things through the PA."

John felt the pain behind his fone begin to throb and intensify. He established a direct connection to the EV's computer and accessed the backups—always synced in real-time from the station's data storage—and located Zisa's maps. He just needed their coordinates to—

Minerva spoke up, as if reading his mind. "You can get our coordinates from the EV console on your left."

"I know, just work on the language." He knew it sounded snippy as soon as it came out. If they were still alive later, he'd apologize.

"I *am* working on the language," Minerva barked, then muttered, "'Optimal suicide.' Just wow. … Okay, I found Ish's main file, dated last week. What? Empty! Ugh! *Her!* Note says 'full update in progress.' Eff me, if she's not already dead—"

"Why the hell would she wipe the old file for an update? That makes no sense. Where's the update? Offline? On her fone?"

"I know. Ish is weird, but not this weird." Minerva turned back to him. "Wasn't she controlling the supply pod that struck the station?"

"I know. It's in the back of my head. Higher priorities right now. So you have *nothing* for us to say to them?"

"Don't *you* know something of the language? Always figured you micromanaged her like you do me."

The sounds at the hatch had elevated to a single, cacophonous jumble, as though eight or more creatures were working on it. Their claws were too thick and blunt. They were using some sort of tools. He'd been right: they would never give up.

John ignored Minerva's ill-timed jab. "I know some, a few basics. Yes, no, stop, go, us, them. But there're different dialects, inflections. Our vocal folds are so different, it might just be gibberish."

"So what, don't try? If you sound even remotely Hynka-like, hell, they might think we're gods or something. How do you say 'stop'?"

John searched his jumbled brain. "Yeah, I got it. Sort of a hocking. Like clearing mucous in the throat."

Minerva raised her eyebrows, pressed her lips together, and lifted the EV's PA mic to his face. "Just pinch the little clip."

They both turned to observe the Hynka staring at them in the portholes. A terrifying intelligence appeared to be at work there. That gaze, fixated on his own eyes, curious but knowing, assessing, imagining. Predators typically focused on grab or kill spots, hobbling opportunities—the neck, the legs to trip up, where to dig in the talons, where to sink the first bite. Or, when significantly larger than their prey, they took in the whole picture, the mass that they'd consume—shark and fish, snake and mouse. Often, they only saw the moving parts. With everything these Hynka could observe through the glass, the creatures appeared acutely focused on Minerva and him—and only their eyes.

John practiced the hocking sound, but found his throat dry.

Minerva said, "The tube by your shoulder."

He reached back and pulled it into his helmet. "I know." He sucked in several gulps.

"You don't have to tell me you know every time."

John attempted the word twice more, then activated the mic.

"Khoh!"

All sounds at the hatch ceased. The Hynka at the portholes looked around outside.

"It worked!" Minerva whispered.

"Maybe. Might just be the first sound they heard come from the EV. They've never heard amplified sound at all."

"Thunder …" Minerva was thinking out loud.

"Something bigger than them …" John had the first inklings of an idea.

"They've no natural predators."

The silence outside continued, even after 30 seconds. John and Minerva leaned to face each other. John said, "How would they respond to that? Being at the top of the food chain, then a new predator is introduced? Do you know of any examples?"

Minerva nodded, a small smile curling at the corners of her mouth. "Hundreds. Apex predators. They adapt quickly, but clueless at first encounter."

The scritching prying sound at the hatch resumed. The Hynka at the portholes began screaming silently and pounding on the glass, smearing the sprayed saliva from their drooling mouths.

"Again," Minerva went on, closing her eyes as if it shut out the noise. "Doesn't matter unless we have a destination. Just a guess, but greater than five hundred meters, less than two-K is probably ideal, assuming passable terrain."

"Right," John said as he continued scrolling through the maps. "Numerous sinkholes around—"

"Probably faster to search on it instead. 'Subterranean, habitable.'"

She was right, of course. He'd normally have thought of it, but the pandemonium had clouded his thoughts. It was one of her documented assets: clarity under pressure. While stabilized by meds, though. Just how long would she remain lucid down here?

"We have flare projectiles," Minerva said as she continued rooting through her SSK. "Red and green."

Before John's face, a subterranean cave rotated between x and y axes. "I think I've got a destination. Sending it to you."

"Awesome. Can you find a secondary while I look at this?"

"Already on it."

The first cavern, 2.2 kilometers away, appeared to be accessible from the bottom of a 15-meter-wide sinkhole. Orbital imaging showed the site during three different seasons. Twice the sinkhole was imaged half-full of rainwater and runoff, and during the dry season, it was entirely evaporated. They'd have to descend 13m into the hole to access the small entrance. If they weren't observed entering, they should be safe, though getting back out would be a different matter.

Minerva asked without any noticeable skepticism, "You're thinking we run to this?"

"As opposed to what?"

"As opposed to rolling the EV halfway there, like a scurry ball, before the uphill grade begins. I don't think either of us have any illusions about getting the skimmers out, set up, and in the air. I assumed you were defaulting to a foot run for our transportation."

"Well, I hadn't thought of the rolling thing. And wouldn't they just follow us?"

"Just voicing thoughts. Didn't say it made any sense. What's our backup?"

John sent her the second site the computer found, and yelled over the growing clamor in front and behind. "Six-K east, and we would have to dig a little through soft humus to access it. A long way, and I don't know if we'd have that kind of time. There's nothing else closer."

Banging, grinding, smashing, shaking ...

The Hynka were attacking any groove or crevice. An exterior panel tore off. Cables and instruments could be heard ripping from inside the shell. They'd finally gotten something. It fed the creatures' resolve. John's fone began throbbing again, in rhythm with his pounding pulse.

Minerva leaned closer and yelled over the noise, startling him. "You think that sinkhole will be full?"

John flipped back to the imagery and checked the dates. "Right time of year."

"We'd save time if we didn't have to rappel down."

"You're saying run and dive straight in? Swim down to the cavern entrance?"

She nodded.

The lights and consoles on her side went black as another panel was breached. Snapping and grinding, flexing metal sheets, constant *twangs* of severed cables. It sounded as if they were right on the other side of Minerva's console, a screen or panel yank away from a giant pair of fingers reaching in and plucking her from her seat.

She glanced toward her console. "I think this is it! Let's transfer the SSKs into the backpacks! You loaded?"

John replied affirmative as they hastily extracted the compressed gray packs, expanded them, and dumped the surface survival kit contents inside. Each connected their suits to the EV water tubes, and pumped the fluid into their suits' veins until full—a theoretical three days' worth of hydration and sustenance.

"Hey." Minerva touched his arm. "I don't want to be eaten to death."

John knew what she meant and snapped a nod. "Same here."

Tubes disconnected, packs on, and the last remnants of protection disintegrating around them, they turned to each other. As Minnie shouted the plan's bullet points, they checked that ammo packs were secured to suits, backpack straps taut, and then shared a brief, silent gaze that conveyed more than words could express.

"Ready," Minerva said.

"Ready," John said.

1.4

Hissing emanated from the frame as pressure built in the hatch's emergency release system. John lay ready, the flare gun aimed at the top of the hatch. Minnie stood at the back of the cabin on the ledge above the seats, multiweapon aimed at what would soon be the center of a wide opening. She hoped the ejecting door would take out a generous portion of Hynka, while stunning the rest.

The lack of information was infuriating. If she'd been the Hynka lead, she'd have had every seemingly trivial behavior detail logged. Then again, maybe Ish did have all that, but kept it to herself. Minnie's mild dislike of Ish continued inflating with high-pressure hatred.

The hatch paused, a low tone ringing around them. Maybe it couldn't blow anymore, the edges so warped and twisted or obstructed by—and then it blew.

John blared through the PA, "*Khoh!*"

The sounds and scents of the outside streamed in. Shrieks, grunting, hisses. Cool, wet, fertile, pungent.

John's flare gun discharged with an echoing twang, the phosphorescent red stream flying off in an arc, drips of frothy glowing clumps falling behind it. Minnie watched with her thermal optic as Hynka heads all moved in sync, following the path of the flare. The horde quickly fell silent. John snatched up the MW from his chest and aimed it out the hatch.

Hynka sounds slowly resumed—quiet at first—their breathy, hiss-and-throat-heavy voices seeming to debate the flare as it disappeared beyond the tips of starlit foliage. The two hulking creatures at either side of the hatch turned to each other, exchanged words, and then snapped their attention back into the EV.

Minnie began hyperventilating. The things were less than a meter from John's feet, 2.5m from her, and even more terrifying in person. Most grew beyond 3m tall, the largest specimens nearing 4m, even with their hunched postures—like mega-sized gorillas, with two rows of serrated teeth hidden within tapered gatoresque snouts. As the purple-black figures reached toward John, Minnie still doubted whether their thick leathery flesh could be penetrated by the multirounds.

Only one way to know …

She aimed at the one on the right and squeezed the trigger.

Following plan, John fired at the one on the left. Both creatures reacted with the same stunned confusion. They halted in place, swaying, and regarded their midsections as if inspecting a newfound stain on a shirt. Broad fingers probed in and around the penetration points.

"Ehswah och!" spoke the one on the right, and pounded its chest before collapsing backward into a seated position.

The other injured Hynka faltered and tripped in place, held up by those nearby. An eerie calm spread through the crowd. Deep, hushed voices seemed to gossip as necks craned to see what was happening.

"Smaller one in the middle there," Minnie said. "He's eyeing you and puffing up."

"I see him. Watch for any others."

"They're acting really odd," she said. "Not retreating at all … waiting. What do we do?"

"Just go with it. We only shoot if they're coming at us."

Minnie watched through thermal as the smaller Hynka, a bit taller than John, sucked in a final breath, and dug its blunt foot claws into the moist soil. "Watch it, he's coming!"

It spread out its long, bulbous arms, snorting and shoving back those around it, then charged straight for the pod opening. Minnie and John both fired. A second round when it didn't stop. John fired a third projectile just as it began slowing, mitts clutching at its chest. That same confusion. It labored to breathe, struck its chest, spun a little and fell on its front.

"We should step out," John said. "I think now's the time. A sign of strength, before they start thinking all this over."

"Before they start testing again," Minnie agreed.

John slowly pulled himself to his feet and stood right in the doorway. Minnie could hear the breathing and whispers of the mob. Her breath went shallow. She fought to uncurl her fingers from the handhold behind her, the pseudo-safety of the EV nearly gone. John lifted a leg over the threshold and planted his boot on the ground.

One small meal for Hynkakind, she thought.

John panned the MW across the expanding circle of creatures, slowly inching backward.

"Keep an eye on the ones on the ground," Minnie said, doing the same. All three appeared to still be alive, only incapacitated.

Minnie stepped out beside him just as one of the Hynka to their left advanced a single pace out of its group, arms crossed against its chest. John aimed his MW.

"Ahh crap," she whispered. "Testing?"

"Just keep your eyes on that side. Even if this one charges."

The cross-armed Hynka called out, *"Khow ayk!"*

Minnie watched her side. The Hynka were no longer backing away, just rocking side to side, eyes intent on the pair. "What did it say?"

"No idea."

"Got a snappy retort?" Minnie asked. "Something that says, 'Whatever you just said, I'm still the boss.'"

"I could shoot him." John kept walking, one leg after the other.

"Just continue moving that way. Keep therm up in case anyone's hiding in the vegetation. I'll watch out for all the ones behind the EV. They may not have witnessed our impressive display firsthand."

"Got it," John said.

As they moved, the crowd continued to retreat and part. Once passed, the Hynka regrouped and followed slowly behind, Minnie holding her MW at the ready. At any moment one of them might shriek a command and everyone would charge. If they did, Minnie and John wouldn't have a chance. This was the highest stakes bluff ever.

"Watch your step," John warned, and Minnie glanced back to see the strewn heaps of dead Hynka—still warm severed limbs, jutting ribcages, ivory blood.

"They're going to keep following us," she said, stepping over a leg. "Once we're in the thick, we'll have to stop that … somehow."

"I know."

John and Minnie continued on through the throngs, back to back, each scanning their own 180° perimeter. 10m from the EV, 30m, 50m. Eventually, the horde thinned and gave way to immense blades of foliage.

As she predicted, the pack followed.

"I have an idea," Minnie said. "Try your 'stop' again. Through your suit's PA."

"Okay, and if they keep coming, we shoot one?"

"Exactly. And then you say it again. I have a feeling you won't have to say it three times."

John glanced back at her. "Then what?"

"Just say it. Loud."

John faced the advancing rank, stood tall, and shouted, *"Khoh!"* then resumed walking away with Minnie.

The front line of Hynka stopped, and then resumed as soon as John and Minnie continued into the foliage.

Minnie fired at the center of the group, striking one of them in the belly, home of their massive breathing organ. It released a wet cough, and they all stopped once more, attention redirected to the injured.

John shouted, *"Khoh!"* and glowing eyes refocused on him. He whispered, "Keep moving!"

Step after step, back to back, the pair moved deeper into the vegetation. The Hynka no longer followed. When Minnie lost sight of the last of them, she said, "Should we run?"

"I think we go slow a little farther. They might hear us if we run."

Minnie's thermal optic could see the group hadn't advanced any closer, but many had circled around the individual she'd shot. They were crouching over it, poking at the wound.

"How far to the sinkhole?" she asked.

"Less than one-K. If we run, I figure we could make it in less than ten minutes."

"And how fast could *they* do it?"

John grunted, "Hell, probably three."

"I think we should run."

John glanced at her and nodded. "Let's do it. But switch on infra and watch the terrain. It's even darker beneath this canopy and we can't afford a single mistake."

John was slow and less than nimble. They had numerous obstacles to traverse or avoid—downed epsequoias, swampy fungal patches, a river. Minnie repeatedly slowed for him to catch up. She switched back to thermal and glanced behind to see if anything had decided to give chase. No one so far, but as she returned her focus forward, a hot spot streaked by in the distance to their left.

"I think we have some stragglers out there," she said. "Not part of the group."

John panted and gasped. "How do you know?"

"Therm."

"I told you to switch to infra!"

"Are you ser—come on! Just shut up and switch to therm! They're going to hear us coming."

"I see them. But one of us needs to stay in infra … the terrain—"

"Fine, you save us from the ground. I'll protect us from the things that want to eat us."

She heard John grumble.

A minute later, the orange and red blobs beyond the blades perked up as the crackles and crunches of their footfalls reached the Hynkas' ears. Minnie raised her MW and patted John's arm to slow down.

"Hang on, hang on … here they come."

John put his hands on his knees, wheezing beside a thin, fan-shaped plant. "Which way? … Dizzy …"

"Two o'clock!"

Two glowing figures galloped toward them with incredible speed. Minnie worried that the one-ton beasts' momentum would carry them on well after several shots. Just ahead, the blobs split up, rounded an epsequoia trunk on either side, and then appeared in stark detail 20m away, four eyes shining in the starlight.

The ground quaked beneath Minnie's feet. She fired two rounds into the first, two in the second, then frantically unloaded on both.

John began firing, too.

The Hynka stumbled but the distance between them continued closing.

John pulled Minnie to the side, tossed her into a patch of undergrowth. When she looked up, the hacking and hissing creatures lay only a few meters away.

John helped her up. "Let's keep moving. And keep that thermal up, huh?"

"Right."

They ran the remaining distance, John gasping and struggling as flat forestland inclined into barren hills. A few moments later, his hand grazed her back, apparently pleading for her to slow down. "It's … coming up … the sinkhole."

Minnie climbed the last few sloped meters and rested on the flat plateau. As John trudged toward the finish line, she surveyed the nightscape with a slow 360° rotation. The sinkhole sat at the top of a gently sloping foothill overlooking healthy forestland to the east. Beyond the forest, a monolithic mountain loomed above the entire area. Behind Minnie, to the west of the sinkhole, the hill rose gradually higher before a towering rock sprang from the ground like some prehistoric skyscraper. Despite her very recent brushes with death, the scene was disarmingly peaceful, disrupted only by John's belabored panting.

"We've got eight to ten more to the south," Minnie pointed. "Maybe two-K away. Some loners here and there. Nothing very close."

Gradually recuperating, John went to the sinkhole and scanned around. "The entrance is definitely underwater. Let me see how we get out of here when needed."

Remaining on guard, Minnie kept her focus on the forest. She zoomed, spotting the original group as a large, morphing amoeba.

"Looks like the horde is all back at the EV. They really listened to you. I wonder if that would work again."

John inhaled a wheezing breath. "I wouldn't count on it. Man … still dizzy. Hard to get air ... out of the *air*."

Minnie sniffed. She'd noticed a sweetness to Epsy's air once away from the Hynka, but it hadn't really clicked. Lower O^2, higher nitrogen and argon. They weren't more than a thousand meters above sea level, but the air here would trigger symptoms like altitude sickness. "You're definitely out of shape, but that's mostly just the air mixture. Drop your visor and use the tank for now, but the sooner you deal with it, the faster you'll get—"

"I'll get used to it. I know." He pointed to an outcropping of rock on the other side of the sinkhole. "I think we could hide a rope over there. Tie it to the rocks, then bury it all the way to the hole. Someone'd have to be looking for it."

Minnie agreed; they set up the rope, tested the weight, and obscured it from view. Back at the hole's cliff edge, John pointed to one side of the glistening pool ten meters below them.

"It's deeper on the left than the right, but I wouldn't dive either way."

"Feet first it is," Minnie said, sealed her visor, and leapt in.

The fall lasted longer than she expected, the impact more jarring. The weight of her gear seemed to balance with the air in her helmet and the compressed minitank in her suit, rendering her buoyancy near neutral. She switched her optic to the highest infra and spotted the cavern entrance a couple meters below her feet.

MINNIE: M's only. Our audio's inop. I'm all clear now. Aim for my landing spot and hold balls. Infra on high.

JOHN: Okay. Clear out of the way.

Minnie kicked and paddled downward into the hole in the side wall. Semi-transparent root-like hairs protruded from the craggy tube's top. Even with the infra, she couldn't see more than a few meters ahead. She accessed her suit controls and enabled the helmet's infra emitters. The tunnel was suddenly alight, blinding like daytime, and she quickly decreased her optic sensitivity.

JOHN: Right behind you.

MINNIE: Just turned on my emitters. You can reduce your sensitivity.

JOHN: Already done. That was blinding.

Minnie sighed, fogging her visor for a moment.

MINNIE: How long is this tunnel?

JOHN: Should curve upward into main cave soon.

Just as his M popped up, the path of the tunnel began sloping upward.

The tube shrank and tightened around her, dangling roots grazing over her visor and helmet like long brittle fingers. Aether's scent entered Minnie's nostrils, Aether's presence beside her, stretched out in their bed, stroking Minnie's hair, helping her to fall asleep.

Her helmet scraped against the jagged roof, jolting her senses. She'd closed her eyes.

He's going to have to say something about that.

JOHN: You okay?

MINNIE: Fine. Cavern ahead. Switching to therm.

The tunnel widened out in all directions like a funnel on its side. Minnie stopped herself a meter below the glassy water surface. John drifted up beside her. She scanned the vast cavern for heat, finding only subtle hotspots on the ceiling and walls.

JOHN: Looks like only plantlife and microbes. We'll still need to sweep the rest of the tunnels and subcaverns.

Minnie deleted her M with the same conclusions and proceeded upwards to the surface.

JOHN: Are we sure the air in here isn't toxic?

MINNIE: You tell me. Does it have any surface supply?

They stepped carefully up the slippery slope until the ground flattened out. Minnie switched back to infra and surveyed the scene. Small puddles and stalagmites carpeted the ground beneath a thousand stalactites. Many had joined into columns thick and thin. As they walked to the other end of the cavern, the walls tapered in as if by a belt at a waist, then widened again into a small subcavern. At the smaller cave's far side, Minnie spotted a concentration of thin columns. The only other tunnel into the cavern was blocked off by a hundred reedy pillars, like delicate prison bars, along with an equal number of unjoined stalagmites and stalactites. It looked like a prehistoric fish mouth full of deadly teeth, but what it meant was nothing larger than a mouse could enter the cavern via that tunnel. All over the cave, the stalagmites jutting from the ground—thousands of years in the making—confirmed they'd never been visited by Hynka, or anything else of concern.

JOHN: The air is fine for now. Also, if you look at the fragile cave features, you can tell nothing's been in here. It's all been undisturbed for centuries, at least.

I know. But I don't need to tell you I know.

Minnie removed her helmet and sucked in a breath of the cool, moist air. There was a subtle sulfuric scent, like old eggs. Eggs. Other than the artificial sensory input of her game, she hadn't smelled anything remotely appetizing in decades.

Food . . .

They'd soon need to recommence ingestion and digestion. They only had three days of supplement-infused water. Fortunately, this had been planned before they left Earth. The SSKs had meds and calorie bars to aid the process, but it'd be painful. The mere idea of swallowing solids made Minnie's throat protest. And they'd eventually need to source sustenance from a planet without much to offer. The SSK only contained a couple weeks' worth of calories.

* * *

Minnie loosened and removed her pack, setting it down in the cave's only area that was flat, dry, and free of head or knee-cracking formations. John was squatting in front of his, fishing around inside. Minnie unsealed the top of her suit and peeled it away from her chest. The cavern air was even colder than she'd expected, but she needed to be out of the suit, free of the added weight. Conceptually, Epsy's 1.5 *g* hadn't seemed all that drastic a change, but paired with the suit and helmet, full water veins, and loaded backpack, it felt like she was carrying around a horse.

John sat down in front of a little contraption, popped it open, and expanded it into a box shape.

"What's that?" she asked. It felt strange to speak again. Strange perhaps because they were, for the time being, safe. They could now discuss things besides that which was immediately required for survival. She could say what *needed* to be said.

"Heater. It's seven-C in here. Probably still best to build the shelter and sleep inside." The device began to glow orange, bathing the cavern in light, probably for the first time ever.

"Right," Minnie said as she stepped out of her boots. "That thing powerful enough to raise the ambient temp in here?"

She glanced down, realized she was in nightclothes, and didn't hear John's lengthy response. She'd just thrown on whatever her hands had found in the wardrobe. Thin PJ pants and a draping top that reached her thighs. It was one of Aether's.

How much time had passed? She looked at her clock. Just one hour ago they'd been in orbit, Minnie sleeping peacefully.

"You know it's only been an hour?" She spoke without intent, simply sharing the surreality.

John merely looked at her eyes for an instant, then picked a little case out of his SSK. He walked into the darkness at the far end of the cavern.

"What are you doing?" she called.

"Launching a dragonfly into the blocked tunnel. See where it leads or if there's anything we need to worry about in there."

The high-pitched buzz of the dragonfly echoed in the cave for a minute as John fumbled with a headlight. His shadow stretched across the damp floor and swept back and forth as he messed with the tiny flying probe. The buzz grew louder as it lifted off his hand, hovered for a beat, then zipped between columns into the dark tunnel. John stood in silence at the end of the cave, presumably watching the dragonfly's progress through his fone.

"Anything interesting?" Minnie called.

"Not yet." He walked back and sat down on the other side of the heater, rubbing his hands together and holding them out to warm up.

The sound of the dragonfly gradually dissipated to nothing. Now there was only the heater's soft, infinite exhale.

John glanced up at her through his eyebrows. "We should probably talk now."

Yes, we should, she thought.

She unwrapped and shook out the survival blanket, allowing its tiny pores to sponge in air and expand. Piling it into a little circle in front of the heater, she sat down on it and folded her legs under each other. John bent his legs in front of him and rested his arms on his knees. His giant shadow stretched out and painted black the cavern behind him.

Minnie began before he could start. "Why aren't we in the Backup Habitat right now, sitting in the mission room doing a postmortem?"

John appeared stunned. He rubbed his right temple as he stammered "Well … I wasn't going to—"

"Who ordered full evac?"

"Well, I did, but—"

"And who determined the station damage was irreparable?"

"Minerva …"

She pointed her finger at him. "There was no time, right? You had to make split-second decisions? Lives were on the line? Am I right?"

He glared at her, blinking rapidly and squeezing his eyelids shut as he pressed his fingers in circles at his temple. "Please stop talking for a second. You weren't there; you don't know what happened …"

"Send it to me! You have a vid of the whole thing. It would have started recording the second the alarm sounded and kept the prior buffered thirty minutes for context."

"No, wireless went down on impact. It never got the signal to record."

Minnie snorted. "Convenient."

"Not really. Now listen to me a minute. I did start recording when I ordered evac …" Minnie was about to speak, but he held up a hand. "Yes, *I* ordered evac, but only *after* consulting with Aether. She agreed we didn't have time to get everyone through the tube to the BH, undock, and reach anything close to a safe distance before the blast. Yes, *maybe* you or Zisa or Ang could have repaired cooling, but who knows how long it would've taken? Zisa was panicked and you were in quarters on the other side of the station. You didn't make it to the EV until a minute before the station blew!"

Minnie was clenching her teeth. She didn't want to hear anything more. He was right on every count, and she needed for him to be wrong. She needed to purge and to see his face betray his regrets.

"Why didn't anyone come get me? Why was I the only one in quarters?"

"Everyone else was already up. Tom was in hygiene when the pod struck, but other than you and him, we were all in Wheel A or below. *Another* reason why the BH wasn't an option … and Aether *wanted* to go get you, but she would have held up her EV, and Qin along with it. I promised her that I would wait for you. In fact, just before you showed up, I'd unstrapped and was on my way out to get you."

Minnie didn't buy it. "Really. To save *me*. The person that *stole* Aether away from you? Leaving you *alone* for the rest of your life?"

John closed his eyelids. He dug his knuckles in, rubbing near his fone.

That was too harsh ...

But she *wanted* to hurt him. She *wanted* him to feel pain. Why should he get to sit there in a protective shell of rationalization and logic? A robot like him needed something long and pointed to pierce through the metallic exterior to the heart.

They sat in silence for a moment, John's head hung between his knees. Minnie wondered if he was crying. She couldn't tell anymore if she felt good or bad about the prospect of John Li tears. But she wouldn't be apologizing either way.

John startled her with a sudden short laugh—a choked sort of outburst. It echoed through the cavern.

Weakly, he said, "I wanted to talk about food." He chuckled quietly to himself.

"I'm sorry," Minnie whispered. The words escaped despite her resistance.

"No ... no you're not. You have a lot of anger and frustration built up against me. It's only natural it come out now."

Minnie dropped her eyes to the powdery floor, the oddly unmoving shadow of the heater. As her forehead warmed, her mind had expected the random flicker of fire.

John went on, "You know, before Aether ... before the two of you ... you were the single highest source of complaints against me in the inbox and in group. Afterwards, well ... you hardly ever say a word in group anymore. I guessed you felt bad, or believed that you'd *won* in some way." He peered up at her with his bio eye, still squeezing the other shut and rubbing around his fone. "Plus, you got *her*. In-house therapy, right? I tried to tell you so many times, I've never harbored adversarial feelings about you. Even after Aether ... That was all on me. My failures. My shortcomings. She stuck with me far longer than she should have. It hurt like hell, but I was happy that she found you. *Surprised* a bit, yes, that it was you ..."

"And not Qin or Pablo or Tom?"

"I suppose. Though probably not why you'd guess. In reality, my relationship with her has been great since then. It was what we needed.

To be the friends we were before one of us decided it should be something more."

Minnie pulled the blanket up over her exposed shoulders. "So you're saying you never miss her? The rest of her?"

"I'm … No, I'm not saying that. Of course there's a … *closeness*, when it's all out there. We don't talk about certain things anymore—probably for fear of triggering the other."

"Of course not." Minnie observed a tenderness in him for the first time. Each of his words required herculean effort, but he was opening up nonetheless. She went on, "Aether is very maternal. I can imagine how that was a comfort sometimes. And something that wouldn't be appropriate now."

John glanced up at her and looked back down just as fast. He nodded and sighed.

Minnie swallowed. "I see it now. And not as a weapon—honestly. I see how lonely it must be for you. I'm sorry if I ever made it harder on you." A thought suddenly popped in Minnie's head and she was helpless to hold it back. "You've got vids of her though, don't you? Gross stuff."

John appeared stunned. "Vids … What? I wouldn't—"

"Nevermind. Don't answer that. I don't want to know."

The cave was quiet for a time, only the sounds of drips and drip echoes, their breathing, the heater's low drone. Even with his head down, Minnie could see John wincing. He'd been nursing an apparent headache on his fone side.

Minnie broke the silence. "What's wrong with your head?"

"Huh?" He looked up at her. She pointed at the fingers pressed into his temple, rubbing in circles. "Oh, right. Something wrong with my fone or housing. Not from evac, though. Been going on for a few weeks."

"Does it go away if you shut down?" John nodded. Minnie flipped a palm upward. "So shut down."

"Upgrade was on that supply pod. Two gens."

"Bummer." She peered around the cave, the silence growing louder with each second. "So … you wanted to talk about food?"

John nodded again, sucked in a deep breath, all too ready to think and talk about something else. He pulled his backpack to him. "We need to start day one meds. The EV water has sups, but I believe we still take the day one tab with three-fifty mils from our suits."

"Two hundred mils is the minimum," Minnie corrected. "We might want to ration until we check that sinkhole water."

"That's fine for now, sure. Tomorrow we'll dive into those bars."

"They're chalk flavored, if I recall correctly."

"Their creators were focused on concentrating calories and nutrients, not taste."

"Cripes, John, it was a joke."

"I know, and I appreciate the attempt at levity, but perhaps now isn't the best time. We've got people up there, you know."

Done. Oh, sweet mother of pearl. So done.

He studied her face. "We on the same page?"

She concealed her murderous ire with a deadpan he could never read. "Absolutely."

"Good. Now, ingestion is going to be uncomfortable, regardless of flavor. Though I don't think we'll be able to taste for a couple weeks." He ran a finger down his smooth, glossy tongue. Their taste buds had seemed to disappear after the first few weeks without solids. "We'll have to be careful when we run out of calorie bars. Rely more on scents as far as spoiling and such goes. Obviously, we have multisensors for chemical content."

"Right."

"And there's one other thing." John gave her a look. The *I hate to bring it up* look. She knew instantly what he was going to say. "Your meds."

"You don't have to worry about that. I'll be fine."

She'd been regulated for so long that it hadn't even occurred to her since evac. Her last HSPD breakdown had taken place at age 15, and it'd been brutal. Tearing through the city, folks couldn't even catch up with her long enough to sedate her.

During her lowest lows after an episode, Minnie's father always tried to console her by offering that "with a brain as bright and active as yours, this is the unfortunate trade-off." Now recalling the quote, John's voice took the place of her father's, ruining the tiny bit of solace those words had always provided. John wouldn't have a damned clue what to do with her if she had an all-out episode in this place. *"Mmm, gosh, Minerva, perhaps now isn't the best time for a mental breakdown. Couldja be a champ and reschedule this one for a later date?"*

With her track record and luck, she'd dive suitless into that tunnel, scale the rope, and set out to be the first human to climb that mountain across the valley.

If only episodes were limited to the physical. Visual hallucinations, voices, paranoia, along with a potent surge of catecholamines from her adrenal glands to fuel it all. Her case was among the most acute: without sedation, she could keep going until she passed out or dropped dead. And it wasn't as simple as adrenal regulation. When triggered, floodgates opened in nearly every gland, closing only after complete depletion, when there was nothing left to release.

"I'll be fine," she repeated.

"Minnie, hyperschizoid perso—"

"I know what I've got, John."

"It won't be what you remember. Just hear me out for a second. The metabed on the way here and your meds have concealed an intensifying disorder. You know how they've got our v-clones in the system? Well before launch, the docs and psychs and I slid each one of us ahead twenty years, forty, a hundred, and we went back and adjusted for post-metabed, various meds, weight gain, environmental changes, exigency measures, etset. So I—and all the docs at the Center—know *exactly* where you're at right now. Metabolically, you're twenty-eight, well past HSPD's peak. We need to figure out some alternative meds for you."

Minnie rubbed her knuckles together and avoided his gaze. He was right, but she still hated when he was right. And more, she hated that she had a *weakness*—something more to worry about.

Childhood episodes dwelled in her memory with strange clarity alongside other key milestones. Her first crush. The episode that ended on the school roof. Her first thesis. Flying a homemade skimmer over her neighborhood and getting caught. The attack during a road trip during which she tried to throw herself from the vehicle at 300 km/h. Ah, memories.

Her regular hallucinations had been harmless enough. A neighbor kid named Otto and his dad that were, retrospectively, far too captivated by her ideas, and always seemed to show up whenever she'd conceived new concepts. Otto and his dad, of course, turned out to be imaginary.

Some illusions were quite enjoyable. Commercial transports from the nearby airport would often change course at Minnie's will, flying in circles or performing impossible stunts. Occasionally, the transports would control Minnie and she'd have to run where they commanded. While still little, this had proven fun. Experts always said that imagination-heavy playtime was a critical component for cognitive development. Perhaps the crazy had made her smart.

The real danger revealed itself when the Hyper in HSPD made its presence known. Minnie only vaguely remembered the imagery—melting walls and sinking floors, hard surfaces turning to slowly enveloping tar or molasses, the slinking, malevolent entities of extreme hallucinogenic drug overdoses—but she clearly recalled the emotions. Crippling fear and panic. Her worst and last attack had introduced her to "chasers," as the psychiatrists called them. Some see insects, others see zombies or some variant of crazed human attackers. Oddly enough, Minnie's chasers turned out to be cats. She wasn't normally afraid of cats, but this was what her capricious brain had decided to conjure. Thousands of yowling cats pursuing, their glowing yellow eyes intent on catching her and licking the flesh from her body until she was only bones.

Her father had at first looked to homeopathic remedies: hyoscyamine, ergot, belladonna, and such. Minnie could function okay on them, but they'd cast a color-dulling overlay on the world, and killed some of the lucidity that made her brilliant. After rejecting countless novel surgery proposals, father and daughter agreed she'd take whatever meds the doctors deemed appropriate.

Minnie's rubbing knuckles were growing sore as she became aware of John's waiting face.

"There's an option," she said. "In Threck Country for sure, but I don't know about here. It's a hallucinogenic fungusflower some farmer Threck consume for entertainment. They call it *alditz*. The effects come from a pure, separate fungus that accumulates on the stigma. Similar chemical makeup to some of my meds. It's widely available ... *if* we could get there. Not that we needed another reason."

"You know all that off the top of your head?"

"One of my first tasks when Angela's probes began populating her botany database. Like I said, I know what I've got. We just weren't supposed to land over here, were we?"

"Good thinking. Probably would've been nice to share that information with your mission commander. You had your last dose about six hours ago, correct?"

"Something like that."

"With zero sedation, your profile says that you could go a week or more without symptoms. Do you agree with that assessment?"

Minnie wrapped the blanket around her tighter. She didn't like beginning a countdown clock. "I guess. And if you're thinking about sedating me—"

"I'm not. Just trying to plan for everything, Minnie."

"Good. Because I'd be useless. And you know I don't like when you call me that."

"Sorry. In the systems, your M's ... It's hard when *everyone* else—" John stopped, apparently recalling he wasn't a member of *everyone else*. He let out a deep breath, nodding. "Right. Sorry, Minerva."

Her irritation with him had reached its traditional peak, but she'd lost the energy to argue. Besides, if she didn't guide them to a new subject, she may just have to kill him. "I didn't mean for that to come out bitchy. It's just that it catches me off-guard every time. Nothing against you personally. I actually don't like it from most people." It was a lie. He had no place using an endearment. "Moving on, do you have any ideas on how we get to the other side of the planet?"

"I was about to ask you the same thing."

Minnie sat up straight. “Good, because I do.”

15

If the Backup Habitat survived the station's destruction, Minnie could use it to communicate with any other survivors on the planet or still in orbit. She had some thoughts about the supply pods as well, but didn't know enough about their subsystems, only the fact that they'd all been repurposed as Epsy's GPS satellites. With the right gear, she could connect to the pod network, but then what? *The right gear*. What were the chances there? How had the EV faired? Once the tasty flesh filling departed, had the Hynkas' interest remain? Had at least one skimmer survived the abuse? When would Minnie's stomach begin aching? What productive task or research could she do on her fone?

She couldn't sleep.

Sharing the cramped tent with John had kept her warm, but her mind raced, refusing to settle. John didn't exactly snore, but his breathing had grown progressively louder and more strained sounding, as if he were lifting a heavy object with each exhale. How could Aether stand sleeping with him for all those years? And then Aether was all she could think about.

It was unlikely that Aether was dead. Objectively, this much was certain, and true as well for the rest of the station team. Even those flung directly away from orbit were not in immediate danger. An EV could sustain two people for at least a week. Water supply was probably the biggest limiting factor. If properly rationed, a pair could stretch an EV's water tank over 8-10 days. They'd all have their SSK supply of calorie bars after reinitiation, but food would outlast water. So dehydration, Minnie determined, was how anyone stuck on an EV would die. That is, if they didn't take other measures first, such as shutting down environmental.

This was how she preferred to think of Aether going: by choice. Not the slow, agonizing churn of dehydration. No, no going, period. No goddamn *going* for Aether.

Eventually, Minnie moved on to a thorough dissection of EV design and evac procedures.

Why had the pod systems been programmed based upon optimal station orientation and coordinates in the first place? Pods should be designed to assume worst-case scenario: station chaos. In what fantasy world did evacs take place under optimal conditions?

EVs should have full propulsion and guidance systems programmed with specific coordinates based upon layers of redundant sources: GPS, magnetic field, land feature recognition, and above all, direct, on-the-spot user input. She knew why they didn't. They were built and coded 35 years ago based directly upon the even-older pods used in local system research. They'd never once received an upgrade and no one on the station ever gave them half a damned thought—Minnie included. And if anyone had, obviously, pod enhancement would forever remain buried beneath an ever-growing mountain of higher priorities.

She could have done something. She was Little Miss Think of Everything.

But as much as her subconscious wanted to lay some amount of blame on her shoulders, she knew that software and guidance systems could only do so much. It wasn't like she could have retrofit the pods with new launching mechanisms or propulsion. EV thrusters were next to useless if a pod experienced a dud launch (detached from dock without a booster blast), or was spinning out of control, or was shot beyond orbital arc by greater than 20°, even in the hands of a skilled pilot.

It was true though, and some small hope, that when it came to piloting, Qin was the most capable of the bunch. John had asserted that EV assignments were based upon "mission factors," not skill and survival probability rating, but it was certainly interesting that the one person on the station that he cared about above all others was assigned to an EV with the individual most able to control and land it. Then again, John pairing himself with Minerva would seem to refute the theory. Despite her consistently superior SP rating, she was the last person he'd want to be stuck with, and vice versa. Oh, how he'd hated being number two at anything. And, oh, look how big of him to congratulate her each time she beat him.

Exhaustion finally dragged Minnie into the black of a dreamless sleep.

She awoke a little over four hours later—groggy, yet with a new determination. Exiting the tent without waking John, she shivered at the still-chilly air and quietly pulled her survival bag out with her.

Two hours later, a list of if-thens continued growing in her fone's project management interface.

Communication with the rest of the crew was paramount, but without the Backup Habitat as a comms relay for the little transmitters in the SSKs, she and John would need to return to the EV to salvage the integrated comms units.

If the BH did survive, then her first task was to attempt contact with it. If she established contact with the BH, then she could initiate comms with the other EVs. If she could communicate with other EVs, she could talk to Aether.

While this seemed like a mission in itself, it wasn't strictly for personal reasons. If Qin could set their EV on a course for entry, he could probably instruct the other errant EVs to do the same. Maybe he was already working on it, or maybe his judgment was clouded and he was sitting by doing nothing useful. They could simply need a nudge from an outside voice.

To even attempt comms with the BH, they needed to leave the cave. And if they were leaving the cave, they might as well return to the EV and salvage all of the laser-based comms components.

If Hynka were still scratching around the EV, then she needed to find a way to draw them well away from the area. If she successfully earned enough time with the EV, they could potentially recover one or both skimmers and fly the equipment back to their hideout. With a single passenger, the skimmers could zoom up to 180 km/h, and if they went out light on equipment, one flyer could support both of them, albeit slower.

So it looked like the EV factored into every branch of her chart. More pure water, comms, power, transportation—the skimmers alone were essential mission assets.

This branch was but one small section of the expansive, growing flow chart, all of its initial boxes splitting off into multiple options based upon various outcomes, and then branching off again and again.

John either found it all too overwhelming or had decided to curb his commentary. Minnie found the process relaxing, centering. Until everything was all laid out, the future—both near and distant—was far too murky and anxietous.

"We're up to fourteen," John proudly proclaimed from the other end of the cavern.

"That's great," Minnie murmured as she sat nestled in her survival bag, leaning against the cavern wall, now fleshing out various foot-travel scenarios in her flow chart, in the event they were unable to recover one or both skimmers.

"It's amazing how quickly the temperature in here normalizes," John said as he moved one of the tiny unisensors onto a head-height stalagmite. "If we're still here in forty hours, I think I can have it stabilized at twenty-two degrees."

"Mm-hm," Minnie replied, and then actually considered what he was saying. She looked up, frowning. "Do you think it's a good idea to be raising the temp in here so much? I mean, it's probably been essentially the same for thousands of years, or more."

John appeared to think it over. "I'm not sure what it could hurt. It's not going to affect structural integrity, no animals to consider—"

"Well, we don't know what kind of microorganisms are in here. Maybe you're affecting something's metabolic rate. Just a thought." She shrugged. "Also, we didn't scan for dormant bacteria or anything. Remember, we still haven't been inoculated against *anything* on Etsy."

"I'm well aware that we haven't been able to do our inocs. And it's true, we could have caught any number of bugs in here. I'll have the heater standby at sixteen."

I know you're well aware.

Minnie shook her head and chuckled quietly, but, in the cave, no sound escaped the other's ears.

"What's funny?" John said, walking back to their little camp area.

"Nothing. Okay, something. It's just that, I know that I'm a know-it-all, but you're like the *definition* of Mr. Know-It-All. I guess it would be less distracting if we could have a conversation wherein you didn't feel the need to assure me of what you already knew, thought, anticipated, etset. It's unnecessary information."

John wasn't amused. "We're all know-it-alls, Minerva, or we wouldn't have been assigned to the mission."

"Yeah, yeah, *I know.* Forget it. Now, please stop talking while I finish polishing this chart."

She could feel him simmering, see his hovering body in her peripheral, wanting so badly to argue with her or at least slip in the last word. But he remained quiet and eventually returned to the other end of the cavern to retrieve his dragonfly. It had followed fourteen different channels thus far, each eventually tapering down to a few centimeters. Now its battery needed a recharge.

Minnie wanted to remind John that without sunlight, the heater unit was their only significant power source, but she was secretly glad he'd warmed the cave. It meant they didn't have to spend another night together in the tent.

She'd sleep "outside" tonight.

* * *

Fully suited up, John stepped carefully into the little pond from which he and Minerva had emerged the day before. Shifting his optics to IR, he opened a new M.

> JOHN: Activating IR emitters in a moment. Be sure
> to

But he stopped and deleted the M. He needed to maintain minimal communication with Minerva. Her sensitivity to anything and everything he said or observed made it challenging to get anything done. It was on him to adjust, filter, and keep their interactions productive. Minerva most certainly would not.

Exchange only the bare minimum of required information. He started the M again:

JOHN: Activating IR emitters.

MINNIE: OK

He crept down the slope, his boot treads gripping the rock despite the slick glaze, and shifted his weight forward to ease all the way into the water. Strangely, it felt good to be swimming again, or maybe it was the warmth and security of the suit.

What might they find outside the cave and around the sinkhole? There was no reason to believe the Hynka horde hadn't tracked their scents to the hole, and now stood around the perimeter with 10,000 more friends. But once he reached the end of the tube, twisted upside down to look up, and flipped through various optics, it became clear that nothing awaited them. At least not near the rim of the sinkhole.

JOHN: All clear out here.

John slid out of the tube and watched Minerva follow. Now vertical, they both looked up and around, daylight illuminating the water and the sinkhole's craggy walls. John kicked his way to the rope, still hanging against the side where they'd left it the night before, and tugged on it to verify it was still secured.

JOHN: I'll go up rope first.

MINNIE: OK

Bare minimum was working nicely.

John repositioned himself, planting his boots on the wall and coiling the rope around one wrist, then the other, and then pulled himself up. It was surprisingly easy despite Epsy's 1.5 *g*. From day one, the station's personal quarters segment had been set to 1.5 *g* to prep their muscles in the event of surface evac. Nevertheless, he'd expected to feel exceedingly weak, especially with the added weight of the suit.

And then he reached the surface of the water and felt like a complete idiot. Of course it had been easy to lift himself while half-submerged in water.

Now with torso above the surface, John replanted his boots, took a deep breath, and strove to pump his resolve.

You've got this! One arm over the next! Keep momentum! Feet in sync, go go go!

But he couldn't move. His arms could scarcely hold half his body above the water. Even his fingers were beginning to lose their grip on the rope. It was as if his bottom half was being dragged down by a 100-kilo weight. This climb wasn't happening.

With the last of his strength, he lowered himself back into the water, Minerva's curious face shining up at him.

MINNIE: What's up?

JOHN: No strength. Can't lift my own weight. Muscle atrophy worse than expected.

MINNIE: I'll give it a shot. Maybe I can pulley you up if I'm able to make it out.

JOHN: Good luck.

John kicked himself back against the far wall and looked up as Minerva made her attempt. Once again, he found it difficult to inhale a satisfying breath, though his tank should be supplying plenty of oxygen. Thirty seconds of exertion and he was this beat?

Minerva's legs slowly disappeared above the water line. Yes, it would be embarrassing for her to successfully scale the rope, but he was much more interested in getting out of the cave and sinkhole. Though a moment ago he hadn't considered their refuge anything other than a safe camping spot, it had abruptly turned into a prison.

A big splash, scattered bubbles, Minerva's flailing feet.

MINNIE: Dammit! Only made it about ¼ up. Arms like jelly.

She floated down to his level and faced him, her frustration visible through her visor. She glanced back up at the resettling rope end.

MINNIE: Maybe if I dump the suit. That'll drop 20kg.

John thought about it for a second and realized that bare hands and feet would negate any benefits of dropping the added weight.

JOHN: Gloves and boots?

MINNIE: Oh, right. And probably not a good idea to de-integrate them from the suit, huh?

They stared at each other in silence for a moment, both contemplating the situation, and both clearly at a loss.

JOHN: I'll set us up a little gym in the cave. We focus on pulls and lifts, squats for our legs. I don't know about your core, but mine seems pretty worthless. Swimming maneuvers in here might be good for us too.

MINNIE: I can't envision any regiment that gets us out of here in less than 10 days.

JOHN: Well, yeah, of course it'll take time.

Minerva's face skipped right past irritation to pure rage. Bubbles burst from her helmet as she screamed. Her visor fogged, but he didn't really have to read her lips. "We don't have that kind of time!" She lurched and swam down to the tunnel entrance, disappearing inside.

John fought the urge to M her, to tell her she needed to calm down, that they had to make the best of their situation, that this wouldn't be their first disappointment, or to cite the bleakest of his own thoughts: now, more than ever, they needed to get along because they may never see another human being for the rest of their lives.

What would be the point? What exactly did he want from her, anyway? He wanted her mentally stable, that much was certain. How much longer would she remain in balance?

Secretly, he hoped for an inkling of respect, but this was a laughable notion. If lucky, he'd settle for being *tolerated.* Whatever provided them both the best chance of survival.

And then there was the rest of the crew. Aether and Qin. Zisa and Pablo. Angela and Tom. Ish. John couldn't help them anymore. Their fates were in their own hands. If he allowed into his mind the horror of their situations, nothing would get done. Perhaps he'd end up as erratic as Minerva.

The only one they could possibly help was Ish. She'd been the sole crewmember to evac alone, and was launched in roughly the same direction as he and Minerva. Wherever Ish ended up, he hoped she wasn't scared or hurt or dying, awaiting a rescue team that wasn't coming anytime soon.

Emerging from the cave's entrance pond, John saw Minerva set her helmet down and crouch to dig into her SSK. He popped his visor and drank of the moist air.

"What's the plan?" he said as he stepped around the little orange tent.

"I need to not hear you right now. Can you not talk?"

She stood, unfolding her multitool into its prybar/hammer configuration. She strode barelegged and barefoot, and without any kind of eye protection, into the subcavern, apparently planning to bash away at the mineral columns blocking the passageway.

Chinking sounds echoed into the main cavern as John strolled after her. Grayscale infrared Minerva was swinging wildly at the formations, her ponytail whipping about the back of her head.

He called over the racket, "Can I help?"

She stopped and looked back, eyes glowing like some fire demon, stance primed as if John might as well be a mineral column. He held out his multitool.

She resumed bashing. "Fine."

As the pair attacked the obstructions, demolishing structures that were surely millions of years old, John paused.

"Hey, do you think you could reprogram a dragonfly to consider itself human? As far as phys dimensions go?"

Minerva stopped after a few more swings, considering. She wiped sweat and fragments from her forehead. "Yes. But not considering itself human so much as establishing operating parameters. Environment must meet xyz requirements. It's a good idea. Though if it leaves DC range you won't be able to tell it what to do if it finds an unanticipated parameter."

"Well, we can have it set to return as soon as the parameters are no longer met *or* until it makes it outside, right? I'm just thinking because it's mapped so many branches already—"

"Yeah yeah, branches. Something we can traverse. You made your point. I said it's a good idea, didn't I? Can we shut up and go with it?"

John smiled as she walked ahead of him into the main cavern, swallowing his suggestion like a bag of sand.

* * *

Lying on her back, Minnie stared at the orange material above her, faintly illuminated by the glowing heater outside. She'd slept alone in the tent for the past six nights—*nights* as in the six-hour sleep periods prescribed by their fones. Outside the cave, days followed Epsy's roughly nineteen-hour cycle, and Minnie frequently checked her fone to see whether it was day or night out there. Station life had long since eroded this association between daylight and waking hours, but she found herself troubled by the knowledge of a warm sun shining down on her EV only a short hike away, just outside—just outside her grasp.

Minnie didn't want to sleep, but her body needed the healing time after each day's rigorous exercise regime. She'd charted out the whole program, rotating between muscle groups, allowing certain areas more time to heal than others. Build maximum strength in minimal time. She'd tried to help John do the same, even sending him his own chart, but he didn't have her discipline or resolve. He refused to push his body, and as a result, progressed slower than her.

In other news, he'd already passed two BMs, and Minnie hadn't defecated once. For some reason, this was John's favorite topic.

Her body definitely seemed to want it. Rolling onto her side, she could feel it in her transverse colon, high in the abdomen and painful, unmoving. Earlier, John had told her it wasn't happening because she didn't want it to happen. She'd replied that if he continued commenting on her lack of movements, he'd soon find one waiting for him in his survival bag. He finally shut up.

There were good days and bad between them—mainly her fault, she knew—but sometimes she just couldn't stomach his voice. Sometimes the little clock looming high atop her fone would remind her how much time had passed since evac. Aether up there, Minnie stuck in this damned cell with tunnels that led nowhere and a mocking rope dangling over the sinkhole, and a man that seemed to lovingly nurture the very worst in her, able to trigger her wrath with only a few words or even the most innocuous of sounds.

Earth's original space programs called it "irrational antagonism" when otherwise great friends, isolated together for an extended period, would grow increasingly irritable, previously nonexistent pet peeves festering into rage-worthy obsessions. Some orbiting Russians even came to blows.

But John was not a great friend to begin with, and he was intentionally annoying, and his sleeping sounds would surely inspire murderous ire in the most angelic of grandmas!

Minnie smiled, rolled onto her back, and closed her eyes. The tent's orange hue remained as a ghost vision behind her eyelids. Like some kind of self-hypnosis, she advised herself that despite John's obnoxious breathing, sleep would come with the fading of the orange. With the last bits of orange, she'd fall into a deep, deep—

Well, that's weird.

John was still asleep outside the tent, but his usual exhale sounds were different. In fact, instead of the familiar straining noises she'd come to expect, he sounded strangely content—moaning pleasantly as if he were receiving a foot massage or having a sex dream. Minnie rolled back onto her side and flipped her optics to thermal, curious if any regions would appear warmer than the rest of him. Maybe he'd dozed off while watching some pervy old vid of Aether that he'd never in a million years admit to having.

What the hell?

His temperature was all over the place—a strange glob of yellow/orange warmth around his side, another concentration around his left thigh, one at his neck, each region surrounded by drastically cooler blue rings. Circulation? Was he ill?

She sat up for a better perspective, counting four of the hotspots. John continued moaning appreciatively. Maybe his survival bag only had him half covered, one leg thrown over the top to cool. The bag was practically invisible through therm, so she switched to biomag.

"No! Oh, crap, John!"

Minnie scrambled out of the tent with a virtual full-light view of the cave, biomag's surreal colorizing casting the place and John's body in embellished tones. He remained asleep despite her yelling, a little smile curled into his cheeks as he sighed with pleasure. But on the left side of his neck, from the edge of his jaw to the armpit, lay a flat, parasitic lifeform apparently feeding on him. A larger one was on his opposite side, stretched out along his ribcage, down to the hipbone. His left thigh bore a smaller creature about the size of her hand, and the last was attached to his right calf. She couldn't tell exactly what they were doing, but it mustn't hurt too much, she imagined, or John would've woken up.

Minnie scanned around the cave in search of others. Indeed, there were many, many more, though only a couple centimeters each, and all over the walls. On the ground around John's mat, several of the tiny worms were making their way to him. This would be happening to her if John hadn't traded, "gallantly" opting to sleep outside the tent. At the time, she'd thought it silly, perhaps a bit sexist or martyrish of him.

She crouched down and slapped his cheek. "John. Wake up. Hey." He licked his lips, sucked in a deep breath, and released a longer satisfied moan. "John," she said louder. "Hey, wake up. Bit of an emergency here! Hello!" She slapped him harder. Poked his chest.

Finally, John stirred and opened a single groggy eye. "Yeah?" He wore a dumb, drunken smile.

"Listen carefully. You have some sort of platyzoa attached to your skin."

"Platyzoa?" he slurred, squeezing his eyes shut and rising up onto his elbows. "I think it's fine. Go ahead."

"John, do you understand what I'm saying? We need to get these parasites off of your body. I don't know what kind of damage they're doing."

John displayed a clownish pout and deepened his voice, mocking, "That sounds *pretty* serious." He rolled onto his left side, pulled the bag up over his shoulder, and nestled back in to sleep. He murmured, "Go away, *Minernie.*"

The parasites must have been releasing some sort of drug into his bloodstream, Minnie surmised, something with a narcotic effect.

He doesn't feel them.

She pulled the top of the bag off his shoulder to examine the large specimen on his ribs, wondering if a type of dermal numbing agent was also at work.

He doesn't feel—

Alarmed anew, Minnie hastily scanned her own body for foreign creatures. Wearing only a tank and undershorts, she ran her hands over every body part she could reach: arms, neck, face, ears, scalp, shoulder blades, armpits, all the way down to her ankles, where she discovered what felt like an old bandage. Hyperaware of the dangerous ground and perhaps even ceiling, Minnie fled into the tent, zipped the door shut, surveyed the place for intruders, and then sat down, examining the tiny thing attached to her ankle. She scratched at its edges with a fingernail, watched it partially detach. It peeled back with surprising ease, writhing like a disturbed slug. She pinched the body between thumb and forefinger, pulling it off the rest of the way, and set it on her palm, inspecting the underside through a series of optics. Magnification exposed rows of tiny cilia, some secreting a viscous fluid, while other extremities appeared to be for absorption. Around the edges she found little articulated hooks searching for something to grab.

She plucked a small container from her kit and deposited the creature inside. Her focus returned to her ankle. The small oval of skin appeared burnt and moist, as if injured and then coated in salve. Still no pain. She was afraid to touch it, but also worried that the parasite's acidic mucous could still be breaking down her skin. After a few swipes with an alkaline medipad, Minnie began to sense the little wound—raw, like the skin beneath a freshly picked scab. She hurriedly finished with an antiseptic cream and slapped a dermal over it.

She needed to rip those things off of John immediately. Who knew how long they'd been on him, or how rapidly they were consuming him? His drugged state suggested they could ingest an entire body without the victim putting up a fight. A brilliant, terrifying design.

Fully suited up, and with the tent closed behind her, Minnie stepped beside John, bent over, and unzipped his survival bag all the way to his feet. With their limited attire, she didn't want to ruin his one pair of enviropants. She tugged them down from his waist with several yanks.

John groaned halfheartedly. "What? … Hey, quit it now ..." One hand blindly grappled for covers he couldn't reach.

With his pants at his ankles, Minnie gained a clear view of the slug on his calf. A subtle wave rolled across its surface from one end to the other, repeating once more. She slipped her gloved fingers beneath one end of it, tightened her grip, and peeled it off. It was definitely more tightly affixed to him than hers had been, like separating strong Velcro. Goopy threads stretched out between the worm's underside and John's leg. The concept of liquefied skin launched a shot of bile up Minnie's throat. She swallowed and tossed the contorting parasite to the wide puddle at the other side of the cave.

She looked down at his calf.

Oh no …

It was bad. An uncontrollable quiver attacked her chest and she inhaled a shaky breath.

No no no.

She rolled him onto his back and ripped the creature from his thigh. It, too, had made it well into the muscle, cauterizing the wound as it delved deeper and deeper into its food. The hunk splashed in the puddle and a sickening revelation hit her. She'd just tossed John's left quadriceps. The wriggling mass had begun as a tiny thing—probably smaller than the one she'd plucked from her ankle—but it had broken down John's flesh, fat, and muscle, converting the matter and expanding its own form. It had felt like a couple kilos when she threw it.

And then there was the ribcage.

The parasite landed somewhere near the last. Tears began to cloud Minnie's eyes. With several ribs half-exposed, she didn't know how John could possibly live through this. Even with the cauterization, burn victims' greatest threat was infection.

"D'you mind?" he said, slowly rolling over. "Some of us're tryin' t'sleep here. What … what time's it?"

Minnie opened her visor a bit more as she studied the worm on his neck. If it had burrowed deep enough, infection would be the least of his worries. "John, you had some parasites on you. I'm pulling off the last one."

"I'm here to help." He was still intoxicated.

"Go ahead and roll all the way toward me, okay?"

He complied with some effort. "I'm itchy. Hey, am I naked?"

Minnie leaned close and pulled back the end attached to his jaw. Indeed, it had made it well into the mandible, bone apparently no more resilient than flesh, but she was more concerned with John's neck. She continued peeling it slowly away, its body compacting as it squirmed in her grip. It had melted away much of the neck muscle, but had yet to reach the carotid or jugular. Farther down she could see that the things seemed to prefer muscle—his pectoral and a bit of deltoid muscle eaten deeper than the surrounding skin.

Fully detached, she flung it away to join the rest.

"Minerva, what ezackly're you doin' t'me right now? Y'know …" He lowered his voice to a slurred whisper. *"I don' really thing of you thi'sway. No 'ffense."*

She looked at his eyes, almost wishing he could remain ignorant of the reality he'd soon comprehend. She patted his chest, examining the ground with biomag. The little ones were everywhere. Fortunately, they moved at a snail's pace. Minnie leaned close to John's face.

"I need to grab some medipads to clean up these wounds and neutralize the acids."

"What're *these wounds*?" He was sounding a trifle more lucid. "Who's hurt? Am *I* hurt?"

"Just sit tight," she said and walked around him, squashing the nearest parasites and twisting her boot into each.

"Jaw stiff. Cheek fills like … dentist. Neck too." He poked at his cheek and she saw him itching around his ribs.

Minnie tried to sound calm for him. "Try not to touch anything, okay?"

As she knelt down and pulled the medikit from his SSK, she knew the instant that full reality kicked in for him.

"Oh … *no* … what, what happened to me?"

She turned to see him straining to sit up, shirt raised, and arm lifted out of the way to inspect his side. Four of his exposed ribs and the meat between them shone in the heater's glow.

16

297 hours on Epsy. 12 Earth days. 15 Epsy days.

If Minnie were somehow still alive in an EV at that moment, adrift or settled into some crazy high elliptical orbit, would she want to go on living? To have survived this long would've meant purifying and drinking urine, gathering condensation, or possibly having had the forethought to kill her podmate on day one, thus keeping all water and solid sustenance for herself.

There remained only two possibilities: Aether was dead, or she and Qin successfully made it to the surface. If the latter were the case, they'd likely try the same things Minnie intended: attempt a link to the BH or—and Qin would be the one to think of it—hack the supply pod network to post a message. Without an EV, Minnie was limited to her suit's comms which reached a mere 3-5K in this sort of terrain. Aether, or any crewmember for that matter, could've been broadcasting for days and Minnie wouldn't know it.

Minnie hadn't given up on comms after all this time, but would others? Would Aether? It depended upon environment and survival concerns. Anyone landing in an arctic region would probably remain focused on the bare necessities of living. But anyone making it to Threck Country, a land full of wild fruits and fungus, rivers and coastline loaded with healthy, edible vertebrates, no significant predators—those people could afford to split their attention.

Perched atop Epsy's equivalent of a redwood—the towering, squishy lichen/fungi that Angela named *epsequoias*—Minnie slowly scanned the landscape. The closest Hynka roamed more than 5K south of her, which was about 7.5K from the EV landing site. There were three of them on the move even farther south. In search of other life forms, she had surveyed the area with various optics, spotting only scattered rodentia until she'd encountered something that paralyzed both mind and body. A monstrosity so ghastly that any thought of Hynka evaporated to nothingness: the Giant Flying Spider Monster.

It had been a big laugh on the station. Those with a healthy distaste for arachnids cringed and squealed when Tom Group-M'd the sped-up loopvid to everyone. One of his dragonflies had caught the thing on camera on an island the team called Badagascar, but which was officially tagged LI 52S-232.

The autonomous dragonfly had clamped itself to a vine about a meter off the ground and aimed its sensors toward a cave. A short time later, a bristly creature emerged from the darkness, skittering on ten long, multi-jointed legs. Its body alone was the size of a beanbag chair, with a single shiny eye as big as a human head. And it moved with unnerving speed, even without the loopvid's playback doubled. But the worst part, the part of the vid that inspired more than one crew member to shriek, laugh, and attempt to flee their own skin, was what happened next.

The hellspawn folded four front legs, leaning forward so its cycloptic head almost touched the ground, extended two pairs of hind appendages, and began excreting a viscous yellow-green fluid, like snot, from some glands in its backside. Saturating its rear legs with the substance, the goop kept coming, and soon after, the thing began inhaling through a wide-open mouth where one would expect a neck, shooting the air out its backside, and inflating the thick fluid like a soap bubble. After a couple minutes, the bubble had grown to twice the creature's size and the light breeze lifted the horrific thing off the ground and out of sight.

There were GM'd replies of Noooooo! and Welp, nothing left to do but burn down the planet. And, of course, Ish—the lover of all that nature had to offer—later blasted the group with a thousand-plus-word finger-wagging on why they'd come in the first place, asking how they can rate by appearance one species' right to exist over another's, and that everyone should be ashamed of themselves. She'd pretty much sucked the fun from the moment and John had to send out an oh-so-serious brief on respecting each other and the research subjects.

When Minnie had begun climbing the epsequoia's spongy layers, confident that any chasing Hynka would be too heavy to make it higher than a few tiers, she'd felt increasingly safe. And then, about three-fourths of the way up the tree, no more than 6m away, a dangling spider monster drifted slowly by, hanging from its bubble, wide-open mouth sucking air as it passed. Minnie had frozen in place, turned her head with it, unblinking eyes tracking the thing until it disappeared into a stand of mushpalms.

Several years had passed since the original discovery, back when they were finding hundreds of new species a day, and the Giant Flying Spider Monster was known to be a harmless consumer of root worms. Despite this fact, and a mind that strove for logic over emotion, seeing one in person had Minnie's neck hairs on end.

But after it was gone, she reminisced and enjoyed a smile. Briefly.

Oh, Ish, did you strand us all on purpose?

From her vantage point atop the area's tallest tree, Minnie studied a recommended course through the forest. A thick red line marked the path, tapering thinner all the way to the EV's previous resting spot. The app flashed warnings in areas where topo was either unknown or known to be hazardous, and she adjusted accordingly until satisfied with the route.

On to mapping a backup option.

JOHN: How's it going out there?

MINNIE: Good morning! I didn't want to wake you.
Want to see where I am?

JOHN: I see where you are in the mapping app.
Congrats on making it up the rope.

MINNIE: Yeah, thanks! But I meant optics.

JOHN: Oh, yes please!

Minnie shared her optics with him and, beginning with a distant shot of the sinkhole entrance behind her, she slowly panned across the scene. He'd yet to see it all in daylight.

JOHN: So far away. Beautiful. Hynka?

MINNIE: None close to the EV site, though I can't seem to pick up the EV itself. Worried they might have taken it somewhere.

JOHN: The beacon?

MINNIE: If you recall, the beacon hasn't been up for over a week. Either too far or they destroyed it.

JOHN: Right. Sorry. Forgot. Well, carry on. Don't let me distract you. Be careful.

MINNIE: Yup. I'll leave optics up for you as long as you don't backseat hike.

John replied with a sealed lips emoji and Minnie began climbing down the flat "branches." She mused that a skydiver with a parachute malfunction would need only target an epsequoia on the ground. Slamming into 100 layers of thick, squishy pads would probably slow them to a safe stop, while breaking off half the pads on the way down.

JOHN: What do those feel like?

MINNIE: Ever walk in arctic moss?

He replied with a smiley face and resumed his silence.

Sometimes conversing with him hurt. Since his injuries, John had become this pleasant, agreeable stranger. It was as though he knew he was dying and saw life through cheerful new eyes. Pain meds may have had something to do with it, but regardless, there was little evidence of the man she'd often despised, and so she frequently found herself assailed with guilt. Perhaps this was who he'd always been. Maybe she'd been such a jealous, egotistical, competitive jerk that she'd never seen the real him.

She reached the ground, unholstered her multiweapon, and activated route guidance. The transparent red line appeared before her, overlaying the terrain. Just ahead, the planned path led around a large boulder, continuing beyond the obstruction as a dashed line. Minnie cracked her visor open to allow in outside air and she broke into a jog.

Running felt good. She noticed her energy level increasing the more time she spent outside the oppressive cavern. In the beginning, the limitations of the cave occasionally provided comfort, like tightly swaddling a newborn that had spent its first nine months in a room no bigger than its body. Hynka aside, the idea of the surface's unfamiliar and boundless expanse had felt wholly unsafe. But after several days, even with the calorie bars and supplements, Minnie had noticed a growing fatigue weighing on her in the cave. She'd felt lazy and unmotivated, useless and depressed. In there, her only consistent drive was handling John's medical needs.

Fresh air, despite the higher nitrogen level, had made all the difference.

One of Epsy's rodentia popped out of a hole just in front of her before startling and disappearing just as quickly. Biologically, the Hynkas' favorite prey were closer to birds, their coats consisting of very fine, downy feather structures like young chicks, but they were millions of years from flight, if that's where they were headed. For now, they behaved much like timid squirrels or rabbits, and the crew fondly referred to them as *bunnies*. Though no one ever put it in an M (as it'd violate conversation topic rules), curiosity abounded on whether or not, this far from Earth, an animal would still "taste like chicken."

As cute as they were, Minnie planned to bring one back for supper. She'd settle the chicken question, once and for all. And this one seemed as appropriate a candidate as any other. She posted over its hole, spun off a length of trapping wire, and fed it into the burrow. When it felt like it reached the end, she snipped the wire, wrapped the ends around her MW's stun posts, and cranked up the voltage. She pulled the trigger. A sad, muffled peep let her know her very first hunt had been successful.

Lying prone in the soil, Minnie stretched her arm into the hole, feeling around for her prize. No such luck. After a quick scan through the soil via biomag, she dug around to widen the entrance. Quite a few flatworms were exposed in the process but, unsure if they were related to the ones from the cave, she disdainfully flung them away. Finally, upon reaching and extracting the electrocuted bunny carcass, Minnie stood up and inspected herself for worms or anything else that might have attached itself to her suit. All clear.

She unzipped a storage pocket, pulled out the crumpled bag attached within, stuffed in the bunny, and sealed it up.

As she continued on to the EV site, she felt a strange mix of pride and guilt about the limp animal bouncing on her thigh. Hooray for a successful first hunt, but it was almost as though she'd killed a puppy.

JOHN: Good job with the rodent.

MINNIE: I forgot you were there. Thank you, but shush.

He resent her the sealed lips.

There weren't many things on Epsy that reminded her of home. The forests were dominated by teal, orange, and yellow megafungi, and the lack of flying insects limited the number of aesthetically Earthlike plants to a few remote locations. But bunnies reminded Minnie of home, and the fact that she'd have to go on killing and eating them reemphasized the fact that she'd never again be at home. A real hunter would probably feel the opposite.

The red guide line ended beyond a dense thicket of green wafer fungi, like the underside of a portabella mushroom, turned on its side and shooting up from the soil like rows of wavy walls. She could have slipped between them as the guide line suggested, but wasn't keen on being coated in spores.

Instead, she took the long way around, observing familiar terrain and the first remains of dead Hynka. If she had more time, a close inspection of a cadaver could prove useful, but her mission was comms.

She passed a worm-riddled behemoth and disregarded the bones of several others. But as she came upon the EV site, trampled and littered with more Hynka bones than EV scraps, she noticed a few interesting things.

The EV was gone.

All of the Hynka remains but a few were practically scoured of meat. The intact ones had been left to the worms and fungus—the Hynka hadn't eaten the individuals she and John had killed.

A not-so-subtle stampede trail led east through trampled foliage; a telltale track marked the middle where the EV had been rolled. The Hynka had taken a prize.

Pieces of small components littered the entire area, many pressed into the soil beneath massive footprints.

Minnie squatted over a little blue component she recognized from the station's rebreathers. In the EVs, these things were mounted deep inside the hull behind the seats, protected along with all of the other life support-related gear. The Hynka must have ripped the inside of the pod to shreds.

JOHN: Sorry, but what is that?

MINNIE: CO_2 biscuit from the scrubbers.

She peered around the site, spotting hundreds of other tiny pieces, like hi-tech confetti.

JOHN: I'm sorry, Minerva.

MINNIE: It's ok. I didn't have high hopes.

JOHN: Are you going to try to go after it?

MINNIE: Just looking around here, it's highly doubtful that any kind of comms gear survived their rage dissection.

JOHN: What about the beacon?

Again with the beacon?

He seemed otherwise lucid, but strange how his memory repeatedly erased the bit about the EV beacon being dead.

MINNIE: Do you not remember us talking about the beacon? That's twice in the past 20 mins.

JOHN: I remember it was out of range. Thought maybe since you were closer now … Shutting up.

Minnie sighed, feeling like she was once again being mean to a severely wounded man. She pulled out her multisensor. She looked directly at the screen so John could see it through her feed, and set the device to listen for emergency signals. The device immediately emitted the three-beep chirp of an affirmative. Range and coordinates of a beacon popped up on the screen.

What the hell?

MINNIE: You see this?

JOHN: I see.
JOHN: I'll stop asking about the beacon now.

Minnie smirked. So a dash of the old John *was* still hanging around in that head.

She couldn't believe it. Not only had just a few kilometers been the difference between sensing the beacon or not, but she was amazed that the emitter was still functional after all the abuse. Then again, they did make those things to survive pretty serious impacts.

Wait a second …

She expanded the beacon signal's details and found ID info. It wasn't EV6; it was EV5.

MINNIE: John?!

JOHN: Wow, I see it!

MINNIE: She's 11K away. I'll route the course and head straight there.
MINNIE: How were Angela's SP scores?

MINNIE: If her beacon's active, they probably didn't find her.

MINNIE: Or maybe our landing distracted them for her.

JOHN: Angela didn't evac in EV5. I guess I never told you. Ish stopped her, volunteered to trade spots so Angela wouldn't have to be alone. She let her go with Tom in EV4.

MINNIE: Oh.

Minnie remembered the *clang* of EV4 launching into open space. She remembered the recroom and Angela hugging Tom from behind, her cheek smushed up between his shoulder blades. Angela giving Minnie a pedicure with probably-toxic enamel paint. "Now if only we could cut the tips off some old runners and glue on a high heel," she'd joked as she fanned Minnie's toes. "She won't be able to resist you." An early date night with Aether.

At least Angela got to be with Tom.

MINNIE: Well, how thoughtful of her in the middle of exigency.

Could Ish have known in the midst of all that chaos that the EVs were launching askew, and deliberately sent Angela to die in her place? Minnie just couldn't see Ish doing something for her fellow humans in a time of crisis. She simply didn't like *people.*

Or what if… was she that *crazy?*

MINNIE: John, how was Ish's last psyche eval?

JOHN: You know I can't talk about that stuff.

MINNIE: Honestly? Even now? Think for a second. Really think about it. I bet you that looner blew up the station on purpose. Killed more than half of the crew. How would she *accidentally* guide the pod in on a collision course without Qin noticing? It would take more than a little planning and strategy to hide what was really going on. No way he left her unsupervised for 2 effing hours.

JOHN: If she was suicidal and meds didn't help, there were numerous systems in place to detect and report anomalous behavior. But she evac'd with the rest of us. She didn't even hesitate. She didn't have a death wish.

MINNIE: No, she *didn't* have a death wish! She wanted to be down here! With her *real* people. Surface evac was the only way. Did the supply pod hit the tube to the BH first?

John didn't respond right away. She knew it had, and she knew he was mulling it over. Minnie paced around the scene, kicking Hynka bones out of the way. Every passing second solidified her suspicions. Ish guided the supply pod to impact the escape tube, and then to destroy the engineering sub-bay. Exigency procedures went into effect and she got her surface evac. As mission psych, though, how could Aether have missed the warning signs? Weekly one-on-ones were as non-opt as group.

JOHN: If she didn't establish superiority via violence like we did, the Hynka would kill her in an instant.

MINNIE: And you know she wouldn't dream of hurting of her babies. My question is, would she *expect* an attack from them? Or do you suppose she might have built up some grand illusions about communicating with them? Establish peaceful relations? Join the tribe?

JOHN: What are you going to do? Won't it be dark soon?

MINNIE: I have 3.25 hours of daylight. I'm going to find EV5 and, if she's not dead, I'm going to find Ish.

17

Minnie's stomach ached for food, a dull pain joining the piercing stabs of her colon. Running through the forest along the red line, she hoped the adrenalin would ease her discomfort. *Tomorrow*, she pleaded with her gut. Halfway to EV5's beacon signal, she certainly wasn't going to stop and go back to the cave to eat.

ALERTS: Terrain 0.5K – 3rd order stream

She ducked beneath a pair of supershrooms and wondered how those babies would taste on a giant grill, drizzled with butter.

Everything's food now, eh?

An image of John lying in the heater's glow, his body slowly morphing into a roasted chicken, like an old-timey cartoon.

"Depth and flow?" she asked her fone, unable to navigate the menu and run simultaneously.

"One to two meters at crossing point!" Superhero emphatically replied in her ear.

She hadn't used audible prompts in ages and couldn't remember why she'd changed it away from the hilariously sexy, breathy Domino voice she always used. The only times she used Superhero was when John sent out long, rambling messages she wanted read to her. It always dampened her irritation to hear his words read in Superhero's deep, melodramatic yell. That must've been why audible was set to him. A fresh dose of guilt.

Superhero went on, "Twenty-three C-F-S flow! Bank soil rigidity unknown!"

"*You* are advising against jumping an obstacle?"

"Rephrase!" Superhero demanded. The mapping system wasn't programmed for idle banter like some of the others. And Superhero probably didn't know he was a superhero, or all that that entailed. Well, Superhero didn't actually *know* anything. He was one of thousands of voices that could speak for her fone.

Minnie dismissed the warning as the river came into view. It was definitely too wide to jump without getting wet, but she was able to walk through without much effort. Beyond the stream, forestland gave way to a relatively flat plain and a wide, distant view. In the distance, a purple mountain overlooked the land, apparently coated in the same mossy lichen that blanketed the plain of river-smoothed rocks around her.

She focused on the center of the mountain and expanded the tiny details icon that appeared. The station's sensors had scanned and mapped the mountain several times a year since their arrival in Epsy orbit. Dormant volcanic, 14 major caves, 29 minor caves, nickel, copper, platinum, and rhodium, and though it wasn't in the files thanks to Ish apparently erasing everything, Minnie remembered a little something about this mountain.

Ish had done a report on it for the team a couple years back. The Hynka called it *Duchroch* and it was apparently their equivalent of Mount Olympus, or any of Earth's other geographically based origin-of-life legends. Minnie had irritated Ish by calling it "duck rock," but now she was glad she'd actually paid attention in the briefing. Though there were signs that early Hynka occupied its caves, it had been considered sacred and untouchable for as long as modern-day Hynka knew.

Minnie resumed running along her guide line, cutting left at the mountain's shrub-littered foothills. 2K to go, and the last leg would have a 300m elevation rise. Peering "through" the mountain in her map overlay, she could see EV5's flashing beacon signal coming from a saddle between a low-lying foothill and the mountain.

Halfway up the rocky slope, 15 minutes later, Minnie paused to catch her breath on a small landing. The next rise wore an apron of rocky debris she wasn't looking forward to climbing. Her abdominal pain had subsided for the time being, but her chest burned. She closed her visor and sucked in a lungful of pure oxygen. John had been silent a while. Asleep, she guessed, as she curled her tongue around her helmet's water tube, pulled it to her lips, and watched her fone's gauge count off as she gulped down 500mils.

Peering back, she saw that she'd reached treetop elevation, a beautiful view of the curving valley behind her. In the distance, the rocky spire that marked their hideout appeared as a rough-edged toothpick before the darkening western sky. She thought about sending John an M to check in, but didn't want to wake him. Besides, she might've been mere minutes from finding Ish camped out in a nearby cave. John didn't need to be involved with wherever that led.

She switched to therm and unholstered her MW, setting it to nonlethal.

Here we go …

She opened her visor and attacked the loose scree slope—two steps forward, one back; one step forward, two back. It felt like paddling up a waterfall. Discovering she needed both hands, she reholstered her MW.

One foot after the next! Get those knees high!

More time on the station's legger would have been advantageous. Hell, fitness minimums should have been double the prescribed total, but she admitted it would've been yet another complaint she'd have sent John's way.

Finally reaching the top of the scree, she huffed more oxygen and waited for the thumping all over her body to wane. She peered left to the floating red guide line gently arcing round a bend.

Beyond the blind curve, the guide continued briefly as a short dashed line before ending abruptly at a white circle. Therm revealed nothing through the dense rock, but upon switching to mag, Minnie held her breath for a beat, swallowed, and proceeded forward.

Dry purple lichen crunched beneath her boots as she moved along the mostly flat terrain. The sky grew darker by the minute. She wasn't worried about her ability to see, but while Hynka weren't strictly nocturnal, most of their prey were, so she figured it's when they'd be most active. It would explain the massive horde that had greeted them upon landing. However, if the glowing green sphere in her optic was as perfectly intact as she thought, she may not need to worry about Hynka tonight.

As she rounded the final bend, Minnie paused and leaned out just enough for a direct view. Indeed, EV5 was not only sitting in a convenient little saucer of a depression, it appeared to be in pristine condition. Its hatch hovered above the opening as if someone had just landed and stepped out. Multicolored lights illuminated the interior and visible porthole. Its parachute had retracted upon its pilot's command during landing, as evidenced by the closed doors at the top of the sphere—an evac step she and John forewent.

Minnie switched back to therm and surveyed the scene for lifeforms. Nothing bigger than a worm for 100m around the hillside. She held her breath and had her sensors listen for disrupts—sounds that defied the local din pattern. Nothing.

Venturing forward, Minnie stepped out and walked cautiously toward the EV, noticing halfway there that the hatch faced the wide mouth of a cave. Her optics wouldn't have picked up anything inside it. She halted, sidestepped to the cave entrance (possibly wide enough to roll the EV into), and ran the same scans. Still no lifeforms, but mag picked up a collection of disparate metals on the ground about 20m in. Minnie activated IR and crept inside, MW held steadily before her.

Just beyond a slight curve, Minnie recognized a familiar glow: the little red LED atop a survival heater. She crouched down and activated her helmet's floodlights. The scene gradually illuminated before her as the floods brightened. Calorie bar wrappers, an opened SSK and backpack, both raided by rodents. She brushed aside the gnawed shreds of foil on top of the SSK and found an untouched, sealed brick of eight bars. The bunnies mustn't have smelled anything of interest. Nor did they appear interested in meds. Ish had left behind some critical items. Indicative of plans to return?

Minnie noted what she didn't see: no MW or ammo packs, no multisensor, no tent or survival bag, no suit or helmet. Ish had taken *some* essentials, though without a backpack. What was she carrying it all in? Suit pockets? Maybe the EV had been supplied for two occupants like all the others.

Skimmers!

Minnie snatched up the brick of bars, medkit, and heater, and walked out of the cave. She set her booty on the ground outside the EV and stepped around to the rear. There she found the empty, zigzagging depression of a skimmer bay: former home of the vehicle Ish had apparently taken on her field trip. But right beside it, in its familiar mirrored position, Minnie beamed up at the exposed edge of the second skimmer, nestled right where it belonged, blending perfectly with the curvature of the EV.

"Well, hello, sexy," she said, and gave the exposed edge two taps. "I'll be back for you shortly."

She returned to the pod's front and peered into the open pod hatch. Apparently unconcerned with power conservation, Ish had left everything on.

Minnie felt nervous excitement tremble in her sternum as she climbed in and connected her fone to the EV's wireless.

ALERTS: ID mismatch.

She enabled security? Wow.

Minnie grunted smugly and connected as a root level account.

ALERTS: ID disabled.

What? Bitch!

Minnie clenched her jaw, her hatred of Ish soaring to a previously uncharted realm. The system had to have been completely wiped and replaced to disable root access. And there was no way that happened down here. Minnie was at a loss. The pod could have received hundreds of new messages from the BH or elsewhere and she'd have no idea without system access.

Well, I don't need access to steal your damned comms.

Minnie plunked down into one of the seats and bent over to access a panel. Behind the sheet, she found the laser comms unit, flipped the four mounts out of the way, and pulled the handle. The unit slid out with a satisfying *shink*.

She had to remove the bottom of the other seat to access the primary comms unit—about ten minutes of work—and soon found herself standing outside the pod with a cache of gear and supplies to take back to John. Thankfully, her body wouldn't have to bear the weight all the way to their hidey hole. The real gem of her find was still parked in its bay. And she decided to *strut* her way back to it.

Reaching up, Minnie twisted the skimmer release knob three times counterclockwise, pressed it inward, and sighed with satisfaction as muffled machinations hummed and whirred, and the transport emerged smoothly from its home. The warning beeps were strangely soothing, grounding—the emblematic call of *all* the magnificent technology that defined her species. And though she hadn't designed the thing herself, she watched with pride as the mounting arm continued outward, fully extending, while the skimmer blossomed like a smooth, white flower.

Fully deployed, the skimmer pad looked like a shiny white disk, flat on the top, and with a convex underside, like a shallow saucer. Noting she could fit her helmet in the space between the pad's outer edge and the ground, Minnie squatted for a peek below. Like an EV, retractable stabilizer legs around the perimeter kept the unit from teetering on its rounded center.

Minnie peered up at the skimmer's curved console, rising from one side of an otherwise wide-open platform. The power supply was fully charged, system checks had come back optimal, and a big blue "READY" shone on the screen. Minnie stood and pressed the release button on the EV. Two claws disengaged and the arm slowly retracted into the empty skimmer bay.

She stepped up onto the pad and ran her gloved fingers across the dashboard's screens. At waist height, just beneath the screens, three extendable safety lines sat in individual chrome recesses. And below them, a row of panel walls concealed the control console's inner workings. Above the dashboard, a short transparent windshield rose just a hand's length higher. Probably the perfect height for Minnie, but maybe a bit low for those of "normal" stature.

Tour complete, Minnie got busy loading Ish's treasure trove of supplies.

Moments later, with all the gear strapped to the pad or secured inside the skimmer's in-floor storage bin, Minnie clipped the safety lines to her suit, and activated flight controls.

On Earth, skimmers had grown more common than cars and cycles for short-distance personal transport, along with other vehicles both open and enclosed, broadly referred to as *threebs*—an odd simplification of "Below 3000," for their flight zone. Legally, you had to be 16 and licensed to fly a threeb. Minnie had *just* turned 16 when she entered mission training, and besides a short-lived joyride on a homemade rig, she'd only been able to operate a skimmer during a few obligatory exigency classes. The training center's vehicles had all sorts of limiters and could be remotely controlled by instructors. No opportunities to "open them up," as they say.

Minnie wrapped her fingers around the thick, cushioned handle grips, testing the steering devices' ranges of motion. She could twist both grips like throttles, rotate the whole assembly like a steering wheel, and move it back or forth a few centimeters. There was, of course, no ID scanner on the dashboard, so Minnie simply activated flight with a tap on the screen, and twisted the altitude grip toward her. The ionic drive engaged with ghostly silence, lifting the skimmer slowly off the ground. She twisted harder, then engaged forward propulsion.

Within seconds, cool wind stung her unprotected eyes and blared in her ears. She quickly locked the altitude to free her left hand and slapped her visor shut.

Much better.

In the starlight, the skimmer whizzed noiselessly over the plain and the river and the epsequoia forest. Minnie's head was a rush of pleasure and guilt. Her mission had been a major success—a first taste of things actually working out as planned (and more!), yet the stars above haunted her.

Tiny white dots in space.

It didn't feel right to celebrate anything. To *enjoy* seemed offensive.

But she couldn't help it. As she neared the spire and sinkhole, slowing and descending for landing less than two minutes from leaving Ish's pod, Minnie decided she'd just have to take the pleasure with a side of shame. She'd made it up the rope, nourished her lungs with energizing fresh air, they had a skimmer now, they could leave the damned worm cave, and they had comms. She remembered she even had a dead bunny hanging at her thigh, its chickenality level yet to be established.

Perhaps, every now and then, it was okay to have a good day.

18

John wouldn't wake up. Water dripped from Minnie's suit onto his face and he didn't even blink. At first she stifled panic, stripping away his survival bag and checking his body for new parasites, then scanned the inside of the tent. But none were present. They didn't have to be, though, did they? The damage had already been done.

Minnie's multisensor showed the same readings it had earlier: John's circulation was poor, blood pressure low, but normal temp, electrolytes, and brain activity. She'd repeatedly sprayed down his wounds with antiseptic before applying organic wound sealant. The goop worked on large gashes, acting as a temporary skin while stem cells regrew flesh at an accelerated rate. She'd watched vids on managing similar-but-lessor wounds and precisely followed the instructions. He hadn't gone into shock, and fever never arrived, so she thought she'd done everything perfectly. It'd simply take time for him to get better. And now that they had a skimmer, they wouldn't be anchored by his inability to walk.

If only he'd wake up.

"John." She patted his cheek. "Come on now, wake up. I've got good news." She flicked his forehead and he uttered a pained groan. "John? Wake up now! Hey! Rise and shine! I found Ish's EV! And we're going to have us a bunnyque for dinner!" He let out an extended whine, as if trapped in a nightmare. She hushed and stopped touching him and he seemed to calm.

She sealed the tent door behind her, rolled back to sit on her empty survival bag, and held her face in her palms.

She whispered, *"Please don't leave me ... Don't leave me here alone."*

She sniffed and gazed at him through blurring tears. A quick swipe with the back of her wrist. He looked best through biomag at its lowest intensity. His unnerving jaw and neck wounds disappeared behind a contrived flesh tone. An illusion of perfect health. His usually close-buzzed hair had grown out a bit and was painted a solid black. The simplified features and estimated colors evoked a doll or action figure and Minnie heard Superhero in her head, but the voice had been drained of humor.

"John?" It hardly left her mouth. Even if he was awake, he wouldn't have heard her. *"I'm sorry."*

She touched his hand through the survival bag. He emitted a standard sleep sigh, as if he'd just rolled from one side to the next in a regular old bed in a house at two in the morning.

Sleep was good for him. Why was she even trying to wake him up? Let him be. Not moving sped healing, right? He'd wake as usual in the morning, right?

Well, what if he didn't? This wasn't normal. She'd always been able to rouse him before. She hadn't changed his pain meds dosage. If he didn't wake up in the next 24 hours, he'd obviously need water. There were, no doubt, hundreds of walk-throughs on setting up an IV drip—she growled suddenly and flushed such thoughts from her mind. Premature. Unnecessary. Unhelpful. Let him be.

She had comms to set up.

Maybe after a quick nap. It'd been a long day. A prosperous day. She deserved a break. It was warm inside the tent. She could curl up next to John and pretend he was Aether.

She shook out her head, her cheeks flapping like a hound's. Pretend he was Aether? Cave fatigue was setting in again.

No ... you can sleep any time! You have comms *gear outside! There could be messages waiting! This could be last chance to say goodb—*

No need to go there either. She just needed to set the damned things up. One thing at a time. More fresh air would be nice, anyway.

She stepped out, zipped the tent shut, and decided to rouse him tomorrow morning.

Back outside, Minnie pulled the Primary Comms Unit out of the skimmer and rigged a probably-unsafe hookup to the heater for power. Separating the laser emitter from its unit proved incredibly easy, and she plugged it into a universal port on the PCU. With the emitter propped up on the flattest section of rock, she enabled autotracking, and let the PCU run through signal establishment protocols.

The little screen scrolled through a series of targets, even listing Earth as an option.

That's interesting.

Could she send a message to Earth from the surface? Even if aimed absolutely precisely, would the beam maintain cohesion on the way out of the atmosphere? Its intensity couldn't possibly be strong enough. The comms tower on the station, the one used to exchange data with Earth, was 50 times more powerful than this little laser.

The lime-green beam turned on, streaking past her and into the sky. Start-up GPS instantly failed, so it proceeded on to constellation ID for its current position, then began searching for orbiting supply pods. The beam ticked side to side like a high-speed metronome, rapidly scanning 10 million cubic kilometers of the planet's exosphere over the course of a few minutes.

NO COMM SOURCES DETECTED

Awesome.

Minnie set it to rescan every 20 minutes and sat down on the skimmer platform. She searched through the flops of instructionals in her fone's archive and came upon a relevant vid. Munching on a calorie bar, she watched this brilliant old bearded guy in Australia outline a process for using a ground-based PCU to communicate beyond local orbit. He even had an earlier model of the very unit sitting at Minnie's feet, the critical components all essentially the same. But she appreciated something else about the vid.

Instead of using a fone, the man wore a head-mounted camera and had happened to record his vid on a sunny Australian day, forty-seven years ago. He had a bunch of tools and gear laid out on a table, and the table pushed up against a wall with a wide mirror. He intermittently looked up at himself in the mirror when addressing the viewer. Behind him was a window to a yard, and in that yard Minnie could see a pair of little girls playing. Sometimes, when he looked up, they were not visible outside, but most of the time they were there, aiming a hose or running through a sprinkler. The man's mic picked up their giggles and shouts, and once or twice, to Minnie's alarm, he appeared to be annoyed and considering whether to stop their play. To Minnie's pleasure, he did not.

She'd participated in such antics when she was very small—before she'd become overly bookish, reclusive, and *crazy*—but she recalled fondly that freedom and unreserved joy.

Cold wind whistled over the skimmer platform and across Minnie's exposed neck. A fresh whiff of mold and decay she was surprised to find herself enjoying.

She composed herself and skipped the vid back several minutes as she realized she'd missed everything the man had said about actually enhancing an emitter.

What time was it? She was cold and tired but didn't want to go to sleep. It was dangerous to be out this late at night. She peered at the sweeping beam of green light shooting up in the sky and wondered if any Hynka would see it from afar. They'd certainly all seen the EV during reentry. Knowing now that the kidney-shaped valley in which they'd landed was not all that popular with the natives, it was amazing how quickly the horde had converged on the EV. Most likely the bad luck of dropping in while a hunting party happened to be passing through, combined with a blazing parachute. But what if someone spotted this beam from, say, 5K, how long would it take for it to run through the forest to her?

Minnie ran a therm scan of the valley, indeed spotting several wandering Hynka scattered about. They seemed to favor groups of 2-4. None appeared to be headed her way. A mental note to re-verify this fact in another 30 seconds.

Halfway through the vid, the PCU on the ground before her sounded an inspiring tone. She spun and dropped to her knees and read the blue strip of screen.

COMM SOURCE DETECTED
LINKING...
LINKING...
COMMS READY

"Yes!" Minnie blurted, then cupped her mouth and resurveyed the panorama. The closest she could see was a glob of indeterminate numbers about 8K away, just beyond Duck Rock Mountain.

Back to the PCU, she held her breath and opened the homepage. This was the first thing anyone connecting to the pod network saw. This was where anyone with half a brain would leave a message for others.

WELCOME TO SP004!!

VER: 14F.01.2D3

POD NETWORK STATUS: SUBOPT

UP: 15 ~ DOWN: 2

HAB LINK: DOWN

BH: DOWN

Default crap, albeit enlightening.

As she suspected, no Backup Habitat. Interesting that two pods were dead. Probably taken out by the station's debris field. Minnie navigated the menu and initiated an unfiltered search, sorting by date to find recently uploaded code. She was certain that the pods would at the very least track changes. They had plenty of onboard storage and, even though no coder ever expected the system to be used this way, it would make no sense for existing code changes to be overwritten without something logging the actions.

There was indeed tracking, but the most recent code change was a firmware update dated three years ago. If this was truly the case, it meant that no one—not a single evacuee—had connected to the only available network that others on the surface or in orbit could access.

The only place where anyone could leave a message. And like any perfectly dumb network, changes were instantly synced across all other nodes, so even if she checked every pod she'd see the same thing.

No one had left a message. Over 300 hours had passed since landing on Epsy.

No one had left a message because everyone was *dead*. Why was she surprised? She'd said all along that none but EV5 and 6 could have survived. Why would there be something new to find here?

Because denial said so. She'd performed a convincing show of certain pessimism, all the while holding out hope to find a surprise message—from Aether, of course—saying how they'd made it back to the BH, everyone was good and safe but worried about her and John, and Qin and Zisa were rigging up some kind of lander that would go down and pick them up so everyone could live happily ever after, though, sadly, in the BH's more confined space. Right. She'd known the truth from the start: EVs launching away from the atmosphere would *not* be able to reestablish a proper trajectory, regardless of piloting skill. It was the equivalent of shooting a person into space with only a pressurized fire extinguisher in hand, and expecting them to make their way back. That was the stuff of lazy science fiction, not reality.

Fortunately, Minnie hadn't wasted too much actual work time on this ridiculous fantasy. If she and John were to survive, those people must be banished from her head. All of them.

Minnie rolled her shoulders and moved on to accessing the pod's homepage source file.

ROOT ACCESS REQUIRED

She tapped in the passcode and the file unlocked. The homepage reappeared in edit mode. As it had been for her, it would now be the cold, insentient purveyor of bad news to unknown others. Syncing across all the orbiting pods, it would forever remain—the last digital communication from one of the disaster's only survivors. If another mission came to this place 50 years from now, they'd know that at least a few people surface evac'd. Maybe their remains could be returned to Earth, as if she gave a crap about that.

She appended the beginning of the homepage, pushing down the oddly cheerful welcome message and status links.

She wrote: Post-station evac, EV6 landed Hynka country 39S112,95E908. Survivors Minerva Sotiras and John Li (level 8 injury post-landing). EV5 discovered today, sans sabotage suspect Ishtab Soleymani. EV6 planning to leave hostile territory for west coast 50N when able.

She read it over once and saved it, initiating a system reboot to force a network sync. A 10-minute countdown clock began—some sort of grace period.

Leaning forward onto her knees to disconnect the rig, Minnie paused, considered, a dry swallow, another safety scan of the landscape. She rolled back onto her rear and reopened the file.

Why? Not sure. She didn't want to think about it—just do. Words—stream of consciousness, no hesitation, no edits—filled the screen before her.

> Zisa: You are so quick, so brilliant, and with so much heart you almost make up for those of us who are more like robots than people. You live on another emotional plane. I suck for every time I tried to knock you down from way up there.
> Tom: An inextinguishable light of positivity. If anyone was keeping score, you're surely responsible for more laughs bursting from my mouth than any single person ever. You're a hundred times smarter and more capable than you give yourself credit for. Lucky to have known you.
> Qin: I loved our every argument. And even though I clearly won 98% of the time (OK, fine, 96%), I'll now confess that you often got in my

head, continuing to present your cases long after I'd ever admit. I may have actually been swayed once or twice, or once. I'll also, painfully, concede that you're smarter than me ... in a couple of trivial areas. Wink.
Angela: You're a bad ass. Watching you in training and our first couple years made me a stronger, more confident person. In reality, John has you to thank for me making his life miserable. Ha ha. I always loved how you owned what you know and said "how the hell should I know?" to what you didn't. Also, I could never tire of the banter between you and Tom. Heart.
Pablo: You know how much I love WYSIWYG, and that has always been you. It's super weird to have one of my best friends doing my OBG checks, but you skillfully made them seem like a haircut. Also, you give great haircuts. No idea why I think of OBG and haircuts first, but I guess I feel so close to you that it doesn't matter. You'd laugh and shrug. Wish you could've bought me that first beer.
Ish: You're super cute. (Wanted to say something nice. I'll save my other thoughts for when I find you, you silly, irrational, selfish, daffy, murderous bitch.)
John: You're less than 50m from me right now, and hurt so badly. But somehow talking to you, real talk, seems like the scariest thing imaginable. Maybe it's because, as much as I've always resisted and denied, you really are like a father to me. This is especially rough for me to swallow, given each other's past and

present relationship statuses. Combine that with your enviable logic, problem-solving, insanely broad knowledgebase, and impenetrable calm, one can see why the psych analytics threw red flags about us from the start. I've often wondered why you went to bat for me to keep me on in training, and whether you later regretted it. And if so, because you're a better person than me, I know that you'd never say so. I couldn't possibly explain it, but I am so thankful to have you with me right now. We're surely the last human beings each other will ever see—the sole remaining connections to our own humanity, because if someone else isn't there to see it, are we still human? I believe I'll disappear. Since we both know I'd never say it aloud: I love you, John.
Aether: I wish we'd met sooner; I could have loved you longer.

19

Beep ... beep ... beep ... beep ...

How long had it been going off? Was it a wake-up alarm? Someone needed to turn it off. Would someone turn it off?

Beep ... beep ... beep ... beep ...

Minnie felt her warm breath reflecting off something just in front of her face. Her whole head lay in a snug cocoon of enchanting warmth.

Beep ... beep ... beep ... beep ...

The sound echoed in the cave.

In the cave, Minnie repeated in her head.

Good grief someone needed to shut that thing off. But who else was there but her?

John.

Could John get up? Was he still hurt? How long had he been healing? Five days? Ten? Thirty? Time felt so inestimable—intangible.

Beep ... beep ... beep ... beep ...

She wished she could snooze it. Just five more minutes, Dad. Five more minutes of sleep was all she needed. Could she wirelessly connect to whatever it was? That would be the ideal. Not leaving the tent—no—that would be the absolute worst-case scenario. No leaving the tent just yet.

A list of available devices popped up in her fone's basic standby interface. Two MWs, one MS, the heater's diagnostics interface, John's suit, Minnie's suit. An orange dot flashed beside John's suit, indicating it was low on power and in powersave mode. He certainly hadn't been moving enough to provide any significant charging. Next to Minnie's suit, the blinking red dot revealed that it was the source of the alert sound. Almost dead power cells? How could she have less power than John? She connected to it and silenced the alarm.

About to disconnect, she reread the alert.

> ENVIRONMENTAL ALERT – Advise close visor, seal suit.

Minnie sat up, bare arms instantly chilled by the frigid air outside her covers. She didn't even remember taking off the suit the night before.

Wait, what time is it?

She fully activated her fone and the usual border of icons filled the top and bottom of her view. It was almost sundown—32 hours had passed since she'd left the message on the supply pod. Something was very wrong. She'd never been able to sleep more than seven hours. And what about urination? Had she gone in the tent? She felt the mat beneath her and it was dry. Her stomach, too, didn't hurt, despite the fact that she still hadn't had her first movement. And why was the suit advising about seals?

Eyes still heavy, a soothing voice encouraged her to relax, to just be glad the beeping had ceased, to go back to sleep for just a little while, that she *deserved* it. Minnie fought the temptation and connected to the multisensor somewhere in the dark outside the tent. She had it run a new environment analysis. At sea level, oxygen was always lower on Epsy than it was on Earth, but in the cave it had apparently gone down 3% over the past two weeks, simulating an extreme rise in altitude. Stranger still, it wasn't replaced by nitrogen or carbon dioxide.

> O_2: 12.2%
> N: 66.8%
> CO_2: 4.6%
> Ar: 1.04
> Oth: 15.36

Well that's a whole lot of "other," Minnie thought, still struggling to focus. *What the hell is it?*

She expanded the "other" line to see what they'd been breathing, but didn't recognize the mixture. Whatever it was, she guessed it was toxic. After downloading the values, she switched to the med app and dropped the gas mixture into a typimale of John's height, weight, and age. It sped through simulations: 5 minutes, 30 minutes, 4 hours, 24 hours, 1 week. It didn't even have to go that far. Right away she grasped that, for humans, the gas mixture would be received as a potent anesthetic.

I wonder ...

The warmth and peace of her bag calling to her, she drove on, running through the list and selecting each compound to pull up the details. Nitrous oxide, propofol, several others without names that would surely have some sort of medical significance back on Earth. She blinked slowly. So much of the past two weeks suddenly seemed to make sense. Maybe. Or maybe this was a dream. Some fresh air would be nice. Some cool outside air ... but it was so far. Maybe after a little more rest.

Cripes ... of course!

She violently slapped her face, unzipped the door, and staggered out of the tent, clumsily pulling on her suit. It was like untangling a hundred cables tied up in fishing net. Eventually, feet found their way to boots, hands made it through sleeves, and her helmet surrendered to her sealing efforts.

After only a few deep breaths, her muddy head already began clearing. And after a few more, some of the "other" elements struck her as familiar, after all. She pulled up the acid slime sample she'd taken from one of John's parasitic worms and compared the elements. The substance contained many more compounds than the air—more than two dozen—but *all* six of the unknowns in the cave air existed in the slime.

The air hadn't always been that way. This was certain. When they'd first arrived, it was only slightly off from the outside mixture.

The heat!

That was absolutely it. Raising the cave temp had activated the worms. She'd even said it. She'd said it and never looked back. But had she inadvertently poisoned the air by killing all the worms? Like carbon from deforestation? She switched to therm and moved her head through a full scan of the floor, walls, and ceiling. All appeared clear until red streaked across her optic as she glanced past the smaller subcavern. She looked back and walked toward it.

Indeed, speckling the subcavern's walls, floor, and ceiling, plus *entirely* coating the half-barricaded tunnel, there were thousands of the things. In therm, it looked like someone had lit up the place with red holiday lights.

Minnie rushed back to the campsite and began shoving their gear into the backpacks. Food, clothes, SSKs, weapons. She needed to carry it all in one trip out. And that'd be the easy part. Getting John into his suit and helmet, dragging him across the cave, out through the underwater tunnel, and then somehow up and out the sinkhole—probably still unconscious the entire time—it all might pose a small challenge.

* * *

An abrupt *scritch*. Again, longer. Nausea. Neck pain, legs sore, side burning, jaw ... so much burning. Hunger. Dry mouth. Unable to swallow.

Strangely, among all the new pain, the pressure behind John's fone was still relentless. He wanted to rip it from his face, but needed it to keep contact with Minnie. Minerva.

Scriiiitch!

The sound pierced his helmet and he suddenly sensed his orientation: upside down and buried beneath something.

His body lurched reflexively when his boot knock something that wasn't a wall. He woke up his fone to see where he was. Low power alert from his suit. Everything felt wrong. Something pushed his feet again and his helmet scratched once more against coarse rock. He was in the water tunnel. How had she gotten him into the tunnel? What was the last thing he remembered? Hadn't he taken off his suit at some point?

JOHN: What's happening?

MINNIE: Hey! Good morning! Just sit tight, okay?

Assigning inflections to text was generally ill-advised, but her M looked downright chipper.

Light appeared at the end of the tunnel. Apparently daytime outside. He used his hands to guide his body through the tunnel and keep himself from banging up against anything. His arms felt tender and weak, as if they'd been punched all over a thousand times. An unseen Minerva continued to push him forward from behind.

MINNIE: Almost there! You still doing OK?

JOHN: For the most part. Care to share the plan/situation here?

She shoved him out of the tube and into the wide pool of green-hued water. He tried to right his body into a proper feet-down orientation, but the attempt only served to reemphasize the uselessness of his muscles and to light up sore spots on his legs, side, neck, and chest. Minerva appeared before him, took hold of his shoulders with her hands, and used her legs to set him upright. Facing helmet to helmet, he saw her grinning face. He watched as her eyes skittered about—movements indicative of typing. A few seconds later, he received the M.

MINNIE: I was going to tie your limp body to the rope and then lift you out. Now, same plan, but with you awake you're much less likely to be *damaged* in the process.

She followed up with a winky face emoji. The only emoji Minerva had ever sent him in the past decade was that of sarcastic slow-clapping hands. He'd long since forgotten what it had been for, but he still remembered those hands, and he remembered the sour mug on Minerva's face when he'd looked at her to inquire. She'd been seriously pissed. While surprised and perplexed by her current friendly nature, he didn't want to do or say anything that would cause it to stop, if at all possible. And knowing himself (and her), it'd only take a single M.

One of her hands moved to the grip on his chest and she began to swim upward, dragging him behind her to the blinding light above.

JOHN: How are you going to lift my weight? I don't think I can contribute much.

MINNIE: The skimmer.

Both of their helmets breeched the surface, water sheeting down their visors as fog formed at the edges. Minerva reached back and produced the soggy end of their rope.

He'd tried to get out before, but failed. His arms had been too weak. Much stronger then than now, but he just couldn't heft himself up.

JOHN: You found the EV.

He watched her face change an instant later when she received the M. She frowned and shook her head.

MINNIE: We apparently have a lot of catching up to do. For now, know that I found EV5 but no Ish, we have comms but no messages, we have an op skimmer, and that we almost died. Several times.

JOHN: I look forward to elaboration. What happens after you lift me out of here?

She began tying gear bags to his waist, followed by the end of the rope around the grip in his chest.

MINNIE: Moving to a safer spot. Mt. Duck Rock. Where Ish was, and might return to if she isn't already a lump of Hynka feces. I'm not sure which one I'd prefer.

John resisted the urge to scold her for such talk. For the time being. He watched as she tested the strength of her knot. The suit tightened around his shoulders and torso, pinching into his right side, and slapping the area with searing pain. His eyes instantly teared up.

Minerva must have seen him wince and flinch.

MINNIE: I'm so sorry!
MINNIE: You OK?

JOHN: Yeah, just surprised by some sensitivity here.

He pointed to his ribcage.

MINNIE: Yeah, that's where the worst wound is.

She glanced up toward the light, considering, then faced him once more, stricken.

MINNIE: I don't know how else I can get you out of here. It's *seriously* going to hurt.

JOHN: It's fine, really. Let's do it.

He forced a confident smile.

MINNIE: I don't know. What if you go into shock?

JOHN: Ready when you are.

He saw the rise and fall of a big sigh and she gave him a concerned mother look before turning and grabbing the rope. She climbed it with impressive ease. Their exercise regimen must have worked out nicely. How long had it been since that failed attempt to get out? He glanced at the clock and date in the upper right corner of his fone.

What the hell? Two weeks?

Minerva's feet disappeared over the top of the sinkhole, her helmeted face reappearing in its place. She flashed an inquiring thumbs up.

MINNIE: Everything still securely attached to you? That's nearly all of our gear.

He looked down, saw the bags floating gently at his sides. The suit pressed at his neck. More agony.

JOHN: I think we're good.

She disappeared again and a moment later he watched his side of the rope slacken and drop, gathering around him. The bottom of a skimmer appeared overhead, about 20m above the top of the sinkhole. The other end of the rope was fastened to an anchor loop and slowly rising, straightening into a perfect bar. He stiffened his body just before the first yank.

He rose a full meter in a second, the wound at his side feeling as though someone ripped a massive piece of duct tape from it. Dangling gear weighed him down and knocked about his legs. Something very bad had happened to his left calf. Still in the water, his boots stirred a circle.

Another upward jolt as Minerva found the proper throttling for a full cargo load, and then everything smoothed out, the vined walls of the sinkhole falling around him.

MINNIE: You OK? I can't see you.

JOHN: Fine, let's finish this.

MINNIE: Meaning set you down? I can set you down, have you lay on the platform, or I can carry you like this to the new spot. It's a 2-minute ride.

JOHN: Just go please.

He was sure he came off terse and snappish, but the pain was unbelievable. She'd make him pay later, but for now he could think of little else but escaping this pulling, stretching, tearing. At any second his flesh would rip free and drop with the gear to the ground, his skinless body somehow remaining bound to the rope.

MINNIE: I'm so sorry! Going now. Just keep taking deep breaths.

A whole new Minerva.

John's body dangled from the chest loop and oscillated as they flew above the forest. To redirect his screaming mind, John tried to imagine how this would look to an observer on the ground. He'd probably appear dead. How high up was he? He didn't want to know. Some other distraction. A song? He couldn't summon a single tune.

His eyes remained shut tight for most of the way, intermittent peeks revealing only a purple mountain, growing larger with each glimpse.

It felt much longer than 2 minutes, but he was counting by *pain time*, an abstract measurement existing outside normal space-time. No, his clock confirmed more than 5 minutes had passed. Probably a 2-minute ride without a spec-defying load.

When his feet finally touched something, his legs followed, folding beneath him, his body spreading out on a crunchy, semi-soft surface until all of his weight rested on his enflamed side. It was as though he'd been lowered into a brim-filled bathtub of agony, and time ceased to exist at all.

* * *

Minnie liked this new cave. Its wide-open nature brought obvious security concerns, and the distance from a water supply was rather inconvenient, but the abundance of life-sustaining air, lack of determined parasites, the ability to come and go without negotiating an obstacle course, and not-to-be-discounted killer *view* made up for it all. They'd moved into the Hynka Country equivalent of a penthouse apartment, and if Ish had been correct about Mount Duck Rock's sacred nature, Minnie and John wouldn't have to worry too much about security. Surely this had been Ish's thinking when she selected this site. Her EV had landed *precisely* where she intended.

Minnie sat leaning against the smooth stone wall at the cave's entrance, watching the sun set on another Epsy day. Far to the north, the towering front of a major storm loomed beyond the mountain valley. According to historical weather patterns, the cell would gain significant strength when it reached the mountains. The new cave was in no danger, but floods were likely in the basins below. Their old sinkhole would surely overflow.

"Hey," John's voice from the darkness. He'd been unconscious for several hours. She'd given him a couple rounds of pain meds.

Minnie smiled and walked inside, grabbing a heater and flipping it on. Orange light slowly brightened the cave. "Welcome to our new abode." She reached the bend and sat down beside him, curling her feet under her legs. She rested a hand on his survival bag. "How's your pain? Best to wait another hour before another dose, but if you're in agony—"

"No, no, I'm fine. How about you?"

"Me? I have no issues at all. I was lucky … well, being in the tent …" She sighed, feeling guilty once more for making him sleep outside the tent. Well, she hadn't *made* him, but by telling him he could have the tent to himself, and then him insisting *she* keep it—she knew it was her fault he was injured. "The parasites only got to you because I didn't want to share a bunk."

John was quiet a moment, tentatively feeling around inside his survival bag. She watched the lump of his hand inspect his side, move down to the left thigh, and then the hand appeared at his neck, gently probing the shiny glaze of sealant she'd sprayed on all of the wounds. He turned his head on the fluffy coat she'd bundled into a pillow for him, and peered up at her.

"I meant, have you been able to … well … *purge?*"

Minnie laughed and slapped a hand over her mouth. His expression suggested she looked like a looner, but it was just so inexplicably great to hear John being John again. "Funny you should mention that. Been handling that business for a while now. Even handled one just a couple hours ago. Feel like a new woman."

He cracked a small smile, then resumed the professional, mature tone. "How's the regularity been? Since the first?"

She shook her head, amused by the preoccupation. "Well, that was only just a few days ago."

"Wow. So—"

"Hey, I know it's your favorite subject matter, but we're done with this topic, boss." She grinned and patted his arm. "Back to your wounds. Sensors show you've regrown about ten percent of the lost tissue. In terms of mobility, it looks like your right calf is still pretty much useless. I don't see that changing without some kind of implant. If Pablo was still around, he might have had better ideas." She watched his face slowly sober. Perhaps she wasn't relaying this news with the best bedside manner, but he already knew most of this, so it shouldn't have come as too much of a surprise. "As for the ribcage, I honestly don't know how that's going to work out. It worries me more than any of the other ones. If not for the sealant on there, the bones would still be exposed."

John blinked purposefully a few times in a row, licked his lips, and tried to speak. "Min—" He grimaced as he tried to swallow. Minnie stuck a straw in his mouth and he drew a few pained gulps of water. "Thanks ... Minerva, but what ... what exactly *happened* to me?"

He didn't remember.

It was all gone.

Minnie spent the following hour recounting the events of the past weeks. John seemed to gradually stow away his surprise and fear, thanking her at the end for everything she'd done to save his life.

Following an uneasy silence, while John peered under a couple of his bandages, Minnie decided to leave him alone with his thoughts and venture out to hunt.

"I'll keep an eye on you in mapping," he said as she left.

In the valley, she came across a pair of bunnies nibbling at a root bulb they'd dug out. With the bunnies in her pocket, she inspected the root. Like most non-fungi plants on Epsy, the seeds grew from roots, acting as both fruit and storage organ, and where they were most accessible to seed-spreading helper animals. This one was a dark aqua hue, had the exterior texture of a carrot, and a squishy tomatoey pulp inside. She unearthed a few that hadn't been nibbled, and brought them back to the cave.

Despite her insistence that he rest, John lay on his side and used one hand to help rig up a rotisserie using the heater and some IR emitters.

After a chemical analysis, it turned out that the root's outer crust was both edible and safe, while the pulp and seeds were human *incomp*. The nontoxic part tasted like a pickled shallot or onion. Unimpressed with their "vegetables," they moved on to the meat. Both agreed that the bunnies, indeed, tasted like chicken.

Minnie setup a drying rack to preserve what they hadn't eaten. Bunny jerky would soon join their expanding diet.

As they fell asleep, cave entrance moaning with the wind, Minnie told John she still planned to track down Ish. Bring her back if she found her alive. John didn't argue. He even suggested a method of pinpointing Ish's skimmer even if it was completely shut down.

The next day would see no search expedition. The storm had arrived.

Neither had appreciated the power of Epsy's major storms. Viewed from above and through sensors, sure, many were stronger than Earth hurricanes, but to experience one first hand for forty straight hours, Minnie and John shared a new respect for Epsy's resilient inhabitants.

On the second night, after eating, John put on his earnest face. "How you doing up here?" He tapped the side of his head. "Almost three weeks."

Minnie looked to her eyebrows, as if conducting a visual inspection. "Looking good!" No amusement in John's expression. She exhaled. "Honest, not even a hint. I've been thinking about it a lot, as each day passed. Maybe my broke got fixed in the metabed on the way here. Or what if every year that went by on meds—years without a single episode—just gave the crazy glands time to heal? Nature tends to fix itself when given time."

"You know it doesn't work that way. What if the neurotoxins from the cave were keeping you in check? Just delaying. You might be on the verge."

Minnie shrugged. "Could be. Or I'm cured. Time will tell. Leave it, okay? I'll let you know if anything even slightly zany pops into my head."

The skies cleared on the third day. Minnie set up her skimmer's onboard scanners while John walked her through the steps from the cave.

By midday, Minnie was flying toward the other skimmer's reactor power signature. Observing that her pathway followed along the curving course of a well-known river, Minnie was keenly aware that this route led directly to the area's largest Hynka village.

JOHN: If we haven't already, we're going to lose DC soon.

MINNIE: Yeah, any second.

JOHN: I know I said it already, but if it looks like you'll be in any danger whatsoever, abort and come back. Do not land that skimmer.

MINNIE: I know. Me and it are your only way out of this giant butt. I won't be hasty.

JOHN: It's not just for me. And it's an order, understand?

Ugh. Old John back in action.

Minnie ignored his last message and, a few seconds later, saw the DC icon flash and break in two, letting her know she'd traveled out of range. Below her, the landscape shifted to an oddly beautiful plain of knobby green waves, like a flash-frozen ocean. She dropped to 10m, gliding across the surface, exhilarated. Upon closer inspection, the lumpy topography appeared to be ancient lava flow coated in lichen moss.

If not for deadly native inhabitants and another human life dependent on her for survival, she'd love to set out exploring this land from coast to coast. So much of it was entirely different from Threck Country. She didn't know why that surprised her. The Threck lived in the geographical equivalent of New Zealand, while the Hynka had a landmass the size of Eurasia to call home. Mountain ranges to canyons, deserts and great lakes. "What a waste," had been Minnie's not-so-quiet original observation, especially given the fact that the Hynka stuck to these premiere upper-middle latitudes.

More fungal forestland approached up ahead, and Minnie returned to her higher elevation. The instant she passed over an especially tall stand of epsequoias, Minnie realized she'd arrived. Throngs of Hynka filled the trampled, near-barren land, moving about like worker ants without the lines. Hundreds carried water in hollowed-out shroom stalks to a vast "well" in the center of the village, while hundreds more streamed in from the forest with arms full of large nut pods, bundles of stringy black leaves, bunnies, and other bounty. Circling over the village, she saw clusters of Hynka in the river catching jellies with their bare hands.

Not so savage at home, eh? Cooperative civilized behavior like this never made it into one of Ish's reports. Why hide it? She'd so desperately wished to convince Minnie and the others that the Hynka were these advanced people—not the frenzied pack animals everyone observed, little more than rudimentary tool-wielding wolves.

But then she was spotted and things returned to familiar territory. Five individuals yelling and pointing grew to ten, which grew to thirty, and before she could zip from the clearing, chests began heaving, heads rolled around on necks, shoulders rose and fell, guttural shrieks rang out, and bodies were ripped apart. For the Hynka, there was no time like a crisis to devour your closest neighbor. Minnie peered back just in time to see that limbs and heads weren't being ripped asunder merely for rage management or food, but for ammo. An arm whizzed by behind her, instantly followed by a head, which actually struck the side of the skimmer.

She accelerated and shot up into the sky another hundred meters, well above body part flinging range. She pulled up the tracking screen in her fone and saw that Ish's skimmer was only 1.5K east. The app had precise coordinates now and Minnie set them as her destination, bringing up the familiar red guide line. It was interesting to see it floating in the sky, like a game, gently arcing toward an unseen location beyond a rocky red outcropping jutting up from dense foliage.

Less than a minute later, Minnie was well away from the hordes of Hynka, but she could still hear the ruckus she'd instigated. There were no Hynka in sight here on the outskirts of the village, but it was quite clearly an area they frequented. The lack of small foragers dispersing a variety of seeds had created a monochrome landscape dominated by a single species of tall, cream-colored, martini-glass-shaped fungus in every direction.

They'd surely seen which way she'd flown. They'd be here soon enough.

Minnie crossed over the 30 meter-high sandstone outcropping, like a natural wall extending from the taller hills on one side, gradually losing height until finally plunging beneath the fungus jungle's (Tom had brilliantly coined "fungle") colorless canopy less than a kilometer away.

Another half-K into dense, seemingly untrodden fungle, the guide line plunged into a small gap in the vegetation. Without an obvious path to land, Minnie switched to biomag. The drab fungi disappeared, revealing the distinctive structure of a parked skimmer, shining green. Clearly the Hynka had yet to come across it.

She surveyed the perimeter, finding no signs of Ish or anything else. Gazing back toward the sandstone wall, Minnie tried to imagine where Ish would've gone first. Heading straight for a crowded area would be patently suicidal, but who knew if Ish would see it that way?

With a now-or-never fire beneath her, Minnie landed, hopped over to Ish's skimmer, powered it on, and enabled pairing. After a quick glance at the small pile of supplies (and Ish's helmet) on the ground, she leapt back to her pad, completed the skimmer pairing, and launched back out of the hideaway. The handling was slightly different than a single vehicle, but not remotely as unwieldy as she'd expected. The two ionic drives seemed to act as a single, giant propulsion surface, even seamlessly correcting for the lack of load on Ish's skimmer.

Keeping low over the fungle canopy, Minnie returned to the rock outcropping and slowly floated above a path of seemingly cleared ground between rock face and vegetation. The trail soon widened out into an unquestionably *created* area.

Hovering above an apparent shrine—a massive, many-pointed star composed of what appeared to be thousands of bones—Minnie slowly rotated the skimmers. The pale bone star had been set up on a level bed of dark gravel. Large, crudely chiseled blocks rose away from the bones and pebbles toward the jutting sandstone—1-high, then a stack of 2, then 3—the initial building blocks of an as-yet unimagined pyramid. The giant steps led to a landing or stage, also built of monolithic blocks, three wide. From there, natural tiering took over, offering access to increasingly steep third and fourth levels, where semi-spherical natural cavities dented the sandstone, like docking ports for 20 EVs.

The whole rock looked to Minnie like pics she'd seen of the Utah desert, and it probably would've been even more reminiscent a thousand years ago, before the Hynka decided to make it their own. No doubt the stone on this side had not always been so pale. Like a seabird flock's favorite offshore rock, the tiers of formerly red sandstone had been bleached white by years of defilement—Hynka blood sheeting down the steps like a gory fountain, or some bizarre "water" feature one might find outside the HQ of the International Milk Farmers Association.

As she imagined the grisly ceremonies that must occur here, something caught Minnie's eye above the bleached layers. On the rocky outcropping, between the highest tier and the peak, Minnie found Ish.

20

EV4's stabilizer legs deployed as the sphere descended slowly toward a vast, featureless plain. Thomas Meier held his breath as he watched the altimeter count down, awaiting the jarring thud of surface contact. Through the porthole above, a mostly clear violet sky implied a beautiful Threck Country day awaited them, though sensors had warned of gusty wind in the projected landing zone.

On the panel before him, a virtual Evacuation Vehicle graphic met the ground's jagged line a few seconds before he felt anything. For an instant, it seemed they'd stopped moving, but then the EV grazed the surface, tilting and wobbling for a few seconds as it bounced and drifted several more meters, then skidded to a stop. Silence followed, emphasizing the eerie, almost sickening sensation of zero motion.

Concerned about the wind and the EV toppling if he retracted the chute, Tom instead hit the chute release. A muffled *ch-kck* overhead signaled its successful detachment, and he turned his head left to see Angela's stunned face. Eyes alert and guarded, her mouth hung open in a frozen smile. They sat there, still, for nearly a minute.

Angela's hushed voice in Tom's helmet broke the silence.

"Strewth … We're actually alive."

"For the moment," he replied with grim earnest. A line from OUTPOST IOTA. "Let's see if there's anything outside that wants to eat us."

She glared at him and lifted her visor. He did the same and began disconnecting his helmet.

"You hole!" She backhanded his chest. "We lived! You can't just celebrate that? Or at least let *me* celebrate it for more than a second?"

Tom sighed and put his hand on her knee. “Honey … *shut up*. That was a quote. And an awesome one at that. Victor Kant. Such a bad ass. But yeah, I wasn’t serious. What I’d like to verify is that there’s nothing that wants to eat *me*.” He winked and unfastened his restraints.

She pulled off her helmet. “I’m so kicking your ass when we’re settled.”

“I love you?” he said in an apologetic singsong.

They leaned close and embraced, both squeezing a bit more firmly than the other had expected. Tom planted his nose into her hair and inhaled.

She pushed him back. “No way. Don’t smell me right now. Five days of funk layered up on this nasty body.”

“I enjoy your nasty body.” A spot-on impression of Welsh actor Vale Bevan, if Tom said so himself.

He set the pod to begin equalizing with the outside air as he and Angela opened their surface survival kit’s to resume evac procedures. Tom clipped the holster onto his suit and pulled his multiweapon from its case. He held it out by the grip, pointing the business end up.

“A man and his gun,” he said.

Angela glanced at him and laughed. “So sexy.”

Tom lifted an amorous eyebrow. “You want another go before we disembark for the rest of our natural lives? Make it a nice even three?”

“Uh, no. Rewind forty-five seconds and pay close attention to the ‘five days of funk’ part. And three is an odd number, doof. We’ve got work to do. For one, we need to track down Aether and Qin. Do you have a fix on them … or Zees and Pablo, for that matter?”

“I lost my DC to Aether when our chute blew. Figured they kept descending for a while before theirs deployed, thus moving out of range.”

“Wait, what if their chute didn’t pop at all?”

Tom waved a dismissive hand. “These things have backups for the backups. Don’t wack out on me.” He studied the EV’s console. “We’re all equalized here. Weather outside is safe. No natural threats in the vicinity. You ready to step out?”

"I feel like we should wait for Aether's instructions."

Tom's hand hovered in front of the hatch lever. "Honey, I'm eighty-eight kilos. Nearly two meters. I've been in this thing with you for almost *ninety* hours, and while the conversation has been riveting, and while I feel that our relationship has reached a beautiful new level—and I don't just mean the fact that we're probably the first people in history to christen an EV, not only once, but twice—and while I love you and *never* wish to be apart from you, I need to get the hell out of this thing before my spine buckles and my brain implodes."

Angela looked up at him with loving eyes and a touched smile. "Okay, sweetie. If you're sure it's safe outside. And I like it when you turn into Mr. Take-Charge, by the way. Uber-sexy. Though I doubt we're the first to defile an EV."

"But during a *real* evac? Hmmm?" Tom rotated the lever and the hatch glided outward before rising up and over the top of the EV. Hot air flowed in.

"Oh wow, that smell!" Angela said as Tom poked his head out and peered around. "So different … Is that sun-dried landfill I detect?"

For a brief moment, Tom thought they'd landed on a dry lake bed, the surface a seemingly perfect flat, almost all the way to the horizon. In the heat-blurred distance rose a low, rolling mountain range. Above, the pale violet sky was painted with stretching cirrus clouds. Gusty summer winds howled and whistled around the EV, the shiny white sphere an alien blemish on the monotonous landscape.

Tom checked the ground before stepping out. "You know where we are?"

"No, you're standing in the way."

"The Parking Lot," Tom said with genuine awe, and moved aside.

"No way."

Like referring to Everest or the Amazon on Earth, Epsy's "Parking Lot" was a renowned land feature. It was one of the 17 Wonders of Epsy, so branded by the station crew. Six years after arriving in orbit, or more precisely, three years after dispatching their initial report and data drop back to Earth, the mission had received its first set of new orders. For Tom, the most intriguing part of the message was not the strange shift in research priorities, but the unexpected intro to their new bosses and colleagues.

At some point during the two decades since launch, the United Exploration Agency had been dissolved, and ongoing responsibility for the projects (and personnel) was split between two private companies, one in Switzerland, the other in Argentina.

Tom knew that 80% of the in-progress missions had been sent to investigate stable Earthlike planets with no known intelligent lifeforms, and that these pre-colonization teams had always ranked higher than his purely-for-science 20%. But he was still shocked to learn of an intense bidding war for the colonization teams while a non-profit organization struggled to drum up interest in the science stations. Fortunately, all of this had been worked out three years before the team received the message.

The transition was delicately explained by Swiss executives in a vid. After a recounting of pertinent recent history, and introductions to other members of their new Earth-side teams, Tom's station was given a list of five high-pri research objectives, one of which was to begin in-depth examination of the Parking Lot. Knowing that these people were the ones who would continue launching semiannual supply pods to the station, the crew were all too happy to oblige their requests. John had wasted no time sending back a formal thanks, enthusiastic acceptance of the new dictate, and a vidtour of the station highlighting each member of the crew, smiling and alive (and clearly hoping to remain so for as long as possible). It'd be another three years before the reply reached Earth, so there was some amount of assumption and good faith on both ends of the comms.

Now, as the laser carrying that message neared the Oort cloud of Earth's solar system, the crew had become quite familiar with the Parking Lot.

Side by side in the open hatch, Angela wrapped an arm around Tom's waist as they slowly took in the panorama. Strewn somewhere across and beneath this barren landscape lay miner probes, dead dragonfly probes, and spikers. Once the crew determined to solve the mystery of a kilometers-wide cement plain, it hadn't taken long to form theories. Either via nearby volcanic activity or an impact event, the native limestone had mixed with fine ash to form this awe-inspiring cement flat. Though its outward appearance eschewed natural formation—especially with the conspicuously straight line of the Lot's eastern border—it only took a few months of focused study to solve the puzzle to the crew's satisfaction. The full report was sent off to Earth. 14 million years old. The product of a now-inert supervolcano. Meters below the surface, spiker sensors had found the remains of a once-fertile marsh, frozen in time.

Tom stepped onto the cement surface first and stretched his arms over his head. Despite the scorching heat and instant sweat, he cried out extravagant pleasure and relief, rolling his neck and twisting at the waist. He bent over and touched his toes, then back up again, reaching for the clouds.

"So good!" he shouted and glanced back at Angela as she planted her first foot on the pale ground. "You know what I wish we had?"

"An air conditioner? A swimming pool? A launch pad and fully fueled interstellar transport ship?"

He interlocked his fingers in front of him and stretched out his back. "Pshh-no. No, what I *really* wish I had was one of those ancient torture racks where they tied your wrists and ankles to either end and just pulled ..." He moved his hands apart as if stretching out dough. "What were those things called? The rack things."

"A rack." She inhaled a deep breath and held the hot air in her lungs.

"No, there's got to be some sort of real name for it. Like *guillotine*."

"Look it up, doof. It's 'rack.'"

"We'll have to agree to disagree."

"No, we don't. We don't have to agree to that at all—"

He pressed a gloved finger against her mouth, uttering a mock-seductive, "Shhhh ..." then hunched down, curled his other hand around her waist, and gazed into her cobalt eyes. "Tell me something. How could you *possibly* be attracted to a gangly beast like me? I mean, look at all this." He glanced up suddenly. "Hang on … what's that sound?"

They froze and listened. A rapid beep emanated from within the EV. Angela climbed back inside and Tom stuck his head in after her.

"Radio!" Angela said as she opened the comms panel and fumbled with the headset. "EV-four here. Go." Tom could hear a tinny voice through the little speaker as Angela listened. She looked up at Tom as she pinched the mic button. "Understood, Zees. Just try to stay calm. I'm handing you over to Tom." She released the button and put the headset in Tom's hand. "They landed in a farm. Several adult Threck approaching from the dwelling. Be cool, she sounds like she's about to droop her poop."

Tom pinched the button. "Hi, Zisa, this is Tom. Listen close, okay? Do you know if you're anywhere near the city, or if this farm is out in the country?"

"Yes!" she replied in an anxious whisper.

"Which? Yes, near the city?"

"No, country," she said, annoyed. Tom heard a garbled something from Pablo. Zisa responded, "I know! We're two-point-two-K west of the river, okay? Just tell us what to do! A proper peace greeting or whatever!"

Tom sighed and gave Angela a grim look. Everyone was supposed to download the emergency maps, language, and customs file before exiting their EVs—something Tom and Angela had also failed to do.

Angela leaned close to Tom to hear the radio.

Tom continued, "You're not going to like this, Zisa, but it's important for you to know. Listen, have Pablo come near the radio so you both hear me, okay?"

"Come here," Zisa said. "He wants you to hear. … Go ahead."

"Here's the deal. These are Country Threck, so they're not as predictable as City Threck, and I'm not too solid on their dialect. You definitely want to keep from making unintentional hand or head gestures. Body movements are nearly half their language, so you could accidentally say something offensive or threatening. Don't turn your back to them. Don't keep your mouth open if you're not talking—"

"Ten meters and slowly closing," Pablo said. "One of them is saying something."

"Just don't interrupt. In a second, you'll need to stop talking to me and focus on only them. *Ee-shaaay-CK.* That's what you're going to say. *Ee-shaaay-CK.* Nothing else. It means 'peaceful greetings' in every Threck dialect. Carry that *a* sound and punch the *CK* at the end. Now, give me your coordinates so we can get to you asap."

Tom saved Zisa and Pablo's location to his fone and DC'd with the EV to download the emergency file he should've picked up in the first place.

Angela was standing in front of him, fanning her face and neck with her hand. "Should I get the skimmers going?"

"Yes, please. Thank you. Don't forget your helmet, though. This heat isn't safe."

A moment later, the full emergency data pack was on his fone and he sealed the EV before joining Angela at the rear to help undock the skimmers.

This wasn't how first contact was supposed to play out. Now they were at an immediate disadvantage.

"You okay, baby?" Angela said as she prepped her skimmer. Tom only shrugged and clenched his jaw as he watched the skimmer slowly lower and twist into shape. "You were good back there. On the radio."

"I wish I'd taken the 'backup' role more seriously," he said as he stepped on his skimmer's platform and powered it on. "Actually, I just wish Minnie was here."

21

Droplets of ocean water dotted EV1's two overhead portholes. The pod's slow rises and falls, combined with early digestion restart, had Aether's stomach in a threatening state. She and Qin should already be on their second calorie bar, providing the fresh bile something to work on, but the idea of eating made her feel even sicker.

Obviously, it would've been preferable to touch down on dry land, but she couldn't blame Qin for that. A) He was the one who'd figured out the fine adjustments required to get the stranded pods rounded up and reentering, saving all of their lives; and B) EV1 only deviated off-course because the main chute hadn't automatically deployed. Instead of landing along Threck Country's lush southern coast, they'd continued hurtling an extra 8K south before the backup chute fired. Now, floating so far from shore, land was but a hazy strip on the northern horizon.

Neither had been keen on the idea of rowing their way ashore, even with their suits' temp regulation systems. In the middle of Epsy's southern hemisphere summer, where temperatures frequently exceeded an unlivable 60 °C, waiting for the current to carry them most of the way would be more than acceptable. That was, if none of the other evacuees felt inclined to amble out their way with a few skimmers to carry them to the rally point.

Aether wasn't holding her breath. The other teams had their given tasks, and unless called upon for emergency assistance, all should have been heading to the rally point and setting up. Once the sun set, the heat would rapidly dissipate, and she and Qin would spend the better part of the evening paddling the EV the rest of the way in.

Qin, face contorted by his growing dread, sat with eyes squeezed shut. While an exceptional pilot, Qin had always been at home in a lab. He despised the outdoors and all that lived within it—animals (whether furry or not), bugs, even plants for some reason. Among all of Aether's crew/patients, she knew Qin would never have issues with cabin fever, irrational antagonism, or space panic. But that was on the station. He loved the station. Now, she wasn't so sure how he'd manage. His SP rating had always been worst, and by a wide margin from the next lowest, Zisa. Since evac, whenever he wasn't busy, Aether had him deep-diving into transitionary input. And that's what he was doing now, brow furrowed with concern as he sat transfixed by Threck Country maps, pics, and vids from the emergency file pack. Minnie had been utterly meticulous with its content.

Minnie.

Yesterday, with 13 orbits remaining out of 74, Qin had worked out EV5's and EV6's trajectories. Minnie, John, and Ish had been headed straight for Hynka Country's middle highlands, chillingly close to one of the savages' most populous villages.

Aether closed her eyes and tried to see the situation as John would. Focus on logic and tasks at hand. Do what could be done while mentally compartmentalizing all she couldn't control. In addition to their top SP ratings, Minnie and John were the most "generally capable" crewmembers, regardless of their differences. If they followed protocol, they'd now be a team of three, with Ish's Hynka expertise at their disposal.

A comms alert rang out, startling both Aether and Qin.

Qin leaned forward and reached the panel first. "We're in range!" He pulled out the old wired-style headset. "It's Zisa. Kind of freaking out. Calling for Tom. Should I tell them where we are?"

Aether shook her head. "Sounds like she might have more pressing concerns. And it's radio. We don't want to step on Tom if he answers. Give it thirty seconds. Relay specifics."

"Angela's on now … handing off to Tom … Zisa and Pablo landed in farmland … several adult Threck approaching … Tom's all over it. So now? Before they go away? Should I tell them? When they're done, you know, maybe they can—" Qin was already bordering on panic just hearing about *others'* distress.

Aether smiled softly and patted the air with a *"settle down"* hand.

She spoke gently. "In a minute. Make sure they're both done transmitting. But no distress call. We'll stick to our plan while they do what they need to do."

Qin waited in fidgety silence for exactly one minute before pinching the mic. "EV-One to Four and Two. In comms range." He relayed their current coordinates and glanced at Aether. "Should we request periodic check-in?" Aether returned a no-nod and motioned him to calmly finish. "We've made a water landing and will meet you all at the rally point tomorrow. Over." He sat and listened.

"Any response?"

"Nothing." He wiped the sweat from his head. "I think you're right. They'll be indisposed for a bit."

"Did it sound like Zisa and Pablo were in serious danger?"

Composure returning, Qin shrugged and gave her a knowing look. "Yeah, *but*."

Aether nodded. Zisa's tone wouldn't be the most accurate indicator of a critsit.

A dull thud struck the EV hull. Aether and Qin looked around and then at each other. A wave? Their motion hadn't been affected. Another thud, this time at the very top of the EV.

"What the hell is that?" Aether said.

"Seabird?"

"No birds on Epsy."

"A fish? Some kind of jumping fish?" Qin's face remembered and said *duh*. "Optics!" He popped up, squatting in his seat and peering around.

Aether followed suit and set her fone to autoglide through spectrums. She paused on the thermag overlap, spotting through the EV gear and walls a group of figures in the water beneath and around the pod. "You see them?"

"Ahh man, I ahh, yeah, I ahh ..." He began hyperventilating, head snapping from figure to figure. "What ahh ... what'd'you ahh ... what'd'you think they're doing?"

The colorful blobs of warmth appeared to be poking at the hull and conversing. Aether counted only five.

She adjusted focus and intensity until the bodies gained definition. "Just checking us out. Slow it down. Remember that these are all peaceful people. In nose, out mouth."

Unconvinced, he tried to watch each individual at once. "Nonono-why? Why us, too? All the way out here? Ah-hey!" He jumped as if to avoid a probing Threck tentacle touching his foot.

Typical phobic behavior. The full meter of gear and hull between him and the Threck in the water below offered no solace. His mind was operating as if the visitors were inside the EV with him.

"Qin, sweetie, look at me." She annunciated as if speaking to a child. "I *really* don't think we need to worry. Not about Sea Threck. These are Sea Threck. You remember Minnie talking about Sea Threck? They're the purist hippie types, right? They reject the modern comforts of the city and return to the water, remember?"

He looked at her, desperate for it to be true. "Yeah, sure, yeah, but doesn't that make them hunters versus farmers?"

"Yes, however we look nothing like fish or crustaceans. Besides, how could they possibly breach the hull? Even if they had the very best bronze weapons from the city, they'd hardly make a dent." She glanced down. "Look, some of them are leaving."

"Great, but some are staying."

Aether watched as three orange figures slowly descended into darkness, tentacles waving gracefully around them. The two that stayed behind appeared to be keeping their distance, floating beneath the EV.

"If you were amphibious," Qin began with a shaky voice. A valiant effort at self-distraction via idle conversation. "Would you 'return to the water' or stick to the city?"

Aether wished she could be more thrilled by this moment. She stood mere meters from another intelligent lifeform—people they'd never expected to see up close with their own eyes. "I think I'd choose the place I didn't yet know."

Qin looked up, wearing an aspiring smiling. "I guess that's *all* of us, huh? Thus the current predicament." He peered back down between his feet. "When they're swimming like this, you can really see how they evolved for land ... the ruined symmetry ... and yet still so suited for the water."

Aether watched the two Threck under the pod. Side by side, they "lay" beneath the surface as if on an invisible hammock. They supported each other with one "arm" tentacle wrapped under the other's back, the unoccupied arm gently waving at their sides to maintain position. On land, the Threck's two front tentacles stretched out below them as legs—thus their wider girth and stiffer structure. Over millennia, the rear appendages had become arms, and the ends—called *pads* or *clubs*, or even *hands* when the team got lazy—evolved increasingly useful features. The arms were thinner and considerably more dexterous than legs, and for precision tasks such as sewing, Threck used the thousands of cilia on their pads as little fingers. A couple years ago, Minnie captured a clip of a Threck artist painting a detailed mural on a city wall. The clubs were dipped into various paints and then gradually slid across the wall as individual cilia hairs applied paint to specific "pixels." The pad was washed, a new paint applied, and more blank areas were filled. "They use them like inkjet printers!" Minnie had enthused.

"Still there," Qin said. "What if they don't leave by nightfall? Then what?"

"I'm hesitant to try and scare them away. Can you verify that, if we do nothing, the current is still leading us close to the rally point?"

"Already done. We're still heading north for several hours before skirting the coast eastward. But if we don't blow the raft when we get close, we'll pass right by, and out to open sea. What if they stay—"

"Hang on," Aether interrupted, holding out a finger to Qin while staring down at her seat. "What the hell is *that?*" Deep beneath the surface, perhaps 100m below the two Sea Threck, hundreds of new heat signatures appeared and grew.

"Ahh yeah, ahh not good ... ahh how many—"

"Does it matter? Wait ..." As the amoebas of heat ascended, Aether could see them combining into larger blobs. It wasn't a bunch of different entities, but a single, extremely large creature, slowly rising toward them.

Qin murmured, observing the same thing, "Ahh man that's some kind of whale ..."

"More like a mollusk ... That's all hard shell just beneath the—oh, I know what it is. Affrik or averik or something like that. It's the big domesticated fishing boat animals. You know, in the harbor?"

Qin just stared downward, inhaling through the nose, exhaling through the mouth.

A moment later, the massive beast stopped its ascent about 40m below. Five Sea Threck appeared from around the thing's edges. The other two that had waited now twisted into action and all seven rose to the surface, surrounding the floating pod.

Two thuds in rapid succession. Something appeared in the porthole over Aether's head. A thick, pink vine. Squeaks and bumps against the hull. The EV tilted, knocking Aether off-balance. She grabbed a handle and steadied herself.

"They're wrapping us up!" Qin said. "Hippies or not, they're not giving up as interesting a prize as this! They're keeping us! They're going to take us somewhere!"

Aether ignored him and watched four figures quickly swim down toward the giant animal. What to do? Blow the hatch and raft, and bail? Initiate contact now? As much as she tried to convince Qin how peaceful these people were, the truth was they didn't have all that much data on Sea Threck. What if they spoke an entirely different language? It seemed likely, given the differences in environments, land and water. Most sounds spoken in one atmosphere wouldn't work at all in the other.

And what if the Sea Threck tried pulling them farther out to sea?

She didn't have to think long about this question. Answering for her, the Sea Threck had their enormous creature submerge once more, dragging the pod beneath the surface with ease.

"Crap! Ah crap!" Qin blurted, clutching two handles as the pod sunk deeper and deeper, sunlight from the surface rapidly dissipating, the glow of the EV's internal lights taking over. He spewed rapidfire thoughts, "Where're they taking us? Wha'd'we do? What if the pressure—"

As the pod continued plunging, it accelerated to the northwest.

Aether tried to remain calm for the both of them. "We don't have to worry about pressure. We equalized on landing, so we'll remain at sea level atmosphere. Also, the EV's can withstand pressure down to … what … two-K?"

Qin was losing it. "I don't know! Is it? Can it? What if we run out of air? Stuck at the bottom … the scrubbers …"

"Calm down!" Aether roared. "Our concerns are no different from being in orbit."

The top of the pod scraped against a rigid surface, sending a grating screech into Aether's head. They'd been dragged beneath something solid. Forward motion slowed.

The EV bobbed side to side as she toggled the console to the external environment variables screen. The altitude gauge had switched to read "Depth." They'd reached 156m below the surface and continued to move northwest, albeit very slowly.

Aether climbed up onto her seat back and peered out the porthole. There, a few meters away, she saw a Sea Threck swimming alongside the EV. A faint green glow was all that lit its bug-eyed face. Aether switched to IR and the area beyond the window appeared in crisp grayscale. They were in an underwater cavern, but not a naturally occurring one.

The EV stopped its forward progress and swung against its line for a moment, drifting forward then backward until the pod's buoyancy held them straight up like a tethered balloon.

"Ahh man, so not good, really not good," Qin murmured under his breath. He was in his seat, gripping the restraints and staring through the instrument cluster. "Wha'd'they want, wha'd'they want …"

"Start adjusting our pressure. I think we need to equalize with this depth, and fast."

"But you said they couldn't—"

"Qin!"

He shut up and turned to the console.

"And make sure your suit and visor are sealed."

Aether climbed down and switched back to thermag, observing what had so rattled Qin. She estimated 30-40 Threck floated before them. Beyond the group of orange figures, the rough outline of a craggy wall appeared in wavy grays, and hundreds of vines grew upward, obscuring the rocky surface like a curtain. Several dark patches marked entrances to tunnels hidden behind the vines. From the vague features discernible through her optics, the whole structure before them looked like a magnified coral reef, whereas behind and above, the cavern appeared fashioned from enormous shells. Perhaps, she thought, shells of the huge mollusks, like the one currently anchoring the EV. They'd built onto a natural structure, creating a concert-hall-sized compound.

To her left, hundreds of small fish swam frantically within a netted enclosure affixed to the wall. Tall vines grew in clusters from small pits. On her right, half a dozen large animals drifted about, tied to the opposite wall. Through thermag, their silhouettes were smooth domes like turtle shells, but with four long, broad fins instead of legs. Could they be young versions of the massive creature that pulled the EV under? The basic anatomy matched.

"I can't believe this," Qin's voice moaned in Aether's helmet speakers. "This is unbelievable. Do you believe this? After *all* that to reenter?"

"It's less than ideal," Aether said. "Can you check our comms status? And after that, assemble a map of this cavern. We need the shortest, safest routes to the surface."

"You expect we'll need to—"

"No, I don't *expect* anything, but we need to plan for everything. Just focus on the tasks, okay?"

Qin quietly echoed her words as he began. "Focus on task ... planning and focusing ..."

Aether climbed around, peeking out the portholes again. The vines were the source of the green glow. Tiny bubble clusters along the stalks, like baby grapes, appeared to be reservoirs for bioluminescent bacteria or fungi. The Sea Threck equivalent of installing street lights, or had they simply grown wild?

Two more Threck figures emerged from the tunnels behind the vine curtain. Aether and Qin watched in silence as the pair appeared to confer with their comrades, then proceeded to swim toward the still-anchored EV. Several other Threck sprang into action, disappearing deep below. The EV lurched, rose minutely, then sunk once more. Aether watched as the giant creature below them slowly exited the area from the direction they'd come, while the pod remained in place, apparently tethered to a new anchor.

"Ho-hey!" Qin exclaimed.

Two Threck now swam just outside the EV, running their long, arm tentacles along the hull. Despite all the vids and pics she'd seen on the station, it was still astounding to see them so close. In the water, with leg tentacles fully extended, they appeared so much taller than all the on-land images—perhaps half a meter longer than an average human male. Out of water, they walked on a calloused bend in the tentacles, sort of shuffling along as if on very low knees. Near the center of Threck City there was a statue of a famous historical Threck leader with his arms in the air and standing on the very ends of his "legs," but Aether wasn't aware of Minnie ever observing someone fully extending their legs to stand or walk on the ends. Perhaps if there were a Threck ballet.

The two Threck swam around the EV, studying the hull, until one made its way to the top and found Qin's porthole. It summoned its companion and another head appeared in the window. Their big eyes, like flesh-hooded billiard balls, touched and slid around each other as they tried to see in at the same time.

Aether made a decision. She stood up and faced the porthole straight-on, holding her arms out at her sides in the shape of an arrow.

This was the City Threck equivalent to waving hello to a distant person. The two Threck gawked at her—not moving for a moment, appearing to consider—then whirled back to life. A third swam forward, passing what appeared to be a small stone to one of the two observers, who then struck the EV hull with it.

"Nononono …" Qin's shaky, whispering voice.

"Just one tap … stay calm." Another tap, harder. "Your suit ran a check, right?"

"Ahh yeah ... it's fine. Hey, do MWs work underwater?"

"Good question," Aether said, checking her waist to verify the multiweapon was still there. "Look it up for us, would you?"

A rapid buzzing alert rang out in the cabin as the ambient light flashed from blue to orange and back.

"What?" a flabbergasted Qin shouted. "He figured out the hatch access!"

Aether peered through the still-sealed hatch and saw one of the Threck fiddling with the opening mechanism. Manipulating it was not an intuitive process, and the Threck's nubby pad just didn't seem up to the task. Then again, those nimble little cilia …

She barked, "Shut off that racket!"

The sound stopped but the lights continued flashing.

The Threck had poked the bar that pushed the semicircular handle out (thus the alarm), but to actually open the hatch they'd have to grip the handle, pull it out a couple centimeters, and rotate it 180° clockwise before pushing it in. Aether crouched close and watched the club struggling with it. Did the Threck know that the thing it was fooling with was an access mechanism? Or was it simply the first moving part they could find? A similar latch resided at the back of the EV for skimmer deployment, but everything else on the hull was tooled on.

"MWs work underwater," Qin said. Aether heard a new determination, as if he'd come to terms with the situation and was ready to suck it up. "Stunshocks auto-disable when submerged. It also advises lethal setting for effective defense as nonlethal is severely diminished. Also, we should reset the EV. Prep it for reentry."

"Why?"

"So the lockdown bars reengage. I just remembered. They can't open the hatch if we reset."

Aether thought about it. "Will *we* be able to? When the time comes? And what about the pressure?"

"Yes, it'll be like a landing simulation as far as those instruments go. The pod's already equalized for this depth, but its environment won't be affected anyway. Plus, our suits are handling environment individually now."

She looked at his intense face through the visor. She'd never seen him panicked before today, and it was good to see and hear him getting it together. "Okay, do it then. Lock us down."

A new alarm sounded, more insistent.

Beep-beep-beep, beep-beep-beep ... and the orange light began to strobe. From the hatch frame, a thin bar of water blasted in, striking Aether's body and helmet, thrusting her against the seat back. She struggled to turn sideways, grasping fruitlessly for the holstered MW.

The gushing water abruptly stopped.

Aether looked down and saw that she was sitting in a shallow pool. She clambered once more to her feet, climbing back onto the seat. Outside the EV, five Sea Threck appeared to be in a heated debate. One poked another in the face. The other returned with a swipe. Two more pulled the poker away. Which one had figured out the hatch access? And why did it stop? Had the external pressure been too great to pull the hatch open more than a crack, or had the ones at the portholes seen the water streaming in and ordered a halt? Aether had suddenly become a goldfish in a little bowl.

Three Threck swam to the top of the pod, pushing down with their legs while pulling at the vines. The EV began to roll in place, sending Qin and Aether scrambling to stay on their feet.

"They're tipping us over!" Qin shrieked, his voice atop a layer of static.

They stepped off of their seats as their world rotated forward, the pool of water splashing over the hatch, consoles, and EV controls, shorting out instruments. Lights flickered and popped off, display panels shut down.

"We might lose intercomms," Aether warned. "Switching to DC."

They stepped lightly onto the systems panels, carefully avoiding kicking any switches or applying weight to sensitive surfaces or screens. What the hell were the Threck doing?

Blue emergency lights activated just as the EV stopped rolling. Aether and Qin stood on instrument panels flanking the hatch and waited, their respective portholes now situated beside their faces. Aether locked eyes with the Threck floating just a half meter outside. Like the mudskippers the Threck partially resembled, its large eyeballs sucked into their sockets and popped back up like an elaborate blink. She glimpsed its siphons moving open and closed like giant nostrils. Minnie had catalogues of Threck facial and body expressions in the language DB, but Aether couldn't bring herself to pull them up. Her eyes were glued to the thing's face, and the reverse appeared true of the Threck beyond the porthole. Beside its head, the occasional tentacle whooshed by. Its own or another's? Too much going on at once.

The EV lurched again and the hatch slowly sank below gurgling salt water. The water level rose and briefly splashed, but only for a few seconds before stabilizing like a moon pool, the air trapped within.

Aether watched the submerged hatch slide silently away. Had this been the Threcks' intention? Had they earlier observed the water spraying in, resealed the hatch, and turned the EV on its side to act as a diving bell, conscious of some beings' need for air, and aware of the moon pool effect?

Without warning, two tentacles splashed up, planting themselves on the hatch frame, and a Threck thrust itself up into the cabin. Aether and Qin fell back against their respective sides as the Threck groped about before finding a bar to grasp, then braced its long legs against two sides. It twisted on its appendages, left, right—the equivalent of turning one's head, and gawked at Qin, then Aether, then back. It reached out and touched the dark fabric of the seats, then the smooth surface of the panels, all the while turning and angling its body in short, rapid movements, like a bird.

While it appeared more curious than aggressive, its boldness was thoroughly disconcerting. It even reached out and ran a cilia-coated tentacle end down Aether's helmet and visor. The little hairs waved in sequence like a field of centipede legs. Aether strove to remain still as it fondled her body, squeezing, poking, and swiping. Then it turned to Qin whose expression made it clear he wouldn't be maintaining such composure during any brief exam.

Aether activated her mic and listened one more time to Minnie's synth voice repeat the sounds in her ear module. The Threck's club patted down Qin's shoulder and arm. Before Qin could lose it entirely, Aether proceeded. *"Ee-shaaay-CK."*

The Threck stopped and twisted with startling speed, ogling Aether with its two bulbous eyes. It repositioned its legs to match the head as the eyes sucked in, disappearing for a second. This eye-hiding rendered the head top a featureless blue dome, save for two nearly invisible slits. Aether almost expected the eyes to reappear inside the two soda can-sized siphon orifices, but they popped back up as fast as they'd dropped, and the Threck thrust both of its clubs onto Aether's visor, seeking to probe her cheeks, nose, lips, eyes. Unable to penetrate the transparent material, it slapped its pads onto each side of the helmet and tried to pull it off.

Awed by its strength, Aether was lifted onto her toes and struggled to keep her footing. She threw up her hands reflexively, shoving the tentacles out and away from her helmet, and slipped, her right glute landing hard against a pointy corner.

"Ow!" Her mic and PA were still active.

"Ah!" the Threck echoed. Clubs dropped to its sides and it moved its face right in front of hers.

She imagined the salty, fishy smell of its skin. It repeated, *"Ah!"* once more, and she could see the muscles move inside the siphon holes. Threck mouths were hidden under their bodies where the four tentacles converged, much like an octopus, and weren't involved with vocalizations.

Sifting through options in the language DB, Aether found and activated the Livetrans app. A little box popped up in the upper left of her view, showing Minnie's virtual Threck, Howard, standing and ready to demonstrate appropriate body language. Livetrans automatically disabled her mic and took over control of her suit's PA speaker. Meanwhile, their guest had begun a close inspection of Aether's neck coupler, its club tips pointed and hovering close, like a doctor moving in for the first incision. Without realizing, Aether had been recoiling from the imposing Threck, and found herself pressed into the wall, feet tripping below her.

Qin, in her helmet: "Should I shoot it?"

"No! What? Just stand quiet and don't move. And put your damned MW away if you have it out!"

Still fidgety and with an intense, methic energy, the Threck looked down, scooted its "knees" to either side of the open hatch, and faced Aether with its hands held out to its sides. "*Ock! Ee-shaaay-CK. Sthaw-ptck tshss-ahh …*" It jabbered on like this, cocking its head sideways, popping in one eye or both, arm gestures and body thrusts, bending and stiffening.

Aether tried to maintain eye contact while also watching the Livetrans app working diligently away. Words appeared and disappeared—correcting based on context and gesture interpretation—and as Aether watched the Threck's message come into focus, she felt incredible relief wash over. Less than two seconds after the visitor stopped speaking, with an 8-out-of-10 confidence score, the app presented Aether its first translation.

> LIVETRANS: Peaceful greetings. [Your] bodies and shelter [are] welcome in [my] water. No danger [for you]. [My] water [is] safe from [unknown] and Threck. Where [is your] mountain? [I am] [unknown]. Where [are you] made? How [you] know Threck words?

Aether input her response as quickly as she could, while the Threck popped its head forward in little fits that Livetrans read as "Now you." It glanced back at Qin.

Aether chided herself for never once attempting Threck language on the station. Her response pre-played in her ear (as if she'd be able to verify its accuracy) and she observed this new synth voice was a variation on the generic Sindy synth, though its pitch range had been extended several octaves higher and lower. As Sindy spoke, Howard the Threck's body moved, demonstrating the associated gestures.

Ah, she thought. *That's why it pre-plays ... so I can see where the gestures fit with the words.*

Aether sucked in a deep breath, as if about to speak the sounds herself, and activated playback through her PA. She mimicked the body language in time with the appropriate syllables. *"Ehh-skwaw fwips-scay peeesss-CK ..."* One fist, two fists, exaggerated blink hopefully understood as an eye hide, hip pop, overlapped hands to chest ... "*Packesheh Aether.*" She pointed her stacked palms past the Threck toward Qin. "*Packesheh Chin.*"

The Threck seemed to struggle with most of what she and Livetrans had said. "*Peess-CK,*" it repeated. "*Peess-CK.*" A head cock.

Aether looked over the translation. She'd supposedly told the Threck she was grateful for the welcome, grateful for safety, that she was from a very far away mountain, had gotten lost, and sought to return there. And, of course, their names. The City Threck were known to use names and titles, and the language this one had spoken was 100% City, so it stood to reason that it would contextually receive "Aether" and "Qin" as names, however unfamiliar.

While confident in Minnie's DB and Livetrans, she knew her gestures (or lack thereof) could have ruined the entire message. Especially given the number of physical modifiers in the language that neither Livetrans nor Aether could incorporate. Speaking during inhale or exhale, siphons open or closed, eye hides—and there were a dizzying number of variables. "Fortunately," Minnie had said in one briefing, "this is one of those exigency preps none of us need worry too much about. Unless the Threck throw together some kind of superduper slingshot and shoot themselves up here, we'll never be face to face with one of these people."

The Threck was still asking about *Peess-CK*. Aether highlighted the sound. It meant "lost." She checked for modifiers. The app indicated it was an inhaled word. She played it again while exaggerating an inhale.

The Threck signaled understanding and looked purposefully to Aether then Qin, pointing. "*Packe Eeser … Tchin.*" It crossed its clubs over its upper legs and said, "*Packesheh EH-skinee.*" It repeated, slower, "*EH-skinnneee.*"

LIVETRANS: [I am] [unknown]. [unknown].

Aether input a response and the translation played through her speaker. "Peaceful greetings, Eh-skinee." She added the Threck's name to the catalogue as Skinny.

"Peaceful greetings, Eeser," Skinny replied with much exuberant head cocking.

Aether smiled and then hoped it wasn't an offensive or threatening gesture to show one's teeth.

"Okay so this all looks great and everything," Qin's voice said in her helmet. But you think you can tell him to take us back up to the surface? Maybe something like we'll only keep talking if you let us go up?"

She ignored Qin and composed her next message to Skinny. What an insane thrill to be conversing, she thought, even through a synth. Skinny, too, appeared more energized. And, apparently, Aether's body language and expressions were sufficient for Skinny to grasp her meaning. Who knew if Minnie would be proud, ashamed, or die laughing at the sight?

"Aether and Qin breathe only air so cannot stay long in Skinny's safe water. Can we talk more on land beach?"

Skinny's eyes hid before peering down at the pool of water. Another pair of eyes and head top had been poking up for an unknown length of time. Aether watched Livetrans.

"Orange People want land," Skinny said to the observer. Apparently, the suits' bright color had become the defining characteristic of humans.

The other Threck rose up so its siphons were above water.

"... danger ... die in water," the Threck at the hatch replied.

Aether had disabled [unknown] words and gesture bracketing from displaying, but she wasn't fond of what remained without them.

Skinny turned back to her. "How much time Aether and Qin live in water?"

"No amount of time," Aether had the synth reply. She needed to make it very clear. "We only live on land. We die in water."

Skinny said, "Threck are on land. Not safe for Aether and Qin."

Threck are on land?

Aether was confused. "Is Skinny not Threck?"

Skinny's eyes hid and body contorted. [Shameful disgust]. The other Threck below disappeared under the water with a little splash.

Aether watched the Livetrans unfold before her as Skinny went into an apparent tirade, voice blaring through wide siphon holes as tentacles slapped consoles.

"This is not kind to speak! You are mountain people from far away! We do not angry for these words not to repeat. Threck are evil! Threck are tricking! Threck take people away to make more Threck! Threck will take Aether and Qin! Skinny protects Aether and Qin from Threck in my water!"

22

Was it wrong to be a little grateful for a station catastrophe? Offensive to internally celebrate a near-death experience—a disaster that may have taken the lives of crewmates and friends? Tom knew that Aether and Qin had made it to the surface (albeit an unstable, liquidy surface commonly known as an *ocean*), however the fates of Minnie, Ish, and John had yet to be determined. Of course he hoped for the best—nay, was near-*certain* of the best!—but zipping through the hot fresh air atop an expedition skimmer, pseudo-racing Angela, his girlfriend and bunkbud of the past several months, lush landscape flashing by below them, with open space stretching off in every direction, well ... it'd been difficult to remain exclusively glum.

Tom glanced down at the nav panel. 39 seconds from EV2's position. In the distance, the terrain appeared to clear. Threck farms in this region typically grew beans or pulp fruits, and, removed from the surrounding backdrop of unearthly blue, pink, and teal vegetation, they could easily be mistaken for farms back home. The Threck's favorite beans even boasted green foliage, an abnormal hue on Epsy where teal had evolved dominance beneath the violet sky.

The wild, vibrant forest gave way to the managed farmland and sporadic, low-profile domed structures characteristic of Country Threck. The crew had yet to determine these simple domiciles' building materials, as opposed to the wood-crafted structures found on farms closer to the city, and managed by City Threck. Not really wood. It was more like dense, petrified mushroom. For simplicity's sake, whenever possible, the crew had agreed to refer to certain things by their closest Earth counterparts. Fungus, lichen, plant, rodentia, worm, mollusk—few were all that accurate. Epsy's rodent population were more closely related to early Earth birds. They were even coldblooded. The crew used the term "fungus" to describe the planet's dominant flora, but epsequoia, toothpicks, pillars, palms, and the rest had no real genetic equivalents on Earth. In reality, nothing living on Epsy had a true Earth equivalent. Epsy life's foundations began similarly to Earth, but a billion years of initial evolution produced different "winners" than on Earth, and so everything thereafter had been built upon common building blocks. In fact, without counteractive supplements, there was little on Epsy that humans could safely consume on a regular basis due to extremely high arsenic and chlorine content. The beans and fruits in the fields before them were literally poison.

"There they are!" Angela's voice in his helmet.

"I see them." EV2's shiny white hull couldn't be missed in the duotone field of brown soil with neat rows of short, green crops. Zisa and Pablo, too, were more than discernible in their orange survival suits. And, as reported, a few Threck stood nearby.

Tom began cramming from memory.

While culturally different from City Threck, Country Threck had rapidly grown dependent upon their coastal cousins. Minnie posited that City Threck had begun by exchanging wagons of seafood for portions of the then-limited crops. Later, they'd brought fresh water via aqueduct to the landlocked region from the distant mountains, reducing Country Threck dependence on the unpredictable rains, and enabling the farmers to multiply their harvests.

But this civil relationship between previously separate cultures hardly suggested that Country or City Threck would behave even remotely accommodating to actual aliens.

As Tom considered the potential danger of the situation he and Angela were about to enter, he self-soothed with a series of recalled images from Minnie's reports: a Country Threck nursing an injured rodent, well-organized teams of City Threck building a dam, groups lounging in a warm mud bath in the city as they debated the existence of "the future." No scenes of war or religious sacrifice or cruelty.

As Tom and Angela descended, the three Threck near the EV suddenly caught sight of the skimmers, and took off running through the field toward their domicile. Tom had never before seen a Threck in a hurry. Those guys could move! They reminded Tom of Jesus Christ lizards running across water ... but in funny outfits. Unlike the common City Threck in their Romanesque robes, Country Threck wore more fitted garb: trousers of canvas-like material and an overlapping short cloak that covered their heads and a bit of tentacle, like a medieval hooded shoulder cape.

Tom watched the farmers bound across the crop rows as he brought the skimmer down near an apparently ecstatic Zisa. He shut down the transport and glanced up to Angela as she descended. To annoy her, he pointed out a landing area in the open space exactly where Angela was headed.

Angela's voice: "Oh, right here? May I? Here's good, you silly ass?"

He glanced back at her as she touched down and saw her wry grin when something suddenly struck his chest, pushing him off-balance, and he almost tumbled off the skimmer platform.

"Zooks, that was *so* close!" Zisa embraced him and he tentatively stroked her back. She was shaking. "Thank you thank you thank you!" she babbled into his chest.

Tom looked up and saw Pablo's *she's exaggerating* expression.

A request appeared in Tom's fone.

ALERTS: Direct Connect request from Pablo.

Tom accepted and an M instantly appeared.

PABLO: No danger. They were just standing there, staring at us.

Tom composed a reply while making fatherly shushing sounds and patting Zisa's back as she cried.

TOM: I figured. How was it the past few days? Pure hell?

PABLO: Surprisingly OK. She talked a lot. I listened. Kind of really connected. We did it. Took turns sleeping.

TOM: Wait. Did it? As in *IT?*

PABLO: Yup. Don't say anything tho. Not even to Ang.

TOM: That's crazy! And don't worry, I won't.

Tom opened a new M to Angela.

TOM: Pablo and Zisa did IT!

ANGELA: NO! You're lying! Are you lying?

Tom copy/pasted his exchange with Pablo into his M to Angela just as she arrived at his side. She rubbed Zisa's back in circles and guided her away from Tom.

"C'mon now, hon," Angela said. "It's all over now. We'll let it all out and get to work, 'kay?"

ANGELA: So it looks like you waited about 3 seconds after promising secrecy before telling me.

TOM: LOL not even 3 seconds.

ANGELA: I'm in awe.

TOM: Me too. I love you.

ANGELA: Love you too. You better not c/p crap I send you.

TOM: Never.
TOM: OK Once.
TOM: OK Rarely.
TOM: OK Sometimes.

ANGELA: I'm gonna kick your ass.

"Thanks for the assist," Pablo said as he shook hands with Tom. "Guessing you guys landed pretty close to here?"

Angela nodded. "About five-K east. Let's get your skimmers undocked so we can tow your EV out of this field."

Tom agreed. "And you two need to finish your exigency procedures. Data files, suit water, SSKs, food. We need to stay on top of that stuff until everyone's at the rally point. Aether and Qin made a water landing and expect to be there tomorrow."

"Yeah, I caught that on comms earlier," Pablo said. "Are we sure they're okay out there?"

"We'll check in with them once we get you guys out of here," Angela called from the other side of the EV. "Just get going on your stuff for now."

Pablo leaned to Tom and cut his eyes toward the EV, whispering, "She's still bossy."

Tom smirked. "Yup. I think she'd like to be gone *before* your three farmer friends stroll back out here. You two eat anything yet?"

Pablo's face twitched a little at the mention of food. Tom empathized. For how many years had it been the ultimate taboo? How long would it take for the stigma to fade?

Pablo replied, "We both had our scheduled calorie bars. You?"

Tom nodded affirmative as Angela called out again, "Tom, could you come back here, please?"

Pablo and Tom shared a lighthearted "uh-oh" face and split up.

"Coming!" Tom walked around the EV just as the first skimmer was unfolding. "I'll start the other one—"

"No, I need you to figure out how to link the skimmers. You know, for loadbearing."

"Right." He walked to his own skimmer, trying to recall the steps.

Up to eight skimmers could be linked and controlled by a single node, and at least three were required to heft the weight of an EV. He dove into his skimmer's settings in search of a link or connect menu, but found it under "Advanced Tasking." Only two other skimmers appeared in the discovery list until Angela got the fourth powered up.

"All set!" Tom gave her a thumbs up. "Let's get the cables out."

A few minutes later, Tom noticed two Threck had reappeared in the field. The pair were lying low behind the row of bean plants closest to their domicile, attempting to covertly observe the team with only their protruding eyes. Tom imagined the species had spent millions of years in such a position, body hidden beneath the sea floor, or more recently, in mud—thus the eyes' position atop the dome-shaped heads.

"We're all hooked up," Zisa said, snapping Tom out of his daze. "You want us on our skimmers or in the EV?"

"Oh, definitely the skimmers," Tom said, observing her face looked especially red and dry. "Just hang onto your grips and don't reinitiate control unless I say so. You doing okay? You're not sweating."

"Plenty of sweat in this suit," she said and tilted her head to the EV. "Pablo's almost done filling his. He already told me I have to drink more water."

"So *are* you?" Tom worried about Zisa manufacturing another illness for sympathy's sake. She'd done it a few times on the station and they couldn't deal with that mess here on the surface.

"Yes, I am," she said like a bratty teen. "Here … see?" She grabbed the tube with her tongue and sucked in several gulps.

"Tom," Angela said, and he glanced back at her.

She was standing on her skimmer, hands on the control bars, but concerned eyes pointed behind him. She cocked her head for him to turn around.

Tom peered back and spotted them: a caravan of City Threck emerging from the shaded road beside the farm's domicile. They marched in two, wide-spaced columns with bright red shades, each held aloft by four tall poles at the corners. As the caravan turned in front of the domicile, the two hiding Country Threck stood up and faced the new arrivals.

"We need to hurry," Tom said. "Pablo? We have to go!" He stepped up onto his own skimmer and Zisa did the same.

"I'm coming!" Pablo's muffled voice from inside the EV. "What's happening?"

"More company!" Angela shouted. "Move your ass!"

The columns of City Threck continued their march in front of the structure, revealing more and more of them, some pushing or pulling stone-wheeled carts for the harvest. Tom estimated at least thirty so far, all covered by the canvas shades, a red hue cast upon the Threck and ground.

"Crapshake," Angela said.

Tom saw it, too: the Country Threck pointed back at them and a group of curious City Threck stretched out higher to see. "Pablo!"

"Just sealing the door! Ten seconds!"

"Too late," Tom said quietly as eight City Threck bounded across the crop rows. Strides of seven to eight meters required little effort from their long legs. Each held up their robes like a Renaissance lady lifting a dress to scale a flight of stairs or cross a puddle.

"I'm on," Pablo shouted from the skimmer behind Angela. "Let's go!"

But the first of the Threck had already stopped a short distance from Tom, its arms held out to its sides. "Peaceful greetings," it said in crisp City dialect. "I am *Dowfwoss Amoss*." Its voice was mesmerizing—similar to the thousands of recordings he'd heard over the years, but so much more dimension. The Threck voice box was buried deep inside the head (the equivalent of humans vocalizing from the chest) and soundwaves traveled up through two widening tubes to their siphon holes, amplified and emitted as if through a short horn. On the station, Tom hadn't given much thought to the harmonics, focusing strictly on the words and gestures during Minnie's often abbreviated lessons. In person, the voice was smooth and deep, like an old-fashioned radio announcer. At least, that was the case with this *Dowfwoss Amoss*.

Tom scrambled to bring up his Livetrans app.

Dowfwoss? Some sort of honorary? C'mon, c'mon!

"Pleasure for all," Amoss went on, though Tom had no idea how much of the message he was interpreting correctly. "Do return home ... group animal life. So much pleasure. With Threck words? Feel them? Now you."

The app had finished loading, but Tom had yet to resync his fone and suit. PA speakers finally activated, Tom stepped down from the skimmer platform, faced the Threck, and pointed his hands out to his sides. This was the moment he'd dreaded for days—an encounter he thought he could delay or even avoid all together.

"Peaceful greetings." Minnie's synth Threck voice worked perfectly as it read the lines Tom had entered. Tom didn't know if he could say the same for his associated gestures and expressions. "I am Tom. My people have different words than Threck, but I know some of yours. Please speak slowly, so that I may understand all of your words. We are peaceful people from faraway place."

Tom watched as all of the Threck behind Amoss leaned to each other and chattered quietly amongst themselves.

"Your words are like moist song I wish to dance," Amoss *may* have said ... Tom checked Livetrans as the Threck went on:

> LIVETRANS: [Your] words flow like beautiful music that could inspire dancing. To speak is to think, [I] think, and Tom speaks Threck words. [Is it] respectful that [I may] call [you] Tom? [Do your] companions know how to speak words? From which winds [is your] faraway land? [Do you] cooperate? [Now you.]

Thank you, Livetrans! Thank you, Minnie!

Minnie had mentioned that Threck could be very "flowery" with their speech. "But," she'd warned, "on the off chance we ever end up down there, don't try to make up your own flourishes. They shouldn't consider it rude—only uneducated, which is understandable for a foreigner, but not worth the risk."

Tom wasn't sure if he was supposed to acknowledge the compliment, and then recalled another of Minnie's tips: "Err on the side of *not* talking." Now, this was mostly due to her assumption that she'd be on the scene in short time—that Tom would only have to stumble along for a moment or two until the real emissary arrived. Regretfully, Tom had expected the same.

"Please do call me Tom. My companions speak only in my language. The north winds come from our land. We do cooperate with each other, if that is your meaning. We are friends and team. We would like to be friends with Threck. How do I respectfully address you?"

Tom rushed out an M to Pablo and Angela.

TOM: Hey guys. Sticking to M's while talking to these folks. If you don't already have Livetrans up, you can listen in on this conversation and learn something. Tell Zisa, too. No DC with her.

ANGELA: Already up. You're doing great! I can't believe this is happening!

PABLO: Will do.

ANGELA: FYI no pressure, but unless something happened elsewhere in the past few years that we don't know about yet, YOU are the first human being to communicate with an alien lifeform.

Angela added an ecstatic emoji to the M.

TOM: It's because I'm suuuper qualified.

Tom inserted a terrified emoji.

Amoss's response began appearing and self-correcting in Tom's fone.

LIVETRANS: To know and speak with Tom is like bathing in warm mud. [You may] address me as Amoss. Dowfwoss … this is [unknown] for achievement, like winner. Does this have meaning for you? [We have] language Tom speaks with talent, but [we have] no such expertise to speak Tom's language. Tom's people [are more] smart than Threck. Such pleasure surges through ourselves at this significant event. The day is dry and hot. May both peoples retreat into [unknown] and continue pleasuring each other with words.

ANGELA: He wants us to pleasure each other.

TOM: You caught that, eh? So should we go with them?

ANGELA: I don't think we've much choice. But my LT couldn't figure out where he's saying he wants us to go, and I'm not bathing in any warm mud, just so you know.

TOM: Mine either. And they're technically all *she.* Ask Pablo and Zisa what they think we should do and see if you can reach Aether while I stall.

"My people would very much enjoy pleasure of more words with Threck people," the synth voice played as Tom swung his arms around and mimed inhales and exhales. Talking to Threck, he determined, was more like performance art than conversation. "We would first like to move our belongings from the farmer field, and setup respectful temporary campsite on Threck land, if acceptable to Threck people."

Amoss emitted an operatic sound Tom recognized. "It's their laughter!" Minnie had gushed when playing the recording during an early mission meeting.

LIVETRANS: [laughter] [You and your] people are merrily considerate ... What are Tom people called? And [you need] never worry about farmer wants. [They are not] Threck. Leave your belongings where you wish, and take what you desire from farmers. [We will] use their [unknown] for respite from dry and hot. Let us go now as there can be no pleasure in this [unknown]. Come along, if you would. [Our] enjoyment of you cannot cease at this time.

ANGELA: Zisa doesn't think it's a good idea that we all go with them, and I agree with her. Pablo tried contacting Aether but hasn't received a response.

TOM: So what the hell do we do?

ANGELA: You and I go with them while Zisa and Pablo transport the EV out of here to the rally point. Zisa says she's flown a cluster before.

TOM: K. Let them know. I'll try to explain to Amoss.

ANGELA: I'll grab our packs.

Amoss was already holding out an insistent, beckoning arm as she took a few steps toward the Country Threck domicile. What had she meant saying farmers weren't Threck? Clearly she considered them lessor beings—perhaps some sort of class system Minnie mentioned and Tom hadn't bothered to remember.

Tom took a few conciliatory steps forward as he composed his response.

"My people are called *scientists*. We live for learning. For *science*. I will enjoy joining you along with my friend, *Angela*, while my other friends continue their important work."

Amoss stopped, her eyes sucked into her head, popped back out, and then peered past Tom to the EV, skimmers, and Zisa and Pablo.

LIVETRANS: Syons People. Some Syons People must work now? No. Let them work later. Come now.

Uh-oh, Tom thought. *Is that annoyance seeping out?*

Tom made a quick decision he wasn't sure was wise. "These two are like farmers. They do not need or deserve pleasure of words with Threck."

LIVETRANS: [laughter] Yes, I see now. Let us leave them to their work while we escape this dry and hot. Come now. Come now.

Tom reached back and accepted his pack from Angela, took her hand, and gingerly stepped over the rows of crops as they followed Amoss and the others toward the domicile.

23

Aether decided it was finally safe to open her visor. The air in the EV was essentially the same as what her suit provided, but a hearty lungful of the pod air somehow tasted fresher.

The EV bobbed subtly left as the giant towing animal below shifted its course to the right. The pod's motion resumed its retchy natural rhythm (the creature propelled itself in bursts, much like a squid), a pool of sea water sloshing about at their feet. Gazing up through her porthole, Aether observed they weren't so far from the ocean surface. Perhaps 20m. Where were the Sea Threck taking them?

Sorry, Skinny, Aether thought. *Sea "People?" When exactly did you stop being Threck? And where the hell are you taking us?*

Skinny had last said, "I show you. You will see," before diving back in the water and trying to shut the EV hatch (Qin had kindly assisted).

Show us what, exactly? How bad the real *Threck are? Show us what happens to people that insult you?*

How could she have thought first contact would ever occur under the silly ideal conditions outlined in the mission guide?

"Essentially same course," Qin said. "Looks like it's navigating around a little island just off the coast. Want to see?"

"Sure," Aether said, and Qin M'd her a map of their position.

"I put a blue dot at the center of Threck City."

They'd apparently traveled several kilometers west—farther and farther from the others—surely out of comms range by now. There was probably a way to improve surface comms, maybe use the supply pod network somehow. Qin or Zisa could possibly figure it out, given the opportunity, but when would that kind of time and focus present itself? After their current communication needs concluded, no doubt.

Aether noted EV4's beacon on Qin's map, but there was no indicator for Zisa and Pablo's pod. "Where's EV2?"

"Just outside the upper right corner. Not too far from Tom and Angela. The map is active. You can pull back and see them."

Aether zoomed out one level and EV2 appeared. "And the rally point?"

"Southeast. Actually not too far from EV4 … let me see … about two-K?"

Aether slid the map over to see the blinking orange dot. An abrupt pain stabbed sideways through her guts and an audible wince escaped.

Qin touched her arm. "You okay?"

"Reinitation pain. I think I need another bar. When was your last?"

"Yeah, I'll eat. The idea is sickening, what with all *this*." He flailed a hand around him as the pod once again lurched softly forward. "But it's definitely been a while. Well before reentry." They both tore into their calorie bar wrappers. "What happens when we run out? As in, we can't eat their crops or meat or anything, right?"

Aether's first bite slid abrasively down her throat. She envisioned a pile of gravel poured into an empty sack. "Not exactly. The arsenic and chlorine levels are high in pretty much every living thing here, but there are exceptions and there's a plan."

"Pablo and Angela."

"Yes."

"They just need time to make us some new meds. In the meantime, it won't kill us to consume meat or most of their fruit crops. The effects would be longer term."

"Yeah, I think I remember that report. Rashes, lesions, diabetes, cancer. At least the water's safe." He shook his SSK's included filter-top bottle. "I just don't get it. Everyone read the reports, so how could she think this was a good idea?"

Qin had spent a fair amount of time in orbit crabbing on Ish. He'd seen her hands on the supply pod's controls in the seconds leading up to impact. Supposedly, her face displayed no alarm whatsoever, even once the pod reached final approach at double speed. Ish may have been responsible, but Qin's harping was less than helpful.

Aether's gaze remained on her food. "We can't say as fact that it was intentional."

"Oh, I can! Happy to! It was intentional. Crazy bitch. Sure, right, the walls are closing in on you, you've got to escape, games aren't enough anymore! Well, it's not an escape if everything down here kills you." His tone stung.

Aether scowled. "That's enough."

Qin looked at her, confused. He didn't get it.

If Ish was the cause, didn't that mean Aether was equally responsible? And blame aside, she loved Ish like a daughter. She loved each of them, faults and all. Ish, Zisa, Angela, Pablo, Tom, Qin … John …

Minnie.

Aether had been selected for her maternal nature. Father figures hadn't been in short supply (not exclusively due to the inherent abundance of male egos in the program), but every mission required a mom. The role carried as much priority as any scientific discipline and, like every other station position, mandated a back-up. In the case of the Epsilon C mission, Zisa had been designated maternal secondary. As laughable as this notion was to the rest of the crew now, Aether knew that Zisa certainly had the emotional depth, if not maturity.

Ironically, if asked one week ago who she thought would best serve as mission mom in her stead, Aether would have said Ish. This only highlighted how out of touch she'd been with her troubled Hynka lead. Months ago, during a regular private session, Aether had brought up Ish's lack of recreational gaming (a strictly quota'd activity for all crew members), and Ish responded calmly, and even with good humor.

"I've developed my own game in the Epsy surface sim. It serves all of the same spatial relief requirements, and …" Ish smiled and tilted her head in that girlish manner that widened her eyes and instantly wiped 20 years from her face. "… it was the cleverest way I could find to overlap work and downtime."

Aether had melted and let it go, hugging Ish tight and kissing her forehead. "I love you, beti."

Ish patted Aether's back. "You too." She'd always been a little timid about physical affection, but especially so after Aether left John for Minnie.

Aether had well understood the awkwardness and scaled back accordingly. It'd take time for everyone to adjust. People would have their thoughts. Mom leaving Dad was one thing, but Mom leaving Dad for the hot young neighbor girl? It was why Aether held off disclosing for so long. Looking back, perhaps it was the reason she missed Ish's warning signs—months spent preoccupied with her own situation and how best to handle the crew. Taking her guilt a painful step further, what if Aether's relationship decision alone had set Ish on her fateful course?

Qin's voice broke into Aether's head. "We're surfacing … approaching shore."

Indeed, a second later, the EV popped atop the ocean surface and rode a series of large swells. Gone was the smooth motion of the deep, replaced now by momentary peaks and sudden drops. Aether and Qin watched below as the sea people disconnected the EV from their towing animal. A moment later, three of them could be seen swimming toward the beach, dragging the slack vines behind them.

"They're about to go taut," Qin said.

"I see."

"You think they're going to be able to pull us up onto the shore?"

Aether looked up toward the island and spotted a new horde of Threck-like people, all converging and walking toward the bobbing EV. "They won't be alone in that effort."

"Whoa, yes, I see! And we're about to hit the waves."

The EV lurched and thrashed for several minutes as the people on shore dragged the pod, little by little, through a series of cresting and crashing waves. Finally, the EV touched land and the people swarmed, pushing it up the sloped sand as one of them—Aether guessed Skinny—directed them. Aether and Qin remained strapped tight to their seats, waiting out the slow, careful rolling and spinning. And then everything stopped just a few degrees from proper orientation.

The slightly-angled hatch clacked and squeaked.

"Visors?" Qin whispered.

"I say closed." They both reached up and secured their visors. Aether activated audio. "Hear me?"

"Yes."

Beeping and a final tell-tale click, and the hatch popped open once more. As it slid up and away, one of the sea people ducked under and entered. Outside, curious eyes competed for a view into the EV.

Aether reactivated Livetrans. Though her audio feed contained only a garbled mess of murmurs and shouts, she had her Livetrans fixed on the one in front of her.

"Welcome to … Aether and Qin. It is safe to depart white egg. Here is for food, for learning, for resist Threck. Skinny will teach Orange People of Threck and … . Come. Come out. Can Orange People walk?" On the right side of Aether's fone, the two unknown words floated in a pink box, awaiting cataloguing or deletion: *Eekareth*, which context implied was the name of this place, and *Seekapock*, evidently something they were to learn about along with their unrequested Threck lesson.

Aether quickly composed her response as she unfastened her restraints. Peripherally, she observed Qin following her lead.

"We're grateful for your welcome and will enjoy walking with Skinny and learning of Threck and 'Seekapock.'" She'd considered including *before we leave you* but decided it was too early to gauge their response to such a statement. Instead, she inserted synths of Skinny's uncatalogued words into her response. "Please, what is meaning of this word, Seekapock? And this place name, Eekareth, does it have meaning?"

Skinny took a step out of the pod as Aether stood up and leaned forward. "Yes, meaning! Eekareth is the base. The home of resist. Home that is not home, but visit place. And Seekapock, these are Skinny. These are all who are not Threck." Skinny pointed at those around him as they spread backward. "These are Seekapock … these

... these ones ... these ... you. Aether and Qin are Seekapock of Orange People of the white egg. Understand?"

"I think I do." Aether's arms waved out, curling in to point at herself—the only way to denote "I" in Threck.

Skinny and several others began singing a single, climbing note, like an opera singer reaching a crescendo.

Qin asked in a spooked voice, "What the hell is that? What's happening?"

Livetrans answered for both of them:

LIVETRANS: [laughter]

Aether felt Qin's hand on her back as she stepped out of the pod and onto solid ground for the first time in nearly 30 years.

"Thing that is alive?" Aether replied after the merriment subsided.

Skinny laughed again. "*Smart* thing that is alive ... that is not Threck."

Aether peered around at dozens of curious eyes.

Qin again: "Some have weapons."

"She says we're here to learn," Aether replied from the corner of her mouth. "She wants to teach us. We're safe, at least for now. Stay calm."

Aether felt her boots slowly sinking into the muddy soil as one of the Seekapock approached and handed the still-nude Skinny a cloak—initiating a rapid dressing process that lasted all of five seconds. Aether watched with fascination as Skinny's leg tentacles suddenly curved inward, spreading into a split until she lay flat in the mud, stretched out between the legs of the crowd. She wiggled for a moment, covering her skin in mud, then rose up partially, arms dipping the cloak into a particularly wet patch of mud, as if cleaning it of its dryness. Finally, Skinny opened the square of cloth, slid it over herself, and popped her head up through a wide slit in the middle. Standing fully upright, Skinny now appeared as all Threck did when venturing outside the city walls: skin and cloak coated in mud. She even appeared taller upon dressing (though Aether's leggy frame had several centimeters on all of them).

"That doesn't look good," Qin said an instant before the crowd of heads all twisted in the same direction.

Aether turned to see another Seekapock stomping their way, thick legs rising and curling and landing with dance-like rhythm. It reminded her of Tom and a loopvid he'd made of precisely this style of walking, captured by an observation unit and synced with risco music. And it reminded her of Minnie, cry-laughing as it repeated endlessly on her fone. "I can't stop watching!"

The approaching stomper had many questions. "What is this? What are these? Why brought here?"

Skinny turned to face the new arrival and stood even taller. "These are new Seekapock—Orange People of the water. They ... white egg ... and travel the ocean. They speak Threck words."

Aether noticed layers of raised, overlapping scars covering every visible swatch of the newcomer's flesh. Even the rubbery folds of eyelid bore the marks of a hundred battles.

Blotchy eyes studied Aether and Qin. "These understand what say I now?"

Aether wasn't sure if she should answer, and so instead let Skinny continue speaking for her.

"Yes! They understand! This is called Aether and this other is Qin." Skinny turned to face Aether. "Orange People, it is your pleasure to meet ... leader of resist. Aether—" Skinny paused. "Is Aether Orange People leader?" Skinny's eyes flipped from Aether to Qin and back.

"Yes, I am leader," Aether replied and queued up Skinny's mention of the leader's name. "It is our pleasure to meet *Eeahso* and to be welcome in this place. Where shall we go to rest and speak more words of each other's history?"

The crowd laughed again, though Aether had no clue what triggered them. She assumed Livetrans had an incorrect translation in there somewhere.

"This one Aether?" an unamused Eeahso asked, and Skinny confirmed. "They look same. How tell apart?"

Skinny peered at the pair once more before concluding that "Aether is bigger of these."

Eeahso turned to face Skinny and grabbed her with both arms. "Listen now. We not have days to spend with these … and watch copy Threck words. We have *imick* at dusk. Distraction only, these, unless they have helping. How you know these not new Threck?"

"This is what I wish to learn," Skinny said. "All of this." And Eeahso stomped off, large globs of mud flinging in every direction, much of it landing on heads and even eyes, but with no one appearing to notice or care.

Skinny turned to Aether and raised a single arm toward her. Aether must have recoiled without realizing it. The club hung in mid-air, strings of silver palm cilia slowly waving side to side, like a stadium full of enthusiastic fans.

"Is it respectful that I touch Aether?"

This was an important moment—not only for the potential precedent her response might establish, but for the fact that Skinny had asked. To be concerned with what is respectful, to view "Orange People" as people with customs or preferences, and to care what those are, these were indications of a highly advanced, civilized people. Aether was beginning to see what Minnie loved about them. They might've been as far along *technologically* as the early Romans, but this regard for strangers—not even of the same species—she wondered how the average human would have behaved during the equivalent era.

Aether reviewed her response, previewed Howard the Threck's associated gesture guide, and played the translation.

"Orange People do exchange limited touches between friends—extremities only. I understand that Seekapock may not appreciate touching of head and especially mouth. This is same with Orange People. May I demonstrate customary greeting?"

Skinny was silent and still for a moment, thinking. Her eyes hid and reappeared twice before, "This I want more than any other thing at this time."

Aether extended her gloved hand in front of her to shake. Skinny ogled it, glanced up to Aether's eyes, then down once more. Skinny's arm twisted counterclockwise so that the cilia-covered palm area faced out, extending it before her in a mirror of Aether's stance. Aether leaned gently forward, easing her hand to Skinny's pad until contact was made. Aether wrapped her thumb softly over the club, but did not squeeze. She didn't know if it would be painful, or even appropriate. As soon as her thumb touched down, several strands of cilia stretched up from the pad and wrapped around the digit, embracing it. Gently, though. It didn't hurt—more like a hundred little thumb hugs.

"Pleasure to meet you," Aether said.

"This is pleasure, truly," Skinny agreed.

Aether released, Skinny followed her lead, and the shake was done.

"Come and follow," Skinny said, and the crowd of onlookers stepped backward, opening a path. "You will eat what I give you."

Whereas Livetrans excelled with its verbal interpretation, it could use some help with deducing inflection and inference. She chuckled internally upon reading the last sentence, and walked after Skinny.

"I capt pics and vid," Qin's voice in her ear as the pair exited the crowd of onlookers. "That was history right there."

"Thanks. Though I suspect Tom has already performed the official first contact. If you're able to maintain link with the EV, and they're in range, please check in and inform them of our situation."

From the crest of a well-trodden dune, Skinny motioned them to follow her inland.

LIVETRANS: [impatience] Come now!

24

Dowfwoss Amoss led Tom and Angela into the farmers' domicile—a dugout section of ground, like a basement. Above, a roof sloped a dozen or so degrees, fashioned of large, overlapping cones with saucer-sized holes in each. At first glance, Tom thought the lampshadesque shells belonged to some ocean mollusk the Threck consumed. Upon closer inspection, they were Threck shells or, perhaps more accurately, their skulls.

Tom and Minnie had spent weeks mapping Threck evolution. While the team had devoted relatively little time to Epsy oceanography, it had been necessary to shed light on the planet's most intelligent lifeforms. Threck, as it turned out, were closely related to most of the dominant ocean species, including their domesticated work animals. From the immense *afvrik* they used for net fishing and sea travel, to the horse-sized *minnit,* they had all branched off from a single, still-present species, the *starclam* (named by Tom, with great pride). All of their skulls bore this same basic design.

Minnie had imagery of Country Threck domiciles, including internal layout, but as far as Tom knew, she'd never identified the building material as the remains of their dead.

Stepping carefully down the wide stairs, Tom closed his bio eye while it adjusted to the darkness. His fone automatically adapted and he observed the new surroundings.

"Out, out with you!" the Threck shouted and waved away the scurrying farmers and their young, like shooing vermin.

Ten or more startled occupants brushed past Tom and Angela on the stairs, forced out into the heat.

One of the farmers protested the rush, if not the eviction. "Need garb. You wait."

"Hurry then!" one of the Threck barked.

ANGELA: Is it just me or are these guys major holes?

TOM: They sure don't seem to think much of the Country Threck. Classism, maybe racism? Might be multiple ethnicities we don't know about.

ANGELA: Disliking our supposed hosts already.

Once the domicile's presumptive owners were gone, the five City Threck appeared somewhat more relaxed. They spent the next few minutes rooting through containers while Tom recorded vid and snapped pics.

"Disgusting," Amoss said as she examined the muddy floor. She turned to Tom and Angela. "Apologies for the unsuitable meeting place."

Another Threck now spoke to Tom for the first time. "Do your people excrete within your shelters?"

Tom wasn't sure how to answer.

Technically, yes?

Amoss, fortunately, raised an arm and laughed.

"No answer, no answer. This is not how we wish to begin our splendid exchange of feeling and ideas. If you are able to forgive the unforgivable odors, perhaps Syons People would enjoy bathing with us?" She gestured toward another carved stairway that led to a recessed loft area.

The other Threck began shedding their cloaks, hanging them over one of the roof support beams, then climbed the stairs in turn. Despite a thorough familiarity with their anatomy, Tom was both fascinated and disturbed by the nude Threck. Only after seeing the way their bodies moved up the steps, legs bending and twisting with seemingly unnatural rotations, did reality smack Tom square in the forehead.

This was an *alien house.*

He was conversing with alien beings on an alien planet and the aliens wanted to bathe with him and to know if his people crapped in their homes. What would he say? How to behave without giving the Threck a bad impression of humankind? The stakes of this encounter were far too high. Wasn't there some clever way he could get out of this? An indefinite deferral? Just run?

If only.

Amoss stood before him, awaiting an answer.

ANGELA: Are we supposed to follow them up there? I don't know if salt-water and the suits would play nice together.

Right, salt-water, Tom thought.

The Threck had built aqueducts in both directions: fresh-water from the mountains to feed the crops, and salt-water from the ocean to the floodplains for drinking and bathing. The farmers' roofs extended over the salt-water channel, providing an ever-flowing in-house bath.

"It is clean and warm," Amoss said. "Constant current. All feces from first farms diluted to nothing."

Ah, Tom thought. *So you're supposed to crap in the drinking water. Not on the floor, which is gross.*

ANGELA: What are we doing? Say something to her!

Tom quickly composed his response to Amoss. "We would be honored to bathe with you."

And then sent an M to Angela:

TOM: We're taking a bath. Strip.

Tom removed his helmet and began opening the suit. Amoss laughed heartily and removed her cloak, tossing it over the beam with the others, but all the while watching Tom and Angela disrobe.

ANGELA: You're lucky I'm an exhibitionist. If Zees were here she'd be filing a harassment suit against you and the entire Threck population.

As Tom set his suit, boots, and helmet on the entrance stairs, away from the mud, he realized they were giving up their MWs, too. The Threck didn't have any weapons in the water, but they didn't need any to be a threat.

Angela handed her things to Tom and he stole a quick look at her bare body. She wore a dubious expression that may have been due to the peculiar situation, unexpected skinny dipping, or the pungent scent. Powerfully pungent. Tom was doing his best to conceal his gag heaves.

"It's going to be fine," he whispered and gagged. "Just a quick bath among new friends."

Angela appeared to be handling the aroma commendably. "If I feel anybody trying to play footsie up there, I'm out."

Tom glanced back and saw Amoss with an arm held out. "Come now, come now."

And then it suddenly occurred to Tom that he'd made a huge mistake. Without the suit, he had no PA system to relay the translations of his input. He was completely on his own to try and speak the complex Threck consonants—sounds best uttered by compressed whipped cream cans and Donald Duck. Perhaps he wouldn't need to speak in the water. Maybe they'd all just relax and enjoy each other's naked company.

"Is that a male reproductive organ?" one of the Threck in the water asked as Tom arched a leg over the craggy rock wall and slipped into the warm salt water.

It was surprisingly deep. Tom found himself touching bottom with the surface at his shoulders. The current was slow but strong. He had to cling to the porous basalt to keep from drifting. At her height, Angela wouldn't be able to stand at all.

Tom turned to her. "It's very deep. You need to hold on."

Angela scowled at him as she slid in, scratching her backside against the rock and grimacing with pain. Tom caught her and curled a hand around her waist. The Threck were saying things, but without looking at them, Tom's Livetrans only captured the vocalizations.

"They grow hairs."

"... moist skin."

"Differing anatomy ..."

Angela whispered, "I think my ass cheek is bleeding. And the water stings."

"Do you require assistance?" Amoss—or the Threck Tom *thought* was Amoss—asked Angela.

Tom put a leg up for Angela to sit on, and they were finally able to settle into a stable position against the wall. Angela apparently noticed their new acquaintances ogling her chest and crossed an arm in front of her.

"What is the purpose of those appendages?" One of the Threck reached across the stream and pointed directly at Angela's breasts. "Did it always have four appendages?"

"An amputation perhaps? Observe the sub-appendages, too."

"Are they talking about my boobs?" Angela whispered, then her eyes opened wide. "Wait ... how are you going to talk to them?"

"I know," Tom sighed, defeated. "I don't know."

The room was quiet for what seemed a long while. Only the soothing sounds of flowing water echoed in the air, like some romantic grotto. The Threcks' giant eyes rolled around as they studied Tom and Angela. The water appeared to relax them, their eyes slow blinking, hiding and unhiding, heads dunking beneath the water then back up, exposing only their eyes and the tops of their domes. They didn't seem to care if their siphon holes were in, out, or half-submerged in the water. Tom tried to match their behaviors, blinking slowly and dipping his head beneath the surface. Awkwardness aside, he could get used to this ritual. There was even a nice, fresh airstream flowing from the thin space between water and roof at Tom's left, to the river's exit at his right—a welcome respite from the noxious odors behind him.

Amoss finally broke the silence, her smooth, deep voice reverberating in the cave-like space.

"Syons People are smarter than Threck. This is fascinating and shocking revelation. Our people have never in our history encountered beings more advanced than us. The Thinkers will be outraged and jubilant. They should like to speak with you at great length."

Amoss stopped speaking and awaited a response. It would be rude to not answer. He needed something short. Something simple. He tried out several brief replies, listening to the synth vocalizations.

Intimidated by pretty much everything he wanted to say, he finally settled on: *Pleasing.*

"Kwadth tem," he said.

Tom felt Angela's hand tighten on his waist and he peripherally saw her head turning slowly toward him.

ANGELA: Pleasing? Wow.

TOM: Hey, if you want to try talking to them, jump in here any time.

ANGELA: They're staring at us. Don't be a wuss.

Tom recalled a guest speaker from the requisite diplomacy training back on Earth. She had said that, despite one's every instinct, in nearly every diplomatic engagement, honesty was invariably the best approach. Skeptical students had challenged her with hypotheticals that she'd deftly swatted away with real-world examples in which an honest dialogue had deescalated a touchy circumstance or secured a desired outcome.

Tom reverted to his original reply and listened once more to Howard the Threck's synth. He inhaled a deep breath and began:

"*Ja-ahshkeh pladtip vrrish …*" but he stopped, thought quickly, revised the text. A new response played in his ear. He spoke the words slowly, purposefully, one at a time, as the phonetics flashed before him, and Howard demonstrated the associated gestures. In Threck, he attempted, "Our speaking parts are different from Threck. While we understand your words, it is difficult to say many. The voice you heard earlier, this is from our garb, which contains technology. They aid us in speaking your words. Without that help, though, this is how I sound. My apologies."

The Threck regarded one another for a moment.

"What is 'building voice?'" one asked another.

"Is it 'speaking tools?'" another said. "'Tools wearing garb?' What does it say?"

Tom pointed to the steps to the entrance. "My garb helps. Makes voice. Speaks words."

Amoss suddenly got it. "Its garb spoke the words before! This now is real Syons People voice! I do not understand, but I understand." She turned to her comrades and explained.

"Yes," Tom labored on. "My Threck words will sound silly, but we want you to know that we will enjoy speaking with the Thinkers, though I am not sure that my people can live up to your flattering assessment of our intelligence."

"Why not sure?" Amoss replied. "Is it not obvious? Syons People speak our language, but we do not speak yours. You have created technology that allows you to float in the sky as if it were ocean. Even your garb, as you say, can speak words like a real Threck and has been fashioned and assembled with precision and skill that our people cannot comprehend. Not only are Syons People smarter than Threck, Syons People *garb* is smarter than Threck! The list of questions I have for you grows with each passing second, and I can foresee no end to them. I think, perhaps, that to Syons People, *we* are the farmers, and Syons People, Threck."

"You are very kind," Tom said.

Angela rubbed his side just as an M from her popped up.

ANGELA: You're doing so good! Proud of you. (And it's *very* attractive)

TOM: I'm sure our friends would love for us to demonstrate how Science People reproduce . . .

ANGELA: Sicko. I'm not *that* much of an exhibitionist.

* * *

Tom and Angela sat (floated) through nearly an hour of questions, from anatomy to the prickly subject of human technology. While the Threck had no reference point for breastfeeding (Epsy's relatively few lactating species lived in Hynka Country—the Hynka themselves among them, though not through a nipple), they seemed to finally understand that Angela's strange torso had neither befallen some tragic accident that had robbed her of a third and fourth arm, nor was there cause for tumor concern.

"Apparently, the entire galaxy is obsessed," Angela quietly observed.

Tom, too, had obtained answers to some of Minnie's top questions. Threck City's population? 36,077 as of yesterday's hatch. Minnie's most recent estimation had been fairly close at 34,500. Reproduction? Fertile individuals could lay 2-3 eggs up to twice a year. Who's in charge? An ever-changing group of individuals comprised of the seniormost members of each city group: Fishing, Farming, Thinkers, Makers, Materials, Nursery, Education, Waters & Sanitation, Exploration, and Expansion.

"You are all with the farming group?" Tom asked.

"Not precisely," Amoss demurred, and emerged from the water. "Let us check on the harvest loading and take our leave if complete." She raised one of her legs, planted it on the wall beside Angela, and then nimbly pushed off the rear wall with the other leg.

Angela turned to Tom. "Let's wait for the rest of them to disembark, shall we?"

"What?" Tom smirked. "Tired of anatomical discussions?"

As it was desirable to remain wet as long as possible, the Threck weren't familiar with towels. In fact, they each dipped their robes into the river to saturate before putting them back on, while Tom and Angela struggled to slide their wet bodies into their clothes and suits.

The Threck resumed bemoaning the place. "A shame there is no unbefouled mud to apply."

"Filthy hynka," another agreed, and Tom noted the term for "savage" describing something other than Ish's beloved civilization.

Outside, throngs of Threck loaded the final baskets of harvested crops onto their filling carts. Amoss and friends—their names were Tatsis, Eskip, Mestthish, and Oose, though each time Tom thought he had a name pegged to a body, he had it wrong ("Once again, I am Eskip, not Tatsis. Are we so indistinct to Syons People?")—spoke to their workers before Amoss and possibly Eskip returned to the domicile entrance.

Relieved by the return of his modern technology, Tom had the PA resume speaking for him. "It was so pleasurable to bathe and speak with you all. We hope that we can one day visit your city and speak with more of your wonderful people."

Both Threck laughed and Amoss replied, "Ah, the sweet perfection of your garb's voice again! Indeed, it is elegant and contenting, but I almost prefer the strange pitch of your true voice. As to your moistening desires, your wish is ours to bestow! Let us be off to the city."

Oh no.

Tom considered his response, searching through Minnie's list of formalities for an inoffensive decline.

> ANGELA: As fun as moistening desires sounds, please, no, my stomach is killing me. We need to take our reinitiation meds and get some calorie bars in us. As nice as possible, as firm as necessary, tell them we're *not* going to the city right now.

* * *

Three hours later…

Amoss pointed to the towering steeple. "Welcome, Syons People, Tom and Angela, to Threck City!"

25

The Sea Threck, or Seekapock, as they preferred to be called, enjoyed three things: eating, rolling in mud, and talking. Their seemingly calm demeanor and relative silence upon first meeting Aether and Qin had been wholly uncharacteristic.

Away from the beach, beyond a sand berm, Skinny had led the group to a vast area shaded entirely by enormous, table-shaped fungi called *wects*. These "trees" were endemic in southern Threck Country, and from orbit appeared as some strange pink snow or ground cover. It was only after sending a probe to investigate that Angela had discovered their true nature and form.

Aether gazed up at the caps' undersides 10-15 meters overhead. The wects' gills hung like fuzzy icicles atop dense, trunk-like stalks above the real ground: a swampy marsh where mudworms thrived—a perfect symbiosis in which falling spores fed the worms whose excrement, in turn, nourished the fungi. It had been an ah-hah moment for the mission. The Threck had clearly evolved from a 100% aquatic species, but what had brought their ancestors—like humankind's fin-walking forebears—out of the water? Even now, millions of years later, the Threck struggled daily with life on land. It was here, Angela had theorized—or a place much like it—that early Threck found an evolution-fostering sanctuary. Frequent rains and storms kept the fertile soil moist, and the pink wects supplied perpetual shade as primitive Threck gorged themselves on mudworms. Minnie believed that the tall trunks had inspired Threck City's Romanesque columns.

Aether labored through the knee-deep mire, her boots sticking with each step. Behind her, Qin was experiencing the same frustration, as evidenced by the groans and his breath streaming through their open channel into her ear. She lowered the volume. Qin's struggles were now replaced by the buzzing drone of a hundred chattering Seekapock. Flopping around in the sludge like fish washed ashore by a rogue wave, the masses seemed to be in the throes of food-bingeing ecstasy.

Aether's Livetrans app couldn't keep up, rapidly framing the heads of the talkers, one after another, as Aether read the words.

LIVETRANS: So good … more … never stop … delicious … great satisfaction … more.

Treading carefully through the mob, Aether was sure she was stepping on tentacles, but no one seemed to mind. Bodies grazed her legs as she tried to keep up with Skinny, who, cognizant of her guests' slow progress, would take two broad strides, then turn and wait.

"Just over here," Skinny assured. "Easier if you move faster."

Aether trudged on without responding. She sent an M to Qin.

AETHER: Were you able to get through to any of the others?

QIN: Yes. Zisa. They're at the rally point.

AETHER: Everyone?

QIN: Sorry, no. Z and P at rally point. T and A went off with Threck.

AETHER: Any other details on that last bit?

QIN: That's it.

Finally, they arrived at a drier area, like the bank of a mud lake, where a few less-animated Seekapock sat draped over stumps and rocks, nibbling on fish from a basket. They, too, wore the usual mud-soaked cloaks.

"You, Orange People," one of them said as she grabbed a thin, white, pancake-shaped fish and stuffed it up between her leg tentacles like a feeding elephant. "Skinny tells you live in egg and travel ocean." Before Aether could finish composing a reply, the eater went on, "And you think us all Threck. You Threck friend?" She turned to Skinny. "Why it no answer? You say it speak."

"Orange People take time before speak. I think maybe they slow think."

When they both appeared to pause, Aether activated her synth. "Peaceful greetings to you. We use egg for travel only. We are from—" Aether's response went on, but the seated Seekapock interrupted, addressing the others.

"It sound like Threck with perfect speak. I dislike."

"It does," another agreed.

"Where it get speak like Threck?" the first asked Skinny.

"Aether," Skinny said. "Eeko wish to know how you learn Threck words."

Aether wasn't sure how to answer. Clearly these people had some quarrel with the City Threck. But then, once more, they just went on eating and talking, as if their questions had been rhetorical.

"Is it big eye head, this?" Eeko pointed at Qin's visor, then reached closer, about to touch the helmet.

"They no like touch," Skinny said as she slapped away the outstretched arm. "I think this like shell. Orange shell but sandy flesh inside. Here, Aether and Qin." Skinny plucked two fish from the basket. "You will eat this."

Aether and Qin both accepted the offerings in their hands, but neither moved to eat.

"Go on, now you eat. Move shell and eat fish."

"We are thankful for this kind offering," Aether said. "But we cannot eat food that is not from our land. It hurts us inside. Do you understand?"

"It ask if understand," Eeko said. "It like Threck in one way more. Why you bring these here, Skinny?"

Skinny twisted and rolled both arms toward Eeko. The translation appeared in Aether's fone like any spoken words would.

LIVETRANS: Be gone. You are purposeless.

Skinny held out an arm to Aether, the end curled inward. Aether took gentle hold and Skinny pulled her from the scene.

"They not respectful," Skinny said as they went. "These is typical Seekapock. These is lazies. They sit all day and eat what is brought until no more food. No work for anything since long time. These no listen when Eeahso teach."

Qin, huffing, "Where's it taking us?"

Aether glanced back and saw him keeping up as the three of them moved farther and farther from the muddy area, the pink wects gradually shrinking to bush size, beams of sunlight piercing through.

Aether agreed with Qin's concern. "Skinny, where are we going now?"

"*Imick.* We join with Eeahso then show you difference of Seekapock and Threck. Good night for you, I think. Seekapock first imick is special."

Qin, in Aether's ear again, "You know we're completely out of EV range now, right? If anyone tries to reach us—"

"I know. And we didn't bring our SSK packs."

"I still have that fish, if you're hungry. Just pretend it's a tortilla. With guts. And bones. And arsenic."

Aether turned round and slapped the fish out of Qin's hand. "I'm going to mute you." She flashed a grin. Good to see Qin relaxed enough to joke.

She triggered her reply to Skinny's last statement. "What is meaning of imick?"

Skinny stopped abruptly and spun round to face Aether. The club that Aether held (or club that held *her*) remained wrapped around her hand, the animate pasta plate of cilia all coiled around her fingers, and Aether felt the arm stiffen to keep her from slamming right into Skinny.

Qin had no such block and Aether felt his hands hit her back. "Whoa, what? Sorry!"

"You know not what this mean? Imick?" Skinny's face was only centimeters from Aether's visor, eyes wide and unblinking.

Aether sent "No" and observed the close-up view of Skinny's flesh. Where the mud had dried and flaked off, the top skin layers appeared semi-transparent with a thousand little bumps, like gecko skin.

After a lengthy stare-down, Skinny's eyes popped down and up and she took a step back, laughing. "This is good. Very good, but curious."

Skinny released Aether's hand and continued strolling through the well-worn jungle path. Aether and Qin shared a puzzled look before resuming.

"Very curious," Skinny repeated without a backward glance.

Aether noted the continued use of associated arm movements, but reversed for Aether to see them.

"I know what Eeahso say ..." Skinny went on. "Eeahso say, 'How Orange People learn Threck words but not know Threck or Seekapock?'"

Aether didn't answer. If pressed, she would tell the "modified truth," as outlined in the exigency first contact procedures. But Skinny hadn't actually asked.

Still walking and facing forward, Skinny said, "How Orange People learn Threck words?"

Of course.

Aether began composing the outlined reply, though leaving out Minnie's bit comparing the crew's research to Threck scientists.

> Our people are learners. We study all things on the ground, in the sky, and in the water. Threck words are one of the things we have learned.

She followed Skinny over a large fallen plant, rereading and fine-tuning the message.

"Eeahso worry for spies," Skinny said. "Threck send spies always. Spies in big group you earlier see, no questions, they there always. This why imick only for most trusted, proven Seekapock."

Aether bounced the message to the drafts queue and rushed out an appropriate response. "We do not wish to intrude upon sacred rite reserved for special Seekapock. Remember, we were simply traveling the ocean before you brought us, and as much as we enjoyed meeting Skinny and others, we would be happy to resume our journey."

Skinny halted again and faced Aether. "This be most clever way to deliver spy. Most clever … Eeahso would say." Skinny paused for a beat and then laughed, speaking quickly once more. "I know you not spy! Orange People learn Threck words from farmers of north! This correct?"

Aether thought quickly. "Orange People *have* had contact with the farmers."

"I am smart!" Skinny said, and walked with new spring.

* * *

They didn't have time for all this right now. Qin had made reference to his level of hunger and/or discomfort at least six times in the past hour, not counting any of the more general "how much longer" type questions. Even though Qin was two years older than her, Aether felt like a bad mother leaving home without snacks for the kids, and without a clue how long the excursion would last. Now, lying prone in a thatch of potentially hazardous vines, the sun having just set, and Epsy's rapid rotation hastily lowering the shroud of darkness upon them, Aether began weighing the risks of ditching Skinny.

"Do you know what we're waiting for?" Qin whispered, though with their visors down, no one could hear them speak.

Aether pointed. "If you switch to therm and zoom out beyond that sand plain, you can see a small group of Skinny's friends slowly creeping up the slope. Looks like they're about to take down a Threck guard."

"Ah yes, I see. What's the guard guarding?"

"I'm guessing the harbor. Or maybe the city in general."

A few meters ahead, Skinny's eyes poked just above a low wall of piled stones, watching her friends near the guard. Without a backward glance, she lifted an arm, spinning it in a specific gesture to Aether.

LIVETRANS: Wait. Not long. Wait.

If they were really about to attack the city, this might be the perfect opportunity for Aether and Qin to sneak away. Just wait for Skinny to be fully distracted. They certainly couldn't beat these people in a foot race. Then again, what if she simply told Skinny, directly, that they had to go? That they would return soon? Aether didn't get the impression that this idea would swim. Thus far, she and Qin had existed somewhere between semi-willing guests and unacknowledged hostages.

Were Zisa and Pablo still okay at the rally point or had they, in an attempt to help others, ventured out of the safe zone? How long before Qin's (or her own) reinitiation pains became overwhelming? What if Tom and Angela were in some sort of trouble? And of highest concern—though Aether didn't wish to acknowledge that her priorities had personal impetus—how long would it take to track down, travel to, and rescue Minnie, John, and Ish? How long could they survive out there?

"Aether," Qin said. "You see that?"

Aether looked up to see the guard being subdued by two Seekapock. Aether closed her bio eye and zoomed in just in time to see one of the attackers shove a sharpened stick up beneath the guard's head, where the mouth was hidden, and where the rigid shell skull offered no protection for the Threck brain. The guard was dead.

"Imick!" Skinny called, and leapt up.

She grabbed Aether's hand once more, heaving her to her feet with little care, and dragged Aether into the wide open.

A high whistle screamed from the torch-lit city, and a few seconds later, a second whistle joined in the alarm.

"Quickly!" one of the Seekapock shouted from the wall, and others appeared from the line of shrubs where Skinny had them hiding.

These Seekapock carried large baskets out into the starlight, scurrying across the sandy field, and up the sloped wall. Big splashes as a few dove into the water on the other side. Shouts and more screeching alarms from other guard stations. Skinny laughed with exhilaration, running too fast for Aether to keep up, but remained clung like a shackle around Aether's wrist and hand. Aether's feet tripped, dragged, managed a step or two, and tripped again. She felt like a ragdoll in a rambunctious little girl's hand.

Qin's panicked voice, "What should I do?"

He'd stepped out of the shrubs and stood behind the low wall. At least *he* could escape.

"Go!" Aether shouted as Skinny hauled her up the hill. "Get to the rally point!"

Skinny stopped at the top of the rise and someone yelled at her. "Why you bring this here? Take away!"

Aether looked up as she struggled to her feet and saw the distinctive cloak and thick arms of Eeahso. The leader was the one that had killed the first guard. Now, from her new vantage point, Aether could see they were standing atop the harbor's inner levee, and several Seekapock farther down the wall were detaching lines from their anchors, and pulling. In the water below, thousands of distressed fish jumped and flipped at the surface as a net tightened around them.

Toward the city, Aether could see in the torchlight a stream of armed Threck pouring out the arched entrances, shouting, "The food bays! Thieves! Stop them!"

Eeahso slapped Skinny's arm and Aether fell back. "Let this go! Join the others! Delay the guards!"

Skinny looked down at Aether for a beat, then toward the guards running along a raised walkway. She made a quick series of gestures before rushing off. "I will return for you, friend."

Now, only Eeahso and Aether remained at the corner of the levee.

Eeahso eyed her for an instant, then called to the Seekapock as they loaded basket after basket with flopping fish. "Hurry! A moment more, then go!"

Aether planted her hands on the ground, pulled her feet beneath her, and scanned the area for the best escape route. Only a meter away, Eeahso didn't appear to care what Aether was doing, focused instead on overseeing her mission. A series of "clangs" rang out from the other end of the levee where it met the city's outer walkways. The Threck guards' long, bronze blades had crossed various Seekapock weapons.

It was time for Aether to go. To the southwest, she could see a mostly clear path that led around the high city wall and, presumably, into an inland jungle. If she were Qin, that's the way she'd have gone—the *only* option, really, that didn't lead back to the Seekapock camp, the ocean, or the fight in progress. She pulled her MW from its holster, stood, and—

Crack!

Something struck her helmet from behind—hard—and she fell forward, toward the steep slope, falling a full 140° before chest and visor crashed into unyielding cement. Wind knocked from her, she slid, scratching downward another few meters before slowing to a stop. She sucked in air, rolled onto her back, and saw a Threck guard standing over her, long, curved blade held at the ready.

She couldn't hear anything, but "What is it?" appeared in Livetrans.

In a blur, a series of tentacles flashed by her on both sides, and she caught a glimpse of Eeahso at the top of the levee, hurling curses as she fought off two guards. "Filthy smug Threck! Die, unthinking fools!"

The Threck above Aether kicked her in the side and stabbed down at Aether's knee—right on the kneecap. Fortunately, the suits had a tough mid-layer of ballistic material, and the Threck weapon was blunt-tipped, but it still felt as though someone had dropped a cinder block on her leg.

Vomit suddenly threatened. Bile seeped into the back of Aether's throat. She swallowed deep and tightened her grip on the MW, pinky and thumb depressing the safety toggles. Was it set to non-lethal? She couldn't remember, and the guard above her appeared poised for a blow to Aether's head. Could the Threck weapon shatter a visor? She didn't think so, but what if it struck her throat?

Bwop! … Bwop-bwop!

The guard flew backward, smashing to the ground, then rolled limp and heavy over Aether's downward inclined body. But Aether hadn't fired.

Qin.

"Let's go!" Qin in her ear.

Aether glanced up and saw him standing at the base of the slope. She looked down toward her feet and saw a guard's weapon take off one of Eeahso's arms with a powerful slash. The tentacle coiled and thrashed and twisted on the ground. The other guard fighting Eeahso turned her attention to Aether and Qin, and before Aether could think or say anything, Qin popped off four more rounds, sending both guards flying out of sight. Successive splashes revealed their fates.

Aether sat up, surveyed the scene, and saw basket-lugging Seekapock fleeing to the jungle, while a few others ran along the levee toward the injured Eeahso.

"Come on!" Qin shouted, grabbing Aether's hand.

He helped her up the rest of the way and they both fled toward the cover of foliage across the field, pain lighting up Aether's right leg with each limped step.

"Now what?" Qin huffed. "Where do we go? Tell me what to do!"

"Just keep going this way," Aether said as they hurdled the low wall and returned to the darkness of the jungle. Aether activated IR. "Let's get a ways in before finding some cov—" she suddenly belched and more acid filled her mouth.

"Are you okay? What's happening?"

Aether slapped her visor up and dropped to her knees, empting her mouth along with everything that came behind it. Throat and stomach burned. Tearing eyes burned. Chest. Everything burned.

Qin's hand rubbed in circles on her back when footfalls came crashing through the jungle behind them. Multiple individuals were closing fast, and it didn't matter if they were Seekapock or Threck. Neither seemed a safe bet anymore. Qin pushed her down, atop her mess, and lay down flat beside her. Frozen in the undergrowth, Aether fought the urge to wipe her stinging eyes. The crackles and snaps of the approaching steps halted right beside her.

"Bad hide place, this is," Skinny said. "Threck will come and find without difficulty. We go move."

* * *

"I made a major mistake, didn't I?" Qin whispered to Aether as they plodded through the dense, untrodden vegetation. "I panicked."

Aether was hot, tired, in pain, and sick. Her drooping eyes watched the hypnotizing rhythm of Skinny's marching legs ahead. "You followed your instincts in a dangerous situation and probably saved my life."

"These are Orange People words?" Skinny asked without turning.

Aether selected and sent the affirmative response from the floating hotlist hovering at the right of her Livetrans app.

"Funny sound," Skinny said. "Like hissing *pikpik*."

Skinny had been walking slower for the last kilometer, apparently no longer concerned about pursuers.

Aether was done with submissive diplomacy. "Skinny, please stop for a moment."

Skinny complied and faced her, eyes wide and clubs pressed together backward.

LIVETRANS: [Curious awaits].

"Here's the thing," Aether's synth began. She'd spent the last few minutes revising her wording. "Us Orange People are pleased to have met Skinny and Seekapock. Everything you have shown us today has been interesting, and we're sorry that Eeahso, Threck people, and any others were injured." Skinny's eyes hid at this. "But now is time for us to go. We have much to do and other Orange People waiting for us. We will certainly return to visit Eekareth in the future, if you will have us again as guests."

Skinny was silent for a moment, but for the deep inhales and exhales through her siphons.

Finally, Skinny replied. "You will come for one more observe. You will follow."

Aether had anticipated resistance. "No. I'm sorry once again. We do look forward to pleasure of seeing you again sometime." She put out her hand to shake.

Skinny looked at the hand, then at Aether, then Qin. Her arm rose and pressed gently against Aether's hand, cilia wrapping tenderly around fingers.

"Qin keep Eeahso alive. Eeahso wish to see Qin and Aether, and express new pleasure to replace old bad." Skinny twisted half a turn and pointed through the vegetation ahead with her free arm to an apparent clearing. "We meet just there. Short time. Then Orange People go be and return sometime. Short time. Short time. After take you fastest way back to Eekareth and white egg."

QIN: Now we're talking.

Aether sighed, apologized to her protesting stomach, and hoped she wouldn't soon regret her decision. "Yes. Let us."

Skinny laughed and released Aether's hand. "Now we must sneak!" She dropped to the ground and proceeded spread out on all-fours, creeping forward smooth and crab-like.

Aether and Qin took to their knees and strove to keep up.

"How are you doing?" Qin asked. "Physically."

"Same. Need meds and food. And don't worry. I set a timer for ten minutes. We're heading back to the EV at that point, whatever happens up ahead."

They reached the clearing a few moments later, and their location was instantly apparent. To the right, above the tops of tall, thin lichen trees, a clear view of Threck City's soaring tower alit with multicolored torches. Skinny had led them along a gradually curving path around the city's outer perimeter. Ahead lay the "Soccer Field"—another Tom designation. Several times a year, the Threck held sporting competitions in this place. Running, leaping, throwing, block stacking, feats of strength. It was like Threck Olympics.

So why had they circled round to the other side of the city?

"Wait, do you realize where we are?" Qin said, and Skinny threw up an arm.

LIVETRANS: Silence!

AETHER: Yes, though I'm not sure why. She said this was to briefly meet up with Eeahso and accept gratitude.

QIN: How would an injured Eeahso have even made it all the way over here ahead of us? There's no way. I say we bail. We need to get those meds in you.

AETHER: And you. Seven more minutes on the clock. Like I said, we go either way.

QIN: You're the boss.

Skinny reached the other side of the field first and, once more hidden by foliage, stood up and helped Aether and Qin to their feet. She stepped back and gestured.

LIVETRANS: Just here. Little farther.

Five more minutes were spent climbing to a rocky hill's crest before edging a quarter of the way down to the other side, stopping on a small, natural balcony. Skinny crept to the edge, peered over the precipice, and then signaled for them to silently take up positions beside her. Frustrated, and with only a minute left on the timer, Aether slinked to the edge as she searched Livetrans for a way to specify a sign-only response. Qin crawled up beside her and peeked out over the ledge.

With no sign of Eeahso, or anyone else for that matter, Aether decided to stick to her guns and call it quits. She lowered her PA volume to a whisper and leaned the speaker close to Skinny.

"Eeahso not here. It is time. We are leaving."

Skinny put up an arm—a sign that no longer required translation. "Wait."

"No, we will wait no longer, Skinny. We are leaving." She reached behind her and tapped Qin on the back before shuffling backward.

"Aether!" Qin whispered. "Look! Is that Tom?"

Aether scrambled back to the edge and peeked out. Below them, beyond the rocky hill's base and past perhaps 50m of wild vegetation, Aether saw a perfectly circular clearing surrounded by tiki-type torches and tall, planted epsequoias, like an arboreal Stonehenge. To the right of the clearing, a paved trail curved off toward the city. But closer, at the end of a separate, unlit path, Aether spotted an apparent observation post.

"Angela too!" Qin hushed. "The Threck have them!"

Indeed, the observation post—about half the distance between the tree circle and Aether's position—contained several individuals, Tom and Angela among them. Among her friends stood three cloaked Threck, and all eyes appeared to be on the circle, including Tom's and Angela's.

Skinny tapped Aether's arm and signed.

LIVETRANS: Any second.

"What's any second?" Aether replied through the hushed PA. "What's going to happen?"

Skinny edged close, placing one of her siphons right up to the visor opening in Aether's helmet. Strange, sour air jetted out as Skinny whispered, "Like I say before. You see difference of Seekapock and Threck."

Aether gazed down at Tom and Angela as she realized her alarm had been flashing in front of her all this time. She dismissed it, tension rising in her neck and forehead. Her stomach gurgled and reminded her that its rage had yet to be quelled.

"Look, there!" Qin breathed.

Aether shifted focus back to the circle of trees and saw a very young Threck slowly entering the lit area from the path. A second later, another Threck child appeared, then a third. Aether watched nervously as all three children went to the center of the ring, each picking up an object from the middle, then separated, spreading out toward the edges. The epsequoias obscured most of their view, but Aether caught fleeting glimpses whenever they crossed the space between trunks. After walking the full perimeter, the three reassembled at the edge of the clearing, opposite the entrance path, and lay down, stretching their appendages out like four-pointed stars. Tentacles overlapping each other's, the children went still.

A small commotion in the observation post. The Threck around Tom and Angela grew excited, pointing toward the tree ring.

Beside Aether's head, Skinny had begun absentmindedly tapping one club against the rock and, upon closer observation, the cilia were in an uproar, dancing wildly like a thousand arms above a concert crowd.

"What are those?" Qin whispered.

Aether glanced back to the children. "What?"

"Are you zoomed? If not, do."

Aether closed her bio eye and zoomed right up to the three young Threck. It took a moment, but she spotted them. Slithering out from the bushes beyond the trees: three little worms, hardly visible in the mossy ground cover, like tiny snakes in high grass. Each moved on a direct course toward a Threck child.

Within a minute, the worms reached the children and disappeared beneath them, presumably to their mouths. And then nothing happened. The young did not appear to react. Not even a slight tentacle movement.

Aether heard Skinny's breath speeding up. She looked over at Skinny's eyes. They appeared focused not on the ring, but beyond it and to the left, and they were widening, creeping almost imperceptibly forward.

Skinny uttered a single, muted syllable: *"Soot."*

LIVETRANS: Now.

And then all hell broke loose.

26

Having taken her meds and eaten, Angela seemed to be in a bit better mood. One might even surmise that she was *excited* about visiting Threck City. After her fury dissipated, Tom enjoyed witnessing her engineer side taking over as they jounced about in a wagon on the main road.

Threck wagons were designed unlike any cart or vehicle in human history, and while the team had detailed schematics and imagery of the peculiar inventions, to see them up close—*to travel upon one*—was no less thrilling for her. The Threck had examples of wheels in various mechanisms (pulleys and such), and yet they relied upon heavy cement spheres for all sorts of on (and off) the ground load bearing and shifting. City gates, carts, and the massive water-wheels around the city all used these large balls. The wagons had a sphere on all four sides and rolled on the front and rear balls for normal forward travel, and the two side balls for side-to-side motion. It was highly impractical considering that without domesticated beasts of burden, propulsion was achieved via teams of Threck, and at any given time, 200 kilos of extra weight must be hauled above and beyond the cargo.

During an obligatory exigency meeting, the team had discussed what sorts of technology advancements the team might offer the Threck in exchange for accommodating the foreigners on their island. Limited medicinal advancements met with mixed reactions, but *the wheel* had been agreed upon unanimously.

"Isn't it funny," Angela smiled, motioning to the weary Threck driving the cart forward, "how once-theoretical negotiations about technology sharing now have a real-life bearing on our own personal comfort?"

Tom was sweating, and not from the heat outside his suit. He *really* needed to move his bowels. "Explaining the wheel to them right now isn't going to smooth this ride or get us there any sooner. Let me concentrate."

"Just say something, you wuss." Angela smacked his shoulder. "We're going to enter those gates in …" she craned her neck toward the gradually growing city, "I'm guessing around ten minutes, and once we're in there, walking around, meeting with honchos, you're *definitely* not going to say anything. I *know* you won't. You're going to end up crapping in your suit or rupturing something internal."

"I think that's a myth. The door would surely give way long before the walls."

"Regardless."

Tom stiffened his posture and raised his chin, speaking in a posh tone. "Apologies, but, notwithstanding this excruciating encumbrance, I'm like an ambassador at present. Someone of my stature does not—
"

"Crap themselves in public," Angela finished for him.

She stood up in the cart, searching for stable footing on the crops. A few seconds later, her Livetrans synth voice played loud enough for Amoss, in the cart ahead of them, to hear over the rolling din.

"Pardon me. One of us requires an excretion stop." She pointed at Tom.

Fifteen minutes later, the carts entered the city's main western gate. In the broad tunnel, the temperature dropped rapidly, and a cool breeze flowed from inside out. It smelled faintly acrid, like overwatered indoor plants with rotting soil. The tunnel widened abruptly and they found themselves in a large dome-shaped room where Threck moved quickly to unload the carts into baskets. Though Tom and Angela hadn't escaped the notice of these new Threck, no one appeared to slow down or hold a glance for long. These people were well-trained and disciplined, executing their assigned duties like hive insects.

A scurrying young Threck carrying two stepstools placed one beside Tom and Angela's cart just as Amoss and another Threck (Oose?) arrived to help them down.

"Come now, Tom and Angela, and follow Tatsis to your waiting place," Amoss said. "Our jubilant Thinkers have been notified of your auspicious presence and currently travel to their celebrated chamber."

"Have Syons People previously observed Threck City?" Tatsis, a somewhat smaller figure with an apparently permanent leftward lean, gestured around the substantial room. "From within or without?"

"Only from the outside," Tom carefully replied.

And it was true. John would have never allowed a dragonfly or any other probes within the city perimeter, no matter how many assurances Minnie offered. But imaging technology certainly had no problem penetrating concrete or the Threck version of waxed canvas. The team had fairly detailed maps of all but the deepest and centermost areas of Threck City, and most everywhere else had been filled in via conversation analysis automations. This, however, did nothing to subtract from Tom's trembling delight to actually be inside.

Boots firmly planted on the wet floor, Tom helped a grinning Angela down from the cart, and the pair followed Tatsis across the busy room. Tom tried to study everything at once. The floor was of particular interest. This was the surface upon which Threck "knee" bends must step and slide every day. While the team had assumed that everything at or below the water table would be mud, it was, in fact, covered in meticulously polished stone, like marble, and each massive slab was lined up perfectly to its neighbors, making the floor, at first glance, appear composed of a single, arena-sized piece. This flooring choice made perfect sense. Smooth against the skin, easy to keep clean, no issues with constant wetness, and surely great for sliding cargo around. Many of the paths outside the city were paved with polished stone slabs, but the crew had no idea of its extensive use inside the city.

Tatsis led them into a long, bright passageway. The tunnel's roof was fashioned of the same purple canvas that swathed the rest of the city, draped over successive stone and mortar archways, and held taut by braided fibers. Generations ago, in the interest of temperature reduction, Threck Thinkers and Materials workers had settled on the color of the sky as the best reflector of heat. Logic dictated that the sun's violet rays carried with them the heat one felt while standing outside. And so, if one wished to reflect these rays, the optimal material color would, of course, be violet. As far as Tom knew, no one had yet questioned this reasoning, and based upon the remarkable coolness of the interior thus far, clearly other design aspects or mechanisms were picking up the slack. The air felt damp, like a bathroom after a shower.

At the passage's end they reached a T, and followed a new hallway left. Passers-by here were not so indifferent to the orange-clad guests' presence.

"What are these?" A Threck stopped in front of Tatsis, even reaching out abruptly to touch Angela's unshielded face.

Tatsis thwacked the arm away. "Guests from another land. Be on your way. City address to come."

The curious Threck stepped back to let them pass, but remained planted in that spot, transfixed by Tom and Angela as they moved on.

The next citizen hindering their progress was not so easily dismissed.

"What are these, Tatsis? And why have I received no notice?" She was a wide one, commanding in both manner and form.

Tatsis froze and appeared to shrink even smaller in front of Tom and Angela. "Dowfwoss Fetz, I've come directly from Dowfwoss Amoss, delivering these to holding—"

The Dowfwoss's eyes studied Tom and Angela as she spoke. "Before what? In wait of what? They walk on two … Where are they from? What are they for?"

"They are for learning them," Tatsis replied, still appearing to shrivel with every passing second.

Fetz continued eyeing them. "Is one for me? Is one to open?"

Tatsis stood upright, twisted round with bulging eyes to observe Tom. She held up both arms to Fetz. "No, no, Dowfwoss! These are smart! These are Tom and Angela of Syons People." Tatsis lowered her voice. "And they know Threck words."

Fetz's eyes hid and returned. She took a step toward Tom and spoke very slowly. "You understand these words?"

"Yes," Tom's synth replied through the PA. "Peaceful greetings, Dowfwoss Fetz. It is great pleasure to meet you and to visit Threck City."

Fetz snapped a presumably stunned look at Tatsis. To Tom again, "You speak our words with enchanting precision! Do it again … more words!"

"We are delighted to be welcomed in your beautiful city."

"Delighted … yes. Did you absorb my exchange with Persheck Tatsis just now?"

Tom considered how delicate to be. Clearly this Fetz was an important citizen. "I did observe this, yes, before our proper introduction."

Fetz burst out with a melodious laugh, continuing for an awkward length. "Apologies!" she finally said. "Forgive my outburstings, as the pleasure your words incite fills my being with rivers of ecstasy! It is as if I am bathing from within! Give these to me now, Tatsis. I must never stop hearing these … *What* are they called?"

"Syons People," Tatsis said. "Tom speaking, and Angela. The Thinkers were to …"

"Later!" Fetz shouted. "The Thinkers can have them later. Now, they will join me and meet the leaders. Perhaps Syons People will discover some small pleasure from us as I have from them. Assemble the council for abrupt conference."

"I will," Tatsis said, and scuttled away.

Fetz began walking sideways along the corridor, eyes alternating between the guests and the walkway ahead. "Come now, Syons People. Follow me and share the tale of your finding. Where did Tatsis discover you?"

"We arrived at one farm today," Tom replied. "Dowfwoss Amoss, Tatsis, and others came shortly after for harvest."

"I see, I see. And you requested visit to Threck City?"

"Not exactly. We sought audience with Threck to request permission to establish small camp on the far northeast end of your land. Somewhere nonintrusive and acceptable to Threck people."

"And what is purpose of this camp?"

"To live quietly and unobtrusively. Syons People land is no longer suitable for living."

Fetz turned into a covered corridor, leading them closer to the city center. "Interesting, interesting. And where is this land?"

"It is very small place, great distance away."

"Interesting."

Fetz led them through a series of rooms and corridors. Tom and Angela caught brief glimpses of fabric weaving, a large, pie slice-shaped room where 100 or more Threck wove both roofing canvas and Threck garb, and then they passed through an identical area in which a smaller number stirred steaming liquid in large vats.

"Coating," was the only explanation Fetz provided.

When asked by curious passers-by, Fetz responded only, "Guests of the council. Move along."

Soon, they reached the city center and a spiral staircase. Like the steps in the farmers' domicile, they all sloped downward before meeting the next higher stair—perfectly contoured for a Threck knee-bend, and designed well to avoid slippage.

The stairs seemed never-ending, and, midway up, Tom and Angela both closed their visors for fresh doses of pure oxygen.

Twenty stairs ahead, and out of sight, Fetz called down. "Do they need assistance?"

Tom ignored her and waved when Fetz returned to view.

"We have reached the council room," Fetz said. "You may wait at the window there and rest your bodies. The leaders have yet to arrive." She turned and slipped through a passage in the wall.

Tom and Angela reached the landing and collapsed against a wall, catching their breath.

"Damn," Angela's voice in his helmet. "That was torture. Any fresh regrets for cheating on the legger machine?"

"I didn't cheat. I always *just* made it to ten percent below substandard and dealt with the monthly John Li frowny face during review. Regrets, though? Yeah." Tom sucked in a final lungful of pure oxygen and opened his visor. "Ooh, look at this." He ran his glove down a thin line of mortar between the wall's large blocks. "From the ground, you can't even tell it's masonry. Do we let them know the place is going to crumble the next time a moderate quake hits?"

"Not necessarily true. If you look, their engineers are actually super sharp—"

A Threck voice came from the doorway behind them. "Is there anything I may provide you pair?" They turned to see a smallish Threck in a spotless, beige cloak. "I am Setkee. Do you drink water?"

"Thank you, Setkee—" Tom began.

The Threck interrupted him, "You do not refer to Setkee as such. This is strange."

Tom sent "Apologies" from his hotlist of terms and phrases. "I am not familiar with the word. How shall I address you?"

"You may address us however you wish."

Tom decided it was safest to abandon the conversation. Without knowing Threck emotive expressions or inflection, he didn't know if this person was angry, mildly offended, being helpful, or messing with him.

Do Threck mess with each other?

"Thank you for the offer," Tom said. "We do not require anything at this time."

"Understood," the Threck said. "If you do, simply beckon Setkee." She turned sideways and slid back through the passage.

"What the hell was that?" Angela said as they walked to a large window. "Oh … wow."

A warm, humid breeze blew against their faces as they gazed out on an unobstructed view of the city's east side, and the lush low hills beyond the walls. Three of the city's seven arcades could be seen sprouting from the tower base like wheel spokes. Straight roads—most of them paved with small stone slabs—extended out from the gated ends of the arcades, on this side leading respectively to a small cluster of farms, the granite mines, and the bay's northernmost shore.

Tom pointed to an open patch in the hilly jungle about 2K northeast. "What's that?" An unfinished circular building could be seen just peeking out at treetop height.

"Some kind of observatory," Angela said. "At least that's what Minnie thought."

She and Tom shared a somber look. Angela had said *thought*, not *thinks*.

Was it what they both believed? Were John, Minnie, and Ish alive? If so, in that environment, how long could they possibly survive? Tom had run through several scenarios while still in orbit. Between the two EV's SSKs, they'd have 480 multirounds against a very close-by Hynka population of a couple hundred thousand, plus several million more across the country. If a skimmer didn't have to stop, it would take sixty hours to fly from Hynka country's mountainous central valley to the western coast, and the EV's skimmers could *maybe* go ten hours between three-hour regens. At best, they'd have to make five stops. Examining all of their mislaid comrades' possible courses, Tom had trouble coupling what was *possible* with what was *likely*. But if there was a way, Minnie and John would find it.

Staring out at the extraordinary panorama, Angela broke the silence. "She'd have absolutely loved this."

Tom only nodded. Evidently, Angela's hopes weren't so high as his.

"Syons People," a Threck voice spoke behind them. "The council wishes for you to enter now."

Tom's Livetrans picked up a barely audible shout from beyond the narrow doorway. "If they are ready!"

"If you are ready," the Threck standing before them echoed. Tom noticed this one wearing the same sort of pressed, unmuddied cloak as the previous Threck, but was much taller. "Is there anything you require prior to meeting the council? I am Setkee."

"We are fine, thank you," Tom replied, and then took the opportunity. "Excuse my limited knowledge of your beautiful language, but what does this word 'Setkee' mean?"

The Threck pulled a quick eye hide and said, "It is the word which describes our status: Threckee, but not Threck."

Tom glanced at Angela, who he noticed was wearing the same polite smile. "And what is the difference?"

Another shout from the room. "Are they coming?"

"One is what we are, the other is to be," the Setkee clarified.

"I see," Tom said, and gestured toward the doorway. "Great. Let's go in."

* * *

The council's floor of the tower—just above the city's voluminous water reservoir and only two levels below the observation post—boasted a vaulted ceiling atop a wide circle of support columns and a substantial center pillar. Otherwise, the room was essentially empty.

As they were led across the smooth marble floor, Tom noticed at once a dozen Threck standing tall in a wide oval. In silence, all eyes tracked Tom and Angela's progress. Upon passing the center pillar, the Setkee guiding them stopped, rotated, and left. Tom froze as well, unsure of protocol. Unfortunately, he couldn't see half of the council members as they were blocked by those standing closer.

But are *they standing?* Tom wondered.

Presumably, one of these people was Fetz, whom he'd met earlier, and who stood about Angela's height, several centimeters shorter than Tom. This group, however, were all significantly taller than Tom. They had to have been standing on the ends of their leg tentacles, like some sort of Threck ballerina stance.

"Continue on," one of the Threck in front said. "We would all like to see you."

"Yes, come forward Syons People!" An arm appeared and waved from the far side of the assembly. "So that I may introduce you to the rest of the leaders."

Ah-hah. Good. At least we know which one is Fetz.

Tom stepped forward and felt Angela grasp his hand as she followed. There was no discernible area where visitors were meant to stand, and the space between each council member looked a bit awkward for the pair to ease into. If he moved into the space between two Threck, his shoulders would practically graze their cloaks. So then, were they intended to stand in the middle of this group, surrounded, spinning round to hear or address any particular individual?

Tom halted just outside the circle. “Peaceful greetings, wise leaders.”

A flurry of translations scrolled up Tom’s fone as the thin source frame bounced from person to person, linking individuals to their respective comments

“It’s true!”

“I still can’t see them.”

“Remarkable.”

“Where are these from?”

“Can’t see. Make them come into middle.”

“No, Packte!” Fetz shouted. “These are delightful guests, not savage prisoners to answer questions and be punished. Apologies, Syons People, the council does not by habit receive guests. The chamber is not exactly suited for more than the twelve.”

“As I mentioned, I have bathed with these people.” Tom realized the new speaker was Dowfwoss Amoss. “And it was beyond fulfilling. Shall we all descend to the tower bath?”

ANGELA: We bathe well with others.

TOM: Yeah. Any *useful* thoughts here? What do we do?

ANGELA: Don’t get snippy with me, mister. Just let them sort it out.

“There is plenty of space in here,” someone said, and Tom watched as this Threck’s apparently dangling legs curled backward, revealing some sort of thin stand beneath the hanging cloak, then she planted her knee-bends onto a connected block behind the stand, and lifted her body up and back. Once she’d stepped off the raised block, taking the cloak with her, Tom finally observed why they’d all appeared so tall: they were actually seated—or rather, *draped* over tall pedestals that supported their full weight, legs dangling just above the floor. None of this had been visible, of course, because their cloaks hung from "shoulder" height, all the way to the floor, presenting each council member as well over 2m tall.

"True Thinker," Fetz quipped, as explained by Livetrans.

LIVETRANS: True Thinker. [Quip]

Fetz stood up from her seat, too, and the others followed. The group moved to a wide open area near the curved wall and spread out in a semicircle, leaving a large space by the room's center pillar for Tom and Angela.

"Much better."

"Let them say more."

"I have many questions."

"Silence, please," Fetz said, waving an arm before her. "Allow me to express proper introduction … you still understand all we say, Tom and Angela?"

Tom took a deep breath, readying himself for what would surely amount to a Threck body language workout session for his weary body. "We do, yes. Peaceful greetings to all of you."

Impressed, satisfied, confused, curious, and other reactions scrolled by in Livetrans.

Fetz introduced each council member by city group, along with sometimes interesting, often incomprehensible anecdotes, such as, "… And here stands Massoss Pakte, overseer of fish accumulation, storage, and dispersal, and patient tolerator of indecisive currents, insolent mains, and visitors both expected and not."

There was Massoss Symee in charge of the Expansion group, Dowfwoss Towtzaw from the Nursery, Massoss this, Dowfwoss that (more Massosses than Dowfwosses, Tom observed), ending with the uniquely-adorned Dowfwoss *ʔnkte*, representing the Thinkers, whose cloak edges were embellished with purple-dyed trim around the head slit, sleeves, and bottom.

Fetz's introduction of her was conspicuously brief, and *ʔnkte* (pronounced from deep down—an "unh" sound, as if one were just punched in the chest, followed by –nkte), said only "Hello" as her sleepy, half-open eyes gazed at Tom and Angela. Specially designed cloak aside, ʔnkte's demeanor stood out among her peers, suggesting that Thinkers may literally think at a higher level than others. And ʔnkte was their leader.

Disgruntled by Livetrans' use of the glottal stop symbol ʔ representing this sound, Tom made a quick replacement. "*Unhkte*" didn't look much better, but he'd deal with it.

Next came the onslaught of questions, civilly from right to left, and, in the beginning, paired with extravagant compliments. Tom answered many of the same basic curiosities he'd provided back in the farmers' domicile. Then came a new line of questioning.

"Having never experienced the pleasure of another wise creature," Massoss Fact from Waters & Sanitation began, "I beg forgiveness for looking upon you with excessively enamored eyes. For my first question, I wish to know if, in Syons People land, with so few inhabitants, if sanitation is of primary concern."

"Sanitation, as in keeping things clean?" Tom asked.

Fact elaborated. "As in disposal of excretions. We are aware that one of you excreted near the *feshoosh* orchards. It is not of concern—Setkee collected the droppings; I believe we now have them down in Sanitation—but we wonder if this is common practice for Syons People, and if so, has there been any hazards associated with large accumulations."

Angela had stifled a choke and now stood holding her breath beside Tom.

Tom had the M sent to Angela before Fact even finished imparting the question.

> TOM: When crapping one's pants begins to sound like the preferable choice. You're so going to pay.

Tom quickly but carefully composed his response, sending it as he wrote.

"I must apologize if this earlier action caused any offense. Syons People have equipment for such things, and are so disinclined to its appearance and scent, that droppings are sent away in an enclosed system which disposes of it without another person ever observing it. Away from our home, lacking this equipment, I was unsure how to appropriately excrete."

"Fascinating," Fact said. "This sounds similar to our system. I would very much like to speak with you further on this subject."

"And it was not offense," Amoss interjected. "You need not apologize for excreting in uninhabited brush."

Tom could see Angela's chest subtly quaking in his peripheral.

ANGELA: Dying ... Literally. Dying. Inside.

"Can you describe other equipment Syons People utilize?" Massoss Artsh of the Makers group.

"This is one of the topics we wish to discuss with the council." Tom used the opportunity to segue back into the mission. Minnie had outlined specific wording for this very moment, and Tom copy/pasted it into Livetrans—a temporarily relief of responsibility. "Our people have learned certain knowledge about living things, and have found unique methods for curing illnesses in people, animals, and grown foods." Intrigue animated his audience. "We would like to work with the Threck to adapt these cures to your people and foods, improving health and longevity, and protecting food sources from often-devastating disease. This is what we wish to offer in exchange for one small, isolated plot of land to live out our lives."

"In the northeast," Amoss added. "Beyond *Tensakoss*."

"We do not travel that far," Artsh said.

"I believe that is the objective," Unhkte of the Thinkers said, speaking for the first time since her introduction. "Unlike the chattel we've made of our farmer friends, when this proposed arrangement is concluded, we're not to be seen again." She turned to Fetz. "I suggest accepting the offer and dismissing the council. This is all I have to say on the matter."

Tom worried about the leader of the Thinkers. Though otherwise quiet, Tom got the impression that she wanted him and Angela gone. What was going on in that head?

"What else can they give us?" Someone asked.

"I say we agree to terms," another suggested.

"They could also help improve sanitation systems," Fact said. "Let us weigh what is most important to the city."

"How are we to know they can deliver anything offered?" Massoss Kwossh, from the Farming group. "We have attempted countless remedies for vine rot and graying disease."

"Let us not doubt wherewithal, nor presume the option to negotiate terms other than that offer which was surely long-devised, and from people clearly our mental superiors," Amoss said. "They make machines which rise from the ground and fly as rocks are thrown. Their *garb* speaks our language with perfect tenor. Tom, setting aside some of my colleagues' fast-accumulating aspirations, can you satisfy doubts about your remedies? Further explanation, perhaps, if you believe it within our capacity."

ANGELA: Wheel.

TOM: Shush.

ANGELA: Just saying. Don't bogart it like you invented the thing.

"I'd be happy to explain," Tom replied. "As you are all very wise, I have no uncertainty as to your capacity to understand." Almost in perfect sync, the council members' eyes dropped and rose.

Comments and body language interpretations scrolled by as Tom composed.

LIVETRANS: Please proceed.
LIVETRANS: I want this.
LIVETRANS: Yes.
LIVETRANS: Proceed now.

"Many generations before my birth, some of the smartest Syons People of our land made this shocking discovery. Like you, we'd always been plagued by illness, both in our people and in our foods. Cities as big as yours were often stricken by invisible killers. The very smartest of them could not discern the source. But one day, one man discovered that these killers were not invisible, but extremely small—so small that they could not be seen by Syons People's eyes."

Threck eyes hid.

Tom hurried to write the rest of the story.

LIVETRANS: Continue.
LIVETRANS: More.
LIVETRANS: Interesting.

"Another smart person, years later, connected these tiny lifeforms to molds that grew on food and to the passage of disease from one animal or plant to another. And finally, yet another researcher discovered that there were ways to kill these things which no one could see, using other little things invisible to the eye. Remedies were created, tested, and sent all over. This series of discoveries improved all Syons People's lives. Now, we need only study your foods and ill, and we can create remedies for the Threck people."

The council was silent, staring.

ANGELA: Well done. Waaaaay more longwinded than necessary, but I think they get it.

Amoss stepped slowly forward as the other council members shared glances. "Tom, where are Syons People from?"

Asked and answered, Tom thought. *Well, answered with a lie, but how would they know?*

"As I said, we are from distant northern land, as far away as one can imagine."

"But this is not true," Amoss said. "Threck have travelled to *all* lands, and unless Syons People live in Hynka Country, there is no place for these Syons cities. So I ask … *where?*"

Tom had no clue how to answer. There was no protocol for this other than to stick to the guns, resting assured that *technically* it was *partially* the truth. They were from an unimaginably distant land.

ANGELA: Crap! Are you going to tell them?

TOM: I can't!

"Tom," Amoss began again, slowly rocking side to side. "How much time have Syons People spent with farmers?"

This he could answer. "Not long. We arrived just before your harvesting group."

"And how much time have Syons People spent with the sea people? Those who call themselves Seekapock?"

"None, no time."

Amoss stopped moving, dark eyes fixed on Tom's. "And how much time have Syons People spent with Threck?"

"As long as we've been here. Since meeting you."

"Yes. So how do Syons People speak Threck language with such delightful precision?"

"We learn from listening. Our garb is able to keep words. Then we say them."

ANGELA: Wow. That was terrible.

He ignored her. He was burying himself and "Syons People" deeper and deeper.

"Enough, Amoss." Unhkte stepped forward. She moved right up to Angela, her droopy eyes shifting up, down, and around, and then turning to Tom for the same once-over. At this distance, Tom observed several faint scars on Unhkte's head, like an old shark that had once tried to eat a ship's propeller. "You know much about Threck, do you not?"

"We know some," Tom replied. "From observation. Probably not as much as you think, though."

Unhkte faced the wall, eyes roaming the ceiling. "Do you know how Threck are born?"

Tom struggled with his response, deleting and rewriting before reluctantly settling. "There is a cycle in fertile individuals. During fertilization, they experience increasing stiffness, leading to full paralysis while eggs—"

"Enough. Stop." Unhkte waved an arm. Tom paused the Livetrans playback. Unhkte turned to the council. "You see?"

"This is reproduction," Fetz said to Tom. "Answer Unhkte's question. How are Threck born?"

"Apologies," Tom said. "I thought you wished to test our knowledge of your physiology. Birth occurs submerged in saturated soil after roughly eighty days' gestation when the egg is—"

"No more," Unhkte stopped him again. "They know nothing of Threck. Let it be, and let us adjourn."

"No," Amoss said, and then shouted, "Setkee!" Young Threck appeared from the stairway that led to the uppermost floors. "Restrain the Syons People and take them to holding room."

"What's going on?" Tom demanded as tentacles constricted around his arms, holding them tight to his body. He could no longer gesture to plead with the council. "Need explain. Tell what want know. Will explain anything."

"Get it off me, Tom!" Angela cried.

A small Threck's body lay flat against Angela's back and its arms and legs wrapped two or three times around her. The same was true of the one on Tom's back. Other Setkee pushed them along toward the stairwell as the council members huddled close to each other.

Livetrans only picked up a few snippets.

> LIVETRANS: Cannot trust.
> LIVETRANS: Find others.
> LIVETRANS: Execute.

* * *

In the "holding" room, Angela gazed upward, fascinated by the door.

An hour earlier, upon arriving at the end of a long subterranean hall, they perceived a sloped stone wall that, if climbed up, would lead only to smacking one's head on the jagged rock ceiling. It wasn't a wall, though, but a rectangular slab of granite, anchored at its middle to the bedrock on both sides. Scaling the 45° surface—bound by tentacles, and with a few other escorts—the top end of the slab had gradually dropped while the end behind them rose, like a trapdoor for a giant snail. Revealed below, a small, bowl-shaped cave with a shallow puddle at its bottom. Their captors released them and scurried out before the massive gate sealed Tom and Angela in the dark.

Now, Tom lay cradled in the curvature of the wall, scratching an itchy head as Angela studied the "door" through various optics. Their helmets lay on the ground beside the puddle.

"I can't find any records of this exact design," Angela marveled. "Of course, the idea of a gate rotating on a single axle has been around forever, but the concept of body weight as the powering force … I mean, in this application, I suppose it's sort of the obvious, sole option, based upon the cave's purpose. You know, this is the kind of stuff you see in history and wonder how the hell people missed the connections. A Threck engineer doesn't just glance at this thing and go 'hey, whoa, our cart wheels are stupid!' and introduce a proper wheel and axle." She glanced back at the quiet Tom. "Are you still moping?"

"It's not moping when your life is in actual danger. In such cases, it's called 'appropriate distress.'"

She splashed through the puddle and flopped down next to him, slapping his knee. "Moping."

He looked at her through thermag, her smiling face a mix of blues and whites. "I seriously don't get how you're so upbeat right now, appreciating the engineering of our jail cell. They could just leave us to die in here. Move on with city life. Dissect our corpses when they get around to it. That's not some pessimistic worst-case scenario. It's highly probable. I screwed us."

"And *that's* the real issue here, I think." She nudged his shoulder with hers. "*Some*body feels like a big fat failure. *All* your anxiety came to fruition. You communicated ineffectively. And damn, not only are *you* effed, but the chick you're *totally* in love with is, too. Funereal, truly."

"Sorry, are you trying to make me feel better?"

She pushed out her lower lip and furrowed her brow. "Aw, am I making you sadder?" She sunk lower, incorporating an utterly maddening baby talk. "Does da widdle guy need mawmaw to make him feew bedder?" Tom pressed his lips together, shaking his head as he battled a creeping smile. "I'm sawwy, my widdle schnookie ookie wookems."

"Oh man, I'm going to flick you in the eye so hard."

"Don't care. Made you smile. Listen to me now. I'm optimistic for several reasons. First, these are pretty reasonable, intelligent people. Sure, they literally crap through their mouths, but *they can't help that.* No anus. If they had a choice in the matter, they'd use another orifice—I believe that deeply. As for us, something was misunderstood, and you'll surely have a chance to straighten it out before we're dragged off to some gallows, which, incidentally, would probably be another captivating example of unprecedented engineering."

"Particularly due to their lack of necks."

She ignored his muttering. "Second, Zisa and Pablo know where we are. They won't just sit there laxing at the rally point, roasting … *whatever*, and one day wonder what happened to us. They'll come, and they'll come packing heat. Which brings me to C."

"Did I miss an A and B?"

She stood up and patted the holstered MW on her thigh. "Roman octopus people have pretty lackluster arrest procedures. If we have to blast our way out of here …" She sprang into a gunslinger stance. "I'm ready for action!"

He looked up at her, acceding to her good cheer. "'Funereal?'"

She smirked. "Thesaurus."

"Have you noticed how we're sort of opposites when it comes to emotional responses?"

"You're *just* noticing that? Such a male."

A resounding creak from above and bright light streamed into the cave. Tom switched back to standard optics. The top of the stone slab slowly descended with a loud crack as its axle protested the shift in weight. He grabbed both helmets, handing Angela hers.

"This thing could fall at any second," Tom said as they both pressed their backs against the wall and squeezed into the helmets, sealing them into their neck receivers.

Angela kept talking, but in a whisper. "Nah, it's a self-reinforcing design. See, the axle is fully encased, and the..."

She faded off when the door stopped rotating, teetering subtly at a horizontal position parallel to the tunnel floor outside, and several silhouetted Threck heads entered the meter-high space beneath. Tom's optics exposure auto-adjusted and the figures materialized.

"Tom and Angela of Syons People," one of the gawking Threck said. "Come out now."

Angela's hand drifted to her MW.

Tom touched her leg and addressed the Threck above. "I respectfully request the wise council's time to explain any misunderstandings that may have arisen during our meeting. Our people have entirely peaceful intentions, wishing only to live in peace somewhere the Threck people find acceptable. In exchange for this generosity, we offer only the help you choose to accept." The onlookers remained silent. "Or we can simply take our belongings, leave your land, and you need never see us again."

There had always been a backup plan should the Threck people decline Minnie's appeal: an uninhabited, J-shaped string of small islands to the north of Threck Country—beyond the horizon, but well within skimmer range. The only problem was fresh water. The evacuees must rely upon seawater desalinization.

"Your sole mistake," the Threck finally said, "was in addressing the council first, and not my group." Tom suddenly noticed the drowsy eyes and the cloak's purple trim.

Unhkte?

Tom pushed off the wall and stood. "I believe that was the objective until we happened upon Dowfwoss Fetz."

"Yes, I am aware," Unhkte said. "Come now. You have nothing more to fear for the time being."

Tom helped Angela up. "The time being?"

"Yes. For the time being you are under the scrutiny of my group. This is maneuver. Do you understand?"

"I'm not sure I do."

"Gesture," Unhkte attempted. "For the council's sake. 'Scrutiny,' we say. Tactical naming to quell concerns while not, ourselves, harboring such concerns. Do you understand?"

Tom got it. The Thinkers—or at least Unhkte—believed Tom innocent, even if the council did not, and had presented some sort of ruse to get them freed.

"I understand," Tom said. "You have our gratitude."

"We shall see. Come out now."

Tom and Angela stepped over the puddle and struggled to find footing on the roughhewn bedrock beneath the exit. Seconds later, unannounced arms from above curled under their armpits and lifted them up and out of the cave.

Angela pulled her suit down at the legs. She sent one of the preset Threck phrases through her suit's PA. "Thank you."

Unhkte slid closer and regarded Angela. "Identical voice. You share this Threck voice."

Earlier in the day, atop the trembling harvest cart, Tom had reviewed vid of the whole bath encounter, cataloguing observations while critiquing his own performance. Dissatisfied with his poor explanation of the whole talking suit thing, a better explanation had occurred to him that he was pleased to now share. "Our garb emits the words we put into it. It is like Threck whistle—producing sound your bodies alone cannot create, and it's the same sound regardless of the user."

ANGELA: Brilliant! You!

"This is the most extraordinary thing I have heard," Unhkte said with two eye hides. "It is shame." She turned and began walking down the torch-lit hall.

"Why 'shame?'" Tom and Angela followed as some Threck closed the holding room while others walked close behind.

"This is not your mistake." Unhkte gestured behind her back, one arm coiling clockwise, close to her body ("is not"), while the other pointed at him ("you"). Tom realized that one had to adopt a simpler type of speech when addressing someone who was not looking. Unhkte started up the tunnel's cramped, semi-spiraled stairway to ground level. "It is simply unfortunate that we cannot spend more time with you. From what little I have heard, the Thinkers and I could blithely halt all current contemplations and dedicate seasons of time just listening."

"Believe," Tom said, and suddenly felt quite moved—strangely—as if the emotion had a physical form stretching out inside his head. He swallowed. "Syons People share this opinion of Threck."

Unhkte paused at the arched exit and turned to face him. Tom had to balance awkwardly on the concave stairs. Angela ran into him and put a hand on his rear. "What could Syons People learn from Threck? It appears that you have already achieved *shyma*."

"I do not know this word *shyma*, but I assure you, there is much that we've *already* learned and can *still* learn from your people."

Unhkte emitted a short laugh. "As Eshkowoss Peekt taught, *shyma* is not end. To reestablish this notion ... my group will be amenable." She continued on, out of the archway, and Tom was relieved to exit the precarious shaft.

He wondered, though, what was this lamenting? She seemed to be implying there remained little time. Had Unhkte negotiated a reprieve from whatever sentence the council had decreed, but they were now to be forever exiled? Tom wanted to ask, but opted for silence. Despite Unhkte's seeming fondness for them, Tom had earned the same esteem from Amoss until he'd talked too much. No, it was back to Minnie's sage directive: say as little as necessary in as few words as possible. Earlier, once the dialogue had begun flowing, he'd disregarded this advice.

They followed Unhkte along one of the wide, canvas-covered passages that connected the arcades and plazas. From above, this was the outermost of the city's concentric circles, and a bustling army of hungry Threck happened to be heading the opposite direction to one of the plazas for mealtime. Tom, Angela, and the Threck walking with them fell in line behind Unhkte as the ground-quaking crowd parted and streamed by on either side. Ostensibly identical sets of curious eyes flicked by like a series of flashing pics of the same person, reminding Tom of some early animation or motion picture.

"What are these?" popped into Livetrans so many times that Tom paused input until the swarm's numbers thinned and the corridor ahead cleared, only muddy tracks remaining.

"This way." Unhkte gestured to a sloped ramp. "To the nursery." She lifted her cloak from the ground and stepped onto the ramp, skating on her knee-bends down the slippery, hooked slide.

If Earth cities had been built with slides everywhere, Pablo had once remarked, *there would be no wars.*

Angela shoved ahead of Tom, crouched down, and launched down the slide on her backside with a "weee." Tom followed after her, the somewhat muddy polished stone banking left and depositing him at ground level, five meters below the previous tier. A set of stairs followed the edge of the slide, obviously for trips back up, but apparently not to descend levels. Tom supposed it made sense. Who would want to go *down* stairs?

The group walked between two high walls that spread away from each other as they approached the doubly tall main city wall. The sound of a rushing waterway echoed in the corridor with a disorienting stereo effect. The air was cooling, and Tom could smell the moisture ... and something else. He peered up as they walked. This alleyway was not shaded, revealing the violet sky's darkening gradient as the East Ocean rose, eclipsing the Epsilon star. The last sunlight would soon leave the atmosphere.

Before reaching the end of the alley, Unhkte cut right through the only exit, an archway that led to a small, mossy riverbank, and the source of the sound. Threck City had been built atop the "Great Flow," the widest and most consistently flowing channel of a large delta system. The city center and tower were situated just south of the channel, which entered the city through fixed bars beneath the outer wall ... just there! A stone's throw away from him! ... and exited the same way at the other end of the city, near the harbor. As a geologist, Tom had devoted much of his time to studying this delta, establishing models that predicted likely and potential shifts and erosion—data he would *not* be sharing with the Threck any time soon. "You're going to have to move your city in the next fifty years" didn't feel like a prudent fun fact to share at the current juncture.

The river flowed powerfully before them, masking the sound of what lay beyond an arched bridge: the source of the nasty smell. Hundreds of very young Threck thrashed wildly in a huge mud pit, jabbering and splashing and laughing.

ANGELA: Smells like the farm house ... times an illion.

"This is the nursery," Unhkte gestured.

Tom glanced around and observed that the mud pit was only a portion of the total area. They followed Unhkte up to the bridge's highpoint, where she stopped once more.

She pointed to the mud pit. "There you have young, ten days to one hundred or more—I'm not confident of the specifics." The bridge led to a low earthen wall that wrapped around the pit all the way to the city wall. A few adult Threck lounged on top of some sort of seats, like stools, and vaguely watched the young. "These are overseers. When old enough, they move newborns from the hatchery," she motioned to a pool of still water about half the size of the mud pit, "to the mud, and from the mud, inside. Come."

They descended the bridge and followed a gravel path to a walled structure's arched entrance. Passing beside the dark pool of shallow water, Tom could dimly perceive the spherical eggs lingering at the bottom.

"I see you swayed Fetz," someone said as Tom trailed Unhkte into the room.

Small torches hung from rafters, illuminating the area and reflecting off dispersed pairs of eyes. On the floor lay 30-40 mid-sized Threck, smaller than the Setkee Tom had seen, but bigger than the largest young in the pit. These young lay flat against the floor, mostly still, with their arms and legs spread out and overlapping each other. Overseers here walked among the children, pacing over them, gingerly stepping in the spaces between outstretched tentacles. Some of the young fidgeted in place, and eyes could be seen popping out to steal a peak. Many appeared asleep, their eyes remaining hidden in their sockets.

ANGELA: Awwwww!! How cute! Bed time!

"Tom and Angela," Unhkte said. "Earlier you met Dowfwoss Towtzaw, leader of Nursery group, in the council chamber."

Towtzaw stepped from behind a table. "Welcome to my nursery, Syons People. As you recall, I was not howling among the afraid."

"Yes," Tom replied, having no idea who was whom in the meeting, besides the few he'd come to recognize. "Thank you."

Unhkte continued, "Towtzaw comprehended as I did that your comments were not intended as threat, but simply due to ignorance."

What to say to that?!

Tom scrambled.

"Truly a misunderstanding," he submitted. "Absolutely no threat."

"Of course," Towtzaw said with a [dismissive] gesture. "Unhkte has shown you the hatchery and pit, I infer, and now you look upon the laying *Sootskee.*"

"Stop!" an overseer yelled, and kicked one of the quivering young.

Zero reaction from Towtzaw or Unhkte.

"You, stop!" from another overseer, who then plucked a long curved rod from the wall and thwacked a child in the head.

ANGELA: WTH? They're kids!

TOM: I know. Just don't say anything. Please.

"As you see," Towtzaw resumed. "This is where Sootskee are prepared."

"I have a question," Angela said via her Livetrans. Tom grabbed her wrist and glared at her. "For how long must the young be still like this?"

"It varies from generation to generation," Towtzaw replied. "Typically, no less than eighty days; no more than two hundred. Individuals incapable of preparation after so long are disqualified from *keepock.*"

TOM: Don't say another word. Step out if you need to.

"Eighty days?" Angela wasn't done. "This is how you treat your own people? I can't imagine what lesson a person learns from beatings and from being prevented from even moving."

TOM: Walk away, Angela. I'm begging you. You're alienating our only advocates.

Fortunately, in her rage, Angela wasn't even attempting to deliver associated gestures. No emotion was conveyed. To Towtzaw, Angela's comments were purely academic.

"Is it not obvious?" Towtzaw replied. "They learn to be *still.*"

Tom closed his eyes.

Crapshake.

"Thank you for showing us the Sootskee," Tom interjected, anxious to get Angela out of this place. "Best wishes with the current generation." He turned and pushed Angela out the door before whatever tirade she was surely writing spat from her PA.

Though oblivious, Towtzaw seemed intent on twisting the blade. "Significant leniencies compared to prior generations. Since retiring spiked prods, young Threck no longer wear the scars of prior generations."

"No such fortune for you or me," Unhkte said to Towtzaw, and ran a palm over her own faint keloid scars. "Are you certain about tonight? They're prepared?"

Unseen by either Threck, Tom slapped Angela's visor shut and pinched the PA speaker on her sternum between thumb and forefinger. He could feel in his fingertips the vibrations from her muted rant. His eyes pleaded as she yelled at him, her visor relegating her voice to a faint babble.

He fired off an M.

TOM: Do you HONESTLY think a foreign species can change a civilization's age-old practices by *yelling* at them? Control your emotions!

Unhkte stepped out of the doorway and looked at Tom, who held Angela behind his back.

An alarm whistle screeched from up high, in the distance. Unhkte looked to the sky and listened. It sounded as if it'd come from the top of the tower. The overseers at the mud pit shouted commands and sprang in with the young, who quickly quieted.

Towtzaw emerged from the doorway, bronze-tipped spear at the ready. She surveyed the nursery area. More whistles screeched in the distance.

"Where is it?" Towtzaw asked as more nursery workers appeared from somewhere at the end of the water pool, torches and weapons held out before them.

Everyone grew still again, waiting for more alerts. Finally, three toots sounded from the tower, followed by the same note, but prolonged a few seconds.

ANGELA: What's happening? Pablo and Zees
coming to get us? Aether and Qin?

Towtzaw and Unhkte appeared to relax. The other Threck, too, lowered their weapons and turned back from whence they came.

"The harbor," Unhkte said to Tom. "Only small number of raiders. Nothing for us to fear. Let us be off to our final—"

Towtzaw interrupted. "Is it prudent? Perhaps tomorrow instead?"

"We cannot keep them here overnight," Unhkte replied. "We must show them what they need to see, and send them back to the farms."

Tom looked at Angela and saw in her expression the same relief he felt. He released her and she remained quiet.

Towtzaw signaled reluctant acceptance and returned to her room.

Unhkte turned back to Tom. "Now we go to the sacred place. At the path's fork, I will signal you to begin silence. There can be no distractions for the prepared Sootskee."

"We understand," Tom said, set his gaze on Angela, and followed Unhkte back to the bridge. His gut felt heavy and taut. Never one to hold her tongue in the presence of a perceived outrage—even relatively minor wrongs—Angela was *especially* triggered by abuse of children and the defenseless. What if the next step in the Threck brand of child rearing was even worse than the last?

* * *

A pair of city guards accompanied Unhkte, Tom, and Angela beyond the northwest gate, outside the main city wall. One walked ahead of the group and the other picked up the rear.

Walking across one of the great mossy fields that surrounded the city ("parks" to the station crew, but cleared by Threck city builders purely for security), the party entered the jungle through a pair of seemingly random shrubs. Inside, the vegetation appeared unmaintained and untrodden, sparking a fresh bubbling of anxiety in Tom's gut.

After a few stream crossings, the guard behind Angela spoke up.

"Will we guards be allowed to observe the *keepock* ritual as well?"

Unhkte's motions indicated annoyance. "You will be present, but your attention should be on your duty, should it not?"

"Of course, Dowfwoss. Duty for certain."

Instead of a translation appearing for the term *keepock*, a link to the wiki appeared in Tom's fone. Definitely eager to know what was in store for them, Tom accessed Minnie's entry on the ritual.

> Keepock – Threck rite of passage consisting of single or multiple (never more than 4) youths aged 2-3yrs (prepubescent—human physequiv 6-10yrs), sent unsupervised to sacred arboreal circle 1.3K NNW of NW gate for 3 nights. Upon completion, youths are advanced from nursery to primary education. *INC.* Compound: *-kee* – as suffix, generally associated with Threck youth (ie *sootskee*, *setkee*, *eskee*); *kee-* – to-date unique usage as prefix sans *Es* (ie *eskee-*) is *keepock*. –pock – animal, self-mobilizing

> lifeform (erroneously inclusive of '<u>thratze</u>' *mykota glacius* "glacier shroom"), poorly defined as *thing which lives and moves of own power and intent.*

Relieved, Tom closed the wiki. While looking forward to bidding farewell to Unhkte, arriving at the rally point, and sleeping ... *oh, please tell me Zisa and Pablo setup more than just their own tents* ... he found himself oddly thrilled by a revelation. How many wiki articles could he correct, expand, or create based upon this day alone? And then the buzz deflated, spluttering off like a balloon. For what purpose? There was no more legion of eager scientists awaiting their periodic influx of Epsilon C data. Or rather, the legion still existed, but the conduit to them had been irrevocably destroyed. Earth wouldn't haven't the faintest clue of a problem for another three years. In six months, and for another twenty-plus years, full supply pods would brush past scattered station debris and probably explode while entering the atmosphere, raining extraterrestrial materials onto the oceans and surface.

An M from Angela.

> ANGELA: I'm sorry. And you know I don't *ever* say that crap. Forgive me?

She must have noticed his malaise and assumed she was to blame.

> TOM: Yes. Of course.

He felt her hand press into the small of his back.

"Now, we have reached the *last walk*," Unhkte said, halting at the beginning of a flagstone-covered path bordered with decorative hedging and unlit stand torches. A light breeze from the coast pushed the city's briny aroma to Tom's nostrils. The lead guard knelt down and opened a small box, extracted some tools and bits of kindling, and set to work lighting a small hand torch. "The prepared Sootskee must find their way here unaided. This is essentially symbolic custom, and the source of much debate. Does one become any less Threck if *guided* to this point? Certainly not, lest Eshkowoss Peekt's first Sootskee would be counted as such." Unhkte looked at Tom. "You know much of Threck, but I wonder if you know history. Are Syons People learned of Eshkowoss Peekt?"

In the Threck emergence mythology, as Minnie had explained on a few occasions, Eshkowoss Peekt was the Threck Adam … or Moses, or all of them combined—the very first Threck. The catalogued story, which Tom pulled up on his fone, recounted the tale of a mindless Threck ancestor getting lost in the jungle near what was now Threck City. She fell asleep—as most of these characters seemed to in *Earth-diver*-type creation myths—and while sleeping, received the gift of awareness from some sort of Mother Earth/Gaea-type God who resided within the jungle. Upon awakening, Eshkowoss Peekt looked on the world with new eyes and comprehension, then ventured forth to share this awareness with all the other dumb animals.

Given recent events, Tom opted to lie to Unhkte. "We do not. Please enlighten us."

Unhkte proceeded slowly up the path as the lead guard used the now-lit hand torch to ignite the first stand torch. "Yes, as we proceed. But I will be brief, as we will soon reach the fork, and must be silent for the duration." Tom agreed and followed along beside Unhkte as, little by little, the path before them brightened beneath the intensifying glow of rekindled torches. "Eshkowoss Peekt was one of many coast-dwellers, no wiser nor slower witted than any other," Unhkte began, the story sounding as though it would probably end up a wordier rephrasing of Minnie's version. "Meandering beyond the riverside dwellings for no particular reason, Eshkowoss Peekt began on this certain course. The path particulars are another source of debate among my colleagues, as if the journey shares relevance with the destination, thus this nonsense with the unguided portion of the walk. Night fell, and without the sun as guide, Eshkowoss Peekt lay down near this particular stand of trees, quickly falling asleep."

Unhkte stopped at the path's fork as one of the guards continued down the right trail, lighting more torches.

"We will wait here for the guard as I summarize. During the night, Eshkowoss Peekt was endowed with *kee*, sleeping through the second night, and then the next. On the third morning, Eshkowoss Peekt awoke, and *understood.* With memories of arriving upon this place from *two different directions*, Eshkowoss Peekt looked at the deep tracks leading back toward the coast and suddenly *knew*—so simply, so obviously—how to return to the coast dwellings. But there was also the memory of arriving from the opposite direction, the undergrowth, and Eshkowoss Peekt spread low, following this strange memory deeper into the thicket, whereupon she discovered a magnificent city surrounded by red flora."

Returning from the lit trail, the lead guard extinguished the hand torch in a water pot just off the path. "The Sootskee will have left the gate already, Dowfwoss."

Unhkte agreed, motioned for silence, and followed the lead guard up the unlit left path. This trailbed consisted only of dry dirt and the sporadic exposed boulder. Though subtle, the path's upward grade reminded Tom's calves and quadriceps that they had yet to recover from the earlier tower climb.

A few minutes later, the path ended at a bend. Tom followed Unhkte down a few rough steps into a small open bunker area, like an observation booth, built into the side of the hill. Piled stones served as low walls on three sides, and four knee-height boulders in a line near the longer wall served as seats.

Unhkte straddled one of the middle boulders and draped herself over it. Tom sat on the boulder beside Unhkte, but found his entire upper body looming well above the wall. He glanced at Unhkte, whose seemingly reproachful eyes steered him to the ground in front of the seat.

Tom turned to advise Angela on proper seating, but she was way ahead of him, tucking her feet in under her knees, and looking like a kindergartner at circle time. She smiled up at him and patted the dirt beside her.

ANGELA: Let's hope this is a quick show. I'm ready to eat, crawl into a tent with you, and sleep for a few days. I *really* hope someone comes to pick us up, though. I am *not* ready for a 20K hike.

TOM: Same here on all counts. Hopefully by now someone's noticed we're late coming home from work.

Settled in his seat between the boulder and low wall, Tom peered out at the view. The observation booth sat on a rise above a wide ravine set between two ridges. In the distance, the hills steepened and merged as they neared the peak of the rain-soaked Mount Tensakoss.

Tom caught Unhkte glance right, and followed her gaze. A small shadow crossed in front of one of the torches on the path, then another. Tom elbowed Angela.

They all watched as, one after another, the three Sootskee entered the ring, walked to the center, and picked up a thin branch from a pile. Each proceeded to the edge of the circle and began a rehearsed march around the perimeter, whacking their branches against every epsequoia trunk as they passed. Upon completing a circle, they lined up in a row on the left side of the circle and knelt low, spreading their arms and legs out until they lay as flat as possible—just as they'd done for months back at the nursery.

Tom heard the distinct sound of three different Threck eye sets hiding and popping up. Unhkte stiffened beside him and air began sucking faster through her siphons. One of the guards stepped into the space on the other side of Angela, pointing excitedly to the clearing. The other quickly emulated the first, and Unhkte threw up her arms for calm and silence.

Unsure what was so thrilling, Tom scanned the clearing for something more than unmoving Threck young. Sure enough, to the left of the Sootskee, three little creatures made their way through the ground cover, each on a course for a specific youth. He closed his bio eye and zoomed in. Wectworms. A common parasite in Threck Country, and creatures the Threck were known to avoid—even exterminate. Tom pulled up the wiki he and Zisa had created about them. As he'd thought, no new entries from Zisa, Minnie, or anyone else mentioning their inclusion in this ritual. It didn't make sense. Wectworms entered hosts through an available orifice, made their way to the brain (in Threck) or central nervous system (dalis, pikpiks, etc.), where they burrowed in for the long haul. The majority of hosts abandoned previous behaviors, compelled instead to find the nearest fresh-water source, drink until practically bursting, and then travel to the nearest wectworm colony. Upon arrival, and with little fanfare, the host lay down and presented their body for mass consumption. In the small percentage of recorded cases in which this last step did *not* occur, the outcome wasn't much better: death within 16 hours. Body eaten by some other lucky worms.

ANGELA: Those are those worms! The zombie ones! WTH?

So the question was, did Unhkte see the parasites approaching? Were the worms the source of the guards' excitement? Was being *infected* actually a part of the keepock rite of passage? Minnie definitely hadn't mentioned anything of the sort. It had to be some kind of discipline test. The Threck must have developed an extraction procedure, carried out before the youths became truly infected.

Indeed, and to Angela's horror (tightening death grip on Tom's right hand), the worms disappeared beneath the three Sootskee, and none of the children moved. Their eyes remained hidden. Unhkte's clubs came slowly together and turned upward.

LIVETRANS: [Contented approval]
ANGELA: This is sick.

TOM: I know. I appreciate you keeping it together. You, me, tent, soon.

ANGELA: Something's coming.

Tom looked up again and saw what she meant. Beyond the epsequoia ring, the tops of bushes thrashed about on course for the circle. He caught movement to the left and saw more commotion there—things moving beneath the jungle canopy. These must have been the Threck overseers, coming to yank those worms out before it was too late.

But Unhkte's shock nullified that idea. She sprang up to full height. "No! Raiders! Guards, get down there!"

An instant later, a naked Threck pounced from between two epsequoias, landed beside the unmoving children, and raised a large club over its head.

"No!" Angela stood and shrieked, but it did no good.

The club came down with all the Threck's strength, smashing the first Sootskee's head deep into the ground.

27

The blur of Skinny's running legs, the crack and breath static of Qin's frantic voice in Aether's ear module as they descended the slope, the open direct-connect request to Tom and Angela blinking in the air before her, shouts and screams—English and Threck, grisly crunches, alarm whistles, blazing jungle flames, coughing up the fire's lung-burning hydrogen chloride smoke, inflammatory and deadly for Epsy non-natives, "Visors! Close visors!", Angela's face—overwhelmed and terrified—Skinny grabbing, Tom resisting, dead Threck, dead Seekapock, more running and climbing and running.

Sweat pumped from Aether's pores, coursing in thin streams and sheets down her back, belly, inner thighs, and forehead. On autopilot, she followed behind Angela. Tom held Angela by the wrist; Skinny had Tom by an unfastened belt strap, like a leash. He'd given up protesting several kilometers ago.

Beside Aether, other Seekapock ran, nudging her and Qin along whenever they fell back. Her bio eye stung, but it wasn't a simple sweat sting. It was getting worse by the second, as was a similar burning around her fone eye. The inner lids and ducts.

"We need to stop," Aether said through her open channel to the team.

Tom hacked between desperate, wheezing breaths. "Tell … that … to this … guy."

"I can't go anymore, either," Angela rasped.

Aether sent a translation through her PA. "Stop. Now." But her volume was still low from earlier. She raised it close to max and resent.

Skinny halted at once and the team collapsed in unison.

"What is it?" Skinny said.

"Why stop?" another said. "Almost close."

Aether ignored the Seekapock. "Get your helmets off. We need to clean our faces and any hair that was exposed back there. Anyone else's eye burning?"

Angela, on hand and knees, grappled about her neck in search of the helmet release. Her voice quavered, deep in her throat—a faltering shot at bravery. "I can't open mine. Searing."

Qin's medic instincts took over. Still panting, he said, "Sit tight and no one rub anything." He crawled past Aether to Angela, patted her arm, and opened her backpack. "It's a good thing *you* two followed procedure." He pulled out the medkit, opened the flaps, and unfolded it on the crunchy mulch ground.

"Up now," Skinny said. "We go."

The other Seekapock paced about the spongy scrub, facing back toward the city.

"We have injuries, Skinny," Aether replied. "We can't move until fixed. Go on without us."

"Try to open them a little as I squirt," Qin said to Angela. "You'll be amazed how fast it's neutralized. Come on … just a peek. I'm starting with your implant—"

"I can't! Just hold on! Do someone else first!"

"Don't be stubborn," Tom said, rubbing Angela's side. "We can all at least open our eyes. If he doesn't get the acid out, it'll keep doing more damage."

"I know," she said, still squeezing her lids shut while curling into a fetal position. She reached up to rub her eyes and Qin pushed her hand back.

"None of that, now. It'll make it worse. Tom, can you …?"

Tom grabbed Angela's wrists and tried to roll her onto her back.

"Qin, Qin," Angela pleaded. "Qin, listen to me … Oh, come on, let go! Thomas, if that's you … I'm serious—"

Struggling through her own pain, Aether saw Qin's eyes blinking rapidly—his bio eye clearly more irritated than his fone lids. She pulled a medipad from the packet and wiped it across Qin's forehead. He flinched a little and looked at her, grateful. She flipped the pad and ran it over his closed eyes.

"Thank you," he said as he fought with a still-belligerent Angela to pry open one eyelid.

"I know I have to and I will!" Angela shouted, tilting her head side to side. "But you can't force me! It makes it worse! You *know* this, Thomas! I'm so kicking your ass! *All* asses!"

"This one is too loud," Skinny said. "Threck certainly coming. Make it stop. Not leaving Orange People. Go now."

Qin got her fone eyelids open and blasted neutralizer. "Yes! Now the other."

Angela snorted and stiffly rolled onto her back. She growled through clenched teeth. "Just let go of my damned arms, please." She stopped fighting and Qin was able to part the eyelids and squeeze in more neutralizer.

Tom slowly eased his grip until loose enough for Angela to yank her wrists free. Qin handed the bottle to Aether and wiped Angela's face and hairline with medipads. Aether passed the bottle to Tom.

"Did you get yourself yet?" Tom asked her.

"I'm fine," Aether said. "Get this stuff in there before you have corneal damage."

Tom accepted the bottle, brow knit. "Thanks, *Mom*." He leaned onto his backside, tilted his head back, and squirted the solution into each eye, wincing and blinking rapidly. "Oh man, it hurts before it doesn't."

Aether crawled around Qin and cradled the back of Tom's head, his chin raised to her like a small child. She smiled inside, hearing his "Thanks, Mom" repeat in her mind while carefully dabbing his eyelids with the pad corners. "Better?"

Tom nodded and grinned, the nurturing moment not lost on him. "It's really good to see you. You know, besides all the crazy and blood and whatnot."

She kissed his forehead. "Just need the rest of my babies safe, too. *All* of them." She released Tom's head and helped Qin lift Angela into a sitting-up position.

"Growing anger," Skinny said. "Go now. No say no."

Aether ignored Skinny and held Angela's face between her palms. "How we doing, mija?"

"It's not crying, you know," Angela said, half joking, as tears streamed out her still-shut eyes. "It's involuntary."

"Yes, yes, of course," Aether said, stroking her hair. "These are purely reflexive. Can you open the bio for me to have a quick look?"

"Not to contradict a physician," Qin said as he rose to his feet. "But she should keep it closed." He stuffed the medkit into Angela's pack before sealing it shut. "Nothing more we can do here. Ang, just hold someone's arm and use your fone for now, okay?"

Everyone helped Angela to her feet despite her protests. "I got it, I got it, I'm fine …" She slowly opened her fone eye, the other side of her face squinched up tight. "Do I look like I had a stroke? Or some old troll?"

"You look," Aether began, biting her lip. "There may be … *opportunities* for appearance tuning."

"Oh, that's good," Tom said. "I'm using that."

"Don't forget your helmets," Aether said as she lowered her own over her head.

Tom grabbed Angela's after sealing his own. "Want me to carry it?"

Angela scowled at him. "Oh, don't think everything's all hunky-dory here, mister. You can carry that, but it won't decrease the severity of your forthcoming ruin. Holding me down …"

"We walk, Skinny," Aether announced as they proceeded forward. "No more running for now."

"We fast walk," Skinny countered. "Run if hear Threck coming. Silence now."

Moments later, Aether received a group M from Tom, sent to all of them.

> TOM: We should probably debrief. Maybe one of you could start with who this "Skinny" is, where we're going, and what that mess was all

about. Angela and I made contact with the Threck council, toured the city, and were just being shown this rite of passage ceremony. I assume that attack was not on our Threck hosts' agenda, and the survivors back there probably think we're aligned with these other Threck.

ANGELA: Let's not forget the imprisoning part.

TOM: Thank you so much for the reminder, my love. There was a misunderstanding, a brief detention, and relations returned to normal.

ANGELA: Or the institutional child abuse.

Aether cut in.

AETHER: Okay, you two. We're a little more than 30 mins from the Seekapock camp (do *not* call them Threck). Let's stick to the essential facts as we sync up.

* * *

Upon exiting the partially starlit jungle into the dark, wide-open, wect-columned sanctuary, Skinny stepped beside one of two Threck torches—the area's only light sources.

She raised both arms in the air and shouted to the muddy masses of Seekapock.

"Victory!"

The crowd fell silent.

One of the others with them stepped into the light with a bundle fashioned from a cloak. She shifted her grip, clutching a single edge, and held it high, the front side falling away and a load of decimated worms dropped into the mud.

Cheers roared from the mob. Tentacles splashed and scrambled as they charged forward, fighting over the worms.

"No!" A shout from the far side of the space, near the only other torch.

Aether zoomed in and saw a small party of Seekapock, one of whom was missing most of an arm, the stump tied off with rope and coated in a muddy paste.

Eeahso tramped through the swarm, swatting obstructive heads and stomping on any limbs in her path. Her posse followed close behind.

"Eskinnee, you are the leader of all fools!" Eeahso said as she stepped close.

"I think not," Skinny said, laughing as she gestured to the dead worms. "No more Threck." Others briefly laughed, too, but Eeahso ended it with a look.

"Imick not for killing Threck," Eeahso said. "Imick for survival, for punishing Threck, for making Seekapock stronger, smarter. You have doomed all Seekapock back to the water."

"We punished Threck," Skinny said with pride and menace modifiers. "For real for first time. And we rescue two more Orange People before Threck make them Threck."

Eeahso looked over the group. "Which Orange People saved me from Threck?"

Skinny turned around and studied the human faces, comparing Aether and Qin, then Qin and Angela, settling on Angela. "This one! Qin! One of my first Orange People." Skinny thrust Angela forward from the group. Eeahso eyed her.

"I'm not …" Angela protested, her bio eye still squinty as she glanced back for help.

"Orange People have mighty throw weapons," Skinny said. "Good for Seekapock when angry Threck come looking for revenge."

"Precisely what comes to us," Eeahso said mournfully. "Even with Orange People weapons, we will not survive attack on land. Tell me, Skinny … tell all … when no more Threck, where do Seekapock get food? Where do Seekapock get trained *afvrik* and *minnit*? Will you keep fish bay filled? Will you train afvrik, grow food, sew garb?"

Skinny was still for a beat, then spoke quietly, with restrained gestures close to the body—a message not intended for the rest of the onlookers. "You say Seekapock *need* Threck for living?"

Eeahso said nothing. She reached across her and lightly probed the stump where her other arm used to be. Her eyes popped in and out, then she made a gesture normally delivered with two arms: "You and me talk later."

Aether finally grasped it all—the Seekapock, Threck, imick, all of it. This was supposed to be the base of some great revolution. Leaders like Eeahso rallied the masses with inflammatory anti-Threck speeches, us against them, fighting the good fight, etset. The Skinnys of the population sucked it up and ate it whole, driven to harass the Threck with raids, stealing fish and produce from the Threck farms, taking clothes and work animals. But Eeahso had created a monster she could no longer control, and with the worms, Skinny had delivered a devastating and irreparable blow to the Threck.

"Skinny," Aether said, and Skinny twisted halfway round to look at her. "What are the worms to the Threck?"

Skinny blinked and fidgeted—the same sort of confused motions from when they'd first met, underwater in the EV. "Worms to Threck . . ."

Aether rephrased, "Why do Threck care about worms?"

This, evidently, was clearer. Skinny's head remained still as her legs untwisted beneath her to fully face Aether. Skinny knelt down and plucked from the mud a squished worm carcass, holding it up before her.

"*This* is Threck. Worm is Threck. Inside. Understand?"

Tom stepped forward, stunned. "The worms go inside and stay in?"

Skinny turned to him. "Yes. Make Threck. You see Threck nursery—Sootskee and younger—Threck care nothing for these. These are not Threck. These are animals. Nothing important. These are things Threck keep alive until old enough to make more Threck."

Tom faced Angela, still standing beside Skinny. "That's what Unhkte was trying to explain to us. She was showing us the final step to become an *actual* Threck, not some rite of passage like a freaky bar mitzvah."

"Unhkte?" Skinny said. "You know Unhkte?"

Tom looked surprised, shocked that Skinny had understood something he'd said.

"We met," Tom replied through the PA once more.

"You meet Towtzaw? At nursery?"

"Yes," Tom said. "You know them?"

"Towtzaw, yes." Skinny said. "From nursery."

"Did you come from the nursery?" Aether asked Skinny.

"Yes. As most Seekapock."

Now, Aether thought, this connection between the two groups began untangling. Minnie had always said that the City Threck looked down on Sea Threck as primitives, as those people from the city who had decided to heed the primal call of ocean life.

"And you escaped?" Tom asked.

Skinny regarded him. "Some we save outside gate, before get to circle. Some are cast into river if never learn how is good Sootskee."

"Is that what happened to you?" Aether asked. "Did they throw you out?"

Skinny's eyes hid and emerged. She surveyed the Orange People, then looked behind her at the throngs of writhing Seekapock, guts filled, content in their mud and seemingly indifferent to the worms. Aether wondered if Skinny could feel disappointment, or rejection, or desolation.

"Wait," Tom's PA said to Skinny. "Did your people kill every single Threck worm?"

"Yes, and we burn worm house to kill eggs. No more Threck." Skinny dove backward into the mud pit, disappearing beneath the chocolaty surface, then climbed out, dripping, with a single, long stride. "We rescue Orange People before they become Threck. Now Orange People will help kill remaining Threck."

Aether rushed out a quick M to the group.

AETHER: Let me handle this.

TOM: They were NOT planning to put those worms in us.

Aether sent the message in sections, as she wrote. "Skinny, we are all grateful for your help. We wish to repay Seekapock with gifts and help, but Orange People do not kill. I hope you understand."

"Qin kill Threck," Skinny countered with a glance toward Angela.

Damn it, Aether thought. *Knew that would come back to us.*

"That was an accident, and to help save people in danger."

"Yes," Skinny agreed. "Seekapock in danger. Threck will come to kill many now, after what Skinny did. Orange People will save Seekapock in danger."

"No, Skinny. I'm sorry. I think you all need to flee to the water and hide in the underwater city you took us to."

"Threck know this place. No say no. Orange People will do as I say." She spun round and called out. "Swineese!"

Seekapock lounging along the mud bank popped up, looking, then grabbed weapons and began running around both sides of the oblivious mud pit occupants.

Aether noticed Tom's posture shift in her peripheral. He was readying for a conflict. She felt Qin's hand between her shoulder blades.

Tom replied to the group M.

TOM: Angela, move slowly away from Skinny.

"Listen to me, Skinny," Aether began.

"No more no!" Skinny yelled as reinforcements surrounded the team.

One of the Seekapock whacked Angela in the shoulder. Angela glanced back with a start and grabbed her MW, waving it at the three twitchy Seekapock behind her.

"Tom!" Angela shouted. "We're not going into another jail pit!"

Aether didn't know how to defuse the situation without agreeing to do whatever Skinny wanted. Maybe that was the key. She wanted to be honest, but it wasn't going to help right now. They'd agree to join *La Revolución* and then escape at the first, best, opportunity.

"Calm down, mija," Aether said as she wrote the capitulation message. "Put it away. Tom, Qin: hands off."

Like the others, Skinny's eyes were wild, bouncing around the scene as if tracking a super-fast fly. Angela still had the MW in her shaking hand, though now held low at her hip. Skinny's eyes suddenly fixed on Angela, and, in a flash, a tentacle swung out like a whip, swatting the MW out of her hand. Before the weapon even hit the ground, Skinny had her other arm planted on Angela's shoulder and kicked off the ground, mounting Angela's head. Aether cried out for Skinny to stop, to get off. She scrambled in her fone to send the half-composed message.

"Now, we understand the Seekapock struggle. We all agree to join the fight against Threck, and we will—"

Skinny wasn't listening. Her tentacles coiled around Angela's shoulders and arms, and tightened. Angela's helmetless head had completely disappeared beneath Skinny's body, and she dropped to her knees, hands flailing helplessly at her hips.

Tom bolted forward and grappled with the tentacles. He shrieked, "Get off! Let go!" and seized the utility knife clipped to his suit, flicking the short blade open. "I said get off!" he screamed, and swiped the blade across two coiled limbs. Skinny simply unwrapped an arm and whipped Tom in the face.

"Watch," Skinny said, and her body trembled for an instant before abruptly compressing, with a muffled crunch, as if an inflated balloon had popped inside her body.

Aether choked, "No …"

Angela crumpled to the ground as Skinny unwrapped herself. "Take their weapons!"

Tom gagged and emit a despairing little squeak as his knees buckled and gave way.

Seekapock grabbed Aether and Qin, wrapping arms low around the waist.

Skinny stood tall and walked before them, proudly. "Now here is one less Orange People. Now you help Seekapock kill Threck. You do what I say."

Aether glowered at Skinny. Eye and fone blurred with stinging tears, throat so dry and tight it felt like it would turn to dust and drop into her stomach, hands throbbing as they spread wide open at her sides, her locked elbows joined the protests blaring from the rest of her joints. Her captor tightened her grip, and Aether's fingers began numbing. She wrote to the beat of her pounding temples—one letter per jolt—until the message was complete.

"Now, we understand the Seekapock struggle. We all agree to join the fight against Threck, and we will happily do what you say."

Hysterical, and trapped in an endlessly cycling sob, Tom dragged himself to Angela's lifeless body, raising a tentative hand above her arm, hesitating there as if a touch might startle her.

Skinny displayed no outward skepticism at Aether's reversal. "Good. This is what I wish. Now, we will go to kill Eeahso and loyal four."

Aether stood and waited, still restrained by the Seekapock behind her. She glanced down at Tom. His MW remained in its holster on his hip. Behind her, to the right, she caught a glimpse of Qin in the same bind as her, but with fingers wrapped firmly around his holstered MW.

QIN: The second my arm is free I'm taking out that one.

AETHER: Not if I get her first.

Skinny stopped pacing and regarded Aether for a moment, as if there may be some source of concern when she and Qin were freed. "They let you free, what you do?"

"I follow Skinny to Eeahso and kill Eeahso. When you say."

Skinny pointed to Qin. "And this one. Do what I say also?"

"Yes," Aether assured.

Skinny peered down at Tom, face buried in Angela's side, muttering garbled words. Aether felt a new wave of panic.

AETHER: Tom, get up right now and pull yourself together. Fake it goddammit.

He didn't respond.

"This one wants that one not dead," Skinny said, pointing at Tom. "Will it want to kill Skinny?"

Aether could feel the tentacles at her waist slowly loosening, a tiny bit every few seconds.

"Absolutely not. Orange People do not think for themselves. We only serve our leader."

"You kill for leader. … Who is leader?" Skinny said with a [Thrilled] modifier: *I already know the answer, I want to hear* you *say it.*

"You are leader," Aether said. Skinny laughed, and Aether felt as though she could almost execute the murderous creature using only the power of malicious thought.

Skinny pointed at Tom, who lay deflated and hardly moving. "This one say who is leader. *Andela* say it."

Aether winced. "This one is *Tom.* Tom is asleep now and will not awaken until sunrise."

"Yes, Tom. I say this one may sleep." Skinny pointed over Aether's shoulder. "This one is Qin … then … *Andela* is dead one?"

Aether kept her eyes fixed on Skinny's. "Yes." She sent Qin the phrase before he was called to recite the pledge of loyalty.

Aether's arms gained more wiggle room beneath the Seekapock's light grip.

Skinny stepped before Qin. "Qin say who is leader."

Qin sent the message through his PA. "You are leader."

"Let them free!" the benevolent Skinny proclaimed.

The arms around Aether and Qin uncoiled, falling out of sight behind them.

Aether pumped her hands open and closed. "Let the killing begin."

28

Arms free, Aether wrapped her fingers around her MW, felt the rapid double-buzz confirming activation, and pulled it from the holster. A tap of the thumb engaged the lethal setting. She aimed as Skinny began walking away, spouting off magnanimous nonsense that rolled unread through Aether's Livetrans.

She sent Qin a last-minute order.

AETHER: Non-lethal on any others.

QIN: What why

AETHER: Because I said.

QIN: Fine

The multirounds left Aether's barrel at supersonic speed—three shots in the span of one second. Aether blinked upon firing, and as her eyes reopened, a cloud of blood, organ matter, and endoshell fragments had already sprayed out the other side of Skinny's face. The macerated body launched forward, legs yanked from the ground, arms flinging backward, trailing Skinny's descent toward the mud pit like streamers from a kite. A splash. Tentacles floundered and coiled reflexively.

Behind her, Aether heard rapidfire pulses from Qin's MW. She spun to see two convulsing Seekapock already on the ground as Qin dove with outstretched arm to reach a third, retreating guard. Two more on the right, near Tom and Angela, hesitated with bronze-tipped Threck weapons dithering before them. The tip of Qin's MW grazed one of the fleer's legs, and the shock could be seen traveling up the tentacle like a mouse scurrying through a tube sock. The beneficiary seized and joined her writhing friends on the ground.

Aether thumbed the toggle and sent a non-lethal round flying toward one of the still-faltering guards. As she'd hoped, the expanded projectile didn't break skin, impacting between the siphons with what probably felt like the force of a supersonic grape. Another one down.

"Drop your weapon!" Aether blasted from her PA.

The last remaining guard tossed the curved spear aside and thrust both arms down and out in a gesture of peace. In the distance, Aether heard the sounds of clanking metal. She peered out beyond the emptying mud pit—panicked Seekapock bathers running wildly from the scene—and saw that even the guards at the far side had given up their weapons, some joining the escaping masses, while others parroted the peace sign.

Aether's gaze returned to the frightened one in front of her. What now? She hadn't thought much about what would happen after killing Skinny. All advice from her beseeching conscience had been thrust aside, eclipsed by pain and rage and blood. Now, the voice of reason slowly emerged, a timid head peeking from behind a wall: *May I come out?* And Aether felt a rush of fear and doubt. What had she done? What would be the consequences? Again … what now?

She looked down at Tom and Angela. Tom's big hand rested on Angela's blood-matted hair. He stared up at Aether—mystified, lost—a shell-shocked child in the middle of a battlefield.

And then Aether's brain kicked in, like a spinning engine wheel catching on a gear, and clarity returned; options and next steps presented themselves, reorganizing into a bulleted list. Her ears reactivated. The docile Seekapock guard stood muttering untranslatable sounds as Qin held his MW muzzle close to her side, his eyes appearing to await some answer from Aether. Her focus returned to Tom and she held out her hand to him. He seemed to ponder the hand for a second, then reached up and took it, long legs unfolding beneath him, boots searching for traction—learning anew to stand in a world with no Angela. Fully upright, he swayed a moment until finding balance, rolling his red eyes and sallow face down toward Aether. A thick bar of Angela's blood stretched from one of his ears, across his cheek, to a small red circle perfectly centered at the tip of his nose.

Aether reached up and casually swiped away most of the blood with the back of her glove, then cradled both of his cheeks in her palms. "We're going to leave this place now, sweetie. Okay? You stay close to me." He blinked mechanically and nodded. She turned her head to Qin. "I'm so sorry, honey, but I need you to do something really difficult." Qin's face was already wracked, yet compliant. "I need you to take care of her … head, get her wrapped up, and carry her to our EV."

"I'll … Yeah, I can get her … *ready*, but, I don't know if I can, um—"

"I'll carry her," Tom said with a soft, shaky voice. Aether looked up at him. "It should be me anyway."

Qin used wraps from a medkit to cover Angela's head, then carefully slid on her helmet, attaching it to her suit and sealing the visor. He took her MW and utility belt, stuffing them in her backpack, and strapped it onto his back. All three helped to tenderly lift Angela up over Tom's shoulder. Tom wrapped his arms around her dangling legs.

Aether stepped in front of him. "You sure you can do this?"

He swallowed and nodded, determined.

She turned to the Seekapock prisoner, still standing stiff, eyes hiding every few seconds. It was time for the next step. "Do you know where Eeahso is?"

"Eeahso leave."

"Yes, I know. Do you know where Eeahso go?"

"Away."

Aether sighed. "Away to where?"

"No."

"You don't know, or you won't tell me?"

"No know."

"Do you know where Eeahso goes *sometimes*? Where Eeahso can sometimes be found?" Vapid eyes. Pulsing siphon holes. "Have you ever seen Eeahso at a place many times? Where Eeahso stays, rests, lives, hides—"

"Eeahso rest beach."

"Yes! Take us there. Now. Go."

Without hesitation, the Seekapock turned toward the mud pit, marching as if programed, in a straight line from the bank, splashing through mud, stomping over piles of fish bones, brushing through thorny, arm-slicing plants, as hiding Seekapock leapt, frightened, from cover, scurrying from the undergrowth. Aether had to call after her repeatedly to slow down until they finally reached the beach.

Arriving on the dune-covered shoreline, their steadfast guide cut left, scaled a sandy ridge, and halted, facing up the coast. The team trudged up the hill, finding at the top a panoramic view of the brightening horizon, low-breaking waves, and a lone EV nestled in a sandy rut.

Their escort pointed to the threshold of beach and jungle beyond the EV. "Eeahso rest."

Aether pointed, too. "Lead on. Go."

Along the sand bar they walked until it sloped down to the beach level, leading them right to the EV.

With no sign of their guide slowing, Aether turned back to a beset Tom. "Why don't you go ahead and set her in the EV. Think you can prep the skimmers for us?"

"Yeah," he said, and headed toward the sealed hatch.

Aether and Qin kept pace with the Seekapock as Qin called back to Tom. "Stay on guard, man. Maybe setup prox alerts, too."

Tom didn't reply, but he appeared relatively lucid.

Ahead, a pair of Seekapock huddled in wet sand, wrestling with a large, zeppelin-shaped shell. They shot looks at Aether and Qin as they passed.

"We catch! We eat inside!"

The pair returned to their labors, unconcerned with the passers-by.

The guide stopped a short stretch later, pointing to the dark space between a tall cone-shaped plant, and a three-story-high rock face. "Eeahso."

Aether flipped through optics, spotting a layer of discarded seashells and bones fanning out across the sand from the gap. Beyond the conical plant, her fone highlighted the distinctive outline of a one-armed Seekapock, eleven meters in from the entrance, lounging inside a small alcove in the rock, legs dangled over the edge. Aether could see no one else anywhere near the area.

"You can go," Aether told the lingering guide. She pointed farther down the beach, the opposite direction of the EV. "That way."

"Yes," she said, and traipsed off.

"Lethal or non?" Qin asked as he readied his MW.

"Non, but put it away. We're not here for a fight. We're here to try and avoid creating enemies in our new home."

"*We?* ... We're not! *They* are! Don't you think it's a little late?"

"Obviously, I don't. Put it away."

Qin sighed and holstered the weapon, though kept his hand resting on it.

Aether walked to the dark gap, crunching over shells and bones. "Eeahso? It's Aether and Qin of the Orange People. May we speak with you?"

A brief pause. In thermag view, Aether saw Eeahso's shape slowly rise in the alcove, legs drawing up from where they'd hung.

Aether took one step into the gap, opting for candor. "We killed Skinny. Skinny is dead." Still no reply. She could see one of Eeahso's arms reach above to another, deeper ledge in the rock, returning with a thick club. "You can put the weapon down. We aren't here to hurt you. When we refused to help attack more Threck, Skinny killed one of our people, then tried to order us to come help kill you." Aether didn't bother with the gestures Howard the Threck was demonstrating as Eeahso couldn't see her from around the passage's bend. She hoped the message was still clear enough.

She watched Eeahso's shape discard the club, climb down from the nook, and walk cautiously to the edge of the cone plant. One eye and arm end appeared. "You kill Skinny?"

"Yes. We refused to be involved with anymore killing. We stopped Skinny from coming to kill you."

Eeahso emerged a little farther, both of her eyes and siphons now visible. "You avenged death of Orange Person."

"That too."

"And what you want from me in return?"

"Only peace," Aether said, taking another step forward, her hands outstretched at her sides. "We're now leaving your beach and going to our own Orange People camp, far away."

Eeahso moved the rest of the way out from behind the bend. "Far from Threck?"

"Far from everything."

"Take me with you?"

"Uh …" Aether stammered aloud.

"Say what?" Qin said. "Is he asking if we planned to, or asking if he can?"

Eeahso went on, "Threck are coming. They care nothing for Seekapock, but they will see me dead for this. They will never stop hunting me."

Qin murmured, "Then why the hell would we want him with us?"

Aether pushed away her knee-jerk rejection of the idea and considered for a moment. She had questions. "You say the Threck don't care about Seekapock, but they know of you?"

"Yes. I've always limited the raids on Threck resources to ensure they didn't escalate from mere annoyances to intolerable harassment."

"Your speech sounds to be improving," Aether said.

"I speak to the level of the listener," Eeahso replied. "Orange People clearly have an impeccable handle on City dialect."

"No insult intended toward your people, but you seem much more intelligent than the others."

"That's because they're not my people," Eeahso said. "They're Seekapock. I am Threck."

* * *

Warm wind belted Aether's chest and neck, circulating into her helmet, around her sides and back, drying her sweat as her half-open suit flapped in the salty torrent. Beneath her skimmer, early morning swells and whitecaps zipped by in streaks. Yesterday, after streaking violently across the sky, her EV had drifted down and landed on this water—not far from this spot—with an anticlimactic clunk. She hadn't even seen a full day here, but she'd already lost one of her babies.

To her left, across 5K of open sea, Threck City's tower appeared as a misty, dreamlike painting. Within those walls lived people who could potentially help save her three loves beyond her reach. But why would the Threck possibly assist after the previous night's atrocities? And without their aid, what was the backup plan for rescuing Ish, John, and Minnie?

Aether glanced at the transparent floor panel behind her. Eeahso was still losing it—siphons pressed up, fogging the hatch, as tightly confined tentacles writhed around the corners. She looked like an octopus crammed in an ill-fitting aquarium.

You said you wanted to come, Aether snarled inside. *You who created Skinny the monster.*

A tone sounded from the skimmer's panel.

SP: 110 – DTD: 5K – ETA: 2:58

ALERTS: Direct Connect request from Pablo.

The instant they'd entered range … Pablo must have setup a constant ping. Aether accepted.

Qin's voice in her ear, "DC from Pablo."

"Yup, got it too. Let me answer."

She sent Pablo an M:

AETHER: Team inbound to rally point. < 3 mins. We have a casualty and a "guest."

PABLO: Got it. Prepping for trauma inbound.

PABLO: Who? And what/how?
PABLO: As many details as you can provide.

AETHER: Angela. No prep req. We lost her.

PABLO: Just get here fast.
PABLO: How long flat vitals?

AETHER: No, sweetie. She's really gone. I'm sorry.
AETHER: < 2 mins.

Aether gazed to her right. Qin stood at the other skimmer's helm. At Qin's feet, she could see only Tom's legs extending out from behind the curved, opaque windshield. Angela's body sat on the opposite side of Qin, out of view. Tom had wanted to sit with her, but the skimmer would've struggled with balance. Aether felt as though Tom's anguish was reaching out through the air between them, breaching her flesh, and wrapping around her already-crushed heart, squeezing the last bits of life from it.

PABLO: Tom?

AETHER: Shattered of course. Residual shock, imminent guilt, rage. He's going to need you, okay? We can't lose him too.

PABLO: Yeah
PABLO: And I'm here for you, too.

Aether clenched her jaw and squeezed her eyes shut—another shot behind the ribs. She knew what she was trying to do with her feelings, and she knew it was typical behavior—especially for a shrink—but it was a grueling fight to discard the sudden misguided anger toward Pablo.

She drove past the pain and hammered out a scratchnote.

He didn't create my feelings by acknowledging them.

She read each word and swiped it to the archive.

A deep breath. The camp in view. Descent. Touchdown. Pablo's face, Zisa's tears and snot, Eeahso whining about the flight, Tom's daggers in return.

"Why'd we have to bring it?" Seething, Tom stepped right up to Eeahso. Rage had definitely taken shock's place.

"Step away, Tom," Aether said, moving between him and the stumbling Eeahso. "Help with Angela." Saying her name worked. Tom's face flinched as if a housefly had grazed his nose. "Go on, sweetie. Let me handle this."

He complied, his eyes once more glassy as they rolled toward Pablo's outstretched arm.

"Come on, man," Pablo said as they walked away. "Let's take care of her … figure out everything she would've wanted."

Aether pivoted to Eeahso. "Is there anything I can get for you before we talk? Water?"

Aether's cold manner was lost on the uneasy outlaw.

Eeahso's eyes tracked Tom and bounced around the scene of EVs, skimmers, work and sleep tents, and other gear. "Water … water, yes. And shade. Where are we?"

"This is where we're staying."

Herself unfamiliar with the lay of the land, Aether surveyed the area, a relatively dry plateau with steep, grassy slopes on two sides, and few sources of natural shade. Back toward the tents, Qin and Tom carried Angela's body on a stretcher as a blubbering Zisa looked on, shooting glances Aether's way. Aether knew what Zisa yearned for—she wanted to come running, bury her face in Aether's front, be embraced, soothed. But Aether couldn't be *that* for Zisa right now. Her stress level at max, Aether could hardly withstand a creeping resentment toward her most fragile girl.

"Is there water here?" Eeahso said. "River or sea, it matters not."

Aether set her eyes on the Threck. She changed her mind about hospitality. "Water later. First we talk." She walked to the base of the steep rise on the camp's west side, shaded from the rising sun. A flat-topped hunk of bedrock made for a good seat. Eeahso opted to stand, skittering nervously, as if on hot sand. "First, explain why you were exiled from the city."

After a series of eye hides and false starts, Eeahso explained. "There was time when Threck believed that *kee* came from our maker, who painted red this small place in the jungle, her tiny eggs laid out to then spread and enter every dumb animal."

"*Kee* … the worms."

"No, the *kee*. Worms are dumbest animal of all." Eeahso alternated swiping at her arms. "This is a dreadful, dry place—"

"Are the *kee* not the worms we saw enter the youths—the Sootskee—at the tree circle? The worms Skinny killed and displayed to your people?"

"No, no, no." Eeahso signed frustration. "These are *threckee* … Worms imbued with *kee*."

Aether, too, grew impatient. "Very well, how are worms imbued with *kee*?" She opened the Threck language DB in edit mode, preparing to add entries.

Must every damned word include "kee"?

"They eat it from the *fshkee*, behind the *keepock* place, where it grows. Orange People do not know most basic creation of Threck? Surely it is same for Orange People. How do you acquire your *kee*?"

She added keepock:Tree Circle to the DB.

"We're born with it, I guess. Forget about Orange People. You're saying that worms eat this stuff, this *kee*, which they then pass on to the young Threck?"

Eeahso signaled continuing frustration and disbelief while her eyes roamed beyond Aether. "I must have water at once. I cannot go on without."

Aether sent an M to Zisa.

AETHER: Can you please bring an open container of water to me?

"Water is coming. Now, forgiving my extreme ignorance, explain as if to some person from another world—some world without Threck or *kee* or worms."

"Worms live all over. Infect animals. Make them die. *Kee* grows on plants. Lives in one place only: the *fshkee*. Worms living near *fshkee* eat *kee*. Change to smart worm: *threckee*. *Threckee* cooperate, live in worm city, send baby worms to eat *kee*, make more *threckee*, worm city grows—"

The kee is a fungus, Aether grasped. *Parasitic worms are taken over by parasitic fungus. Hyperparasitism.*

kee:Parasitic Fungus [USE kee fungus]
fshkee:Parasitic Fungus Site [USE kee fungus site]
threckee:Infected Worm

"And this worm city is what Skinny burned?"

"Yes ... No ... I don't know. Unimportant. We say city, but this is really house on ground. Walls, tunnels, egg cave. We say smart worm, but this is still dumb animal. It is only when the three dumb animals become one, inside the body of the young Sootskee, that truly smart animals are made. Threck. I disbelieve Skinny destroyed entire worm city or got to eggs, but this is unimportant.

"Worms are everywhere, but they are not Infected Worm without *kee fungus*. Skinny burned the *kee fungus site*, which means no more worms can be made Infected Worm, and with no new Infected Worm, there can be no new Threck. Threck City will die when the last of the Setkee have grown old and died."

Aether sat back in awe. *The miracles of nature. The series of events that had to fall into place ... Three-stage parasitism.*

Aether recalled Earth's "zombie ants," spiny ants in Thailand that wake up one day to find themselves compelled to travel to a specific destination. The culprit turned out to be a fungus—one of thousands of varieties all over the world that infect certain indigenous insects, from ants to bees. After the fungus took over, the spiny ant would make its way to a location with precise conditions—the underside of a particular leaf, 25cm from the jungle floor, pointed north-northwest, and at a fixed time: solar noon. There, the infected ant would bite down on the leaf's main vein and wait to die a horrible death—the fungus building up massive pressure within the head, and then exploding out its spore stalk, like some ghastly jester's hat.

According to Eeahso, the *kee*, which the Threck considered their souls, infected its neighboring parasitic wectworms, but unlike its malicious Earth equivalent, the *kee* fungus *improved* its hosts. The worms had been upgraded from fend-for-yourself individuals to a nest-building colony.

Cooperate, Aether thought. *Threck always talk about cooperating.*

What if one of Earth's "zombie fungi" had happened to infect a parasitic insect, like tapeworms or blood flukes—organisms known to reach the human brain?

Zisa arrived at Aether's side, sniffing, with a large bowl of water.

Aether took the bowl. "Thank you. I'll come see you later, okay?"

Zisa nodded and left as Eeahso rushed forward, carefully grabbed the bowl, and dumped the entirety against her siphons. It looked to Aether that perhaps a quarter of the water had gone in, the rest splashing and dripping away.

"More," Eeahso demanded. "I need more."

"Later. Now, you were going to tell me about your exile."

AETHER: Zisa, what's our water status?

ZISA: 3 drums/600 L. The lake is close when we need more.

"Yes, my people formerly believed that the *kee fungus* was purposeful and for all. Many Threck thought it imperative to give to other animals. They collected animals from all over Threck Country and the sea, failing every time to see results. Perhaps it was the Infected Worms not working inside these other animals. Surely the worms had been infecting Seekapock for as long as there were Seekapock, and also other animals, but only certain of these were made smarter, and not much smarter. *Afvrik* given Infected Worms: nothing. But *afvrik* given only the *kee fungus* alone, these *afvrik* could be trained.

"The Special group did this work. They received permission to open dead Threck and see how Infected Worms lived inside. They opened other animals and compared. They collected *kee fungus,* by itself, from the *kee fungus site*, and gave to the young Sootskee, wishing to know if worms were necessary to make Threck. These *kee fungus*-infected people are the farmers now—*most* of them, that is, as offspring do not inherit the *kee fungus* from parent. The farmers, you may notice, are not so wild as my Seekapock you met, but not so smart as Threck. Threck train the farmers like they train *afvrik,* to do work in places no Threck wish to live."

"And you believed all of these experiments were wrong?" Aether guessed.

"Wrong? Wrong as with rules?"

"The testing, the farmers … You thought it shouldn't be done? That Threck had to change?"

Eeahso signed confusion. "No. Why change?"

"Forget it. Continue. How did all this lead to your exile?"

"One of my experiments was to determine if Threck could have two Infected Worms inside, thus becoming doubly smart. This was not unheard of experiment. Our leader, Amoss, attempted to insert *kee fungus* directly into several of us, with no effect. Long before me, Threck had gone to lay in the Tree Circle, but the Infected Worms disregarded anyone already imbued with *kee fungus*. I continued to the logical next step: I consumed Infected Worms."

"And you were caught."

"Caught? This was not in secret. I announced my plans and performed the experiment before Amoss and others in my group. Only after many days passed without success signs did Amoss inform others. The council reacted as if I had killed someone, and Amoss put stop on all experiments with *kee fungus* or Infected Worms. Days passed without event before I was forced to leave—I, the one to absorb blame and punishment for all of the group's members, for all of the group's actions."

"Well," Aether replied. "Your *new* group really got them back, didn't they?"

Eeahso considered this unironically. "Yes, but the outcome for all is bad."

"You believe the Threck council will have you hunted down and killed. How do you think they would respond if I—if Orange People—went to them and explained that you weren't involved? That it was only Skinny responsible, and that *you* executed Skinny for this offense?"

The layer of water on Eeahso's skin and cloak had mostly evaporated. She was growing antsy and distracted once again. "I don't know if Threck believe things Orange People say."

"Assume they do. Would it matter? Would they still need person to blame, to present to the population in same way they did with you and your group's experiment?"

This idea seemed to strike Eeahso, her eyes bulging as her arms signed newfound recognition, her thirst and discomfort forgotten. "Orange People are smarter than Thinkers! This is remarkable ability, seeing all choices—"

"Yes, fine, what is the answer? I need to return to my tasks."

"This is what they will want most," Eeahso said with enthusiasm. "A liable wrongdoer. This is truly wise thinking, connecting past acts to present context."

"So if we drop Skinny's dead body on Threck City's theater stage, that will be enough?"

Shock and confusion returned to Eeahso. "This would not be effective. This would only confuse … Dead body from the sky like rain …" She glanced at the nearby skimmers. "What holds the flying things off the ground? What carries it—"

"Obviously, we would not drop the body on the city and fly away. I meant that if we give them Skinny, explaining what happened, as I said before, they would accept this and peace with Orange People could resume?"

"And me," Eeahso added. "It is possible, peace."

Minutes later, Aether stepped up to Pablo, squatting before compression bags filled with linens. Aether watched Pablo's eyes shift from the bags, to Aether, to Eeahso as she arrived at Aether's side. Spellbound, he stood up.

"I have a task for you," Aether said, and Pablo's eyebrows snapped up. Aether turned to Eeahso. "This one is called Pablo. He is going to experiment on you."

* * *

Warm wind gusts surged at the team's backs, intensified by the cliff edge behind them, then streaming over the peninsula's flat surface, before returning to the open air of a large bay. On a low pile of non-toxic branches and bark, Angela's body lay wrapped in a white cotton sheet. From the crew's perspective on slightly lower ground, she appeared as a glowing giant, stretched out across the island's northeast mountain range as the sun set somewhere beyond.

Aether tried to remain present as a jumble of thoughts and worries and emotions assaulted her brain. She tried to listen intently as Pablo read the words everyone had sent him, but she kept thinking that the current sentence was the last, and that Qin would then light the pyre, and Angela would begin to burn away to nothing. Aether wished they'd buried Angela, but Tom had insisted she didn't want it—that she'd always been terrified of being eaten by little things. She'd alluded once or twice to her ashes.

Aether wondered if she'd be able to sleep. She thought about tomorrow, returning to Threck City. She wondered what Minnie was doing at that very second. And John and Ish, too, of course ... of course ... Because, of course, all of them were still alive, and doing things.

Zisa snorted out a sudden laugh and sniffed as Pablo read Qin's prepared words. "'... or complained about the sappiness of any of our tributes, and if she could right now, she'd probably shoot a horribly inappropriate M to only Pablo'—to *me*—'to make *me* laugh at the worst possible moment...'"

Aether stroked Tom's back as he wept quietly beside her. She glanced behind him to the unnatural glow from their camp, down the hill. What was Eeahso up to? Aether had warned her that if she touched anything, they'd boot her off the cliff, and Eeahso appeared to believe it.

Tom had taken to conspicuously ignoring Eeahso's presence. He'd never been the violent type, even under the worst duress, but Aether didn't feel good about leaving the camp with both Tom and Eeahso there. More importantly, she needed Tom with her in Threck City. He was the one that established first contact, built a rapport with key individuals, and knew from experience what verbal pitfalls to avoid. In less than twelve hours, she and Tom would audaciously request help—*tremendous,* unmerited help—from people who may currently wish them all dead. And for this feat, she would rely on a delicate, grieving, potentially hateful Tom.

Aether felt Tom's back shift and tense. The pyre had been lit.

The team watched in silence as the flames quickly grew, stoked by the blustery wind. On Aether's left, Qin joined Zisa and Pablo, standing arm in arm. Aether curled her hand around Tom's waist, pulling him tighter to her side, as she wrapped her other arm around Qin's back, joining all five into a single line. Angela's sheet caught, and the flames rose madly into the air.

29

As Eeahso predicted, Skinny's mud-soaked carcass lay undisturbed in the pit where they'd left it, the entire area deserted by Seekapock. Eeahso had confidently proclaimed the clan would be in the undersea fortress—a site she'd persistently branded as safe haven to her flock.

Later, substantiating the Threck exile's third presumption, the city's harbor was abuzz with activity. Four colossal afvrik floated in a line along one of the artificial jetties, their amber-hued shells lying motionless above the surface like a string of sandbars.

Aether slowed the skimmer and veered right toward the assembled Threck as they waited to board. The maneuver certainly caught their attention. Arms whirled and flailed like the cilia of a giant Threck hand. A dissonant, seabird chorus rose from the crowd as Aether swung the skimmer left, zoomed over the walled fish enclosures, and landed in the wide dirt field outside the southeast city gate. The alarm whistles were already blaring.

"Here we go," Aether said to Tom, and he sprang into action while Aether kept an eye on the gate and harbor.

With a look of abject disgust, Tom unclipped the tie-downs, freeing Skinny's limp body, and kicked it toward the edge of the pad. A runny mud streak traced the path. The flaccid heap did not exactly *fall* over the edge as much as *pour*, piling up a short distance below with the sound of splattering vomit. It was difficult for Aether to reconcile the blob in the dirt with the first non-human, intelligent lifeform she'd met.

Tom grabbed a passenger grip. "Clear."

Aether twisted the lift throttle and brought the skimmer up to five meters. "This should be well out of reach, right?"

Tom peered over the side. "Not if they start throwing stuff."

"Well, hopefully we can avert that." She set the skimmer to hold, released the controls, and nodded to the opening gate. "Here we go."

Armed Threck streamed from the corridor, fanning out in every direction. Aether glanced back as small squads of guards around the fish bay performed a well-practiced maneuver, splitting up and reassembling at the bay's two exposed sides. Threck from the gate had traversed the field, half now passing the skimmer (without getting to close), and circling around in two organized ranks.

"Do they ever throw those things?" Aether asked, referring to the bronze-tipped staffs.

Tom's fatigued eyes surveyed an area of troops. "Not that I've seen. Only melee use … Then again, one could always improvise—hey look, some folks hanging back at the gate. I'd say that's your audience."

Tapping at the console, Aether fed her Livetrans output through the skimmer's more impressive PA. She turned back to Tom before sending her first prepared announcement. "*Sy-onz* People?"

"Yeah … like science … it's all in there. You merged our DBs, right? I can talk to them if you really need me to. You know, it's just—"

Aether shook her head. "It's fine." She eyed once again the hundred or more Threck surrounding them. "You're on lookout."

Aether crouched down and clutched the handle in the floor at her feet, raising the booster platform used by shorter pilots. She stepped up onto it, rolled her shoulders to stretch, and sent the message.

"Peaceful greetings, Threck friends. Two nights ago, barbaric atrocities took place during your sacred keepock ritual." A few figures emerged from the shaded gateway, gesturing as Aether's message continued. "This offense was planned by one raider, who then ordered dumb, misguided followers to execute the plan." The waving Threck from the gate—not quite so fast as the guards—plodded nearer, their waves more evidently gestures. "In the interest of ongoing peace and relations between us, we Syons People bring this villain to you, dead, killed by—"

"I think you need to pause," Tom interrupted. "None of these people know what you're talking about."

Aether paused the reading at once. "As in, don't understand because I'm saying it wrong, or that no one knows?"

"Look." Tom pointed at the parting circle of guards in front of them, the three Threck stepping inside the ring.

LIVETRANS: No more.
LIVETRANS: Come in.
LIVETRANS: Come follow. Talk inside.

The three halted below them, regarding Skinny's corpse with vague interest before peering up. One of them reached out with both arms, feeling the air beneath the skimmer as if some invisible pedestal supported it.

LIVETRANS: What holds it?
LIVETRANS: What is it on?

Aether turned to Tom, hands on the console as he leaned over it to see below. "They want us to go with them inside."

"Yeah, I got that. I think that's what they were saying all along. Before they heard anything we had to say."

"So what do you think?"

Tom shrugged. "That I'm not big on you being around any of them."

"If they're willing to help us cross the ocean, I'm going to be spending plenty of time with them. You said yourself that some were reasonable, and we know now why they freaked out about your description of how antibiotics work."

"Right."

"So the question is," Aether said. "Do you trust that they only wish to talk? That this isn't some trap?"

"Honestly, I don't think they're capable of lying, or at least successfully. They seem unable to conceal their feelings. Subconscious body language. Just send the second section and watch."

Aether leaned over the console to see the beckoning Threck below. "We wish to speak with Dowfwoss Unhkte, who was present during the tragic event—" The three launched into a new flurry of gestures, pointing back toward the gate.

Aether looked up and saw a Threck form standing just inside the doorway. "They're pointing at the entrance. Do you happen to recognize that person?" Aether zoomed in and her lighting auto-adjusted. As if only a meter away, she could see the Threck figure (and a few others, deeper in the shadow), eyes inebriated, head adorned with scars of varying size, a few little divots missing from her siphons' outer edges, and cloak adorned with purple trim.

"That's Unhkte," Tom said upon inspection. Aether thought she heard a spark of relief.

"Great, but I don't like that we're still surrounded by armed guards."

"Maybe tell them to leave?"

Aether looked at Tom. He shrugged. She returned focus to the emissaries below. "Send away these guards so that we may come down to talk."

The three conversed briefly with no attempt at secrecy, and ordered the guards to disperse. In an instant, the troops split into four groups, one heading for the harbor, two toward either side of the field, and one toward the gate.

Aether tapped her fingers on the panel and chewed the inside of her cheek. "They could just be waiting for us inside. We don't have time—and I don't have the patience—for even a brief detention." Tom only nodded absently. She studied him. "Hey, if something starts going down, you can't start shooting people. We're all stuck here."

"You made that clear earlier. I'm not some psycho, you know."

She reached out and pulled him against her, hugging tight. "I know that, hon. I'm just nervous about this whole situation, okay?"

He nodded sheepishly and gently pushed away from her. "Not in front of the aliens, Mom." She saw a small, fleeting smile curl into his cheek, and she felt for the first time that he would one day recover.

"Sorry." She sucked in a deep breath, checked their surroundings once more, and brought the skimmer down close to the gate and main wall.

Unhkte stepped out into the sunlight. "I had questioned Amoss's eyes when describing your cloud machine." She extended an arm to touch a handrail, but stopped before making contact. "Truly your powers are beyond our comprehension." Aether stepped down from the platform, followed by Tom. Unhkte regarded both of their bodies and faces. She then set her eyes on Tom. "Welcome back, Tom. Who is this you've brought with you?"

"This is our leader, Aether."

Unhkte turned to Aether. "*Eether* … is that so? This is enticing and disturbing name. Come inside. We have much to discuss."

* * *

Through empty halls and busy arcades they walked as Unhkte recounted the events of two nights ago. A single Setkee and guard followed behind, but without weapons.

"It was clear to me that your people were as surprised and upset as we …"

TOM: I looked it up. "Eether" is their word for "the layer of mucus that forms outside the egg cavity at the beginning of a reproductive cycle." That's the stuff we thought might be the vessel for genetic conjugation, along with mud. If you were wondering.

AETHER: That's great. "Enticing and disturbing" indeed.

Unhkte spoke constantly as they walked. "… convinced the Council that our people's future interrelations would best be conducted by the Thinkers, who, I note, are tense and delighted in anticipation …"

Aether was growing concerned with how deep into the city they were walking, now having traversed a bridge and climbed three tiers. She'd hoped to step inside the gate, sit down, and talk—the exit and skimmer within reach if demanded.

"Apologies, Dowfwoss Unhkte, but could we stop somewhere nearby and begin our talk? We wished to address three important subjects."

"Of course," Unhkte said without a break in stride. "Our chamber is just this way."

They rounded a columned corner and were struck with an awe-inspiring view.

TOM: We've never seen this. Not even in the maps.

Like some warped Roman hypostyle, enormous stone columns stood like ancient redwoods. Arranged in two curved, parenthetical rows, they jutted straight up from gray bedrock, and, at their tops, held a single afvrik shell as roof. The builders had cut a circular skylight into the shell center, evoking some impossibly huge Threck endoshell. Outside of the enormous columns, still-impressive rows of standard Threck pillars lined the room's outer edges, large canvas panels stretched out between them as walls, with archetypal historical murals painted on their inward facing surfaces.

Following Unhkte between the oversized columns, Aether noted the cuboid plinths between each—pedestals for various artifacts. The bonded skeleton of an intimidating, dolphin-sized fish; a petrified, bisected fungus trunk with bored-out tunnels, as if from termites; a giant flatworm, two meters long and hanging from a frame, its underside sliced with an X and pinned open, exposing internals. It appeared to be coated with some shiny preservative.

And then, the preeminent treasure of the collection, suspended by several lines between the last pair of columns: an immense Hynka skeleton. Like a dinosaur museum exhibit, the beast had been reassembled and posed as if frozen mid-attack—long, crocodilian jaw open just enough to show off its inner rows of teeth, thick arm bones stretching out before it as if some juicy prey floated a hair's length out of reach.

Aether stopped in front of it, daunted by the thought of her loved ones in a land swarming with these killing machines.

"Hard-fought prize from distant land," Unhkte said.

Aether snapped out of her daze and saw Tom and the others waiting for her. She replied, "Hynka Country, correct?"

"Have you been there?" Unhkte asked.

"Not me, but some of my people are trapped there as we speak. It's one of the subjects we wish to discuss."

Unhkte stepped to the skeleton and ran her palm down the star-shaped kneecap. "If they are not floating in the sky on one of your cloud things, your people are undoubtedly dead. We lost seventy Threck before capturing this one."

"We have some unique survival skills," Aether said. "How did you catch it?"

"Food trap, set near beach. After several failures—too many for this mere prize, I say—they attached immense rope chain to submerged afvrik, placed captured prey animals in middle of netted circle, and waited. They didn't wait long. Many came bursting from the jungle, and the afvrik was ordered to swim out to open sea. This one was not caught, so much as it refused to let food escape. It clung to the retreating rope, dragging through crashing waves, all the time tearing at the net, stuffing freed rodents under mouth, in neck space, to hold. Even as it plunged deeper and deeper, it refused to forfeit its meal. Finally, it filled with water and died. The joyous Threck towed the thing all the way back across the sea, fending off attacks from sea predators that wished to steal the hard-earned prize. Upon their return, Eshkowoss Peekt ordered it studied, then to be displayed in this way, with the other unique creatures our people have found. Our founder, and subsequently *we*, believe there are groups of related animals. This worm, for instance, shares nearly every internal—"

Baffled, Tom cut in. "Eshkowoss Peekt? The very first Threck?"

"Yes, the first."

Tom continued. "How long ago was this?"

"Not so long ..." Unhkte considered, and turned to one of the other Threck with them. "Were you Setkee then?"

The Threck signed recollection. "Soon after. In my second wind."

Unhkte calculated, "Approximately eighty-eight years."

Tom shared a stunned look with Aether. "Eshkowoss Peekt was still alive eighty-eight years ago?"

"And today," a new voice spoke nearby, thick and husky, "to disdain of learned colleagues."

Aether spun round to see a pair of deep purple curtains, hanging from roof height, and parted at the bottom. Between them, two Threck stood holding between them a sort of litter, and spread across its wide surface lay a dark, bloated Threck—Eshkowoss Peekt.

Unhkte sprang forth with previously unseen vitality, striding across the room to the curtains. "You came! Will you remain? We can have your bath brought at once."

"No, no, stop. Let visitors come close. Certainly day stubborn body awaited. Bring. Heard only wondrous voice uttering words created."

Livetrans was struggling with the elderly Threck's speech.

"Yes," Unhkte said with cheer. "*Your* words."

Already walking from the Hynka display, Aether and Tom marveled at the giant Threck spread across the litter's flat platform.

TOM: This makes no sense. This is supposed to be the *first* Threck.

AETHER: Maybe like a reincarnated pharaoh? Someone new inherits the title and name after the previous one dies? In their case, what if the original parasite is actually transferred to a new host body?

TOM: That's actually not a bad theory. Let's see.

Unhkte gestured to a spot directly in front of the city's supposed founder and Aether and Tom stepped up, shoulder to shoulder. The aged Threck's wide eyes were marbled spheres of creamy yellow and brown, with hundreds of splintering cracks across the surface, like shattered glass.

"Smell," Eshkowoss Peekt said, one meaty club rising feebly to gesture. "Can touch?"

She'd lost the ability to sign, thus the stunted translations. This was how Livetrans speech would come across to the Threck if Aether omitted gestures.

Unhkte turned to them, affecting a more formal speech. "Syons People, Aether and Tom, you are standing before the parent of all Threck, Eshkowoss Peekt, who has exhausted the sense of sight. Would physical touch examination be acceptable?"

Tom's PA announced a response before Aether could answer. "No. No touching."

Aether glowered his way. She understood his reasoning—the fears behind it—but that sort of rejection could damage their attempt at friendly relations, and more critically, the chances of securing Threck help. He refused to look at her, resolve stamped on his face.

Aether sent a more tactful response. "Tom has sensitivity to touch, but I would be honored to be examined by Eshkowoss Peekt."

"No, you won't," Tom said aloud, then echoed via Livetrans, "No, she won't."

"Stop this now, Thomas," Aether growled. "She's a frail, old lady, and you are *condemning* our friends to *death*. Don't say another word."

Tom's chest shuddered as his face contorted from anguish to dogged obstinacy to desperation.

Unhkte cut in. "If there are concerns of disease, Eshkowoss Peekt merely bears the burdens of age. All of those fortunate enough to receive this gift of touch receive no consequences in return, all present included." She gestured to the two litter bearers and others behind Tom and Aether.

"Our apologies," Aether said. "We have no such fears. Tom simply finds the honor so high—an undeserved gift." Aether stepped forward on one foot to kneel before Eshkowoss Peekt. "You may proceed—"

Tom grabbed her arm, pulling her back. "No."

Aether clenched her fists, tiny explosions firing behind her eyes. She shouldn't have brought him! Why did she bring him? What was she thinking? Protect Eeahso? Screw Eeahso! Minnie, John, and Ish were her priority!

"*I* would like to accept this honor," Tom declared as he removed his helmet and took Aether's place, kneeling before the aged foremother.

Unhkte looked on with approval as an aide guided Eshkowoss Peekt's brawny appendages—first one, then the other—onto Tom's head. Like oversized hunks of steak, they slid down his head, over his ears, and then enveloped his entire face, lingering there as cilia scanned every detail.

Aether held her breath as she watched, knowing what Tom must be feeling, wondering if he was thinking of Angela's final seconds. She wanted to send him supportive words, or to reach out and touch him—let him know she was there beside him, distract his senses away from his face and thoughts.

Eshkowoss Peekt narrated as she explored. "Holes … breath … spikes … moist flesh … more fur …" Finally, after several minutes, the examination was over, and Eshkowoss Peekt asked to be returned to her home, adding as she was carried off, "Pleasure courses through, much delight to sustain. Listen, Unhkte … listen learn all from Syons People. City grows from thinking, not bricks."

Unhkte gawked at Tom and Aether. "This was a matchless gift for Eshkowoss Peekt—a thing ungivable by any Threck. The pleasure was mine to observe."

Tom wiped his face on his sleeves as he returned to his feet. "I'm certain the pleasure was all mine." His ironic, traumatized eyes rolled toward Aether.

"Let us continue in." Unhkte pulled one of the curtains wide, revealing a large chamber full of awaiting Thinkers, all clad in purple-trimmed cloaks.

* * *

The Thinkers' chamber was designed as a vertical cylinder, like a grain silo, with immense stone blocks for walls. The tiered basin floor had been carved into the bedrock, a bowl mirroring another afvrik shell roof. A shallow pool of water within the deepest tier reflected the roof's circular skylight.

There were far more Thinkers than council members, Tom had informed Aether as they'd entered the crowded room. Now, standing with Tom at one shoulder and Unhkte at the other, Aether tried to keep up with the scrolling feed of translations. Unhkte made no effort to quiet or control the hundred-plus Thinkers' exchanges. Gazing around at all the adorned cloaks, Aether guessed that the free flow of conversation was customary, but she didn't have time for this.

LIVETRANS: Observe the head shell ...
LIVETRANS: Amoss was allowed garbless viewing. Will we?
LIVETRANS: This dialogue should be focused solely on philosophy.
LIVETRANS: Agreed!
LIVETRANS: Be mindful ... they understand all we say.
LIVETRANS: Technology demonstration should be first.

Aether turned to Unhkte. "Would it be possible for us to begin?" The din of the lounging crowd hushed in seconds. "There is much to discuss."

"Certainly," Unhkte said, raising her arms to subdue the remaining chatter. "I observe from my learned colleagues that your garb will be the first topic, however superficial ... let us put it behind us." Unhkte slid across the polished rock surface, pointing an arm at Aether. "This one is the leader of the Syons People, called Aether." Stifled surprised laughter from a few individuals. Unhkte signed harsh disapproval in three directions, then slid to Tom. "This one is called Tom, emissary with strong medicine knowledge, and one of our initial visitors, met with council. You may direct questions to either, or both for one to answer, or both for both to answer. We will queue by admittance—newest to oldest."

Throaty hocking sounds and gestures conveyed the elder members' disapproval.

Over Aether's right shoulder, a small, Setkee-sized Threck, halfway up the natural bleachers, stood. Her cloak was clearly the brightest of the bunch, purple trim freshly dyed and attached. "Peaceful greetings to Syons People. I am the newest Thinker, admitted the day before your first arrival. I am called Atzik. My first question, for this the subject of garb, addressed to both for one to answer: Do Syons People wear one garb, whether in your home or when out exploring other lands?"

Like silent applause, the membership signed unanimous approval of the question by pressing their palms together.

"Well thought and well said," Unhkte replied. "One *modt* for Atzik." She turned to Aether. "One of you may now answer for both."

Aether stared out at the mass of onlookers, all presumably waiting for their turn to ask a question about *clothes* ... the *first* topic of this apparent interview session. She imagined hours of probing—perhaps even some brief breaks—and it hadn't escaped Tom, either.

TOM: This doesn't bode well for time.

AETHER: Right?! How to avoid being rude? There's obviously no way we can do this right now.

TOM: Promise an unrestricted interview at a later date?

AETHER: What I don't understand—why aren't we talking about the kee burning and threckee and all that? Do you think that *none* of these people know what happened?

Unhkte explained to the audience, "Syons People speech is often delayed. We will address when onto language topic."

TOM: I know. Weird.

AETHER: Unhelpful.

TOM: I'm happy to be the hole. I'll cut in and explain that your time is precious or something. Like an assistant keeping tabs on the schedule. Say the word.

Tom's offer didn't instill much confidence. Delivery could be crucial.

"Well-thought question," Aether sent to fill the air as she devised a hopefully judicious statement. She sent as she wrote, hoping for the best. "Syons People are open, honest, and obliging people. We see and appreciate your group's cravings for knowledge and understanding—traits we deeply share. All Syons People are Thinkers, and we desire this same sort of session wherein we ask of you questions that fill in the gaps of knowledge we have regarding your city and people and history." This was met with enthusiastic—though silent—praise. "However, today we have come here not to this end, but to discuss three specific subjects. Because these subjects are urgent, we wish to delay the start of our delightful exchange of knowledge to some future day."

Aether observed a wave of mixed reactions circulate through the audience, though most appeared promising: curiosity, surprise, anticipation, impatience, "More."

Unhkte appeared to absorb and interpret the consensus, then addressed Aether. "You may announce these urgent subjects."

Aether inhaled deep as she pulled up the precomposed list, dropping it into her Livetrans queue.

"Gratitude," Aether signed. "The first subject is that of the atrocities two nights ago. We wish to explain our experience and the events following." Mindful of the earlier guards' apparent lack of familiarity, she added, "If we may."

The Thinkers bore no such puzzlement. The majority looked on without outward reaction, while a scant few beckoned her to continue. Their conspicuous lack of reaction exuded an unprecedented intensity. Unhkte motioned for Aether to proceed.

Aether unpaused the recounting. "Two nights ago, barbaric atrocities took place during your sacred keepock ritual ..." concluding with "... As evidenced by the wrongdoer's execution, Eeahso condemns this act and seeks peace, vowing to permanently end all raids on the city."

A handful of solitary Threck bodies rose from the assembly and waited.

Unhkte pointed to one. "Proceed."

"Where is Eeahso now?"

Half of the standers sunk back into the ranks of heads and eyes, leaving only three standing.

"Eeahso is in hiding," Aether replied.

Unhkte pointed to another. "Hiding somewhere you know?"

Aether had expected this line of questioning, but hadn't formulated a definitive response. She had figured she'd wing it.

She'd said her piece and decided to move on. They could return to it after, if still insistent. "The second subject is that of stranded Syons People. Across the sea, in the place you call Hynka Country, three of our people got lost, ending up in this dangerous place. Our flying machines can travel far, but not so far as the sea. We wish not to endanger Threck lives in addition to our own, so we're not asking for any of your people to come ashore. Your afvrik would stop as soon as land is in sight. We would require three to six days to find and return with our people, and then be transported back across the sea."

The Thinkers chatted quietly amongst themselves, motioning to Unhkte that this subject "Is not ours."

Unhkte addressed Aether. "This request is not for Thinkers group. Afvrik are tool of Fishing group. Your third subject?"

"The third was previously introduced by Tom, but never answered—"

"Request to build city in Threck Country," Unhkte interrupted. "This was delegated by the Council to the Thinkers for consideration and advisement. This is why all await continuation of questioning. We must have all information prior to submitting our advice."

Aether glanced at Tom, irritation creeping from the back of her head to her temples. She turned back to Unhkte. "The Thinkers must know what garb we wear in our homes? This is how you will come to your decision on whether to allow my people to survive or to turn us away?"

Unhkte seemed to stammer. "This is not only … This is one of many … It was well-thought question …" She leaned close to Aether, normally droopy eyes wide with intensity.

"Allow," Unhkte muttered.

The sound had been inaudible to Aether, but Livetrans picked it up. Aether didn't know what it was supposed to mean.

"If one of your people …" Aether began again, "… happened upon Syons People land, became lost, and lay in the sun, drying out, dying, would you find it reasonable for us to ask one hundred questions and deliberate before deciding whether to apply shade and water?"

"Syons People are not dying," Unhkte countered for all to hear, and gestured for Aether to let her continue.

"Yes we are!" Tom blared from his PA. Aether raised a hand to protest, but paused. "Angela, the one with me at the Council, was *killed* by Skinny just two nights ago. In Hynka Country, there are three more of us who could suffer the same fate from creatures your people know well. They are, right now, lying in the sun without water or shade, waiting for *this* group to decide if they live or die."

The assembly's movements revealed an even mix of confusion, alarm, pity, and thirst. All this talk of dry and hot …

Unhkte was silent.

Aether elected to resume. "In exchange for Threck help with these matters, Syons People will use our knowledge of small life to resurrect your lost kee, make new kee, and establish new fshkee where we can ensure the kee thrives. This we offer because we are in Threck Country, and while Syons People may live here temporarily—if permitted—it is Threck who must live on, flourish, and grow your city."

Unhkte peered around the room, observing the group's feedback as she slid around the circular pool.

TOM: Well-thought, well-said.

A rare eye-hide from Unhkte as she completed her lap and stood to face Aether and Tom. Another whispered address, intended only for them. "You should have allowed me to help." She backed away and resumed full volume for the entire room. "The Thinkers consider the logic of things. All pieces. You wish not to provide these pieces. If I am dying—unshaded and dry beneath your symbol sun—I do not attempt to set conditions of my rescue. As you stand nearby with shade and water, I do whatever is required of me—all that I am still able to accomplish—to satisfy your requirements for help."

"Of course—" Aether attempted, cut off with a wave from Unhkte.

"You wish to trade life for life," Unhkte went on. "You offer kee—substantial trade if the very foundation of our people were destroyed—but the risk of single fshkee was recognized long ago. There are many fshkee, all full of ample kee. Our people are in no danger of vanishing. Thus, it would seem to the Thinkers that Syons People need many things from Threck, but Threck need nothing from Syons People."

3.0

Minnie's paired skimmers hovered over the Hynka bone shrine, drifting right while rotating counterclockwise. Beyond the tiered rock wall, the rumble of stampeding Hynka grew louder, their shrieks and hissy, throaty calls echoing over the snaps and crashes of innocent vegetation. Minnie yanked her eyes from the mesmerizing, unfathomable sight of Ish, up to the unpromising view of a thrashing jungle canopy. Reaching Ish before the first of the horde arrived would be impossible. Her gaze returned to Ish and she began recording, zooming in to capture the details before taking her leave.

The Hynka had been meticulous. From the near-perfect circle Ish's body formed, like a serial killer's Christmas wreath, Minnie guessed that every one of her former colleague's bones had been pulverized—crushed to tiny bits and powder. All but her head. Aside from a few bruises and lacerations, and missing clumps of hair torn from her scalp, Ish's head was intact, set right-side-up at the grisly circle's six o'clock, her blackened neck stretched and twisted and folded like a deflated tire. She'd been stripped nude, her suit shredded into the thin bands used to truss her devastated body and to bind her wrists to her ankles, forming the circle. And finally, the display: raised and suspended there by three bundles of multicolored wire at 10, 12, and 2 o'clock. The wire had to be from the missing EV.

Hectic movement entered Minnie's peripheral. Ten more seconds—five to be safe. She needed to know if it was still there … zooming closer, closer still, a quaking view of Ish's nearly shut, drooping right eyelid. Spectrum switch to mag. A glowing green ball appeared inside the yellow housing mounted to the ocular cavity. Ish's fone was still in there, and from the looks of it, intact.

Bits of sandstone dust trickled from cracks in the rock and Minnie heard the thumping beat of too-close Hynka footfalls. Without wasting a second to glance left, Minnie throttled the skimmer up and right, the high g-force testing her subopt muscles and sore knees. She returned her optics to default as she ascended, glimpsing the amassing crowd of vexed Hynka below, arms thrust upward as if to pull her back down with some invisible line. Others scaled the tiers of chiseled blocks toward the Ish wreath. Minnie held at 60 meters and watched, hoping they'd leave the body alone.

Upon reaching the fourth level, the first Hynka reached up to Ish's body and gingerly poked an exposed armpit.

Yup, she's still there, buddy. All's good. Head on home now, y'hear? Take your friends.

Two more joined the first below Ish, reaching up to touch her, but met with *"no picking at the cake"* swats from the first. All three turned their attention to the strange white object in the sky, probably yearning to snatch another orange-suited wall decoration.

Minnie zoomed back in. These three behaved unlike the frantic crowd still beating their way through the jungle to be directly under her. They simply stared. There had been composed ones like this when she and John had first touched down, their bronze eyes exuding measured intensity, implying a chilling intellect. Had the horde captured Ish due to her lunacy eclipsing any remnants of good sense, or had they somehow outwitted her? It'd be foolish for Minnie to consider her own survival skills among these creatures to be more worthy than Ish's, especially while she lacked the Hynka specialist's research catalogue.

Foolish indeed, Minnie thought, what with the ridiculous nature of her new plan. She brought the skimmers around to face south, tightened her grip on the controls, and—

But what does it mean?

Her own voice in her head, but unlike an ordinary thought. She'd literally *heard* her voice, but a bit deeper, a little older, perhaps, wiser, like an insightful future self, sent back in time to advise at a critical moment.

Minnie replied in her head: What do you mean, 'what does it mean?' I'm supposed to interpret the brutal acts of a primitive, violence-based race? Who cares what it '*means*' to them?

The voice was more than a voice. Minnie perceived a disappointed sigh, the reproachful no-nod of a virtual head.

Minnie persisted, Well what then? Do *you* know?

Wise Minnie put a hand on Minnie's shoulder. *Your cosms got all silo'd, babe. Macro, micro ... you've completely lost the big picture.*

It was true. She'd been wrapped up in linear tasks. Hadn't taken a moment to step back and change scale. But what did Ish have to do with it all? Was she some huge keystone to the bigger picture?

Wise Minnie answered without being directly asked. *The complexity of this thing goes so far beyond Ish. Yes, she's a keystone—one of many—but to say "bigger picture," as if there was but a single image to grasp, it screams naiveté.*

"Screw you!" Minnie yelled aloud. "*You* said big picture first! ... Oh sakes, I'm yelling at myself. What the hell is going—"

And then she caught it. The final dregs of meds had left her body. Or John had been right. The cave worm emissions obviously had psychotropic effects, but could they have been managing all the key systems to keep her HSPD fully in line? The notion wasn't entirely implausible. If her regular meds were given to some Sane Janes, they'd be climbing the walls and scratching the skin from their faces. If John was correct, the worms that had ravaged his body might just save her life.

Minnie said aloud, "So, you're one of *them*, eh?"

Everyone has a conscience, babe.

Peering at the nav panel, Minnie watched as the digits in the proximity box decreased with smooth, writhing transitions—8 uncurling and morphing into 7. The orange digits looked like snakes, or impossibly nimble belly dancers. Yeah, belly dancers. The readout complied and five rexic orange women bent and twisted into ever-shifting, often applause-worthy, numeric poses. Minnie was mesmerized.

How could you ever wish to suppress this? You are superhuman.

The dancers sang out in hypnotic harmony, "Ooooooooo …"

An alert. A prox alert!

"Shut the hell up, you!" Minnie shouted to both Wise Minnie and the console.

She shook out her head as the sights and sounds of the world recommenced. Her skimmer pair had drifted dangerously close to the nearby mountain. She reversed and peered back, spotting a reinvigorated (if they were ever de-invigorated) legion of Hynka tearing up the hillside. If she hadn't snapped out of it, they'd have been on her in under a minute.

"Wow, you almost got me killed," Minnie said as she banked the skimmers right and zipped south.

Smooth and sultry, Wise Minnie vamped, *Can't blame me. I'm the one trying to pull the blinders off your face. You're busy studying blue flowers.*

"Don't try to use my own metaphors against—" Minnie closed her mouth, pressing her lips tightly shut.

Minnie slowed and reduced altitude, giving the Hynka time to catch up. She suddenly realized she was smiling. A wide, toothy, uncontainable grin. How narcissistic was it to find such enjoyment in hearing her own voice talking in her head? In sparring with herself? Too fun! And the air … it smelled so good, felt amazing in her lungs, as if there existed breathing—regular old "Hey, look at me, I'm alive." type breathing—and then there was *this*. Dessert breath. Yes! Inhaling a delicacy.

A foggy euphoria crept up the sides of her neck and lit up her brain. Her chest tightened, like she couldn't get enough of the delicious air. But it still felt good—really, really good … *however* …

She knew what this meant. Despite the ages passed since the last episode, she knew this sensation all too well. She understood the physiological mechanisms behind it. She knew all of the little intricacies of her "unique" central nervous system, pituitary gland, spinal cord, adrenal glands, blood, and neurons when an episode was building, peaking, and falling, and remembered well the aftereffects. At present, her pulse was rising as beta-endorphins flooded into her spinal cord and brain capillaries, so now was the time that her astrocytes would mosey out for their coffee break, eliminating the crucial blood-brain barrier, and waving a green flag to the revving meltdown engines at the starting line. The adrenergic storm would soon follow, throwing fuel on the fire, and crossing the point of no return. It was like opposite day in there, where all the checks and balances evolution had put in place and refined over millennia, rebelled with a haughty "Nay."

When caught early enough, she'd successfully talked herself down from episodes, but it had been so long since she'd felt *this*. It was the same old ploy, she knew, baiting her with soothing, reassuring whispers: *You've let it go longer than this before and still pulled out. You deserve this one little dalliance after a decade of self-denial. You're safe right now. It won't be like it was before. You're stronger now … smarter …*

Her eyes had closed at some point. A distant, hollow biostat alert in her fone and ear module tried to catch her attention, but its feeble buzzing hadn't presented her a compelling case. Biostats, I'd like you to meet **Disabled**.

She slid down from the console and settled in against the warm panel door, like some cozy, enveloping pillow. A bent knee pressed in at her chest while the other leg lay flat, stretched out to the center of the pad. Fingers wrapped around her neck, seductively caressing, while the other hand pressed in between her legs.

Enjoy. There's not another human in the world who gets to feel this.

* * *

Nothing new from Minerva since their DC broke. She'd managed to take care of both of them all this time with no help whatsoever from him, but John still worried, still felt that simmering dread in his gut. He had zero control over her fate. He was effectively useless. And when she'd last asked him to rate his pain, he'd replied with the trusty old five. It'd been more like a strong seven at the time, and now ranked a steady, searing eight.

Curled in his sleeping bag, heavy head pressed into the packed bag Minerva had thoughtfully slid beneath him before leaving, he rolled a capsule between thumb and forefinger. It was one of twenty-eight remaining diclomorph pills from their combined reserve. They'd already squandered twenty-two on him. Half of the medipads gone. Stem cream, antibiotics, gauze, tape, etset—all intended for a lifetime of rationing. Even if he had a chance at long-term survival, it'd be as a convalescent, a mouth to feed, an anchor, a *risk*. If they were somehow able to escape this lions' den, Minerva would be forced to live out her days as a caretaker, and he as a burden.

John elbowed away the top of the survival bag and slowly raised his head. His ruined neck protested and punished. It hurt less to turn it the other way, but he could only lie on his back or left side.

His eyes adjusted to the glare from the cave opening and Ish's EV sharpened into focus. Was Minerva deliberately keeping the medkits away from him? Wise, if so, but what if she didn't return, or came back much later than anticipated? She'd only left him two pills. The first he'd taken shortly after she left; the second lay in the bowl of his upturned palm, nagging him for a trip down the hatch. How many more would it take to slam the door on existence, once and for all? Four? Five to be certain? Five more pills spent from Minerva's lifetime supply. Or a single multiround from his MW. Another irreplaceable asset; however, not so scarce as meds. Though in two to three more days, those five pills would be used on him anyway.

John sucked in a deep breath and held it, gathered himself, and rolled onto his back as he let the air blast from his lungs. Acid seemed to spray at his wounds from the inside. The agony was worst on his torso and thigh, where the sensation of tearing flesh made him freeze in a full body grimace. He forced himself to sip tiny breaths as he waited for the pain scale to drop from 10 to 9 … even just 9.5.

It took a long time. So long that the possibility occurred to him that it may never go back down. That he'd be stuck there like an overturned turtle, a dose of relief clenched in the fist at his side, unable to bring it to his mouth. But it did go down … 9.9, 9.75, 9.5, 8.5, all quite quickly once the peak had released its grip. The opportunity presented, he didn't hesitate to fling the pill to the back of his throat. He swallowed, stuck his water tube in, and then slurped enough liquid to dissolve the capsule. T-minus twenty minutes until relief.

He once again lifted his head enough to see past his chest to the EV outside. His fone pegged it at 10.06 meters. He labored through raising his legs, planting both boots on the gritty floor, and used his left arm as a third lever to turn his body around. Pivoting on his back, he rotated, powering through without stopping, until the top of his head pointed out the cave.

Dust and gravel rolled beneath his back with a deep scritching sound as he slid, little by little, across the surface. Pushing his legs downward hurt worse than sideways. His right thigh screamed at him to stop, to at least take a break as re-formed and half-healed muscle fibers pulled and tore, delicate embryonic flesh detaching at the edges, leaking fluid.

Back up to 9.5, his body surrendered before his mind agreed. Stinging tears streamed from the corners of his eyes, into and around his ears.

He breathed and waited.

They say suicide is a coward's escape. Partially true in this instance. He wished to be free from agony, to head off the unavoidably miserable existence ahead, the despair of a driven personality reduced to irrelevance. On the other hand, there was the freeing of Minerva, both physically and mentally, the preservation of her supplies, increased chances of survival. Still, there was a catch to all this.

He resumed sliding. Outside now. Three more meters. Thin clouds overhead. Two meters. One. The front of the EV moved slowly into view like a massive white sister planet eclipsing the violet sky. Zero.

Now for sitting up. Fortunately, the new pill was kicking in, overlapping with the meds already in his system. It would still hurt like hell, but at the very least his murky brain would care less. He wedged his fingers into a hull crevice, pulled with his abs while pushing with his better leg, and folded himself upward 90°.

A moment later, the hatch glided up over the roof, revealing the medkit on the floor, just inside. With a guilty sense of triumph, he grasped the handle and set the kit in the dirt at his side.

What if Minerva had considered the possibility of him attempting to self-medicate and overdosing—accidentally or otherwise? What if she'd hid the meds somewhere else? These thoughts clumsied his fingers as he groped at the latches.

Open.

All meds present and accounted for. It wouldn't be long now. He sighed relief, but it was short-lived. There was still that catch.

Assuming Ish had met with a less-than-pleasant fate, if John died, Minerva would be all alone, with only herself to support. This fact had fallen into the "pros" column of suicide contemplation, as his absence bolstered her ability to travel, eliminated the need to feed, house, and nurse a burdensome companion. However, absent those very liabilities, she could easily lose the will to survive. She might carry on for a time, try to make it to the coast on the slim chance that, despite the lack of any communication, others had actually survived evac and may come for her. That hope would dwindle away as weeks elapsed. Maybe she'd one day get on the skimmer, point it out to sea, toward Threck Country, knowing full well it wouldn't make an eighth of the journey on a full charge. Or more likely, she'd intentionally set off her HSPD. Let it run its full course. A self-produced overdose.

She needed a reason to live. She needed hope.

* * *

Minnie purred as cool water streamed down her forehead, beading and sheeting over her face. A light breeze chilled it further. Her hand oozed lazily from her neck to her chest.

No one else knows this feeling.

Not another human in the world …

Another human …

Aether …

… gone.

John.

She opened her eyes. The throbbing in her chest began to ache, sharp and stabby, or maybe it'd hurt all along. She was hot—so hot. A tiny glimmer of clarity. Fingers grappled at her suit collar. The suit needed to be opened. She could cool down in the wind. But heat was only a symptom, not the real problem.

She closed her eyes once more, pulled her feet in, spread her knees wide, and rested her palms on them. Slow breaths. Prime numbers and ... black holes. Primes and black holes, go.

2, NGC 1277, 3, Guthrie 13.09, 5, Cygnus X-1, 7 ...

After a few minutes, her pulse responded, slowing. Continuing meditation, she felt it safe to pull up biostats to monitor herself. Heart rate: 177. O^2 level: 86%. Tyramine, dopamine, ABG, pH, SR, friction, metab: all gradually stabilizing. She ceased meditation at *1039, Messier 77*. She'd won. Her mind was stronger than the evil hormones and electrochemical demons.

Ah, but this perception in itself was an instrument of the trap. The fallacy of mental strength and personal responsibility. To succumb was no more a sign of weakness than when an unrelenting cancer finally overpowered a body. Especially since this allegedly strong brain was one of the many organs working against her. Doctors had tried to drill that point into her head, while others wished to literally drill into her head. In a world where few uncured or unmanaged afflictions remained, a medical field wherein DNA transplants had long since taken the fun out of the profession, Minnie had been a captivating specimen for otherwise thumb-twiddling researchers desperate for a problem to solve.

"What if we make her all new thyroid, pituitary, and adrenal glands? Hell, throw in kidneys, thymus, pineal, and pancreas while we're at it. Or maybe we should fill her brain with bots, rewire the offending synapses, neurons, and axons." Her father wouldn't have any of it. Once Minnie's shrink had honed in on the right meds, Dad yanked her out of every study. He wouldn't risk detriment to her brain—identified before birth as an extremely rare H-class, hypothesized to be the type possessed by all of history's famed polymaths.

"If the world ever collapses to a point where people can't get meds," he'd told her with a pinch of her chin, "we've probably got bigger worries than your attacks."

Bigger worries indeed.

Hovering at 30m, with doubly tall ridges on either flank, the echoes of a thousand raving Hynka bounced to and fro with surreal stereo effects. It sounded as though they'd grown wings: two nightmarish swarms closing in.

Minnie grasped a handhold over her head and pulled herself up. Still dizzy, fingers and toes prickly, butt numb, headache from hell sinking its dagger fingers through her skull. Nausea—instantaneous—plopped down into her stomach like she'd swallowed a 10-kilo bucket of rocks and vomit.

"Well, that was nice," she said. "You still there?"

No responses from imaginary friends.

She took in her surroundings, didn't remember entering this wide canyon. Below the skimmers, what looked to be the entire local Hynka population had ripped apart the jungle floor, creating a wide clearing. In the middle of the horde she spotted a semi-pyramid of struggling beasts, like ants, or the universe's most terrifying cheerleading team. They'd reached four standing bodies high but couldn't seem to pull off a fifth. It'd take quite a bit of practice before they hit the eight or nine required to reach her, but she applauded their effort as the skimmers once more accelerated through the canyon. Glancing back to be sure they were still dedicated to their pursuit, Minnie could see she'd triggered a new bloodbath. They had a serious problem with frustration.

Once the killing had stopped and feeding begun, Minnie switched on an emergency alert to recapture their attention.

Wow, Minnie mused, *I could do this for another few hours and thin the population down to one.*

At 30K from the village, Minnie waited for the tiring stragglers to catch up. Knowing these guys could run faster than a thoroughbred—up to 80 km/h across flat, unobstructed ground—she'd brought them far enough to give her ten minutes to fly back, and at least ten more to fetch Ish's fone. She may have even exhausted them so much that they'd be gone for hours. That didn't mean the village would be empty. She fully expected to run into some wily stay-behinds. If they were anywhere near that shrine, though, they'd find a couple multirounds in their chests. Minnie didn't have time for a stealthier approach.

Ten minutes later, she flew in low with high-sensitivity thermag activated on her fone. She counted roughly thirty Hynka still wandering the village, but most were spread out well beyond the bone shrine. They wouldn't see or hear her.

On Ish's side of the rock, three Hynka had indeed lingered. On the ground, two could be seen restoring the vandalized bone shrine. The third lounged on its side up at the rock wall's third tier. Its position was disturbingly human, one arm bent up, and cheek resting on hand—like a child lying on a carpeted floor watching a show or reading a book. This one was the first to spot her.

Minnie quickly programmed a final approach and landing, gripped her MW, and verified it was set to lethal. The skimmer took over and Minnie set sights on her first target, the larger of the two Hynka at the shrine. Descending and curving in, she aimed at a shoulder until the chest came into view. A bark from the lounger, two *bwops* from her MW, a stunned, faltering Hynka scratching at its new holes. 6m from the ground, spinning right, barrel pointed at the second target, Minnie hesitated a beat. The skimmers touched down. In the corner of her eye she could see the dark shape of her first victim collapse. The one now standing before her held out its big hands, as if to block the next shot, or to say "Don't shoot!" But she sensed the third, up on the ledge to her right, on the move.

Bwop-bwop!

The second cried out, began spluttering deducible words. Minnie spun toward the rock face. The last had stood and turned its back and now climbed toward the fourth tier as it called out.

"Ahsa-craht-ye! Ahsa-craht-ye!"

Minnie twirled for a full scan. If this guy was calling for help, there wasn't anyone close enough to hear. It made it to the fourth tier and reached up to the hanging body, two thick fingers wrapping all the way around Ish's bundled legs. Minnie watched, unsure how to proceed, as the Hynka yanked at Ish's body, warping the circle into a stretched oval until one of the ties snapped free. A sudden gag seized in Minnie's throat. Ish was like fresh bread dough, her bound limbs and torso bending and squishing in impossible, appalling ways, head bobbing as if mounted on a flimsy spring.

Steeling her mind and body, Minnie trained her MW on the center of the Hynka's back. Another yank and jerk. Minnie was afraid that Ish's legs would give before the bundled cables. A loud snap from over the top of the rock. A thick branch shot out, cable streaming behind it, and both flew all the way down to the edge of the bone shrine, a few meters from Minnie's feet.

What was this Hynka's goal? Was it trying to take the sacred Ish away so Minnie couldn't have her?

With the breaking of the third cable, Minnie's question was answered. The Hynka turned around with Ish dangling from two hands.

It extended its arms out. "Ahsa-craht-ye. Craht-ye-ngoh."

Minnie took a few steps backward and gestured to the ground before her. "Okay, sure … send her on down, buddy."

But instead of gently handing her off to gravity, the Hynka folded Ish into a single shaft, raised her over its head with both arms, and hurled her downward with all its might. Minnie dove to the side. The body careened off the formerly organized bones and clipped one of her boots. Minnie landed ungracefully in a medley of Hynka parts, flipping herself right over to monitor the sneaky bastard, and watched as it jumped from the fourth level down to the second. It squatted for a flying leap at Minnie, and, stunned again by such speed and dexterity from the hulking creatures, she impulsively shut her eyes and popped off a flurry of shots. 10? 15? She had no idea—still expected a crushing impact, claws and teeth, and the unremitting grip of a two-fingered demolition machine.

Bones rattled. Gurgling coughs. Minnie opened her eyes to see the Hynka much farther than she'd expected. It lay to her left, flat on its chest with a leg kicking out behind it, shunting away the bones forming the shrine's outer circle. It hadn't leapt toward her, but to the path that led away from the shrine. Ish had been a last-ditch distraction before a planned flee attempt. It had expected Minnie to kill it even after she got Ish. A revealing outlook. It meant there wasn't any negotiating with Hynka.

Minnie stood and scrutinized the immobilized Hynka, ensuring no one was about to spring up and grab her horror-film style. Satisfied by their dead or dyingness, she strode to Ish's body where it'd come to rest at the edge of the clearing.

Oh, perfect.

The head had come to rest facing down. No quick pluck and run for Minnie.

She knelt down, breathed through only her mouth, and focused on the mechanics of lifting, turning, and setting the head down. That face … the expression …

She had to keep going, get it done, unclip multitool, flip open scoop tool, finger the eyelids open, ignore vile peeling of flesh bonded by dried fluids, insert tool at outside corner—no looking at face, stop looking at face—pry fone from housing.

The ball dropped from her fingers into an empty cargo pocket. Pocket sealed.

Minnie ran back to the skimmers, hopped up, and stopped her hands before they touched anything. Her gloves had been tainted in the worst possible way. She thought she could feel both germs and creeps burrowing through the fabric, dead-set on reaching her skin.

She tore out the release lines and yanked the gloves off, flinging them behind her.

The skimmer pressed up at her feet, the paired units launching as a single unit, straight up in the air. First to the west, instead of directly back north. Hynka would definitely see her leave, and she didn't want to guide them back toward the mountain cave.

The controls had a nice, grippy rubber texture she realized she'd never touched with bare skin. It was dumb to have left her gloves. Purely an emotional decision. They could've been cleaned of any dangerous or disturbing matter. Now she had an unsealable suit.

Stupid, stupid, stupid. Should she turn back? Was there still time? Perhaps, but she didn't alter her course for 15K, at which point she veered north toward "home."

31

Agitated sand and dust shifted outside the cave, but without the usual accompaniment of a hollow wind tone. John pulled in the corner of his survival bag to have a peek just in time to see the white edge of a skimmer touchdown outside. Minerva was back. She'd made it, of course. The endless string of speculation that tormented his mind had all been silly.

"Sorry I took so long," Minerva's voice echoed through the cavern. "How we doing? Where's your pain at?" She crouched down beside him, set a hand on his shoulder.

The question struck John funny. He chuckled a little, felt a dull pressure in his right ribcage that would've normally been pain. "I don't know … two?"

Minnie's compassionate smile disappeared, replaced with fret. "Oh no … you didn't—" She sprang to her feet and surveyed the area, frantic. Her cute little fairy face left behind ghostly tracers as it darted about.

She really was cute. But not in a lusting older guy kind of way. More of a *"You know, I can admit that's a good-looking girl"* kind of way. He'd seen her coming out of the shower half-covered (and not really caring) enough times to assemble an imaginary full picture if he'd wanted to, but this line of thought assailed him with an instant bout of self-loathing.

"Sorry," he said, but her concerned face thought he was talking about the drugs. That was good. No need to correct her. Mind purged.

She squatted back down, lifted the top of his survival bag, and found his stash. "How many did you take? How long ago?"

He tightened his arm around the little case, though she had yet to try and pull it away.

"You're cute."

Oops. That was out loud. Stop it! What's with this cute stuff?

"That's great, John. Appreciate it, really. How many damn pills did you take?"

It was two. Well, two recently. How many at the EV? One. No, one on way there, one on way back?

"Sorry," he said, trying to unmuddle his thoughts. "I think … how long've you been gone?"

"About four hours. You took one a little before I left, and I gave you two more for—wait, how did you even—" She peered back outside, probably spotting the drag trail leading to the EV. "Oh no … *John* … I'm so sorry! How bad was it? I can't believe you pulled yourself all the way—Oh crap, your wounds! Let me look at you!"

She unzipped the survival bag to the bottom and carefully peeled away the top. The case of meds slid from his cradling arm, tossed aside to a pile of supplies on the opposite wall. As she hunched over him, examining the damage he'd done to all her hard work, his hypnotized eyes hovered on her orange hip. Beyond that curve lay his meds. Not so far. He could get there in a quarter the time it took to reach the EV. *If* she left them there. Oh, but there was no way now. He'd never see that case again.

"Wrecked, John," she murmured, dragging the medkit across the floor. "Just wrecked. It's all my fault. We can't head north tomorrow. Not now."

A cloud floated aside, exposing a small patch of clear thought. He looked up at her as she tried to sop up his leaky body with sponge pads.

"Hey," he said. Fraught eyes locked onto his. "Not your fault. I said five. Was much worse. Thought I could handle, I guess. Stupid." She dabbed the sweat from his head with a clean sponge. "Listen … I have to tell you something. A secret I've kept a long time."

Minerva's face scrunched. "Oh please, no. I don't need any secrets right now. Save it for when your judgment's on a bit more solid ground."

"No, nothing weird. There's nothing like that. I promise. Now listen … listen before I start *swimming* again. A decade—no. A decade and a *half* after launch, a pod was sent up. Special pod. Huge. Inside, an RRM—Rapid Return Module. Major upgrades all around. All over. Back to Earth in almost half the time to take to get here. To took. Ah, dammit … half the time *it took!* Eleven years."

Minerva's expression had morphed into a familiar chilly intensity. "When is it supposed to arrive?"

"Fourteen months."

Calculations seemed to scroll across her eyes. "Fourteen months until *orbit*. Until it attempts to dock with a nonexistent station. A hell of a lot of good it'll do us down here."

"No, that's the thing …" A wave of euphoria drifted through his brain. He shut his eyes for a second … juuuust a second—a light slap from Minerva on his good cheek. Eyes open. "Right … look, it has a lander. Full escape capability. If it can't dock with station, it automatically sends the lander to our original rally point."

She considered this information. "BS. Why exactly are you feeding me this crap? We hadn't even arrived when your supposed RRM launched. I didn't set our rally point until seven years later."

"Retro update, Minerva." He smirked. "Remember that whole thing we all learned about the speed of light? *Laser* comms?" The term *escape capability* struck him funny. He murmured it to himself. "Escape capability. Escape cape. Scapecape."

"So this isn't a load of crap?" Her hopeful gaze searched his face. "Then hang on. How long have you know this?"

"Only a few years."

"Only? Dammit! Do you realize that none of this would have happened if you'd just shared this tidbit of info? If that looner bitch knew there was a way home—an escape from walls and tiny rooms and monotony—she wouldn't have felt the need to blow the place up! She'd still be alive. My *friends—Aether*—would still be alive!"

This was true. He hadn't been thinking about this quite disturbing hypothetical.

Hypothetical … Ish would still be alive?

"You found Ish," he said. Minerva nodded, stone-faced. "Dead."

"Thoroughly," she said. "Thanks to secrets and effing rules."

"We don't know it would've made a difference."

"Oh, good one! That's brilliant. When *were* you going to tell us? Or was it supposed to be a last-second surprise? 'Hey folks, guess what's showing up in ten goddamn minutes?'"

His head was again sinking into a muddy abyss. Vision blurring. "Two months … orders … not before ETA twelve months."

Minerva slapped both hands over her face and produced a stifled maniacal laugh. "Two months. Eff me ... eff *you*. Hahaha, ridiculous."

She struggled to her feet, all strength appearing to have drained from her body. Her boots skidded across gravel as she shuffled outside. John thought he could hear her weeping as she left, but his ears had dipped below the surface. The real world returned to some intangible realm just out of reach. And he didn't mind so much.

* * *

Minnie set her bag on the kitchen counter, slid open the pantry, and browsed the empty shelves for a snack. On to cold storage. Equally vacant, of course. The shelves and coldstore existed here solely as décor. If she cared to take the time plugging in Qin's food hack, she could slap a full banquet across every counter and gorge herself into a coma. If she was hungry.

She walked into the living room and peered out the panoramic window to the dock and lake. Some kids were standing in a canoe, playing balance. So carefree in their perfect world. Well, it probably helped to be only a vis. The kids were, essentially, animated paintings with zero AI. That would change if she went outside and actually interacted with them.

"Meh," she said, plopping down on one of her crescent sofas. Across from her, she spotted a bundle of luxurious silver fur. Emilie was curled up between two pillows on the opposite sofa, sleeping as usual.

"Wake up, you," Minnie said, and lazy lids rolled slowly upward to reveal a pair of lethargic cat eyes. "I'm home!"

Emilie stretched out a leg, splayed the paw and claws, began to purr, and settled back into an even more luxurious slumber.

Minnie threw a pillow at her. "You suck. Where's Noodle?"

Emilie opened one eye. "Probably destroying something," she said. "Check the attic. You see I'm trying to nap here, right?"

"I'm up here!" Noodle called from the attic, appearing a second later, orange tail swinging as he dangled by a single paw. He let go, dropping to the hall floor, and skittered into the living room. He hopped into Minnie's lap, curling and twisting, his incredibly soft fur caressing her hands. "Where've you been? It's been weeks!"

He arched his back, white belly on full display for an overdue rub n' scratch. Minnie smiled and obliged.

Noodle raised his head and gazed at Minnie, remorseful. "We thought maybe … like maybe you were punishing us."

"We?" Emilie sneered.

"No, no." Minnie cradled his head in both hands and scratched his cheeks with her thumbs. "Nothing like that—I'd never. Just some bad days at work. You missed me?"

"To put it mildly," Noodle said as Minnie etched circles into his tummy fur. "Ferrets are highly social creatures. *This* girl," he nodded to Emilie, "can't be bothered. I wanted to play chess."

"Takes too long," Emilie said without opening her eyes. "And you're terrible at it. I don't even have to cheat."

Minnie smiled and turned on the tube. The media options appeared in the air between the sofas. "What do you guys want to watch?"

Emilie ignored her.

"Whatever you want," Noodle said as he spun around on her lap, tail whipping across her arm.

Minnie let the tube pick. A semi-recent series played from her archive. All presumably famous actors she'd never seen or heard of.

Noodle cleared his throat like a person. "I know you can watch and scratch at the same time."

Minnie loved her pets. Maybe she'd adopt a few more. But why? To fill the emptiness? Why not get a mate like others? A kid or two? Even Aether had a husband and daughter in her game. Oliver and Trista. Minnie had never met them—never wanted to. Whatever Aether had gotten from them were clearly things Minnie couldn't provide. Plus, they'd been around long before Minnie had come into the picture. Maybe even before John?

John.

She'd come here to escape from him, and yet here he was. What to think of this return module situation? If they could make it across this continent, build a boat, get to Threck Country, and make it another year, they could actually go home. They'd sleep the whole way, so the time would pass like nothing. Probably dock in Earth orbit, deal with some company folks—debriefs and whatnot, take a shuttle down to the surface. See her dad again. He'd be, what, a spry young 85? She'd probably travel the world, give speeches, plant roots somewhere, and be a professor. The idea of going back wasn't entirely unappealing, but she'd spent so long disassociating from Earth, *knowing* she'd never go back, knowing that the game would forever be her sole experience of her former home. The game, and actual human interaction. Her friends.

Oh, how she hoped they didn't suffer. Hoped they weren't scared. Hoped that Aether, as she drifted into the black, didn't only try to be a mom to Qin. She better not have waited for the painful, suffocating, dehydrated end. They would've had ample meds and access to the air mixture so as to avoid inevitable agony.

Meds.

John again.

Had he tried to kill himself, or had it been an accident? He was too stubborn, too sure of himself for suicide. Then again, being disabled, no longer able to take care of himself—what did that sort of thing do to a proud, bigheaded personality like his?

Minnie looked down at Noodle, writhing in delight as she absentmindedly pet him from neck to belly. "I gotta go, guys."

Noodle was outraged. "What? No!"

"I was just about to go over there," Emilie said, stretching her back. "I don't mind if you pet me now. If you want."

Minnie grinned. "I love you two. I'll be back."

She closed the game and opened her eyes. The inside of Ish's EV was still illuminated from the two portholes above. She'd been gone less than 30 minutes. A thermag glance through the wall revealed a still-idle John in the cave. His temp appeared normal, heart rate fine. He wouldn't be truly lucid for a few hours. In the meantime ...

Minnie plucked Ish's fone from her pocket. A quick thrice-over with a few wetwipes. She held the device up before her, facing the optics toward her, "eye to eye." Ish's familiar pale yellow-brown iris, or rather, a reproduction of it. Up close, one could detect a fone's lack of ridges and canyons, the replica iris and surrounding white sclera were merely a convex disc bonded to the inner casing. The optics orifice contained several lens layers behind a tinted concealer, without which someone could see inside. Minnie preferred to think of the data within the device before her, not the bio organ it resembled, the person it represented, the body from which it'd been extracted.

She set the fone on a console, reached into the medkit at her feet, pulling out the extractor—a simple, silicoated tool that looked like a warped eyelash curler—and turned to face her reflection in a shiny black display.

She opened her fone's manual command interface. One of a few functions that had to be manually sight-typed for safety and security.

Shutdown.

ALERTS: FONE - Confirm full shutdown.

Yes.

Shutting down ...

Blackout. Her ear module emit a tiny crack as it too powered down.

Stereovision gone. Optics gone. No HUD, no alerts, no apps, no access. She was cut off and helpless—in shock at the reality of being truly *disconnected*. It felt quiet, dull, unnatural, *wrong*. What the hell did people do before fones?

Focus on task. Get it over with.

She spread her lids wide, held her breath, and slid in the two circular ends, one on top and one beneath her fone. A gentle, scissoring squeeze, and she tilted her head back while steadily moving the extractor away. The gross (though not all that painful) final popping sensation shot a quick shiver down her spine. She moved the orb in front of her bio eye, giving it a brief inspection. Not too much film built up on the back, but she'd give it a thorough cleaning before reinstalling.

Ish's fone drew in with the usual *slorp* Minnie had never grown used to. Her top eyelid folded in with the device and she had to pinch and pull out the flap. Preboot had begun upon contact with her housing, but it halted as expected a few seconds later with a white passcode prompt on a black background. Even with a mated housing, this was a standard safeguard.

Minnie hoped that one of the root accounts would've been set on their fones as part of exigency protocols.

?4rT~2^3eQ|ρ8

Nope.

She tried all of the others she knew. No access. All she could see in Ish's fone was station time and batt level. 2% and slowly rising, Minnie's electrolytes trickling in through her housing.

Such easy access would've been nice, albeit unexpected. On to Plan B.

* * *

John moaned. His cheeks tightened. It appeared his dreams were unpleasant. Minnie nudged him again.

"Hey, just wake up for a second. One question and you can go back to sleep."

His chin constricted, mouth set into a grumpy toddler frown. A more assertive protest groan.

She poked his shoulder repeatedly. "I'm not going anywhere, John! One question! It's your ticket back to dreamland. Wake up. You don't even have to open your eyes. Okay?"

A quivering sniff like he was going to cry. Finally, a scratchy "What?"

"What's Ish's fone passcode?"

"Dunno."

"Yes, you do."

"No."

"Yes. Tell me now. I'll enter it right in and you go back to sweet, sweet, comforting sleep."

One eye opened—his bio eye. It wobbled and blinked and found her. "You … you took her fone?"

Minnie smiled and widened her lids around the unmatched fone, cocking her head right for him to catch a glimpse.

Fog appearing to lift, he tried to sit up.

She pressed down on his shoulder. "No, no, no, relax. You'll hurt yourself. Just give me the passcode. Once I'm in, I'll dump it all to the EV system and we can both pull it off of there."

"Minerva, we can't just … every private moment, journals, pics and vids—"

"Yeah, exactly, all that stuff. Trust me, she'll never know."

"We have no proof that she did anything to—"

"Stop!" Her irritation with this man had once more bubbled up over the top of her patience pot. The woman was dead. *Everyone* was dead. And he was trying to protect, what, the dignity of Ish's memory? She fought to unclench her jaw. "Give me the damned passcode. Let me grab her last few vids, prove her innocence for you, clear her name, set things right."

John closed his eyes. "I don't think she's innocent."

"Regardless of what you think, there's more at stake here than what she did or didn't do. I guarantee you her entire Hynka wiki is in here. Language and dialects, other villages and concentrations, spiritual beliefs, triggers, behavioral patterns, favorite hunting grounds, geographic research notes. All of which is data we're *supposed* to have right now! That's mission data! For whatever reason, she wiped it all clean. There's your criminal act—justification for a fone recovery. Right?"

She'd gotten him. He was making the acquiescing face. "S'true. We have to get that data out."

"Yes, indeed. Passcode me, boss."

"No."

"No?"

He shook his head weakly. "I can't just give you full access to her life. I'll go in. Copy the wiki and work notes, last week of vids, dump it all in the EV."

Minnie wanted to punch him in the nose. She *needed* into that fone! Some of the most important material was surely in non-work files. But she was powerless. No alternatives.

Maybe after they reviewed the vids—vids of dead crewmembers before they were murdered, of Ish effectively pulling the trigger—John might lose a bit of that self-righteous conviction and, finally appropriately outraged, be inspired to delve deeper into the loon cauldron.

She went to fetch the extractor.

32

Ishtab Soleymani flung aside the weighty fur blanket, rising from her stately bed of piled skins. Her fingertips parted the dangling curtain of piquant vines. A stand of trussed bones bore her long skin stole. She hung it over her neck, draping the wide, black strips in front.

Flanking her bedchamber's tall, isosceles doorway, her servants bowed their heads as she approached. She presented a hand to one of the Lessers. He obliged the gesture by gently sandwiching the hand between his four thick fingers. Ishtab rewarded this obedience by stepping behind the servant, peeling open the protective skin pouch, and sliding her arm in, down to her elbow, until she'd found the hidden organ inside. Her servant twisted and squirmed, hissing his gratitude and undying loyalty.

The other would receive only a stroke of the snout this time. He squatted low, hunching down to Ishtab's raised hand.

"You good," she said, and walked out into the sunlight.

In the shadow of her great palace stood crushing throngs of her disciples, Lessers and Greaters, all eyes glued to her. She raised her arms in a V, silencing the energized chatter.

"This day!" Ishtab shouted. "Westers join. We make. Strong us." She allowed a lengthy outburst of approval. "Bring me. Now go."

The masses cheered. The chests of a thousand Greaters expanded and contracted as they huffed the power breath. Dozens of Lessers fell for the clan, their bodies claimed for vital meat, destinies finally fulfilled. Once their bones had been scraped clean, broken, and drained of marrow, the clan set off to conquer the neighboring village.

Ishtab descended the staircase of short blocks, crafted for her height. Her bare feet reached the compacted dirt ground. She glided across the central court, stepping over bones and overlooked gore, a gentle breeze sending her stole under her arms and fluttering behind her. Lessers with other duties strolled through the village. In passing, Ishtab raised a preemptive hand before these faithful souls could ask if their queen required anything.

In the Greaters' shades, Ishtab walked among the beleaguered expecting, and weary recent birthers. Newborns, not much smaller than her, nursed from the porous skinfolds in their mothers' armpits.

"Good," Ishtab told each mother as she passed. "Good."

At the end of a row, outside the shades, she spotted a small cluster of birthers, apparently ejected into the harsh sunlight. Ishtab approached.

"Why here?"

One of the three mothers turned her head, regarding Ishtab with respect, and then lifted her arm to expose her nursing newborn. The baby's small feet and ashen sides answered the question. These Greater mothers had birthed Lessers.

Ishtab regarded mother and child for a moment and then hailed a passing Lesser.

Pointing to the baby, she said, "Take. Follow."

The Lesser complied without hesitation, throwing the sapped mother's arm aside, and snatching away the baby. The mother's prattles and howls faded as Ishtab strode across the field to the Lessers' shades, baby and carrier behind her. Here she looked upon five times the birthers and expecting.

Ishtab addressed a conscious birther. "Greaters?"

The mother peered up at her, offered respects, and rolled her eyes down the jagged aisle.

Halfway down the row, Ishtab found what she sought. A Lesser birther, asleep, with a Greater infant.

She turned to the Lesser carrying the baby, and motioned to the dozing mother. "Give. Take."

The babies were swapped, then the newborn Greater was carried to the Greaters' shades, to the distraught mother outside. With a look of confusion, the mother inspected the baby from head to toes, sniffing the distinct scent of Lesser, and then proceeded to cleanse the new delivery with saliva and gray milk.

The mother eyed the observing Ishtab and said, "Good."

* * *

Ish closed her game, flung aside the sheet and fuzzy blanket, wedged her feet into her slips, and stepped to the sink. She leaned close to the mirror. A puffy bag under one eye received a resentful poke. She stepped back, tilted her head into the refresher nook, and her foot found the peddle. Microjets sprayed hot mist on her face as warm air and renewer blasted through her hair. The facials cooled to warm and then cold, finishing with a ten-second rush of enriched air. She ran a brush through her hair, worked into a fresh tank, shorts, and top, and traded her slips for runners.

"Morning," Angela said as they both entered the corridor. "After you."

In the lab, Tom was sitting on Minnie's side, gnawing on a chewstick, engrossed with whatever was displayed on one of the screens. His music ticked and thumped from the sides of his headphones.

Ish unbolted one of her own stools and slid it to the farthest screen in the opposite corner of the lab. She sat down, linked in her fone, and navigated into the supply pod tracking system. 133 hours before the next pod's arrival. It had already decelerated to half its cruising speed.

A glance to Tom, focus unchanged.

The trajectory map expanded before her, solid red pipe leading from the pod to the target docking bay. Indicating velocity, the pipe was thickest at the incoming pod's end, tapering to a thin dashed line for the final docking approach. She brushed her finger over a hidden icon in the middle of open space and a new blue pipe appeared, eclipsing the red on the pod side, but then arcing slightly upward, targeting the center of the Backup Habitat. Its speed tapered somewhat, but never slowed enough to prompt a dashed line. The blue trajectory would impact the Backup Habitat at precisely 135 km/h.

Ish copied the pod's most recent position and stats into her simulation and re-hid the alternate course. She closed the app.

Accessing her surface probe catalogue, she filtered down to visuals, and bumped four units onto the large, movable screen to her right. She pinched the panel's edge, angling the screen toward her. Her eyes locked in on the upper-right quarter where a probe lay on the ground outside a tall hut, pointed into a dark doorway. She tapped the black area inside the hut. The camera's exposure corrected. Inside, now visible, a clan chieftain lay atop a bed of stacked Hynka skins. Ish leaned closer to the screen, bumped away the three other quarters so the doorway filled the display, and zoomed the camera until the hut's outer walls disappeared.

She moved her face nearer still, her fone auto-compensating for focus, and watched for a while as the chieftain nibbled on a tiny bone.

* * *

John and Aether stepped out of the CO, quietly chatting. Only "Minnie" and "insisting" were audible. John noticed Ish coming up the hall and touched Aether's elbow.

"Hi, Ish," he said. "I *just* started going over your most recent report. You mind if I get back to you Wednesday? If that's not enough time, you can absolutely add it to Thursday's package as is. You know I trust you."

"It's fine," she replied, stopping in front of them. "You caught that missing reference vid last time. I always appreciate your help."

John returned a smile and modest shrug. He turned to Aether. "After group?"

Aether nodded and faced Ish as John slipped behind her, into the common room. She put her hands on Ish's shoulders, lowered her chin, explored her eyes, a warm smile. "Talk to me."

"What about? All is well."

Aether wasn't buying it, but she didn't press. "You know we haven't hung out in forever, just us? Besides one-on-ones, you know? If it's my quarters—if it's Minnie—you know I can come to you. Or," she raised a conspiratorial eyebrow, "I could always kick her out of our room."

"Sure, that sounds nice."

Unassuaged concern weighed on Aether's face. "You know I love you, beti."

"You, too."

Aether clearly wished to embrace her, but others had entered the hall from both ends. Aether waved Ish into the common room where group would soon begin.

John and Zisa sat at opposite sides of the big round table, while Minnie filled a cup of water from the dispensary. John and Zisa both had the telling, zoned-out faces of fone rapture. Ish sat down as others streamed in, talking too loud for the quiet room.

Suddenly, Zisa blurted out, "What the pip?" silencing the room.

Minnie snorted. "Pip? Is that what *people are saying?*" Minnie liked to mock Zisa's obsession with Earth pop culture. "Or rather, what they *were* saying?" Everything they received was nearly two decades old, and likely obsolete, but Zisa loved it all and tried not to be bothered by the slights.

"Shut up," Zisa said, her gaze still fixed on a blank wall. "The pod!"

Ish's focus snapped from the table to Zisa.

"What about it?" Qin said as he mounted a stool.

"I've been going over the manifest," Zisa replied. "There's a song—a number-one hit—called *Rape Dance*."

Gasps and laughs.

Minnie plunked down beside Zisa. "That's amazing. Who's the artist?"

"Um … oh, well, it matches … *The Tampon Fuses*."

Everyone cackled, even John, but Zisa didn't appear so amused. "Guys, how is this funny? Think about what this means. Think about what it says about Earth culture if the *majority* of people were into a song like this."

"Come on, Zees," Tom said. "It could be satirical. You have no idea."

"Yeah," Pablo said. "Plus it's twenty years old. We'll just have to wait for the pod to get here and all listen to it. Hey, let's open next week's group with it. But nobody gets to listen to it before that! It'll be a bonding experience."

Zisa's gripes and the others' chuckles slowly faded from Ish's ears as the game loaded in her fone. She focused her eyes on the bare wall between Tom and Zisa, and enabled her avatar.

Flinging aside the weighty fur blanket, she rose from the bed.

* * *

Ish set down the helmet beside the utility belt on the supply boxes, and pulled her hair out the back of her suit. She slid off the hairband and shook her head, fluffing away the oppressively taut ponytail she'd worn for so long. Her curly locks drank in the humidity and would soon swell into a striking headdress.

As she hiked through the underbrush toward the great city of Er Khosh, she severed her gloves from the suit, pitching them into bushes without a backward glance. She unzipped the top of her survival suit down to the waist, leaving only her halter bra above the waist. Cool air grazed her bare midriff, shoulders, and arms.

Set to autoglide, her optics transitioned through spectrums. Foliage shifted from white to orange, from purple to black, red-outlined, translucent, entirely invisible. Still strolling at a leisurely pace, she flipped back to biotherm, having caught sight of a distance lifeform. 10 o'clock, 33m ahead … a false alarm. A large carnivorous plant. Her pace quickened.

Mapping guided her along a route she'd planned weeks ago, circumnavigating the bone-laden shrine of Hwahxo, two kilometers along the sundrenched crest of a hidden pass, and then a half-K down to an unobstructed overlook of Er Khosh.

As she sauntered to the overlook's tip, a growing panorama broadened before her. Hundreds of strident Greaters and timid Lessers hustled about the barren field, unaware of her presence. At the cliff's edge, she slid her palms up her sweat-glazed forehead into her frizzed hair, filled her lungs as she hurled her arms out before her, and called to them.

"Greaters!"

Those nearest halted first, scanning about for the strange voice's source. Just as their gazes found her, the next farthest cluster froze, and then the next, until time had appeared to stop across the entire expanse. She looked out at the hushed masses, hearing only the sigh of a gentle breeze.

"Know all! Fear all! Here Shroosh!"

The congregation dropped to their backsides in succession, like dominoes. Muted chatter bustled through the electrified horde.

"All change! Er Khosh change!"

Submissive heads sneaked upward glances at the Goddess of Floods incarnate, no doubt pondering whether the deity they so feared would choose to bless them, or choose to damn.

Shroosh lowered her arms to her sides and stepped back from the precipice. With regal strides she returned to the slope, descending the foothill's gravelly base, boots sinking in the scree as she slid. On firm soil, she continued on toward her docile subjects. With heads still hung close to the ground, their uneasy eyes glinted from the shadows while tracking her progress.

She paused a stone's throw from the first line, sizing up the nearest Greaters. A young adult male caught her eye. Unlike the others, he wouldn't dare behold the visage before him. His focus gripped the ground as Shroosh sauntered his way. Without hesitation, she stepped right up to him, wiry shoulder hairs prickling her bare abdomen. The young Greater flinched as Shroosh laid a hand on his back. She inhaled a deep, intoxicating breath, caressing her subject's skin, his hairs gathering between her fingers and brushing beneath her palm like sapling pine needles. Her eyes wandered down his back to the intact cloacal pouch.

"Move no," she commanded as she leaned forward, her hand sliding toward the virginal slit.

"Shroosh you?" the male quietly asked as Shroosh's fingers explored the pouch's shallow crevice, in search of a weak spot to breach.

"Yes."

The sky streaked forward and she was on her back, biostats alerts flashing and buzzing. Her boot had been crushed into her foot and ankle, and each second—as fast as it could update—new damage sites appended the list.

ALERTS: BIOSTAT – Tibial shaft fracture
ALERTS: BIOSTAT – Multiple fractures
ALERTS: BIOSTAT – Severe musculoskeletal trauma
ALERTS: BIOSTAT – Circulatory
ALERTS: BIOSTAT – Circulatory Critical
ALERTS: BIOSTAT – Pulmonary contusion
ALERTS: BIOSTAT – Critical
ALERTS: BIOSTAT – Cardiopulmonary Arrest

Ish's body rolled, flipped, twisted, and crushed—her face, for an instant, pressed into the small of her own back. Greaters' faces and bodies flashed by in a never-ending blur until one hand pulled her from the frenzied swarm, lifted her high overhead, twirling the mangled body in the air as it was sprinted from the scene.

3.3

Wiping her sweaty face on a dusty sleeve, Minerva burst into the cave. "We have to leave. Now."

Startled, John sat up too fast. Ribs, neck, shoulder. He gasped and cringed. "What's happened?"

Minerva unclipped the string of bunnies dangling from her waist and tossed them in a supply bin. "Ran into some roving hunters ..." She scuttled about, grabbing strewn gear and throwing it into bins. "Spread out over a few kilometers. Thought there were only three. Kept an eye out, making sure I wouldn't be corralled in. But there was a fourth. The instant it came into optic range, they started closing—*all four*. Like they knew where I was. Like they were in communication—coordinated!" She began stuffing her sleeping bag into its sack.

John began easing out of his bag, eyes trained on the cave opening. "Are they … are they coming? Were you followed?"

"Coming, yes. Followed, no. I killed three of them. Tried to get the last one, but it fled. Couldn't catch up enough for a shot. Not even close. I fully expect he's fetching some friends at this very second. I also suspect they can smell us from a *long* way out." Minerva hefted a bin and turned to go load it on the skimmer. "Ugh, *always* paid attention to wind before!"

John began stuffing his bag, catching a potent whiff as she breezed by, like ammonia and fresh cat urine. "I can smell you from here, actually." She paused at the entrance, peering back—only a silhouette, but he could imagine her expression. "No really, it's sharp … biting. Have you had any attacks? Presymptoms? Your profile indicated that hormonal—"

"Not now." She resumed to the skimmer, murmuring. "'Presymptoms hormonal bleh bleh' … damned things practically on our doorstep …"

John sighed. Never now. She refused to discuss it. Better to pretend it didn't exist! And it'd remain her biggest liability, worse even than his burdensome, ruined body. He'd wanted to make her leave without him, had rehearsed the words and bolstered his resolve, no matter what she argued (*if* she argued—he was fairly certain she would) or bargained. She'd believed his story about a return vehicle, but now he wasn't so sure it'd make a difference, even if she didn't have him slowing her down and exhausting resources.

She dashed back in, grabbed the comms unit, and filled her other hand with gear. John threw his packed bag on a pile.

Before he could utter another syllable, Minerva cut him off. "I'm serious. Not now. Just sit tight for a few minutes and keep watch."

John bit his tongue but his mind raced on. She'd already slammed shut the medkit full of his pills. He could see exactly how this played out if he told her to leave him behind. She'd stay and argue, even as an army of Hynka stampeded up the hillside. It'd turn into a gory last stand, both of them torn to bits.

And then there was Ish and her flops of Hynka data, language, vids, and maps, as yet untransferred to the EV or Minerva's fone. She needed every possible resource to boost her chances of surviving a trek across this continent.

Only garbage and a few empty cartons remained when Minerva stooped down on his better side. She looked in his eyes. "You ready?"

John hung his left arm over her neck and pulled his feet in close. She gathered and clutched the material in the small of his back. A count of three, nodded in sync. White and red painted the insides of his eyelids as they rose. He wanted to pause there a moment, let the burning subside, but it wouldn't make the march to the skimmer any easier, and Minerva wasn't wasting a second. His feet skipped and shuffled as they went, contributing but a few pitiful steps along the way, Minerva's little body bearing the bulk of his weight.

On the pad, she crouched slowly and let him grip a handhold as they eased him down to a seated position. Her clammy face was centimeters from his. He could feel her heat radiating against his cheek. He wanted to thank her, to apologize for existing, to tell her something she'd like.

"Minerva—"

"They're coming," she mouthed, her gaze fixed on the panel over his shoulder—optics penetrating metal, plastic, wires, and trees, revealing an apparently disturbing scene John could only imagine. She took his hand from her back and placed it on a bar. "Hold tight."

She jumped away—a brief panic surging over his scalp as he thought she'd run off to confront the horde, but she'd simply hopped to a second skimmer. They had two skimmers. Had he known this?

John curled one arm around a firmly strapped bin and clutched the grip bar with the other. The pad quaked beneath him, the skimmer's pairing tones sounded, and the rumble intensified.

A few meters away, Minerva's mouth whispered pleading, encouraging words to her skimmer.

John closed his eyes and waited for the ready tone, but never heard it. A chorus of cracking branches, thundering feet, and a single, commanding Hynka voice, roaring *"Hwasso-AAAH!"* eclipsed every other sound, but the abrupt crush of what felt like 10 *g* left no question as to whether the skimmer had been ready.

The pressure tapered down quickly, John's gut rising in his body cavity with nauseating force. He dared a peek below. Ish's EV already suffered in their stead. They'd left the hatch open, so white fragments, large and small, filled the air above the amassing horde like harried seagulls over chummed water. Giant bodies fought to squeeze into the cave as innumerable others joined the dark crunch. A few individuals stood down the hill, away from the swelling crowd, tracking the skimmers across the sky with unnerving composure, as if their prey, as planned, had set out on a direct course to some cunning trap.

* * *

Five-and-a-half hours of northwesterly flight presented stunning new landscapes. The continent's largest freshwater lake stretched off to the horizon before they followed its source, a glacier and river-cut chasm where sporadic herds of *dalis* fed and drank in blissful ignorance of the predatory nightmare to the south—an idyllic *before* pic of inevitable extinction. Hynka migration models had this species wiped out within a few short generations.

A slight course deviation took the pair over one of Epsy's renowned Wonders: The Great Bubble Bath. Eons of geothermal activity in the area had cooked fossilized organic material into a vast soup cauldron, feeding a lively population of hyperthermophiles. Foamy bubbles of saplike matter (the original matter combined with the organisms' waste) trapped gases and frothed, rising from porous bedrock, gurgling out over previous layers, and solidified in the frosty air. The perpetual phenomena continued coating an area the size of a small city, re-melting vent walls and sinking in pockets, while adjacent lather hills remained 100m deep and growing. Gases released in the area were poisonous, and the smell was awful.

John choked. "Beautiful, but can we go?"

"Sorry," Minnie said, observing John's pallor.

She released the skimmers' hover lock and steered them upwind toward the nearest fresh air. Once clear, she resumed west and engaged the autopilot, opting for low altitude travel. The frigid air this far north was cold enough without adding the icy insult of higher elevations. The skimmers would consume more energy, but it'd be worth it.

Combing through the data John had uploaded to her fone, Minnie had identified a sizable swath of land where Ish had never observed Hynka. Adventurous (or lost) individuals had been spotted roaming higher latitudes, but Minnie wasn't concerned with the odd loner.

According to Ish's recent maps, Minnie's target campsite's nearest village was a three-week journey at top Hynka running speed. Serious peace of mind. A full night's sleep awaited them. A night free of anxiety, and, if Minnie had her way, a night without more lecturing from John. He'd been relentless for the first couple hours. Minnie's bittersweet triumph at proving Ish's guilt had been short-lived. She'd earned but a few fleeting minutes of gloating before the subject veered.

She shouldn't have admitted to the episode. The man didn't need more things to worry about. Despite his troubling, repetitive assertions that she could and *should* carry on without him "if anything should happen," Minnie's convictions were unshakable. She'd get them to the coast. She'd build them a sturdy boat. They'd make it to Threck Country.

As if she needed more motivation than mere survival, John had tried to reignite her love and fascination with Threck culture, clumsily quoting proverbs, and sending her her own pics. But she didn't snub his efforts. She thanked him and oohed, aah'd, even gasping at pics that had never left her consciousness, as if viewed for the first time. "Wow, is that one of *mine?*" Because she *got* it. He felt like baggage. A liability. He needed to contribute to the task at hand, like stuffing a single survival bag among a hundred other tasks.

Fortunately, she'd rewarded his inspiration efforts enough to satisfy him. Either that, or his meds had taken over. His back leaned against the access panel below the other skimmer's console, he'd been mostly quiet for hours. Eyes attentive, observing the transient scenery, but with nothing to say.

She wondered if he was watching more Ish vids or reading journals—ones he hadn't copied to Minnie's fone. Despite that whole privacy rant, he was the type that wanted every minute detail. It wasn't yet clear how long Ish had been *sunk* in her game, living a second life as God-Queen of virtual Hynka. Minnie didn't care. What happened happened, and she needed no additional explanation, no analysis of the root psychosis, missed cues, or turning point. If Aether was still alive she'd no doubt blame herself, but Minnie was now satisfied with what they'd learned, and content in the knowledge of where Ish's plot had led her.

As knowledgeable as Ish had been about her beloved beasties, she died for lack of the very depth-of-field diversity Minnie was trying to evangelize. *"Context is everything, context can be nothing, scale is infinite."* Ish wasn't some noob overlooking a subtle detail. She'd fully immersed herself in that society, and yet missed the very underpinnings of Hynka spirituality. They didn't fear and respect their gods. They despised them. And like any other external power they beheld, they wished to conquer the gods. They'd hung their vanquished Goddess of Floods above the shrine to Death. *"Warning: We're stronger than you."*

John had been quick to highlight that Ish's scheme hadn't worked out as planned—as if her ghost needed a lawyer—emphasizing that she had no intention to injure, strand, or kill other station crew. The pod was only supposed to strike the Backup Habitat, not the main station (how sweet of her!). Apparently, without a functional BH, frontline safeguards were automatically removed from the EV's. Whenever the dust settled, days or weeks later, Ish would isolate one of the EV's systems, hack in a bogus exigency event, and launch solo to the surface, free to bring her twisted fantasies to life.

Minnie sent John an M.

MINNIE: You awake?

He peered over at her, eyes squinted against the sun. For an instant, he looked like a little boy.

MINNIE: Where's your pain? You good for another 30 or so mins?

He nodded and returned to whatever zone he'd been in, remaining there until they reached their new campsite.

* * *

Dark, low-hanging clouds blanketed the region, soaking the skimmers and everything on them. Minnie had to wipe the moisture from her visor every few seconds as she flew several passes over the area, scanning as far as optics allowed. John, too, helped to survey the scene from his vantage point, agreeing that the area appeared safe.

The paired skimmers descended into a flat plain, patches of snow dotting the mostly barren landscape. Here they'd find no natural protection from beast or weather, but with this came the benefit of unobscured surroundings. The area's largest plantlife were sparse orange shrubs, each standing alone, dozens of meters from another sprout. Growing only a meter or two high, they wore their dense foliage close to a central trunk.

Stretched sideways across a skimmer pad, John observed Minnie in front of one of the bushes. "They're perfect camouflage for evac'd crew."

Minnie glanced behind her, noticing the shade matched her survival suit. "Just stand up real straight and be still, right?"

She resumed setting up the tent.

Late afternoon dropped a few light waves of snow, and it appeared they'd make it through the night without any more serious systems rolling in. Fearful of sending smoke with the southerly winds, each ate one of their few remaining calorie bars. With prox alerts on guard duty, the exhausted pair turned in before the last light had left the sky.

Minnie awoke with a start.

John was snoring loud beside her. She had to pee. How long had she slept? The ever-present clock on her fone revealed it'd been less than two hours. Minnie groaned. It was so cold outside. They'd both layered up their clothes before bed. She closed her eyes and played out in her head the arduous undressing process she'd have to go through just to pee. The freezing air. Why hadn't they made survival suits with some sort of nifty flap you could easily undo, like that old-style full-body underwear? And why in perfect hell had she drunk so much water?

Because calorie bars are like eating a brick of chalk.

Exactly.

Maybe she could fall back asleep—hold the pee for morning.

Yeah, right.

Shut up, it's possible.

John's version of snoring was maddening. He'd go quiet for what seemed like forever, done with the straining sounds and breathing normally, but with each stretch of silence, just when she thought she could finally doze back off, he'd groan as if constipated and striving to release a gigantic crap. It'd been like this every time he'd slept—

especially so with the diclomorph—but, aside from their original cave, she hadn't been trying to sleep at the same time. Aether must've worn canceler plugs every night.

Uh-oh.

What uh-oh?

Nothing, just go back to sleep.

With the snoring and the pee and now you? Impossible. Just say it. Is it about Aether? Ear plugs?

I shouldn't say. It's too soon for you to know.

A bolt of pain shot out from her groin. Overfull. She reached down and pressed in. Waited too long. Now the idea of sitting up, of folding her body, compressing her bladder, standing up, the cold outside—it was all too much. And she couldn't just let it go in her clothes. It wouldn't just be a little dribble; she'd be soaked, and that was dangerous in this sub-zero environment.

And they had a little wide-mouthed bottle they'd designated for this purpose! Where was it? Buried in a bin somewhere, *outside!*

Another violent groan from John.

This was hell frozen over. She knew it now: hell was the stabbing pain of an adamant bladder, and the inability to resolve it.

Just go! Get up and go!

"Fine!" she blurted, and fumbled with her bag's zipper.

She'd disturbed John but didn't care. He sucked in a fast breath, croaked on the exhale, and fell right back into his breathing pattern. Minnie wasn't quiet about leaving the tent. She groused and grumbled, swore at the stubborn door zipper, and crunched across a thin layer of snow to the nearest shrub. Cold wrapped her head like a vise and tightened.

Wrestling off the top of her suit with one hand, she tried to keep pressure on with the other. With gravity against her, she couldn't hold it any more.

Come on, hurry up! Almost there!

"Shut it! I'm not just taking my time here!"

She threw the top of her suit behind her, bent over, and pulled it through her legs, out of the line of fire. Dancing from foot to foot, she unsnapped the environment shirt from the trousers, and then, in one swoop of her thumbs, dropped her suit bottom, environment trousers, base layer, and undershorts. One hand on the shrub for stability, stinging cold raking at her exposed skin, all she could focus on was the too-slow draining. The pain had yet to subside.

There you go … yes … halfway home …

Bliss replaced anguish as the last few drops cut through the rising steam. Heaven was the relief of an emptied bladder, and she'd arrived at the gates. Not even the breeze nipping at her legs and backside could lessen her joy. It actually wasn't so cold, now that she was in it.

She pulled up her shorts as she stood—too fast—a potent head rush. A glance down at the crumple of clothes at her ankles. What a mess. Too much to deal with right now, and besides, she was a little hot anyway. The cool air felt nice on her face, neck, and bare knees. No need for all those layers right now.

She shuffled toward the tent, suit bottom bunched around her ankles, top dragging behind her as she snickered at how this would look to a passer-by.

No passers-by out here, that's for sure.

"Right? You know Aether would die laugh—"

Ouch. Poor choice of words there, babe.

A couple meters from the swaying tent door, Minnie stopped. With a flashing biostat alert filling her fone view, Minnie stared at the tent, at the space she knew John currently filled. She could feel her pulse in her fingers and toes, chest beating.

Feels like a big one coming on, hon. Probably best to run it out.

"Dad said never try to run it out. Said lay down."

Dad said not to think of him. Kind of messed up, really, but I'd say the advice applies here. Feel like running?

"Yes."

So run.

"Okay."

She tried to start, tripping on her suit, and yanked a foot from one boot, planting the socked foot in snow. And fell over. Her hand crushed the thin sheet of snow and landed on an unseen sharp sticker.

"Dammit!"

She plucked the thing from her palm and kicked violently at the suit bunch ensnaring her other ankle. The foot broke free, and *she* was free.

Long-sleeved environment shirt over a tank, plus undershorts and a pair of thick envirosocks. Probably underdressed for the weather, but she'd be running, generating her own heat, and wouldn't be gone for long.

The first few strides felt good, the next few even better. Glands rewarded her for her cooperation. A fresh wave of euphoria. She knew exactly what was happening, and sped up her pace.

Of course you know. And you're doing what you need to. You're doing goooood.

"Now you have to tell," Minnie said with steamy breath.

Tell what?

"Whatever it's too soon for me to know. Tell or I'll stop and go back."

So demanding … very well. You were right. It's about Aether.

Minnie dodged an orange shrub at the last second. She realized her biostat alert was still flashing, obscuring her vision. Real helpful. She tried to shut it off, but it wouldn't go away. What a stupid design. A few more strides and she realized the thing was also buzzing in her ear.

"Goodnight, fone." She enabled optical pass-through and the world regained clarity. "You were saying?"

Aether. But I'm not sure you want to know this—

"So help me, I swear I'm gonna turn—"

It was never real.

Minnie continued running, chewing on this. She hopped a decaying epsequoia trunk.

"Expound. Real what? Real for who?"

Her. Of course it was real for you. You loved her with all your heart. Still do.

This line of thought wasn't entirely new. She'd worried in the beginning, couldn't believe she'd found real love, couldn't understand what Aether saw in her, thought she'd come to her senses at any second and say, "Whoa, sorry everybody! John is definitely the love of my life. My mistake!" But Wise Minnie was making it sound like some sort of conspiracy.

Private moments with Aether flashed through Minnie's head as she skipped left-right-left across an outcropping of round-headed rocks. Aether's skin and hair and lips and breath. Heady conversations, sore-gut laughter, M's.

"You're wrong. It was real."

Yeah, you're probably right. Let's forget about the whole thing.

There was something more. What was she trying to hide?

Nothing. Focus on your footing.

Minnie skidded to a stop and headed back to camp.

Fine! Look, you were doing so well until a couple years back! Remember that review?

She reversed again, resuming south. "Damned John and his stringent BS—"

You started isolating yourself, went all passive-aggressive with quotas …

"Hahah … if I made a quota I was pissed. I think I only hit my water that first month."

Right, but exercise, game, missed meetings, hygiene, going silent in group …

"Childish, but those were good times. Drove John crazy, I'm sure."

Not just John. Everybody was worried! You're the lynchpin of the team! It was bringing down everybody's morale. Something had to be done.

Minnie slowed to a jog, trying to remember. It hadn't seemed like others were worried … everything seemed fine otherwise. Only John was gnashing.

When did your behavior change? When did your quotas return to normal?

Minnie felt a pinecone in her throat. She knew exactly when she'd shaped up. Her biweekly one-on-one with Aether. Something was different, from the second Minnie closed the office door. Aether had said—

"I need to tell you something ..."

"... and I'm afraid of the consequences ..."

"... but I can't go another day without telling you how I feel."

"I've fought it."

"I've taken meds."

"She laughed with a little tear forming in her eye and said how she'd consulted with a sim therapist in her game. And I still had no idea where she was going with it."

She leaned forward in her chair, put one hand on your hand and the other on your cheek.

"*That's* when I thought I knew where she was going! But I still couldn't believe it."

And then she said ...

"I'm madly in love with you."

Minnie stopped to catch her breath. She was shaking violently.

Don't stop! Not yet!

"You're crazy. That was the realest moment of my life."

I know, hon. Just not the realest in hers. You know that she and John would've sacrificed anything for the good of the mission and crew. Remember that time, a week after she moved in—

"In the hall outside John's office."

They were so close, his hand in the small of her back, their heads low, sad.

"She told me he was begging her to reconsider."

Is that what it looked like?

"No."

Minnie ran.

Something was coming. Thousands of them. She dared not a backward glance. Hynka or cats or the knobby stilt legs of an infinite *dali* herd, they were chasing her, and she had to speed up.

* * *

Warm gusts against nose and lips. Body so cold. Minnie couldn't feel her legs anymore. She supposed she was through with legs. Used them all up.

A thick drop on her upper lip. It crawled toward her cheek and streamed slowly down. She didn't know where she was, but the crispy crackles beneath her back felt like a pile of potato chips whenever she moved. Petrified lichen? Snow, but her skin had gone numb?

An awful odor.

The warm puffs brought her cheeks back to life. Suddenly, she actively felt the pain of the cold, no longer in some vague, intangible manner. She was freezing to death. Her body rotated on its own, rolling to the side. Was she doing this? Still couldn't feel her legs. Was she in motion, rolling and sliding down some hill?

And then she *was* in motion. No question. She was being carried.

Some body parts were being heated while others suffered against an increasingly frigid wind. Was she on a skimmer?

It didn't matter.

Body hurt, sick, done. Brain fried.

Let someone else be in charge for once.

She faded out.

* * *

Leg cramped, headache, thirsty, weak, suffocating heat, hollow gut. Minnie's legs were crossed in an awkward sort of twist, one foot pinned beneath something, preventing her from shifting. Her hair and face were soggy, probably from whatever cloth was being dabbed against her face. Not cloth. A water bag? And not being dabbed. *She* was being moved up to it. The sensations all over her body suddenly made sense. Her back lay atop an arm, her rear cradled in a pair of giant fingers, her arms across her chest and wedged between an immense thumb and her belly. Her face, more wet pressing on her mouth.

The urge to cry, chest quaking with fear of impending agony.

She dared a peek.

Hazy sunlight from somewhere. A blurry shine. Dark cave—some strange, moist nook. The *smell!* Though lacking firsthand experience, she concluded with certainty that *this* was the stench found behind an overactive bull's testicles.

"Rrloch-tss."

Her host had seen Minnie's eyes open, felt her body come to life. Another pair of fingers moved near Minnie's face, like leathery Dobermans with conical claws for heads, and pinched at its wrinkly drapes of armpit skin, pressing it against Minnie's lips. Thick, gray milk percolated from a hundred lactiferous ducts. The Hynka was trying to nurse her.

Relief flushed through her. She cast aside visions of her own body thrashed about like Ish's, and turned her fone back on. She couldn't see anything but purple-black skin, had no idea if she'd been carried into the middle of a bustling village or was still somewhere near her campsite.

Nine hours had passed.

Pressing her lips shut against the increasingly insistent Hynka, Minnie's fone reacquired GPS and established position 14.4K from John and the campsite.

John! He must be losing it!

Had she brought the medkit into the tent the night before? Would he be able to take his morning dose? Or had Hynka gotten to him, too?

Minnie switched optics and rolled her eyes around. She was in an above-ground burrow set between a mature epsequoia trunk and one felled long ago. At her current angle, she could see no other mobile lifeforms in the area.

"Rrloch-tss!" The Hynka gave Minnie's ribs a near-crushing squeeze.

A scary thought: even if "Mama" wished only benevolence upon her new adopted daughter, Hynka were accustomed to a much more rugged offspring. Even their newborn's bones were three times denser than a human's. Mama wanted Baby to nurse. Baby wasn't cooperating. Mama was getting mad.

Crapshake, Minnie thought, and regretted the ironic expletive.

She steadied her nerves, pried apart chapped lips, shut her eyes, and felt Mama raise her body once more, pressing the skin flap to her mouth.

Breathe through nose, don't let it in mouth, don't swallow, don't taste … like a stage kiss … the galaxy's most vile stage kiss …

The ducts didn't just seep, though. After a few seconds, a gush of fluid sprayed to the back of her throat and she choked.

Mama rubbed Minnie's tummy with her thumb and uttered approval, or maybe soothing. *"Otch … otch …"*

Minnie let the overflowing milk ooze out the sides of her mouth. Ducts flowed like a broken shower head—starts and stops, jarring blasts. Minnie was being soaked. It saturated her shirt, spreading down her front and back.

At least she was warm. And Mama seemed content, rolling onto her back and easing the pressure on Minnie's body. Now, Minnie stood on hands and knees in a nest of dry litterfall, between Mama's side and arm, face still buried in spurting armpit. The milk streamed from the corners of Minnie's mouth, coursed down to her chin, and ran like a faucet to the ground. Surely Mama would soon run dry.

And then what? To both plan and distract herself, Minnie inventoried her assets. At some point she'd lost her suit, and with it all sorts of essentials: water, personal climate, multitool, mini medkit, boots, PA, signal boosters. She was practically naked in only environment shirt, tank, and undershorts. A toe wiggle divulged a single sock's presence.

Her brain and fone would be her sole resources. But within that little device, she had Ish's data, and a 2,611-word Hynka core language DB, with a regional dialect sub-catalogue of another 601 words.

Without warning, a thick glob slopped into Minnie's mouth with a gaseous splutter—like a shot of pudding or expired milk chunk—and she gagged, blowing away the sour air while trying to eject the lump out the side of her mouth. Her tongue only spread and split the dollop apart. Still heaving, she pulled her face away and spat.

At least the milk had ceased flowing.

Mama disapproved, hissing, *"Onykyah! Rwitz!"* as she smacked the back of Minnie's head—a smack that felt like a medicine ball.

Minnie's face and upper body crumpled into the crunchy, soaked floor. A giant digit slid beneath her chest and she was flipped like a ragdoll, the back of her head striking a solid object on the burrow's side wall. Milk and sludge coated her face, bits of dead twig, spore, and foliage adhering. Mama brushed away the outer mess on Minnie's cheeks and nose, finding little globs of the rejected goop, and guided it all back toward Minnie's lips. She poked at Minnie's sealed mouth with a single, dull-tipped claw—a thick, stubby rhinoceros horn jabbing against tender flesh, cutting lips on teeth—and Mama directed the substance back into Minnie's bleeding mouth, bit by bit.

The Hynka jerked Minnie into the crook of an arm, reaching with the opposite hand into the soup of spilled milk and compost below. Minnie had evidently spat out a vital shot of nutrients. Mama's determined bronze eyes shimmered in a dusty bar of sunlight as she brought a filthy thumbclaw to Minnie's mouth, carefully peeled down Baby's bloody lower lip, and pressed, sliding. A bitter cereal of kindling and mammary snot scraped across Minnie's teeth and filled her cheek. She yelped as the claw slid too far, stretching her lips near to tearing. The thumb was withdrawn as Mama stared.

Minnie had most certainly already swallowed a few drops of the sludge, along with dirt and lichen dust, yeasty flecks, and throat-scoring bark chips. Most still lingered in her throat. Her parched mouth refused to provide more than a pinhead of saliva. She needed water. She needed an MW to blast a multiround into well-meaning Mama's chest cavity.

You probably saved my life and all, but this just isn't going to work.

Satisfied with the quantity of goop that had entered (and not re-exited) Minnie's mouth, Mama reclined once more, this time dragging Minnie across her fuzzy belly and resting a hefty hand on her back. Minnie was sprawled out like a dead man draped over an enormous horse's back, and with comparable odds of escape.

* * *

The Hynka had been asleep for a while. Unable to delicately wriggle free, Minnie began an intermittent DC request to any other node that entered range. She delved into Ish's maps and data. Based upon now-obvious features, Minnie identified Mama as a member of the Lesser breed of Hynka. The Lessers were far from docile, but didn't possess several trademark Greater traits, such as the adrenal surges they seemed to share with Minnie. And Lessers *never* attacked Greaters, only vice-versa.

Could that be why Minnie wasn't immediately gobbled up upon discovery, found with chest heaving like a panting Greater oxygenating its lungs? If this was the only reason Minnie was still alive, or if Mama had half a brain, she'd eventually notice her little find smelled more like food than family.

One bit of good news: there were no villages nearby, and the hunting grounds for the closest clan fanned out southward. Perhaps Mama had gotten lost or, hell, escaped of her own volition from a life destined to end with limbs ripped from her body. Ish had a record of a small Lesser pack living a nomadic life, but they ended up finding a mixed village and joined them.

While an explanation for Mama's presence would be interesting enough, Minnie's *survival*-focused side was more interested in Lessers' physical weaknesses. Was there some magical pressure point Minnie could jab and Mama would plunge into an incapacitating seizure? Or maybe a period in the sleep cycle where nothing could wake her, during which even intense thrashing beneath her hand and the sudden absence of 50 kilos from her belly would go unnoticed? Ish had recorded no such convenient tidbits. Much of her notes in this area focused on Hynka sex acts and associated physiology.

Minnie explored Angela's botanical DB in search of potential sedatives or poisons. There were a few hits, but mostly in tropical regions, and nothing remotely this far north.

She was losing hope for getting out of this without help. Could John make it onto a skimmer by himself? Stand up and *stay* up to fly it? No way.

No one was coming to rescue her. John would either be killed or die out there alone. The return module would touch down at the rally point in Threck Country, be discovered at some point by confounded Threck who'd never receive anything close to an explanation. Maybe it would become the underpinning of a new religion. Or even better, a Threck boards it, she has no clue what the insistent synth voice is repeating while she's launched into space, and then equally unable to grasp that the trail of animated floor lights lead to a metabed that, well, *might* keep her alive for the journey. Eleven years later, some Earth station dock workers scratch their heads at the long-dead, decayed corpse of a poor starved and suffocated alien.

Minnie sighed. Frustration simmered as she grew increasingly antsy. Silly, no-chance-of-success ideas began flashing through her mind, masquerading as low-to-medium-chance-of-success ideas. What if she didn't need a plan, but only patience? Perhaps Mama would simply let her go after a nice nap.

Her head and joints still ached from the HSPD attack; her muscles were depleted of strength. She'd slept for days after prior episodes as her body slowly recovered. Obviously not an option at present. She'd have to stay awake. Seize whatever opportunity window presented itself.

But her eyelids did need a rest.

No harm in closing them for a couple minutes.

Mama sure as hell wasn't going anywhere anytime soon. The big belly rose and fell with a small boat's rhythm.

Minnie turned her head sideways, one ear nestling into the abrasive hair. The sound of Mama's breaths resonated below the thick skin. Each inhale produced a long, muffled shushing. Outside the burrow, there was only the serene rustle of epsequoia pads rubbing against their neighbors, and a wet trickling Minnie guessed was melting snow or ice flowing down the trunk.

She surprised herself with a little smile. Was this actually a *nice* moment?

The belly slowly rose and fell. *"Shhhhhhhhhh …"*

* * *

Minnie awoke to another forced nursing session. One of her arms had been wrapped awkwardly behind her back—unmovable in Mama's firm grip. As soon as Minnie realized what was happening, she opened her mouth and latched onto the skin flap, appeasing Mama in hopes of it once more earning her slack.

Indeed, the Hynka sank into her bowl-shaped bed and let her arm rest away from her body. Minnie was once more completely unrestrained. Now in the opposite armpit, she had her feet planted on the ground, one hand on Mama's arm and the other on the wooly chest. The milk flow had picked up and Minnie used her same trick, letting it escape out the corners and drip from her chin. But she was thirsty, probably severely dehydrated, especially after the episode. Surely the majority of this fluid was water …

Still breathing through her nose, she dared a small gulp. Her body instantly demanded another, but she wanted to wait—see if her stomach rejected it. The last thing she needed right now was to vomit out what little fluids she had. She watched a minute pass on the clock, noting the time, as well. Late afternoon. She'd slept more than five hours.

Her stomach was fine, pleading for more. Why wait? Another gulp. Mama's approving hand began rubbing Minnie's back. Despite herself, Minnie waited only ten seconds before cutting loose and guzzling the milk. She even forgot to avoid tasting it.

Hm … like rancid walnuts and spoiled goat cheese.

She gagged but persevered until her stomach seized and threatened revolt. Minnie halted and gasped for air. Mama stuck a finger behind Minnie's head, pinched the wet flap of skin, and pressed the two back together. Minnie could see a lump moving in the skin curtain. Mama didn't want Baby to miss out on the best part.

Oh no … already sick! How to get out of this?

She thought fast, reached up, and grabbed the skin with both hands, taking it away from Mama, who offered no resistance. If Baby was ready to handle her business on her own, so be it.

Minnie turned her head, blocking the view of the flap, and pinched it between her chin and neck, attempting to simulate the feeling of a mouth. An instant later, the revolting dessert spewed into her neck, and she tugged her shirt collar open to let it slide into hiding. She simulated a deep gulp and released the fold.

As per their new family tradition, Mama dragged Minnie up over her belly. This time, lying head below stomach didn't sit well. Bile gurgled up; she fought it back. Tears streamed from her eyes and tickled down her nose. Maybe the milk was toxic after all. Maybe she shouldn't fight it.

The choice was taken from her when Mama plopped her heavy hand onto Minnie's back, squishing guts and sending an irrepressible surge up her throat. Minnie coughed and gagged and milk spilled down Mama's side.

Mama wasn't happy.

She pushed off her insolent child, Minnie landing on the burrow floor, where she continued retching. There was no stopping it at this point. Her stomach seemed intent on a full evac. Mama rolled upright, scooped both hands under Minnie's knees—along with layers of now-tainted nest floor—and hurled the load outside.

Minnie landed first on face and shoulder before her feet hurdled overhead—back twisting—and her whole body crashed down facing up, knocking the wind from her. She lay there a beat, catching her breath and offering her gut a chance to orient itself before it decided whether to pick up where it left off.

What was Mama doing? Was she coming? Was this Minnie's chance to escape? Had she been disowned for her disobedience?

A good, solid breath filled her lungs and her stomach felt relatively still. She tilted her chin up to observe the burrow entrance, but a dark shroud consumed her entire head and dragged her away.

She found herself back in the burrow, face smothered in the fold between Mama's seated belly and leg. Minnie's arms scrabbled and groped and she pulled her knees in to try and push herself free. She couldn't tell what Mama was doing up there, but every little movement compressed Minnie's skull to a terrifying degree. Finally, Mama stopped moving and Minnie stopped fighting. Though her nose was squished and pinched shut, the Hynka's skin crease formed a little channel in front of Minnie's mouth, and she was finally able to inhale another full breath. Though she'd be held fast until Mama decided otherwise.

A hard poke at her ankle bone. Surely a claw tip. It slid up her bare leg, tugging the shorts upward a little before the claw rose away. What next? Not knowing was even more maddening. A pinch of her thigh—two claws, one in front, one in back. Her environment shirt and tank brushed up, exposing her waist and back. Hot breath sniffed her skin. Prodding at her waist.

Her air channel thinned to nothing and Minnie held the half-lungful of air.

Now the head—a painful pair of mallet taps on the side of her skull. Swirls around her scalp. The claw lifted away. Tugging at a few locks of hair. A sudden jerk and thin clumps were torn from her head. Minnie moaned and whimpered her final exhale into the wall of flesh.

But Mama leaned back a little, and Minnie caught a rush of cool air, her head finally freed from its confines.

She had to do something. Take control of her own fate.

She accessed Ish's language DB and dropped it into Livetrans. The input prompt flashed ready. What to say? Stop it? That was dumb. She needed to make an instant impact. Scare her, if possible. Back in the catalogue Minnie searched for Hynka lore and superstition.

Come on … who's your personal boogeyman?

Mama flapped Minnie's ear.

> Hwahxo: Universal; Death. (specific to Greaters, see Sssuhke: Lesser Death)
> Shroosh: Southwestern goddess; a shapeshifter; source of seasonal flooding. Metaphoric: "Come/go/went … like Shroosh" (quickly and with irresistible force, as in an invasion)

Sssuhke: Universal; Death (specific to Lessers, see Hwahxo: Greater Death), a blessing on a clan, surges through Greaters, empowering, frees Lessers for rebirth.

A quick glance at Ish's goddess of choice and it was back to the drawing board. No mythology.

She wished she'd spent a bit more time nosing into Ish's research back on the station. Now, especially, with Mama endeavoring to pinch Minnie's ear between thumb and finger claws too dull to succeed. She gave up, instead hunching over to sniff it. Gusts of breath sent static into Minnie's ear canal and she cocked her head out of the line of fire.

Mama whispered, "Ohswe."

LIVETRANS: No move.

Oh, hey there, Livetrans!

Minnie kept her head still, as requested, but rolled her eyes left, spotting Mama's snout—close and moving closer, mouth opening. A drip of hot saliva.

A pair of lengthy incisors scooped slowly behind Minnie's ear, and then the mouth began shutting, the opposite row of teeth pressing into the ridges and caves inside the ear, clamping down, pressing tighter, pinching.

Minnie shut her eyes and held her breath. This was it. The beginning of the end. Just when she thought the first tooth would pierce flesh and spill blood—the bite stopped. Minnie exhaled. Mama rested a hand on Minnie's shoulder and began slowly sitting up, half a dozen teeth still firmly rooted in the ear. She wasn't letting go.

A ring of burning flesh.

Panic struck, and Minnie moved her head up with it as far as she could, but at the end of her reach the skin began pulling once again—unrelenting.

Searing, unbearable pain at the sudden *pop* of the first tear, behind the ear, and the rest of the ring quickly followed, ripping away effortlessly as Minnie screamed.

3.4

259 hours since evac. 10 Earth days. 13 Epsy days.

Aether stood beside Zisa and Pablo, all three's focus locked on Eeahso as tentacles curled and frolicked, smearing her skin with the fresh batches of petroleum jelly and glycerol.

Zisa averted her eyes. "I feel like I'm watching something I shouldn't."

Pablo laughed. "With you there. It's like porn for mermen."

"Quiet guys," Aether said, and sent Livetrans to Eeahso. "How does it feel? Are you able to compare the two sides?"

"Good," Eeahso said—her eyes hidden, arms sliding over her head, one after the other, as if greasing back hair. "All good!"

Zisa sighed and pointed a hand at Eeahso. "He's mixing them together with all the squirming! There's no way we can do an A-B test this way."

"She," Pablo corrected. "And she had them separate for a while there. We'd at least see any allergic reactions, right?"

"There's no way I can say for sure. Not at this point. We need at least a week with the final recipe. Plus, only the PJ has UV protectant right now. I need to synthesize another base to bond it with the glycerol, cook a batch, test." She turned to Aether. "You also said you wanted a native fragrance in there."

Aether's gaze held on Eeahso, sun beating down on the shiny, coated Threck skin as elated murmurs hummed from her siphons. Aether wouldn't wait another week, and the formula didn't need to be perfect right now.

Aether turned to Zisa and Pablo. "How long to make a five-liter bucket of each, as is?"

The pair looked at each other, briefly debated their estimates, and then agreed on a couple hours.

"Perfect," Aether said. "And Pablo, you're coming with me."

"Well yeah, we already agreed I would demonstr—"

"No, I mean the rescue mission." Aether said.

Dread landed on his face, weighing down his features. He and Zisa shared a tense look, and Zisa rested her fingers on Pablo's abdomen. An intimate gesture for Aether's benefit?

Aether cocked her head toward the EVs. "I'll have Qin pack you up so you can stay on task."

Expression aside, Pablo didn't argue.

Zisa was another matter. Now that they were all linked in to the EVs' wireless, M's had been free-flowing at the camp.

ZISA: I know you're zetabusy…

Aether ignored her as she strode to the EVs to find Qin.

ZISA: I have to talk to you about something.

What was she supposed to do, adjust assignments based on Zisa's relationship status?

ZISA: It's just that there's something you should really know.

Pablo was a physician—far better than Aether ever was—*and,* for what it was worth, he was the backup Hynka specialist. Who would Zisa have her bring across the ocean instead? Who was better suited? Grieving Tom? Terrified Qin? Why not Zisa herself?

ZISA: I'm pregnant.

Aether halted and covered her eyes.

Of course you are.

Wait …

AETHER: Stay where you are.

Marching back, she could see the fear oozing from Zisa. Pablo glanced down at Zisa's arm curling and tightening around his waist, caught her look, then followed her eyes to see Aether approaching.

He knew at once what she'd done. "Babe! You told her? We talked about this!"

Aether planted her boots before them, her expression surely murderous. "How do we know this?"

A nervous laugh from Zisa. "Kinda unceremonious, actually. Biostat alert: you're pregnant."

Aether's glare shifted to Pablo. "Confirmed, I presume?"

A guilty nod.

"How the hell is this possible? You'd have to have—" She counted in her head. Evac, orbiting for ninety-four hours, two days stuck with Skinny, rally camp, the Thinkers, and now four days making this damned balm. Thirteen days since evac. She was reasonably certain these two hadn't done anything prior to evac— "Wow. In orbit?" She waved them off before either could answer. "Hang on. It still doesn't make sense. With the meds, you wouldn't be fertile for a couple cycles."

Both tried to answer at once.

"She's actually—"

"I've never been on BC," Zisa said.

Pablo resumed. "She was supposed to be infertile. Multiple checks before and at the training center."

Aether was still aghast. She looked at their faces, back and forth, no words.

Pablo interpreted her shock as continuing disbelief. "Honestly, trust me, if I ever suspected—I mean, she's never even menstruated!"

Zisa faced him. "Well, that's not true."

Now it was Pablo's turn to be shocked. "Not … What do you mean?"

Aether sighed, pivoted, and walked away.

"Like, I've never been regular, but it'll come here and there."

"Here and there? What? How could I not know this?"

"'Cause it was none of your business. I feel like you're yelling at me."

"None of my …"

* * *

The theater of rapt Thinkers looked on as Pablo moved down the second line with the glycerol bucket, applying the balm to the second set of five volunteers. On the other side of the center pool, the five already coated from the PJ bucket caressed their slimy skin.

Calls from the audience:

"How does it feel?"

"Is it cold?"

"Is it the same?"

"Like mud?"

Pablo paid special attention to the last volunteer—not a Thinker, but there by Aether's request: Massoss Pakte, leader of the Fishing group. Pablo slathered on the glycerol from his dwindling bucket, plopping a fist-sized heap into Pakte's awaiting palms. Like the others, she carefully smeared the balm over her head and into the creases between tentacles. And like the others, she signed "unmatched pleasure."

Having earlier agreed to only a single arm of PJ, Dowfwoss Unhkte rubbed her other arm against the first as she addressed Aether. "Where did you find this golden mud?"

"It is not mud and cannot be found," Aether replied. "It is thing that Syons People know how to *make*."

"You will show Threck how to make?" Unhkte asked.

Aether could tell Unhkte was trying to feed her appropriate answers, but Aether had her own plans. Now, witnessing the balm's wider reception—equal to Eeahso's reaction—she was confident in her position.

"No. We will not show Threck how to make. We will make it for you. This is very dirty, tiring task to create it. Like inland farming. We would not come and demonstrate the wonderful benefits of our cream, and then place this unpleasant burden on your people."

Unhkte's eyes lingered on her. She seemed to have gathered Aether's intentions.

Another Thinker stood and Unhkte pointed for her to speak. "The golden mud is grown on a farm?"

"No," Aether replied, trying to find the best analog in Threck society. "I say 'farm' only to indicate hot, unpleasant effort. We make it like Threck make cement, only far more complex, especially in enough quantity for the entire city. Like mud, the cream must be reapplied often, only much less often, and cream's benefits continue long after application, unlike mud which, once dry, saps the flesh of moisture."

Aether patiently fielded the flood of questions, conscious of the Thinkers' need to beat a topic to death before coming to a decision. The jubilant volunteers, too, presented their best efforts at describing the sensation to a roomful of highly envious spectators.

Perfectly, and as if to intentionally augment Aether's position, the final volunteer's thoughtful answer sent the crowd into grumbles of agreement and anticipation. "While *similar* to fresh mud—only *first contact* with fresh mud, before drying begins—this is inadequate comparison. The sensation *cannot* be described, but only understood through direct experience."

Unhkte had gathered the Thinkers' consensus. "How soon could you create and deliver enough for all?"

Aether's prepared response had awaited this. "The *golden mud's* effectiveness comes from its purity. To produce more than two buckets, we require appropriate facility near where our new home will be built. Obviously, the faster we construct homes and facilities, the sooner we may deliver more golden mud."

Ever sharp, Unhkte grasped at once Aether's subtext, addressing both Aether and the spectators. "Perhaps if Threck Makers and Materials groups offered their expert aid and considerable numbers, these facilities could be completed in shorter time than Syons People alone."

Aether shared a smug look with Pablo before agreeing. "This is true. Their aid would certainly increase construction speed. Alone, Syons People would need two to three years to build facilities, then additional two years to make enough golden mud for *initial* batch. As I said, you will require *constant* supply. The addition of our three stranded members would significantly hasten our work and increase output."

Pakte spoke on cue. "You required two afvrik from the Fishing group to locate your people?"

"Yes, and the best navigators to control them."

Pakte addressed Unhkte. "Fishing offers the resources required of our group. Afvriks and handlers will be ready for departure in two days' time. We will not be source of delay."

The spectators sounded off pleasure and gratitude as they streamed down from the tiered rows, bombarding the volunteers with sample requests. Others surrounded Pablo for a peek inside his buckets. Pablo gave Aether a pleading look.

Unhkte wedged her way in, shooed away the lot encircling Pablo, and gestured to the buckets. "Do you have enough remaining to demonstrate for two others? Massoss Artsh and Massoss Feesap must be convinced to divert attention from new aqueduct and bridge."

Pablo peered into the buckets. He held up three fingers.

"We have enough," Aether said. "But if, like you, we coat only one arm, perhaps we could avoid any further potential gaps in support."

Unhkte regarded her before grasping her meaning. "The council."

Aether signed, "Yes."

* * *

Aether stood waiting on her loaded skimmer pad, pondering what else they might need on the journey, or other tasks Zisa, Qin, and Tom should focus on in her absence.

She glanced behind her at the clear hatch over the pad's internal storage bay. A pressed tentacle slithered across the hatch, smearing PJ.

Eeahso was probably cooking in there. A preview of Eeahso's farm-life to come, the sun would be at mid-afternoon intensity when they dropped her off. Though the council had agreed to spare her, the proviso of a life spent toiling in the fields was unlikely to play out as they expected. Aether pictured Eeahso lounging in a cool domicile each day, simpleminded farmers waiting on her with food, water, and massages. Aether didn't care either way. She just needed her out of everyone's hair, especially Tom's.

Aether turned to Zisa and Pablo, still standing with hands clasped behind the other's back, face to face, whispering, weeping, laughing. They looked like a pair of teenagers heading home to distant cities after a summer of love.

She opened an M to Pablo, about to put an end to it, and then thought of a task for Qin. He and Tom were nowhere to be seen. She activated audio to Qin.

"Hey, is there a way for you to track our progress out there? The supply pods can see skimmers, right?"

An instant reply. "I should be able to, yes. If you give me a few minutes I'll tell you before you have to leave. Walking to P and Z's EV now."

A moment of silence. Beyond the beige tent tops, she saw EV2's hatch rise and slide up over its roof. She refocused on Zisa and Pablo, their faces fused at the mouth. She yelled, "Wrap it up, kids! You have two minutes."

Qin's voice in her ear, "You need to come over here."

"It's okay if it's too much trouble. Just do what you can. We've got two loaded Threck boat-fish-things waiting for us at the harbor."

"Not that. Please come to EV-two."

Well, that sounded serious. What could it be? Aether popped open the floor hatch, allowing Eeahso to flop out.

"What happens?" Eeahso called after her.

Aether breezed past Zisa and Pablo, around the work tents, and strode to EV2's open hatch. She poked her head in. Qin was already standing up. He moved aside and nodded toward a console. Aether climbed in, sat down, and tried to understand what she was looking at.

Before she could ask, Qin said, "That's the supply pod network's homepage."

Aether read.

> Post-station evac, EV6 landed Hynka country
>
> . . .

A moment later, her eyes hung on Minnie's final words—reserved for Aether—eloquent in its brevity, paralyzing in its depth.

> I wish we'd met sooner; I could have loved you longer.

She read it over and over.

Qin finally broke the silence. "Says John's hurt pretty badly."

Aether's senses returned and she scrolled back to the top. Level 8. No other specifics. All she could know was that his injuries were life-threatening and/or involved organ failure or loss of limb. Or at least that was the case when the message was left. When had Minnie written all this?

Qin added, "Seems pretty convinced about Ish—"

"When is this from?" Aether interrupted. "There's no date."

"Let me see." He navigated on his fone, both eyes twitching as if following a fly. "Wow. File updated just yesterday."

They were still alive—at least John and Minnie. They'd made it fifteen days! How difficult would another week be? Possibly very. Minnie had offered no indication of their security conditions, but the fact that she thought John would soon be well enough to travel, that was something.

The voice, though … the *tone* of the message, the mixed use of present and past tense ... It was a farewell letter, ripe with nostalgia, naval gazing, and regret. It suggested that, besides John and Ish, Minnie didn't expect to ever see them again. Did it mean she thought them dead, or that she doubted her own continued survival?

"How do we respond to this?" Aether asked with a new resolve. "Leave a new message right here?"

Qin hummed uncertainty. "I honestly don't know how she did it. The homepage is strictly locked down. I could mess with another file, but no one would see it unless they looked for it—a search by recent modification."

Aether wiped a hand down her face. "You have *zero* clue how to do this?"

Qin threw up his hands. "I'm not Minnie, okay? Hold on … let me see if Tom knows anything."

Aether reread the message as she waited for Qin to consult Tom. Keenly aware of the Threck crews waiting for her at the harbor, she hoped that the promise of miraculous skin cream afforded her some leeway.

Qin sat down in the other seat. "Tom says she had root level passcodes." He activated another console and began tapping away.

Aether smiled and felt a fresh rush of adoration—love seeping through a cracked door she'd fought to keep sealed since evac.

Of course root level passcodes.

"I assume I don't have any of those?"

Tom appeared in the EV doorway. "You might, actually. I'm thinking with all the dumps that happen during exigency procedures that that'd be a big one to include."

Qin cheered, "We do! I just remembered! Wireless was down, but ours and John's became 'Leadership' EVs on evac. Everything down to root would be in there from the hardwire. You just need your regular AC account to access it! Hold on, so we don't have to walk over there." He navigated on the console. "Okay, accept that prompt."

An access request popped up in Aether's fone. She accepted, resisting the urge to point out the poor timing of Qin's revelation. It was simply how his brain worked. If she'd thought to ask him about transglobal comms when they were floating off the coast, all this would have occurred to him then. They'd have established contact sooner. Minnie would know they'd survived.

How frightened and alone Minnie must feel. Cut off from everyone and everything. And what of her stability? Two weeks without meds …

Aether sucked in a deep breath. The message was from yesterday. For all the worst case scenarios she'd imagined, she had to accept this for the great news it was.

"I'm in our EV's systems," Aether said. "Tell me how to find the code you need. I'll send you the message I want put up. Like hers, it needs to be the first thing someone sees if they access the pod UI." Another glance at the bottom of Minnie's message. "And don't overwrite this … *please*. Just add what I give you to the top of the homepage."

35

He supposed this was *it*. The end of his story, the end of Minerva's, the end of the mission. Humans would surely come to this place again and they'd be eager to know what had happened at Epsilon C. People loved tragedy and cautionary tales. The question in John's mind, the one whose relevance he found suspect: how much of the *real* story would future visitors piece together?

Why did it matter to him so much? Were these merely the long-established, conventional deliberations of imminent mortality? Meaning and purpose, impact and legacy? How dull. John had always fantasized for himself the also-well-known, though far-less-frequently-successful *blaze of glory*.

Blown apart on the station. Burned up on reentry or disintegrated across the surface when the parachute failed. Torn to shreds in an epic final showdown with Hynka, taking dozens with him as Minerva made a narrow escape ... thanks to him. In practice, none of it sounded all that appealing. It sounded awful, terrifying. He just wasn't the hero type, if such a thing existed outside fiction. He was a bookish scientist and engineer. The only reason he'd ended up a leader was that he wasn't good enough at any one thing to specialize. Standard executive practice—put the generalists in charge. DNA and psych tests said he'd always be patient and paternal.

A lot of good it did him now. His last living "daughter" had flown the coop at some point last night. Now another night approached and still no sign of her. She'd left her suit and environment pants in a heap outside the tent. Wherever she'd gone—*if* she was still alive—was most likely more than 5K away, and she'd be barefoot and barelegged, with zero survival gear, and the overnight temp would surely dip again to -

15 °C. On top of all that, he reasoned that she'd experienced a full HSPD attack, and that her body would be wasted for days. On her own out there, her survival chances had actually plunged below John's. And no one would be coming to help either of them.

His pain approached a high 7, and his reluctance to waste drugs on himself had suddenly become sad and pointless. He scooped a finger into the pouch and dropped a pill to the back of his throat. Maybe he'd take a few more in a bit. No one would ever know his weakness at the end.

They wouldn't know anything else, either. All that data. Those hypothetical future human visitors would have to be satisfied with the last data sent home, along with whatever they could glean from orbiting fragments … *or the contents of EVs found adrift in space.* They'd know nothing of what he and Minerva had learned since evac. None of Ish's flops of unreported data, or the sordid fallout of a disturbed crewmember's missed or ignored red flags. Would the preservation of such knowledge render his life—his entire *team's* lives—any more meaningful? They'd all ended up dying for this work.

John's blaze of glory wouldn't be as blazing as he'd hoped, but maybe he could persuade himself to die with a purpose—something more than as a convalescing heap in a tent. He had a good idea.

Forty minutes later, despite the frigid air of sunset, John sat sweating on one of the skimmer pads, his back against the panel wall. In his lap, the PCU confirmed signal establishment as the fluttering laser emitter beside him froze, casting the lime-green bar of light to a single point in the darkening sky. The pod's homepage replaced the PCU's control interface, and Minerva's message filled the screen. But it wasn't Minerva's message.

> Msg rec'd. Rally Camp est. by survivors Zisa Grafa, Pablo Birala, Thomas Meier, Aether Quintana, and Qin Shubao. 1st contact with native pop, friendly coop rel est. Recovery team AQ/PB/native team OB to HyCo WC 50N, ETA 95hrs. Confirm.

Chills pulsed from his very bones.

Alive.

It was posted six days ago. 95 hours … yesterday. They'd expected to arrive yesterday.

Dazed, John looked around the site. Even if Minerva were here, they were still days from reaching the coast. Absent anyone to rescue, would Aether and Pablo venture inland? John couldn't allow it. Absolutely not. They'd made it down safe! The whole damned—

His eyes skimmed over the names again. No Angela. Couldn't be an oversight.

Oh, Tom … Aether.

Their pain drilled into his sternum.

He reread the message. A little smile. The Threck people were actually helping his team. That was some kind of history right there! He flicked the message upward to verify there wasn't more off-screen, and indeed, more appeared. But not from the team. Minerva's message was essentially what he remembered Minerva telling him. He was surprised to see she'd only called Ish a "suspect" at the time.

The tips of still more letters dotted the bottom of the screen. John scrolled to find yet another unexpected note.

> Zisa: You are so quick, so brilliant, and with so much heart …

John wasn't supposed to see these words, addressed to him but intended for no one. A gaping window into a well-fortified heart. He'd never written anything so personal, not even in an offline journal.

He looked up from the screen. His bio eye began adjusting to the darkness while optics displayed a crisp, enhanced world. Orange points rose from the white plain like giant carrots stabbed through paper. Still-foreign constellations patterned the sky. A charcoal cloud wall loomed above the plains to the east. Heavy snowfall would surely come with it. It was already -2 °C. Minerva was out there somewhere. Aether would scour this land until she found them, or until their fates were certain.

John pushed the PCU from his lap and slumped over on his side, reaching for the medkit. His wounded ribs stretched. Raw, budding new flesh split apart. With the destructive crawl from the tent and now this, Minerva would be furious. He slid the pack across the skimmer pad as he sat back up and rifled through the meds. In his fone, he scanned through treatments for the most severe trauma, unresponsive patients, and stopped hearts, then searched for misdiagnoses and misadministration.

The three bulb injectors sat on his palm, each sealed within its own cautionary red casing. He stuffed two into a breast pocket, trading them for one of the diclomorph tabs.

Pill down the hatch, three gulps from his suit, and he unsealed the injector case. More fearful of wasting the meds than inadvertently killing himself, John found the pulse in his neck. It was critical to stick the jugular—not the carotid. A mirror would've been helpful. A medical team would've been more helpful. A fully functional body.

He pierced his skin, believing he was on target, and squeezed the bulb.

Wow, that was quick.

His mind and body came to life. Heat ripples rolled out to the ends of his extremities, bouncing back like sound waves.

Somehow he'd expected that he would head out with one of the skimmers to find Minerva, pick her up, bring her back to the site, and promptly drop dead. Now he realized he could not only rescue Minerva, but endure on—returning to re-pair with the second skimmer, load up all their gear, and go streaking through the air, all the way to the damned *coast*, where Aether and Pablo would take things from there.

He gripped the bar above him, pulled himself to his feet, and powered on one skimmer. This was going to work!

Wait … the suit. She'd need her suit.

No problem. He locked in on the clothes heap, stepped down from the pad with a dull tug in his thigh, and limped to the pile, undaunted. Bend, clutch, lift, turn. Back to the pad.

He hung her suit over the main grip bar, took the controls in hand, and ascended into the brisk evening air.

3.6

Minnie's wild flailing and screams sent Mama into a tizzy. She pinned Minnie's arms to her body and pressed the ear against the bleeding wound, as if to reattach it. Minnie squealed with each movement as Mama delicately nudged the ear around with her snout.

"Owjt … toh … toh …"

LIVETRANS: Quiet. Fix. Fix.

Minnie focused on her own breath, tried to quell the panic, slow the hyperventilation. A mistake. Mama had made a mistake. She wasn't being eaten. This didn't have to be the end. Not yet.

The weight of Mama's hand lightened and Minnie dared a peek. The toothy snout loomed right beside Minnie's head; attentive, dilated eyes shone in the ambient light. Minnie could see the sandy texture of the iris all the way into the ocular cylinder's dim inner wall. Like many organs with common roots across Epsy, the eye had evolved in its own unique manner. A fascinating topic, but Minnie was more interested in its sensitivity to damage. If unobstructed, could she thrust her fingers in there? Could she destroy both eyes in a swift attack? And most importantly, would a blinded Mama still come after her?

Minnie slowly slid an arm up from her side, timidly probing the side of her head. Her hair was wet with blood, but the wound wasn't gushing. Mama had actually set the ear fairly close to right. With measured breaths, Minnie's flat hand trembled near the ear—closer, contact, stinging, pressing—she rotated until it slid into its familiar orientation. Raw tissue burned, but she pushed harder and held there.

"Toh." Mama repeated.

Yeah, fixed. Got a needle and thread?

As if all was now well, Mama scooped Minnie from her lap and set her in the dry nest bed. Minnie stiffened her body and was able to keep her hand pressed against her head. She didn't know the likelihood of her ear simply healing without additional surgery, but it probably wouldn't hurt to wrap her head in gauze. She considered her one remaining sock, but it seemed a tad too short, plus she'd been stuffing her other foot in there for warmth.

Mama busied herself with old critter bones, splintering them lengthwise and sucking out the dregs of marrow. It sounded like someone cracking nut shells or giant sunflower seeds, followed by gnawing, and then the desperate slurping of an all but clean soup bowl.

Keeping one hand on her ear, Minnie pulled an arm into her shirt, then back out over the top of her first tank strap. A careful handoff, and she followed with the other arm. She wriggled the tank down her body, Mama glancing over periodically with vague interest, until Minnie extracted her second foot, and the tank was free. Some fancy maneuvering, agony, and tears later, Minnie's head was wrapped tight.

So what was it going to be? A perilous eyeball assault? A mad, futile dash out the door? Prior to the ingested and regurged gutful of exotic bodily fluids, and before she'd learned what it was like to lose a body part, she'd elected to wait it out—watch for escape opportunities. The approach hadn't worked out so well.

Mama flung another bone shard and it slid down the wall to Minnie's feet. Minnie eyed it, then peered up at Mama, still absorbed with extracting a calorie or two from every animal scrap in the burrow. The bone had a nice, dense knuckle at one end, tapering to an impressive point at the other. This was one of those auspicious decision moments. To grab or not to grab?

Minnie knew her strength still wasn't close to normal. How much damage could she realistically do with that thing? Then again, what if this was her one opportunity? What if Mama's frustration swelled with each unsatisfying slurp of marrow? Hynka were cheerfully cannibalistic; at what point did hunger trump maternal instinct?

Minnie flexed her fingers. She pumped her fists to test her grip strength.

Without warning, Mama swung around with a grunt, pinching Minnie's legs between fingers, and dragged her away from the wall, releasing her near the burrow's center. Was this it? Where was the bone? Minnie grasped about where it'd been, blindly searching.

Mama huddled over her, staring for a long second, and then reached down with both arms, digging into the nest floor. Minnie slid into the depression and Mama shoveled two giant heaps of tree litter over top, burying her.

Clamping her mouth shut, unsure if she'd be able to breathe, Minnie held onto the air in her lungs. She switched optics and looked around through closed eyelid.

Mama had left the burrow.

Minnie tried to move her arms beneath the load of particles. Surprisingly easy. She wasn't all that deep. Without exhaling what she'd already reserved, she tested a sniff through her nose. Yes, plenty of air filtered into the loose pack. She could breathe. Could she sit up? Her hands worked their way down beside her as she shimmied and wormed her body. After another minute of work, she'd gotten her head and torso vertical, a foot planted on firm ground, and could see sprinkles of light overhead.

A quick countdown, the extension of sore leg muscles, and she breached the surface, her head, arms, and shoulders free.

Mama?

She found the lumbering figure southeast of her, glowing pink and yellow, and gaining distance. No other animals were in view.

With near-constant glances toward Mama's shrinking glow, Minnie dug in with desperate gusto, scooping handfuls away from her chest. She placed her hands on either side of her and squirmed upward a few centimeters at a time, dug some more, pushed, until finally at thigh depth, she was able to kick herself completely free.

Her body was racked but her spirit renewed.

Beyond hundreds of overlapping gray-blue tree trunks and two low knolls, Mama was a featureless speck of yellow confetti. Minnie's fone ranged the Hynka at 3.6K and still retreating. It was time to go.

Maintaining a steady (if slow) jog, Minnie headed due north. The camp was northeast of her, but distance from Mama still had priority over proximity to camp. And Minnie was fairly certain she was leaving behind a traceable scent trail.

The soil shifted from soft, saturated tree litter to dryer, pricklier bits. She cursed her dainty, callous-free station feet, and her absurd, defective glands.

Want to ditch your suit and boots? Pshh yeah. Who the hell needs all that crap?

She winced and paused, skipping on her drenched sock foot to pluck a sticker from its mate. Safety scan. Not even a blip of rootless life.

Unsure if it would make any difference for scent tracking, Minnie skittered up a leaning, semi-bare epsequoia trunk, hopped to a large snowcapped boulder, and slid down the other side. She continued on in this way, with random turns, and scaling unnecessary obstacles, until all of the skin below her shorts burned with the growing chill of sunset.

Three more kilometers behind her. No more snow-free soil patches to relieve her throbbing feet. Though her calves no longer seemed to offer heat, she stopped every twenty or so paces to alternate pressing the bottoms of her feet against them. Her jog had long since downgraded to a shabby hobble. On the bright side, the aching on the side of her head had subsided. Maybe the ear had frozen. Maybe it was now just acting as a pretty gross bandage.

No longer paying attention, route guidance surprised her with a ping.

She'd traveled to the same latitude as the camp. Less than 5K to go, due east. She might even be able to DC with John. Give him a heads up before she shambled into the site. Nope. Her looping DC request was still reaching out every ten seconds. He could be asleep. Hopefully he hadn't sunk his paws into the med cookie jar again.

4K. Snow coming down from her left. Scary clouds overhead. Legs pattering along on autopilot. She'd probably move just as fast with long walking strides, but she was determined to keep her heart rate up. She fantasized about the heater. How outraged would John be if she brought it into her sleeping bag with her? *"Fire hazard and rules and razzle frazzle grumple!"* She smiled and felt her stiff cheeks tremble. A violent palm rub on the numb tip of her nose. She better not have frostbite on top of everything else. Man, her feet ... how could they *not* be ruined forever?

2K. Safety scan. Still not even a blip of—

John?

No.

No life in thermal view. Gear was visible in mag. She could see the side of a skimmer. Cases. Her pace quickened.

There was zero sign of John. The outline of the tent was visible but no body inside, not even a dead one. As the distance closed, she noticed the missing skimmer. He'd left the site, gone out looking for her.

Dammit, John!

But how the hell had he managed that?

* * *

Two layers of fresh, dry clothes, envirocap, pairs of gloves and runners, and with a few teasing minutes of glorious heater time, Minnie hastily tore down the filled tent, stuffing the bundle between other gear on the second skimmer, and launching into a hostile sky. The blizzard had yet to reach its full fury, but visibility was already nil, and abrupt up- and downdrafts had the skimmer console insisting she immediately land.

"UNSAFE CONDITIONS! LAND WITHOUT DELAY!"

Repeated slaps failed to silence the obnoxious alerts. She tuned it out, instead training her thermag focus on the air all around her. The skimmer, too, maintained a constant watch for other active units, whether aloft or grounded.

The heater in the tent had been off but still warm. John couldn't have been gone for long. Minnie's main challenge was in not knowing the direction John had traveled. Her shoulders buttressed against the wind, deft snowflakes still slunk their way into her collar, trickling down her chest and back. Riding the skimmer like a surfjet over wild breakers, she oscillated her head and eyes for a near-360° view.

It didn't take long to find a sign of John. He'd left a trail.

A mere half-K west of the camp, a stack of thin gold and salmon bands in an epsequoia revealed the scattered remains of their medkit—the case itself lying wide on a high pad, while its contents littered layers of lower pads below. They'd need all of it, but no time to land and gather it all now. Minnie placed a pin in her map and continued on, slower, following the line created by their campsite and the medkit location.

Not even 100m west, a splayed survival suit, half-buried in a snowdrift. It was Minnie's suit with the boots still attached. Another pin.

Snow in her eyes. Incessant body shakes. She pressed her hips to the warm panel.

A sharp dodge around an especially tall, swaying tree.

"UNSAFE CONDITIONS! LAND WITHOUT DELAY!"

Her heart thumped. Three more glowing points quivered in thermag, laid out ahead in the swirling whiteout like landing lights on some remote runway. The farthest was the biggest. Accelerating, Minnie streaked past the first two without a glance.

She banked round with eyes fixed on the scene. One quarter through the circle, her life drew up into her throat, compressing and withering there all at once—an unrealized seedpod decaying atop rock.

John's rugged skimmer had come out mostly unscathed, only splitting in two: pad and console assembly, still clinging to each other by outstretched cables and glistening fiber ribbons. Their pilot, however, lay twisted and broken, half covered by the skimmer pad. A dark crown of hair and a single gloved hand, draped on the overturned pad, were all that remained unburied by snow.

As she descended beside him, his remaining body heat dropped into single digits.

Her skimmer was pleased she'd finally complied. "NOW SEEK SHELTER!"

Slogging through deep snow to John's side, she disabled enhanced optics for the grisly view beneath the surface it kept trying to show her. Now, there remained only a few orange knuckles and the back of his head, persistent flurries set to finish the job any minute.

She dropped to her knees and set a gloved hand on his head.

Tears freezing at her eye corners, she shouted over the wind. "You were right about my problem affecting us both. Can't deny this is my fault."

Minnie brushed loose snow off his shoulder and back, nudged her legs in beside his body, and set her cheek against the back of his icy suit. There was no warmth here, but she imagined there was. She slid her buried hand up to her chest, wedging it between them, then reached over him with her free arm to grab his stiff hand off the skimmer, pulling it in. A solid, unnatural *tok* sound she pretended she didn't hear—a frozen finger or knuckle grazing the skimmer's plastic corner bumper. No, none of that. This was all quite normal. She'd had a nightmare, crawled into Dad's bed. He wouldn't notice until morning. Eyes closed for bedtime.

tok

The haunting sound echoed in her head. A noise created by the impact of two inhuman things. No, an inhuman thing struck by flesh frozen so stiff it could pass for wood. It was how her own body would soon solidify.

tok

Tok? With a glove on?

Minnie moved her hand around John's, probing the underside of his palm. Empty.

She opened her eyes, reactivated mag, and peered through his body. It materialized instantly in the wall of snow between John and the skimmer pad—all alone, as if hovering in the air. Minnie sat up enough to extend her reach, thrust her hand into the snow, and plucked John's fone from where it'd fallen. She held it in front of her face.

He'd extracted it, had it under his hand on the skimmer for her to find. Something he wanted her to see. But what? Something leaderly, of course. An inspirational sermon about driving on, assurances that this wasn't her fault … or *ick,* a full on I-told-you-so condemnation and *orders* to make it right by saving herself, returning to Earth to tell the whole tale.

Whatever his dying mind had wanted her to see, it didn't matter. Even if she wanted to, there was no way for her to access his fone. He would've had to—

Hmm …

Minnie sat up the rest of the way, shaking out her head and elbowing away the thickening white blanket. She dropped his fone into a zippered inside pocket, freeing her hands to wipe off the edge of the skimmer. After reaching an ice coat, a moment of scratching and striking chipped it away, revealing a few jagged scratches. A numeral 1 or lowercase L. A lightning bolt … maybe a 3 or Z, or the start of an S. A backslash. And that was it. He'd tried to give her his passcode, but failed.

Or maybe he'd realized the carving approach wasn't working out. Minnie looked for his multitool and found its hot pink outline deep beneath the snow between him and the skimmer. Now on her knees, one hand on John's back, she jammed her other hand down, returning with the tool. She noticed it at once. The blade had been folded back in, and the marker tip protruded from the other end. He'd written the passcode somewhere.

The question of whether she even *wanted* to know John's final thoughts had yielded to the primal impulse to solve a puzzle, the deciphering of clues, and this new quest was an energizing—if cheerless—prolongation of their relationship.

She wiped more snow from the edge of the skimmer, digging out the underside, and dipped her head beneath for a look. Nothing. Flipping through optics, she searched around him for some buried fragment. Still no … maybe his suit …

Despite a dogged new resolve, her raw emotions refused to be buried as clumps of snow flew aside, exposing his contorted body. She climbed out of the pocket, shuffled around over his head, and banged her knee into a hidden boulder—the rock on which John's face rested.

Numb to any new pain, she clutched his suit behind the shoulders, and threw her weight back. His upper half slid out above the snow. She averted her eyes from the impossible twist at his waist, rolling him onto his back. Her hands swiped across his chest, dusting the snow from around pockets and seams, intentionally disregarding the pack on his face.

She examined the front of his suit and sighed. He'd only had the one hand free to write. Maybe it'd been too late. Maybe he'd only managed to slide out the marker tip before succumbing.

Or …

She lifted the arm that had held the fone, grabbed the gloved hand, and turned the palm to her face. There it was in the most logical location, scrawled but legible enough, from pinky to thumb: 1SVr+33<oH. She snapped a pic and looked at the vague mold of his face beneath caked snow, imagining a smug little smile fixed there forever.

Wind howled across the skimmer and an enormous mound of snow crashed a few meters away, startling her. Through the whirling air she spotted a recently relieved epsequoia pad bobbing up and down.

Sensing anew the vise-like crush on her skull and joints, Minnie realized how utterly done she was with cold.

An incomplete plan coalesced.

She ripped the glove release line from his wrist, separating it from the suit, slid the glove off, and took the other as well. Her hands fit well despite the size, owing to her existing gloves. She clipped his multitool inside her collar, regretting it at once. The icy clip found a better home on her waist.

A hand on his chest, she closed her eyes.

You've never been interested in apologies, so just thank you. We'll chat soon, I guess. I love you.

Her runners plowed through the loose pack, finding her skimmer pad completely buried. She stepped up, kicked off enough for traction, and set out toward the pin she'd dropped on her suit's location.

* * *

Bunny jerky tore between her teeth as the heater thawed her legs. Some skin patches burned, others relished the warmth, while a few concerning spots felt nothing, even when poked with a knife. She didn't want to think about that right now. She was doing everything she could for herself, given the snap decision to leave behind the medkit and its strewn contents. Her suit's regulators would do a more thorough, uniform job thawing her, but it was still soaked, hanging on the skimmer, just outside her new shelter.

She aimed a wary eye through the gap in the ice. The visible strip of skimmer had her second guessing herself. If it somehow fell, she'd be utterly done for.

Maybe some kind of tether. There were certainly enough solid anchor points in the vast undercutting behind the frozen waterfall. But unless its residual warmth melted away its parking ledge, the thing wasn't going anywhere. Or was that just her desire to stay by the heater talking?

She rose with a moan, tiptoed down the chilly, sloped, granite floor, and poked her head outside. Only a couple-hundred-meter drop to the rock-hard plunge pool below. She set her optics to kinetic—a setting rarely used outside a lab—and knelt down on the ice sheet. Focusing beneath the skimmer, kinetic drew a zoned surface map with color-coded highlights for active quadrants. The ice shelf under the skimmer wasn't melting at all, nor had any slippage occurred since landing. The only detected motion was inside the skimmer's battery, and to be expected.

Ducking below the side of the console, she grabbed a water bottle from a bin. Its contents were solid, of course, so she scurried back to the heater, set the container down beside it, and retreated into her still-warm survival bag.

She pressed a hand to her chest—a motion repeated no less than twenty times over the past several hours. John's fone obviously hadn't gone anywhere since she zipped it into the pocket. It certainly hadn't gone into her housing. She was too afraid to see what he'd left for her.

Afraid he hadn't left anything at all, other than whatever data he considered important for any future human visitors.

Legacy.

It'd be classic John to use up the last bits of oxygen in his brain to think about the mission.

Minnie rolled onto her feet and grabbed the water bottle, slurping a few melted drops. She returned it to the heater's side and ripped off another string of jerky. By now, her arsenic levels would probably be concerning to a doctor. No lesions or hyperpigmentation, as far as she knew. Her swollen ankles could certainly be a symptom.

Oh, well. Slow poisoning death or fast starvation?

Her fingers traced the lump in her pocket—the second time in under a minute.

Maybe it was time.

It was time.

Once everything was moved into the tent, and John's fone installed, Minnie curled up on her side, with John's glove lying before her resting head. She watched the fone preboot give way to the passcode prompt.

There were a few different ambiguous characters on the glove—1 or l or |, + or t—but she got it right on the second attempt.

His home screen shook her.

She blinked and swallowed and pinched her bottom lip between her fingers.

Minerva Anyone else

She stared at her name, concentrating on *not* accidentally selecting it, unable to fathom why she was so thoroughly terrified to follow the link.

With the survival bag pulled tight over her head, she closed her eyes and forced herself to proceed.

A pic filled her view, eclipsing the tent's warm glow. It was so unexpected that it took a moment to understand what she was looking at. It'd clearly been grabbed from some recent fone vid. She recognized the screen bezel as the PCU she'd snatched from Ish's EV. Above the screen, a tiny sliver view of two orange-suited legs, stretching out from under the PCU. And on the glowing screen, this was what John had wanted her to see. The supply pod network homepage.

For an instant, scanning without truly reading, she thought John had overwritten her message with one of his own, an update on their situation, a list of those lost. With disbelieving eyes she read each surreal word in order.

Her message had been received.

The rally camp had been established.

Survivors. All but Angela. Something had happened to Angela.

First contact with the Threck.

Friendly relationship established.

Rescue team on the way: Aether, Pablo, Threck.

If their ETA was accurate, they'd have arrived yesterday.

The ground tilted beneath Minnie's body, her mind overflowing with invasive new data attempting to overwrite fixed, read-only memory. She didn't need to read it again, the entire message was now branded into her brain. It repeated in her head, read aloud in Aether's official voice—not her shrink voice, or her personal chat voice, or her real voice.

Wait.

It couldn't be real. This was absolute BS. They were all dead. She'd already come to terms with that incontrovertible fact. If everything over in Threckville was all cake and coffee, why would they have waited so long to post a message? Sheer fabrication. A cruel, heartless lie.

Rage boiling up her neck, fizzing beneath her skin, Minnie rolled onto her back and shoved finger and thumb into her eye socket, dug filthy nails into the fone, and yanked it from her face. She hurled it away, blindly aiming for the breached ice wall and a terminal plunge. It bounced off the sealed tent door with a contemptible *theh*, dropping somewhere near her feet.

Fuming chaos. *Why?* Cursing John. No escape from these thoughts; this despair, renewed with insult; half-mended wounds torn open and acid vomit blasted in; a new call for the sweet respite of death, the only true escape from evil tormenters.

She scrambled to her feet, attacked the tent zipper—curses streaming out and echoing through the stone cavity—and marched downslope, through the ice gap, to the side of the skimmer. Wind struck her face and blew her hair behind her, 200 meters of unobstructed freefall flashing by like she was soaring on great eagle wings. Sans depth perception, the 30m-thick ice basin seemed to hurtle closer, sink deeper, zoom near.

With only her bare heels teetering on the glassy ledge, her hand slipped off the side of the ice wall, and her other hand caught her weight on the slick skimmer arm, woozy body tilting out over the sheer face, eye staring down at an increasingly real, petrifying abyss.

Why, John?

She pushed herself back, stumbled from ice to granite, and allowed her legs to give. Sitting, she hugged her knees to her chest and rocked. He'd written it to inspire her on, figuring the promise of returning to Earth wouldn't be enough to keep her going on her own for a full year and a half. He'd made that up, too—that much was now clear. A good liar drilled in the detail; a great liar inspired with grace. He surely rationalized the heartless tale. The ends justified the means. Get her to the coast. Alarmed after days of no-shows, she'd fall back to the boat plan, get herself seaworthy, head to Threck Country. Even after finding the rally point empty, she'd still hold out hope. Head to the city, make first contact, discover the truth—the lie—but then she wouldn't be alone anymore, would she? It was her absolute best chance of survival, so reasoned a desperate, dying John.

How could she hate him for that? It wasn't a heartless scheme; it came *straight* from his heart. Knowing full well she'd despise him for it, he'd ranked her survival over his memory. And she hated him for it. And she loved him for it.

She missed being robotic. Emotions were exhausting.

A resigned breath, a flicked-away tear, she groaned as she stood. Her feet slapped up the rise, tent door thwacked aside, and she stepped in, stooping to find the chucked sphere. It was nestled at the foot of her survival bag.

Once more ensconced in warmth, she delved back into John's fone to see what he'd left for "Anyone else." Predictably, the link simply opened an extensive file catalogue. With an indifferent scroll, Minnie recognized familiar data from Ish's fone intermingling with much of Minnie's own work.

She closed the catalogue and considered the "Minerva" link, her mental image of the pic returning to her consciousness. What additional harm could the real image inflict? She selected the link.

The message hadn't changed, of course, still glowing on the PCU, still transparent in its aims. It *was* strange, the omission of Angela. What was the thinking behind that? An insinuation of tragedy to lend credence to the rest of the message? And why Angela? Why was *she* the sacrificial lamb? Had he actually *measured* each crewmember's "worth" or maybe his perception of their relationship with Minnie, settling on Angela to instill a specific measure of loss, dinging the too-perfect, potentially doubtable perfection of zero losses? *Ugh*, it seemed almost too manipulative for John. In his haste, he'd probably just missed her name. A simple flub.

She closed the pic and found a big scratchnote floating behind it, tacked in the air.

Oh crap, not more ...

> Hi Minerva, I guess my busted body proved less capable than my deluded mind. I blame the drugs (a bunch of drugs). Maybe a tinge of swollen ego. So don't get all down on yourself as if this is your fault. I've been trying to skedaddle from this crapfest for a while, just didn't want you losing the will to go on. Figured you'd need something to keep you motivated after I said farewell. Guilty confession: there's no return module coming. Completely fabricated. I'm awfully sorry for lying to you

about that. If Earth were to send anything (which I doubt), it'd be after our silence was noticed a few years from now, and then it'd show up 20+ years later. Don't hold your breath there. Colonization-ready planets have always had priority. That aside, as you saw from the pic there, my dumb lies were unnecessary. You've got an epic hug waiting for you on the coast. A hug I wish I could've felt one last time. Please, as awkweird as it is, could you give her one for me? And **tell** her it's from me? And tell her I never stopped loving her? She knows, and I know she knows, and coming from you it'll be embarrassing, but it's my dying wish so you have no choice. Ha ha. My only fear is that you don't get this message. Please get this message. Pull through whatever you're going through out there. Keep putting that vaunted SP rating of yours to work. Go lead the team. Build a colony for the long term, with no illusions about help coming. I love you, too.

PS: Don't bother searching for those files you were worried about. I just deleted all vids. Wink.

Once more, Minnie sank into a drowning pool.

Aether *was* alive. Aether was looking for her, waiting for her. The revelation ripped through Minnie's head. Panic slipped in behind it. Aether was alive, and too far, and a million different things could take her away again.

She wanted to pack up and leave right that second. Brave the weather, push the skimmer to its limits, flout the dwindling power meter.

Unable to be still, she exited the tent and paced circles around the cavern. She cried with desperation, with elation, with pessimistic what-ifs. She cried for John, for Angela—what had happened to Angela? And then she tightened her fists.

"Get a grip!" she barked.

Now was a time for practicality, for logic, for planning, organization, sharp focus. Assume Aether would stay and wait in place, or conduct a search before turning back. No less than three days. Assume Aether would be out of harm's way. What were the fewest, safest steps to reuniting? Because nothing after that mattered, and only good could follow.

37

In the icy canyon below, one of the riverbears paused, sniffing the frosty ground bordering a plant's trunk.

Minnie tracked their movements from high above.

Whatcha lookin' for, cuties?

Nothing of interest there, evidently. Both animals moved on to the next.

Long ago, Threck explorers visited this expansive coastline, encountering creatures somewhat less unnerving than those they'd discovered in the South. They tagged these creatures with the highly creative title, *stoopock* (snow animal). A lone Hynka clan residing in the northwestern-most village had encountered these same snow animals—distant cousins of Hynka, in fact—enough times to give them a name: *grarlar*. The word shared no root or correlating sounds with the local dialect, so it was presumed the beasts had been named for the sounds they made, perhaps while being chased or devoured by their larger relatives. Early in the mission, attempting to catalog hundreds of newfound species each day, Zisa had chosen the rather generic *silver riverbear*.

Upon arriving here, Minnie had spotted from a distance a riverbear mating pair, believing them to be more damned inescapable effing Hynka. Yet again, the mission's scrupulous research had been wrong. Why *not* inaccurate Hynka environmental tolerances, too?

Dear old Mama had ventured a whole 20K north of the Hynka comfort zone. Minnie was now *1800K* from Hynka-hospitable latitudes, the distance from New York City to Greenland. There were no Hynka present after all, but it didn't mean there was nothing to fear. Silver riverbears were a bit larger than an adult grizzly, with each hand boasting two 20cm claws protruding from short nubs, and a long opposable thumb. Unlike the toothy Hynka, riverbears had no teeth in their independent jaw bones. Instead, the mandibles themselves jutted from gums, sharp-edged and powerful, chomping food like a giant nail clipper. In their aesthetic favor: a thick silver-white fur coat and big black circles for eyes. The faces reminded Minnie of a baby seal.

With her white environment shirt, pants, and gloves wrapped tightly over her suit, only the bright orange back of her helmet stood out among this colorless world. Lying prone atop a high glacier ridge, Minnie surveyed the canyon that lay southeast of her isolated new camp. Dense deposits of iron and gold filled the hills beneath the glacier, limiting her ground-level visibility to under 1K.

She closed her bio eye and zoomed in. One of the riverbears, large rump in the air, was digging out the frost beneath a megabulb. Megabulb or frostbulb? She couldn't tell the difference. Wistful, Minnie knew how thrilled Angela would've been to see Minnie's vids of her temporary camp, surrounded by the strange organisms.

Vids.

A fleeting smirk as John's cheeky postscript popped back in her head.

Perv. I knew you had goddamn vids.

The second riverbear grew more animated and alert as the bulb's thick, veiny base became exposed, dark permafrost soil staining the white surface. It guarded the opposite side as if something might spring out at any second.

It didn't so much spring as *swim*, slithering up and out for a last-ditch escape. As the second riverbear trapped the eelish thing between four feet, dancing atop it like a cat on a jingly ball, Minnie's own campsite felt a notch less safe than only a second earlier. Within 20m of her tent, no less than a dozen bulbs sprouted from the permafrost, like giant golf balls balancing on little tees. These snake things didn't match any species in the master catalogue, and were probably dangerous, given Minnie's track record thus far. Even if they weren't, they were part of a riverbear's nutritious breakfast, and legitimate cause for concern.

She watched the first riverbear join the second, cordially dividing the convulsing serpent between them. Minnie zoomed in all the way to their gobbling mouths. The silvery creature looked more like a long fish than snake. Tailfin, dorsal fin, eyes—only the pelvic/pectoral fins appeared adapted for surface mobility. This organism could very well offer an eye-opening peek into Epsy's evolutionary history.

Shrug.

Minnie wasn't a scientist anymore. She was just another animal fighting for survival. With any luck, she'd have some help with that soon.

The skimmer sat parked on a clear beach straddling the 50th parallel, three different beacons rigged and silently blaring for anyone with even just a fone. Aether was either three days late, or had already come and gone before Minnie's arrival yesterday.

Minnie refused to believe that.

Sated for the moment, the riverbears engaged in a conscientious, leave-no-trace ritual, repacking the soil around the bulb's base, then the frost, until the surface returned to a seemingly undisturbed state. Minnie's focus centered on those claws as the pair ambled to the next bulb, sniffing around. Remorse already tugged at her gut, but she'd decided that her own life would remain priority one, even if it called for preemptive action. These animals were not endangered (yet), and like everything else alive, they'd meet their end one way or another. Prox sensors or not, she wouldn't be able to sleep tonight knowing those things were wandering the area.

She slid back, rolled over, and sat up, pulling out her MW. Ample power, still plenty of ammo. She aimed at the ground nearby and fired a test shot on lethal. A tiny piece of the glacier's frost coat flinched. She stood up and magviewed through the surface. The round had fragmented and dispersed in the proper starburst shape. Cold didn't appear to be an issue for the weapon or multirounds. Still fearful of a malfunction, she wanted the other MW and a spare cartridge on her.

Descending the icy slope, she took a few precarious steps before deciding it'd be safer on her knees. She dropped down, sliding the rest of the way to her saucer-shaped safe zone. At ground level, she jogged a wavy course through the bulb grove, optics flashing toward each bulb's subsurface root stock. Indeed, roughly half of them were home to an unmoving coiled serpent, mouth clamped on a vein. Ugly, but seemingly inert when left alone.

Her camp was as she'd left it. Supply bins and gear stacked up as a wall between two bulbs. The tent stood only a couple meters from the wall, and before it sat her symbolic campfire—the heater on a metal container lid—along with John's survival bag stuffed into a squishy chair.

She found the second MW and a spare cartridge, affixing the holster to her free hip like a gunfighter. An insulated case supplied a bottle of water she'd earlier melted. She unsealed her suit and poured the water in to top off. A few strips of bunny jerky remained in her pocket, but she grabbed a couple more, just in case. She wouldn't be caught unprepared again. No more overconfidence. No more presumption about *"quick"* excursions. Her eyes touched each container as a mental inventory scrolled. There didn't seem to be anything else she'd need.

But . . .

She turned to the "campfire" and had an idea. The heater's charge was at max. She set it to medium power, then stood, peering west through bulbs and a low permafrost crest. Just beyond the dark crest, the skimmer shone yellow and green in thermag, yellow in pure therm, and pale blue in mag. If Aether or Pablo showed up and stood near that skimmer, surveying the area with optics, the heater would light up like the sun through pretty much any go-to optic. They'd then hike over the little ridge, walk the short distance to her camp, and see that she'd only just stepped out. Satisfied, she set out toward the glacial rift.

* * *

The riverbears had moved fast, leaving the adjacent valley for another farther south. By the time she finally caught up, premature remorse had swelled to a tormenting new level. The animals were *leaving*, possibly calling it a night. As the sun set on the glacier, the temperature rapidly dropped. They were now more than 5K from her camp and still moving. What if they'd just grabbed a final snack before some great seasonal migration? Or they could be stopping into the den to check on the kids before heading back north to hunt in the *nighttime* field, AKA Minnie's camp.

Keep telling yourself that, she thought as she stalked near the couple.

Creeping close, with only a single bulb between her MW and a riverbear ass, Minnie chose to focus only on those claws, and a vision of being dragged from her tent before her body was bisected for a polite, even-steven meal. She strove to ignore the beasts' somewhat adorable trotting before her, hind legs prancing like a pair of dressage horses.

She darted right, through the open, and alongside another bulb. A few shots to the hindquarters would surely be devastating, but this needed to be a quick death for both. Their pace steady, Minnie ran ahead, obscured by the tall orbs, and then cut back left to head them off. She stopped, raised her visor to listen, counted two beats—listening for their thumping canter—and realized something was wrong. Without a glance, she pushed her body away from the bulb, diving and twisting, rolling and spinning about, landing on foot and knee, MW in the air and ready.

Her senses sound, the riverbears had indeed noticed Minnie and snuck right up behind her. All four eyes fixed on her, broad bodies advancing with the fearless audacity of a true apex predator.

"Hey!" Minnie roared, hustling to her feet.

Both paused, confused. Minnie's finger tightened on the trigger. The one on the right tilted its head, like a puppy unsure what master wants. Minnie growled inside.

Shoot, idiot!

But her finger wouldn't squeeze any tighter. She stomped a foot forward and shouted again. "Haurgh!"

Both riverbears recoiled with a start, retreating backward, skirting behind the bulb Minnie had last used for cover, and back toward Minnie's camp.

Well, if you're not going to shoot the damned things, at least scare them off in the right direction!

Minnie gave chase around the bulb, screaming like a looner and clapping her free hand against the side of the MW. Like herding sheep, she had to run out ahead and guide them back on course, *away* from her site. The riverbears huffed and spat, but continued running with their heads hung low. Still anxious about a potentially unwise decision, Minnie deliberated as the duo reached a straightaway between bulbs and accelerated. She couldn't keep up with their burst of speed. Last chance.

She fired a single shot, non-lethal, toward the space between their joggling rumps. The multiround exploded behind them, casting forth blunt fragments. Projectiles struck home, eliciting pained warbles, tripping their pace, before they galloped on with no sign of slowing.

Minnie blew the muzzle tip, mock twirled the weapon around her finger, and shoved it into the holster. She refrained from an ill-fated *"They won't be coming back,"* shut her visor, and headed west toward the shoreline.

* * *

The frozen white surface gave way to mossy permafrost, sloping gradually upward to a dwindling cliff above the beach. Minnie glanced down the shore to the skimmer's little yellow dot (still there), then slowly scanned the horizon from end to end. Still no sign of Aether's rescue team. They were just taking a *bit* longer than they'd thought. Just had to fight against tougher opposing tides than usual. No reason for alarm.

She sat down on the cliff edge, cracked her visor open to invite in some misty sea air, and broke off a handful of frozen soil, playing with it in her lap.

There *was* reason for alarm. Without a PCU or the other gear that fell from John's skimmer, she had no way to connect to the supply pods. No way to confirm receipt of a message that ended with *"Confirm."* No way to see if a new message had been uploaded: *"Dear Friends, hurricane wiped out area. Not coming yet. Standby for 90 days."* Had she known, she would've defied the blizzard and stopped to pick up the gear. She could have gone back, though. She *should* have gone back. When she found out at the waterfall, only a day trip away, that's when she should've backtracked for the PCU.

And then the bigger cause for concern: the predictable return of Minnie's HSPD. With her glands and levels nearly normalized, good old Uncle Huspid would come knocking again anywhere from tomorrow at the earliest, all the way to an optimistic ten days out. Without some kind of sedative—hell, any meds whatsoever—averting an attack in the next seven days seemed pretty implausible. Maybe they'd show tomorrow, Pablo handing her a nasty trial med milkshake of fungus spore. He'd tell her to drink the whole thing, warning her not to puke, because *"That's all there is right now."*

She should've gone back for the medkit.

Impossible, Minnie scoffed. To discover Aether was alive and probably already waiting for her on the coast? Given this revelation, Minnie was supposed to fly in the *opposite* direction for supplies? *Yeah, right.*

Minnie reclined onto the mossy ground cover and looked at the stars. The sun was in the right spot to catch a supply pod, but in that moment she preferred the organic calm of nature—Threck constellations—the Great Afvrik, descending on a small cluster of crustaceans. The tip of one fin shared the double star, Mintaka, with Orion's Belt, but from this perspective, one would never guess. The remaining stars of Orion were irrevocably scattered into other images.

Aroused by hunger pangs, somehow still unanticipated, Minnie sat up, edged over to a safer drop-off spot, and leapt down to the slope of decaying sandstone, surfing the last few meters. From cliff to shore, the beach was coated in tide-smoothed rocks. Each crashing wave clattered and cracked as if not water, but stones, made up the ocean.

When she finally reached the skimmer, Minnie peeked at the status panel. Beacons still beaconing. And plenty of juice to last well beyond sunrise. Time for food.

Remembering the heater she'd left on, Minnie stepped back to the skimmer and reactivated her optics. She faced her camp, verifying the heater was as obvious as she'd earlier assumed.

Oh, dammit.

She had guests, and not the slender little human kind. The warm blobs of three riverbears merged and warped around the heater's static glow. They better not have gotten into her damned food, or she'd be replenishing her stockpile with fatty riverbear meat.

MW in hand, she scuttled up the crest. Upon reaching the peak, she saw her heater's glow illuminating the megabulb tops, also spotting the stretched shadow of a soon-to-be-crapping-itself riverbear. Down the slope she ran, dodging around a young bulb, and into the grove. She slowed a little as she neared, noting that they weren't exactly rifling through her things, just sort of hanging around. Maybe they just liked the heater. Cold wanderers happening upon an abandoned smoldering campfire.

'Happen upon.' Keep telling yourself that, idiot.

The heater's glow was visible from every part of her little valley, and from every surrounding ridge. It'd been stupid to leave it on.

With only a few bulbs between her and her camp, Minnie raised the MW before her, inflated her lungs, opened her visor wide, and burst on the scene with her fearsome, anti-riverbear shriek. *"Haauuurrrgh!!"*

She skated to a stop at the edge of her camp clearing. Her mouth clamped shut, a small residual howl croaking in her throat. Her eyes darted around the site, a thumping bass drum in her ears.

Two of the three immediately rose from their huddled positions. The third lay slumped on its side, close to the heater, slack-jawed and panting, with semi-conscious eyes.

Not riverbears.

The two standing Hynka stared at Minnie as she stared back. Both appeared to be calculating as Minnie calculated. Her little thumb was always just out of reach of the MW's lethal toggle. She'd have to run backward, reach up quickly with her other hand, or slowly shift her grip until her thumb reached. It's how she usually toggled it, but her hand didn't feel all that keen on loosening.

The one standing to her left—fingers twitching as it stink-eyed her—was less than a Hynka stride away. If it moved now, before she could switch to lethal, she wouldn't have a chance. The other, a pace and a half. She couldn't wait for them to make the first move.

"Ayk-yra," the farther muttered.

The closer shot a glance at the farther, then back at Minnie. *"Arp tprik khoh."*

Minnie recognized the word. *Khoh.* Stop. They were discussing the situation, assessing, probably wondering if she was a threat. She'd come screaming before them like a looner and had yet to run away.

Remaining still, she fumbled through her fone to activate Livetrans.

And then the one on the ground spoke, faint and gargling, as if it was dying. *"Ha-aykh … uh-possyr."*

The other two looked at the third, startled, as the translation popped up in Minnie's app.

LIVETRANS: No kill. It [unknown].

No kill sounded good. Minnie allowed herself to breathe and took the opportunity to slowly shift her grip, sliding her thumb over the toggle. The little indicator light changed from orange to red. Now she could most likely take out both primary threats.

She studied the visitors. All three wore multiple riverbear furs over their heads and shoulders. Though not visibly connected to each other, the furs overlapped and made up a sort of hooded cloak. Hynka had never been observed with any type of clothing. Then again, as she'd erroneously consoled herself earlier, they'd also never been observed anywhere close to this far north. Yes, Hynka stretched their boundaries in search of food, but these three would've found food aplenty—and certainly better weather—2,000K south of this place.

Whatever the motivation, once they'd reached this latitude, it certainly made sense to stick around. Those bulbs didn't grow anywhere else in the world, and nothing else grew in this region for hundreds of kilometers in every direction.

Bulbs drew the snake things to their root system.

Snake things drew riverbears.

Hynka apparently enjoyed riverbears. And *warmth.*

The closer Hynka studied Minnie once more before turning to the farther.

LIVETRANS: It home. Not we.

Farther replied, angry—sounding much more like a typical representative of its people—gesturing at the one on the ground.

LIVETRANS: [unknown] with! Hot [unknown] [unknown]!

These guys clearly had their own regional dialect. Minnie wondered if they'd even understand words from Ish's DB. Fascinated by the relatively composed discourse before her, she elected to attempt communication over all of the other sketchy options she'd thrown around. She linked Livetrans to her suit PA and prepared for an unexpected response. Hell, Livetrans might speak to them in the accent of their mortal enemies' clan. There was no way to predict their reaction.

She composed a greeting and watched Livetrans simplify it, paring down 33 words to the 10 that conveyed the basic sentiment.

She waited for their current exchange of countless *unknowns* to end, then sent the message through her PA.

"No kill. Hot stay. Home mine. Home we. Down we."

Their gawking stares sent chills down her legs. Even the sick one's eyes widened and found Minnie's face as all stood in awestruck silence.

The one on the ground lurched and began breathing heavily once more, then murmured.

LIVETRANS: [unknown] speaks.

Without a single step taken toward her over the past two inexplicable minutes, Minnie dared a weakening of her position. She slowly lowered the MW (that they wouldn't know to be threatened by, anyway), and began a gradual squat, repeating the end of her message.

"Down we."

The one closest to her began bending its legs, then shot a look at the other standing Hynka, and growled the same words.

LIVETRANS: Down we!

The other complied and Minnie's head buzzed with delight as all three standing individuals eased into seated positions around the heater. The Hynka still towered over her, losing a mere quarter of their height while Minnie reduced to half. She felt like a mouse sitting with cats.

Minnie had rehearsed this moment since she was 14 years old. She readied Livetrans and stretched an arm out sideways, bringing her palm back to her chest.

"Call Minnie."

The one closest to her worked its long mouth around, trying the sounds, then said carefully, "Nn-neee."

Right, no M *without lips. Ninnee will do just fine.*

Minnie heard the sick one faintly say it as well, before resuming its labored breathing. The farther, largest Hynka scooted closer to its ill comrade and pressed a hand on its back.

The Hynka beside Minnie shared its own name.

"Call *Fitchsher*."

Trying her best to remain present in the moment, head above the surreal, Minnie felt her chest quaking as she attempted it on her own. "Fitch-sher."

Fitchsher's head rolled around, fingernail tips poking the frost excitedly. Fitchsher pointed to the groaning Hynka on his other side.

"Baby in. Call *Leeg*." Not sick. She was in labor. Fitchsher pointed to the last of the three. "*Leeg … Onjr.*"

Minnie looked at the female and said, "Leeg." She turned to the male she guessed was the baby's father. "Onjr."

Leeg began howling from deep inside, like wind from the far end of a tunnel. Onjr continued playing the supportive birthing room husband, tapping Leeg's back and pulling her arm up, then dropping it to her side … helpfully?

Fitchsher placed his fists on the ground, rotating on his backside to face Minnie. Somehow, despite this killing machine's size and weapon array, in that instant he appeared as a kindergartner.

"Nnn-neee."

"Yes," Minnie sent via Livetrans, hoping no one would notice the difference in voices or the fact that her mouth didn't move.

"Greater you? Lesser you?"

Did he think she was Hynka? Minnie also noticed the sudden lack of unknown DB hits in his speech. Coincidence, or had he adopted whatever dialect she'd spoken? So how to answer? She couldn't tell their breed in this light, and all covered in riverbear furs. *Was* there a right answer?

She decided.

Her PA spoke the reply. "Greater no. Lesser no." And then she said aloud, "Hooman."

"Hoonan," Fitchsher repeated. "*Hooo*nan."

Minnie returned the question. "Greater you? Lesser you?"

"Lesser Fitchsher," Fitchsher replied without hesitation, then gestured to his comrades. "Lesser Onjr. Greater Leeg. Two Lesser. One Greater."

"Two Greater," Leeg moaned. "Baby Greater."

Both Fitchsher and Onjr appeared troubled by Leeg's statement, their eyes rolling about, tongues moving in their mouths. Minnie had seen in Ish's game that Greaters could birth Lessers, and vice-versa, but hadn't realized the two breeds actually interbred. She'd thought of it like a black dog giving birth to both black and golden puppies.

After several moments dominated by Leeg's wheezing, Fitchsher stared at the heater for a time, then broke the silence. "Fire in?"

Minnie knew no better way to explain the device. "Yes." Mindful of an even exchange, she decided she could now ask another question. She wished to know why they'd traveled so incredibly far from a village, but was skeptical of Livetrans' simplification, unsure if her meaning would be grasped, "Fitchsher far. Village far."

"No kill," Fitchsher replied, and Onjr echoed a second later.

"No kill."

Reasonable. They didn't want the two Lessers of the group to die. But they could've settled 1,500K south of here, and remained safe—probably *safer*, given environmental concerns.

"Cold kill," Minnie continued. "Hot there." She pointed south.

"Yes," Fitchsher agreed, and Minnie noted the vague body language of an affirmative: a subtle shoulder dip, elbows moved outward ever so slightly. "Greaters there. Greaters come."

They were being followed? Were more Hynka on their way? And why weren't the two males concerned about the Greater among them?

"Greaters come here?" Minnie asked.

Leeg piped in again, a single word between each labored huff. "Greaters … no … stop."

Minnie emulated the affirmative gesture. Apparently, Leeg was as worried about Greaters as her friends, and all three believed Hynka would never stop spreading, so they'd continue heading north. Forever, it seemed. She wondered if they realized that their unwavering drive for survival was leading them to certain death. Then again, they seemed to be doing okay so far.

Onjr twisted and reached behind him, hand returning with a drape of solidified meat, sheets and dots of frozen blood flaking off. Minnie's eyes conjured a skinned human, and Ish's mangled body flashed in her head. Onjr tore off a small piece, exposing what looked like a scapula or pelvic bone. He hunched over and placed the portion before Leeg's mouth, wedging it in as if force-feeding her. She opened a crack, displaying a live reminder of all those teeth, but quickly hissed and spat a series of unknown words mixed with others.

"… hard … no … bad."

Onjr took the piece back and slipped it under his armpit.

"Onjr," Minnie said, and pointed to the metal disc beneath the heater. Onjr appeared startled to hear his name again. "Hot here."

Fitchsher agreed, "Yes. Put."

Onjr snorted and threw the hunk in front of the heater. Perhaps a little too close, it sizzled and steamed. She didn't know how they'd feel about cooked meat, but it smelled damn good.

"Grarlar?" Minnie asked. Fitchsher and Onjr stared at her. She pointed at the meat. "Grarlar?"

Fitchsher pointed a thumb toward the thawing hunk. "Food."

Minnie gestured to the riverbear skin on his nearest shoulder. "Call this?"

Fitchsher crooked his neck to it, then pinched the edge of the fur. *"Possyr."*

It was a word one of them had earlier spoken, Minnie had *thought* in reference to her. Did it mean fur? Protection? Their term for riverbear? The DB had no similar entries.

Onjr leaned forward and slid the smoking meat away from the heater.

Minnie pointed at the slab again. *"Possyr?"*

Fitchsher looked at the hunk as it steamed atop the frost, cooling. "Yes *possyr.* Onjr kill. No *possyr.* Food."

Minnie felt the same warm rush of adrenalin that always hit her when working linguistics. Each new word was a mystery to be solved, and each word defined was a clue toward the next, and all the pieces together would solve the puzzle entire. This meat *was* a *possyr* before it was killed, but no longer. The fur was still a *possyr*, so it couldn't mean *living* or *alive*. Perhaps a generic noun.

Process of elimination. She touched her own chest. "Minnie *possyr*?"

After a pause and glance to Onjr, who was again trying to feed Leeg, Fitchsher confirmed. "Yes."

And with that, Minnie decided to ask her most pressing question. "Kill Minnie?"

Even Leeg went quiet.

Fitchsher stared at Minnie with eyes that appeared to have a million more thoughts than his limited vocabulary could express.

With still no answer, she persisted. "Kill Minnie? Minnie food?"

Fitchsher opened his mouth to speak, then closed it as if to rethink.

Onjr's head appeared from behind Leeg's back. "Nnn-neee scent food taste."

He talking about the half-cooked meat or saying that I smell delicious?

Fitchsher spun round, flinging an arm toward Onjr, snarling, "No!" followed by a string of unknown words. Onjr returned, popping to his feet, and stepped toward Fitchsher, throwing an open hand to Fitchsher's face. Onjr's foot accidentally nudged the metal lid and the heater toppled onto its side. Minnie grabbed the MW from her lap and scurried to her feet, backing away from the commotion. The two wrestled around, arguing and slapping each other over the quietly moaning Leeg. Onjr had the size advantage, but Fitchsher appeared faster.

Standing beyond the bulbs, Minnie's legs remained primed to bolt. What seemed apparent was that Onjr considered her food, and Fitchsher was defending her. In the bustle, the heater was kicked again, rolling and skidding away with steaming footprints. When it came to rest, it hissed and whistled, slowly sinking into the frost. Water at its perimeter began boiling and Minnie wondered if it would soon submerge itself and short out.

Onjr was on top of Fitchsher, one leg pinning his face to the ground, a knee on a thigh, fingers clutching and twisting the loose skin beneath Fitchsher's arm. Fitchsher screeched and yapped.

Minnie darted to the heater, grabbed the handle, and set it upright away from the shallow new rectangle pool. Keeping an eye on the brawl, she shut it off and dashed back to a safe distance.

"Stop!" Fitchsher cried from under Onjr. "Onjr win!"

That can't be good.

Onjr stood up, gave Fitchsher a little kick to the head, and peered round the area. His eyes found Minnie. She gripped the MW, raising it higher. Onjr took a step toward her, then looked around at the ground.

"Cold," Leeg whimpered.

Onjr stomped forward and Minnie prepared to fire, but he was heading to the heater. He huddled over it, crushed two nubby claws into each side, and took it back to Leeg. He plopped down and set two fingers in front of the heater as Fitchsher strained to sit up, rubbing his side and head.

"Hot no," Onjr snarled to no one in particular. "Fire leave."

Leeg emitted a terrible, shrill scream, arching backward before rolling onto her stomach. Minnie switched optics and observed the female's massively swollen lower back. Similar to marsupials, Hynka birthed an under-developed fetus to then carry in a pouch for several months. However, a face-attached umbilical remained bonded, and the birth canal squeezed the fetus directly into the bottom of the pouch. From the lumpy look of Leeg's pouch, her baby had either already arrived, or was making solid progress.

Onjr turned his back to Minnie, tending to Leeg.

Fitchsher poked a thumb at the heater and searched for Minnie. "Nnn-neee," he called.

Minnie took a few steps toward the clearing.

"Fire in?" he said.

"Fire no," Minnie replied. "Onjr kill fire. Onjr kill Minnie."

"No kill," Fitchsher said, standing and facing her. Minnie stepped back again. "Onjr no."

Right, she thought. *Like I didn't just witness that fight.*

Fitchsher persisted. "Onjr no kill. Onjr …" he seemed to search for the words. "… speak smell. Nnn-nee food smell. Food no. Smell yes." He turned and slapped Onjr's back. Onjr grumbled, pushed him away, returning his focus to Leeg. Fitchsher barked at him in mostly uncatalogued words. "Speak … Nnn-neee … smell … kill."

Onjr reared up, shoved Fitchsher, and faced Minnie. "No kill! Nnn-nee Onjr no kill!" He kicked the heater. "Fire in!" He returned to Leeg's side, where she now breathed slower, almost purring with each exhalation.

Fitchsher took a tentative step toward Minnie, disarmingly human in his pleading. "Yes? Fire in?"

Resigned to her own weakness, Minnie walked to the heater and picked it up, reactivating it. She kicked the metal disc back into the icy depression it had earlier formed, setting the heater down facing the backs of Onjr's ankles, and beyond them, Leeg. Onjr moved an arm and peeked at Minnie through the gap. She kept her eyes fixed on his, and the MW primed.

"Move," Minnie said to him as she withdrew backward. *"Leeg* fire."

Onjr snorted and leaned right onto a knee, shuffling from between the heater and Leeg. Leeg murmured something to him and he continued around to her other side. Thick fingers wedged under her, and Onjr lifted Leeg's far side, rolling her until she ordered him to stop. Now, her back—and the fetus in the pouch—faced the heater.

Minnie gazed through the wall of flesh to the writhing being inside, already the size of a human preteen. She could see the membrane gluing its toothless gums to a thick umbilical tube. There was a bit of a kink between baby and the quivering sphincter from which it'd come, and Leeg seemed to be aware of the danger. She'd reached behind her and was smushing sections of pouch next to the baby, trying to spin it around to face downward.

"Turn," she said, and Onjr obeyed, using both hands to reorient the fetus.

Minnie heard the crackling of joints and glanced Fitchsher's way, observing him sitting down. She hadn't been paying attention to him all this time, subconsciously trusting that she had nothing to fear from him, but this was foolish of her. She moved back a few more steps and also sat.

"Baby turn," Fitchsher said. "Baby hot." Perhaps it was a thank you.

Onjr rolled around beside Leeg's head, took a riverbear skin from one of his shoulders, and lay it over Leeg's exposed face. With her baby and back to the fire, her front would be feeling the bite of midnight cold. Onjr settled onto his rump and faced the heater, peering over it to Minnie, his eyes unreadable and disconcerting.

After a few moments of silence, with everyone's focus on the heater—like any classic, late-night campfire scene, orange glow casting shadows—Fitchsher broke the silence.

"Baby kill all."

Onjr stole a glance his way, then back to the heater.

Fitchsher went on. "Leeg birthed *Udartsh. Udartsh* Lesser. Udartsh no turn. Udartsh die small. Leeg birthed Fitchsher. Fitchsher Lesser. Fitchsher turn. Fitchsher big." His shining eyes turned to Minnie. "Leeg birth Greater baby. Greater baby turn. Greater baby big. Greater baby kill Fitchsher, kill Onjr."

Leeg turned her slumped head a degree, and uttered with a feeble, defeated voice, "Greater baby kill Leeg."

Minnie unclasped her sore fingers from the MW, curled her arms around her knees, and pulled them to her chest. Fitchsher's gaze drifted back to the heater, unblinking eyes alight with emotion. Minnie didn't think she was only imagining it, or projecting her own feelings: the bleak bewilderment, the absolute *horror* of knowing with certainty that one's sibling—and for Leeg and Onjr, one's own child—would grow, mature, and eventually slaughter their entire family.

3.8

Their afvrik handler, Heshper, was a real hole. Even the fourteen crewmembers seemed to despise her, for as much as a labor class Threck would reveal such feelings. Their responses were usually subtle—a delayed response to an order, or reconfirming they'd heard her orders correctly, voicing their objection in the least direct manner possible.

"You two: go down, find bottom-grabbers, and bring back up. You that way, you the other."

A beat.

A crewmember replies, *"We go separate. Down there … for bottom-grabbers."*

"Yes," Heshper confirms.

"In this water, away from harbor safety, we go down alone."

"Yes. Quickly!"

And then they comply.

Aether had a firm grasp on her own conflicts with the handler. Heshper had legitimate complaints, and Aether wished she'd been exhaustively explicit about their travel needs with Massoss Pakte. Not only had misunderstandings created an antagonism between Aether and Heshper, their ETA to the recovery location had been tremendously underestimated.

Fishing and exploratory voyages had never been restricted to the ocean surface. In fact, afvrik spent very little time above water. The bands of rope that crossed the top of every afvrik were used by handlers and crew as anchoring points. The crew coiled their legs several times around these *holds*, and the afvrik would swim as usual, with only slight drag from the tagalongs' profiles. Threck even slept this way underwater—quite enjoyably, it seemed—tapping into some primal comfort source. Submerged, afvrik rotated so their broad fins faced behind them, their thrust system obviously at its optimal output with this orientation. Compared to propulsion on the surface, it was the difference between powerboat and paddle.

Further, afvrik had to eat. Go figure. Normally, this was accomplished by the creature descending to lightless depth, opening its mouth wide, and drifting downward over dense concentrations of tiny sea life, much like many whales or the whale shark. This fact wasn't shared until well after losing sight of land, when Heshper told Aether and Pablo that it was time to *"stick"* so the afvrik could feed. While the suits and supply bins were fully sealable, and they technically could have gone under long enough for their vessel to feed, the skimmer strapped to the holds at the center of the afvrik's back eliminated immersion from the realm of possibility. Skimmers were weather resistant, but neither Aether nor Pablo believed they could survive a full plunge.

Heshper had threatened to turn around, call off the voyage. Aether had to repeatedly emphasize the conditions of her arrangement with the Thinkers and Council, highlighting the fact that *hundreds* of Makers and Materials workers were on their way north to begin construction. That *all* these moving parts hinged on this rescue mission.

Three days later, without any warning, Heshper had called for the second afvrik to approach, ordering everyone, including Aether and Pablo, to untie the skimmer, tent, and supply bins, and move it all over. Heshper was simply done with this ridiculous arrangement and the admittedly arduous task of hand-feeding their afvrik. To make things worse, apparently the second afvrik had been flaunting its freedom, swimming below them, twirling around, and emitting the equivalent of yummy sounds upon ascending from a feeding.

Halfway through transferring the bins, Tunhkset, the second afvrik's handler, couldn't keep her animal at the surface. It submerged a couple meters before anything had been strapped down. Most of the bins floated, and the two that sank were quickly retrieved by swift crewmembers. Unhkset apologized (more to Aether than Heshper), submitting her afvrik's relative youth for clemency, followed by a curt commendation of Heshper's masterful handling skills.

Now, eleven days into the journey—the past four spent following along the Hynka Country coast—and after several deviations in course to fish in *"legendary waters,"* Aether had lost her patience on enough occasions that Heshper was no longer speaking to her.

Heshper popped up in the frothy wash at the afvrik's front, deftly found her footing, and walked to Pablo, sitting against the front of the skimmer. "How much longer north?" Heshper asked, her wide siphon holes sputtering water. "She is getting too cold. Obviously, submerging would help."

After days of acting as go-between, Pablo no longer seemed concerned with his Livetrans proficiency, and he'd caught on to the key ingredients of Aether's responses to the point where she now rarely needed to send them to him. And Heshper never seemed to catch on that she was being fed the same formulaic appeasements.

Lying on the skimmer pad, mostly sheltered from wind and mist behind the console riser, Aether saw the Livetrans pop up in her fone, and rolled over on her mat cushion, watching the exchange from the skimmer's side.

"We apologize for the magnificent afvrik's discomfort," Pablo's PA announced. "And our gratitude to you for your patience and dedication cannot be overstated." Aether smiled. His BS placation skills were flourishing. "It appears that today is still our arrival day. Only three gaps remain." He'd also mastered their gauge of daylight time—imprecisely calculated via the sun's movement, measured with tentacle clubs held together in the air with an almond-shaped gap between the pads.

Hold on, Aether thought. *Three gaps?*

Was that all? Little more than an hour?

"This is certain? Three and we begin return?"

Vigilant, Aether zipped out an M.

AETHER: Hold reply!

AETHER: Remind her three to *arrive,* then *uncertain time* for us to fly ashore and search.

PABLO: Got it.

As if this oft-repeated detail had never been conveyed, Heshper put on a histrionic show of exasperation before sending a crewmember to notify the other afvrik of this "troubling new report."

On the bright side, Heshper was well aware of their distance from home, and so the threats of turning back had long since diminished to halfhearted grumbling.

Aether stood and observed the coastline 5K off their starboard side, the indistinct cliffs faintly bobbing with the swells. This close to the coordinates, she could very well be passing her people. Though both John and Minnie were sticklers for detail, if the 50th parallel crossed the shore at inhospitable terrain, they'd likely make camp somewhere south of point zero.

She magnified, hazy cliffs sharpening into rich, layered textures of strata—bands of rock, soil, ice, and eroding permafrost. Intimidating surf crashed against a sheer face, white spray misting the air above. If the shoreline remained this treacherous over the next 10K, they'd undoubtedly camp elsewhere.

While a stubborn whisper strove to dissuade Aether, even since before leaving Threck Country *(they'll never make it across Hynka Country)*, there persisted in her a strange faith—confident perhaps to a foolish degree—affording her a decisive calm as far as John and Minnie were concerned. Even as locusts of doubt plagued her own journey, those two would do what they set out to do. She wavered around 50/50 on Ish.

But here they were! This was truly the last mile. Soon, they might even pick up an emergency beacon.

No more than three minutes after the word *beacon* floated through her head, a tone sounded in Aether's ear module, and a little red exclamation point flashed at the top of her HUD. In her peripheral, Aether caught Pablo's head spin toward her.

"You see that?" he shouted, searching the coastline. Aether nodded absently as the alert opened mapping. "They're here!"

"What do you see?" Heshper said, stepping onto the platform and gazing toward shore. "You see your people?"

Aether ignored her, focusing on the signal source. Mapping was all screwed up, attempting to locate mountains in the area. The signal wasn't ground based.

Up?

Aether squinted at the sky, then felt dumb. It was a bounce. They'd aimed a transponder at the atmosphere to extend its range. A very *John* scheme. A grin spread across her face. She knew he'd pull through.

Heshper was still talking. "… don't see what you see. Is it this way? There? Will you fly now? Go get people and return."

Aether faced Heshper. "Not yet. We don't see them yet, but we know they're close. We will prepare for flying and go when we have better idea where they are."

Thirty minutes later, a second alert activated. This one was direct—a skimmer—EV5's B skimmer. Ish's. Had they ever found her?

Now they had precise coordinates. Mapping put the skimmer on a nearby beach.

Finally able to give Heshper something to do, Aether pointed. "Please head toward shore. That way."

Surprisingly absent of grievance, Heshper went to the afvrik's trailing side and dipped her arms into the two reproductive slits, cilia tickling the tender membranes within, signaling the order to turn. As always, the afvrik complied, gradually shifting course to the precise direction. Behind them, Tunhkset steered the other afvrik to follow.

With everything moved off and away from the skimmer and resecured directly to the holds, Aether was ready to take to the sky. Pablo, on the other hand, kept thinking of more supplies he wanted to bring. What if someone had hypothermia, or frostbite, or gangrene? What if he needed to board someone for a spinal? Once his backpack had filled, he consolidated food into a single bin, and began filling the empty.

“It’s probably a two-minute flight,” Aether pleaded. “If we can’t just bring them back here, I’ll come back for *anything* you need!”

Obstinate, Pablo shook his head as he inventoried the additional gear. “Nope. Level eight injury. No such thing as overprep.”

“Agreed,” Aether said. “And I’ll refrain from mentioning you’ve had *twelve days* to prepare for this moment.”

“That sounded like the opposite of refrain. That was frain if I’ve ever heard it.”

Even with talk of serious injuries, a giddiness had charged the air. 27 days had passed since station evac. They were mere minutes from reunifying with family. Aether’s heart thumped like she’d done 20 minutes on a legger. She watched as Pablo went to seal the bin, thought of something, peeked in, slid the lid back on, and pulled it away again.

She powered on the skimmer. “I’m leaving without you.”

He was unmoved. “No, you’re not. Let me just grab some calorie bars. We don’t know how their food intake’s been.”

The fresh rush of launching stalled, Aether’s mind drifted into the reeds of superstition, as though relief and excitement would cue a trapdoor to open beneath her. And then a clamor arose around her. Threck crewmembers scurried from all sides of the afvrik, hurdling over bins and the skimmer to amass at the front.

Translations streamed into her fone.

“Do you see them?”

“What are these?”

“Hynka!”

“Real ones, Hynka, alive!”

“Can’t see! Move!”

Her head well above the wall of Threck cloaks, Aether scanned the shoreline in a panic, spotting the small group of enormous creatures walking south. She closed her eye and zoomed to max magnification. A band of three individuals, one with a pronounced hunch and arthritic gait. All three wore thick, silvery furs.

“What do we do?” Pablo said. He’d joined her on the skimmer at some point. “She doesn’t look worried.”

Aether looked at him. "She who? Which? What are you talking about?"

He gawked. "Minnie! You didn't see her?"

She blinked, choked and coughed, and shot her gaze back to shore.

"Behind them," Pablo urged. "Maybe five meters."

And there she was, full suit and helmet, eyes on her footing, hands free. Aether could even see the spritely outline of her face behind the visor's glare. The delicate, if boyish, saunter. Pablo was talking. The Threck were talking. But it was all a distant drone. What was happening there on shore? She panned right, back to the Hynka. Still lumbering forward, one gestured down the beach, glanced back to Minnie, saying something. Minnie's head rose, a second's delay—maybe reading a Livetrans—and then she pointed the same way. The Hynka carried on.

More furor around Aether. Streaks of tentacles and rope.

"Can you please tell them it's a terrible idea?" Pablo implored. "You heard what happened when they tried before!"

Aether surveyed the scene, watched Heshper doling out orders, Threck diving into the water with lengths of rope and stretching out one of the fishing nets. She scrolled through the stacks of unread Livetrans.

"Capture one ... bring back alive ... we'll be celebrated ... ready the nets ... tighten the holds..."

Aether spotted Heshper, arms in the afvrik slits, shouting commands. Aether stabbed a finger to Pablo, shouted "Watch Minnie!" and marched straight to Heshper. "You're going to try to catch one?"

"Yes," Heshper said without looking up. "The journey will now have true purpose."

"The journey didn't need any more *purpose* than what was already *ordered* by Massoss Pakte. You're going to get everyone here killed. Have you not heard the story of the bones in the Thinkers Hall?"

"All know this story," Heshper replied. "These were not Fishers. Fishers capture afvrik bigger than six of those."

"Afvrik don't pull Fishers to shore and rip them to pieces! You think you're just going to send some Threck to shore with rope, tie up one Hynka, and escort it back out here?"

Heshper's eyes finally rolled up to Aether. "No. *You* will fly net over top, drop on head, and we will all pull."

"So you wish to drown another one? Drag another big dead thing into the harbor? Is that what the city needs? Another set of bones to face the first?"

"We will bring it alive, as others could not" Heshper said coolly. "You will drop net, fly other rope to Tunhkset, both afvrik swim out, keep Hynka in net in middle."

"That isn't happening," Aether said.

"We will see."

"We will *not* see. We will not be flying any net or rope or anything other than our people."

Heshper pulled her hands from the slits and stood up. "You will do as I order."

"I will not."

Flustered, Heshper eyed the crew, all now standing around to see how this exchange played out. Aether suspected they weren't rooting for their boss.

Heshper poked Aether's chest. "I will leave you here!"

Aether set a hand on her holstered MW. This moron wasn't going to strand them all here just to bring back a stupid trophy—setting aside the pure absurdity of delivering an unstoppable killing machine to the city. This was now a matter of stubbornness, control, ego.

"Heshper," Aether said with calmed posture. "Have you felt the skin coating my people are going to make for your entire city? It's not so hot here, but your skin is visibly drying."

"I know of it," Heshper said, indifferent. "Slow-drying mud."

Aether turned to Pablo, gaze fixed on the shore. "She still okay?"

"Yeah. They're scoping out some kind of cave."

"How much of the PJ did you bring?"

"None," he said. "I … I didn't know—Hang on! I have a tub of the *real* stuff in the medkit! From *Earth*."

Wide-eyed, Aether beckoned him on. He pulled off his backpack, digging inside a moment before producing a fist-sized canister.

Aether opened it and scooped out a large glob, turning to Heshper. "May I? You should really feel what has the Thinkers and Council so eager for us to return and start making more."

Heshper's eyes popped in and out before slowly presenting an arm. Aether applied a thick layer to the driest area. The other Threck moved closer, beguiled.

"So you see?" Aether continued. "This is all we have left of it, but when we get back—*all* of us—we will deliver *cartloads*."

"How does it feel?" an eager crewmember inquired.

Heshper touched it with her opposite club, held it up to a siphon hole. "Unpleasant scent." She rubbed some more, spreading the edges thinner to reach uncoated flesh. "Better than mud … perhaps."

Aether seized the moment. "Note the deep penetration, not just surface coating. While you consider, Pablo and I are going to discuss how to safely retrieve our friends." She stepped away, yet containing her fury.

Twelve more days to relish with this jerk.

It was too bad this had to be Minnie's first encounter with these people.

Aether joined Pablo on the humming skimmer. It was still on. "How is she?" She scanned the beach. The afvrik was much closer to shore—under 300m. No sign of Minnie or Hynka.

"Dark rhombus below rusty rock there. They're inside. It's not deep. I can see them all. She's been conversing the whole time, back and forth. She looks like a real estate agent showing monsters an open house. What do we do? Nervous about just skimming on in there. No clue how the things'll react."

Minnie and one of the Hynka stepped out of the cave, side by side, into the sunlight. She looked so tiny beside it. Behind her, the other two emerged, looming above Minnie's head like gorillas with a kitten. She trusted them enough to walk before them—to turn her back. Aether's smile returned. *Of course* she'd established her own first contact.

"*She'll* know."

Aether went to max mag once more—Minnie's body filling her view from helmet top to waist, as if she stood but a few steps away. She was looking up at the fur-clad Hynka beside her, elaborate hand gestures though her mouth wasn't moving. Livetrans talking through her PA.

Aether set her focus directly on Minnie's face, held her breath, eyes wide, no blinking, and sent a Direct Connect request.

Minnie's head popped back, eyes fluttering as if someone had flicked water in her face. Her head spun toward the sea, eyes hunting, shoulders rotating, a hand brought up to block the sun, her gaze passing Aether by, a blink, and *there* was the look. Stunned. Comprehending. Searching again, and then … eye contact. There *she* was. Awed, her hands went to cover her mouth, abruptly blocked by her helmet and visor. She glanced down, confused, and then looked back up at Aether, laughing, knowing she'd seen the blunder.

The DC, my love…

Minnie shook out her face, put her hands on top of her helmet, and began pacing just as the DC acceptance toned in Aether's ear, and an instant later, the first M.

MINNIE: No wrds
MINNIE: o.M
MINNIE: OMG

AETHER: Well hello, stranger.

MINNIE: GET THE EFF OVER HERE, YOU.
MINNIE: Before I swim out there. I swear I will.

AETHER: You made some new friends…

With a start, Minnie turned to the Hynka, squinted at the two afvrik, and then spoke to the three seemingly confused brutes. Aether watched and waited. First one, then the other two, looked out to the water, one lifting a meaty, two-fingered hand to block the sun as Minnie had. Their eyes found the floating things, chock full of strange people and foreign things, and their mouths moved, no doubt with many questions.

"Syons People!" someone suddenly shouted. Aether observed that one of the crew had lost interest in Heshper and the cream, and had spotted Minnie among the Hynka.

Others flooded back to the front.

"It's with the Hynka!"

"They are friends!"

Heshper climbed onto the skimmer—only *she* felt so bold—and surveyed the scene on the beach.

"Syons People," Heshper began, "*talk* to Hynka. Friends. This is why we mustn't capture. Or ..." Heshper took a frightened step backward. "Or have *we* been *brought* to Hynka? Syons People trade cream with Threck. What do Syons People trade with Hynka so they do not kill?"

"That's nonsense," Aether replied. "We're just as surprised as you are that they didn't kill our friend on sight. Just calm down, keep us right here, and wait for our friend to let us know when it's safe."

"We will *not* wait. The Thinkers and Council certainly knew nothing of these."

"Yeah yeah yeah," Aether murmured, sending Minnie a new M.

AETHER: We've got some jumpy Threck over here.
You're buddies going to scram or what?
Tell me what we should do.

Heshper called, "Bring in the ropes and net!"

Aether and Pablo fell forward, catching themselves with the skimmer console. Heshper had her arms buried in the afvrik's slits and was reversing away from land.

On shore, the two healthier Hynka helped the third, all three hobbling south, away from Minnie.

Aether pointed ashore. "See that? They're running away! They want nothing to do with Syons People."

MINNIE: All clear. My camp is inland. Tons of supplies. Or should I leave them? I honestly don't care at this point.

AETHER: Where's John? Ish?

Aether watched Minnie's face turn grim, head turning with a slow no-nod.

MINNIE: It's just me.

How … how … How could he be gone? Truly *gone?*

AETHER: Are you sure?

A stupid question. Of course she was sure.

Aether fought to maintain. Her face wanted nothing more than to shrivel and hide.

MINNIE: Yes. I'm so sorry.

She forced her eyes open. Focus on Minnie, alive, so close.

MINNIE: I have something to give you from him.

Poor Minnie. Poor John. Ish.

"Aether?" Pablo was freaked. Something was happening.

Someone grabbed Aether's arm. A surge of tentacles converging.

What the hell?

Behind the M screen, a set of Livetrans.

"Throw them off! They wish to feed us to Hynka! Push them, quickly!"

In seconds, her legs were hauled out from under her, body raised in the air, and then hurled, crashing into the sea. Painfully cold water flooded into her unsealed visor, the weight of her suit and pack pulling her under. She slapped the visor shut, pressed it tight, and the inflow stopped. But the water level was already above her nose. It was like an icepack against the bottom half of her face. She hadn't been able to snatch a full breath, and the impact had knocked out a fair amount.

A nudge of her leg. A knee to a glute. An arm around the waist. Her helmet breached the surface and she popped the visor open. Water flooded out as cold air sucked in, biting at her chilled face. She reoriented herself. Pablo was below the surface, kicking, holding her up, giving her time to clear her helmet. She leaned forward and let the reservoir below her chin pour out, then slapped the visor shut, confirmed seal, and reached down to tap Pablo's shoulder. He eased her into the water, waited for her to take on her own weight, and then surfaced himself.

They struggled to keep afloat until Pablo remembered something. He turned to Aether, mouthed "Sorry," and began pawing around her left breast. A few seconds later, a blast of air whooshed into floatation channels in Aether's suit. Pablo's suit swelled taut as well, and the pair looked to the retreating afvrik, Threck crewmembers coiling their limbs around the holds.

Pablo instinctively shouted a muffled "Wait!" then blasted the translation through his PA. "Wait! My thing! The sack!"

The afvrik began submerging, secured bins of gear descending with it, along with a not-so-secured skimmer. A sympathetic crewmember unwrapped from her hold, skittered to the pad, grabbed Pablo's pack, and flung it into the water. She dashed back to her position through a hailstorm of gripes from Heshper.

Pablo swam toward the orange backpack as it began descending in sync with the afvrik. A meter away, the pack's last visible strap dipped below. The afvrik dissolved into a pool of white froth, only the tops of bins, Threck heads, and the entire skimmer remained. Pablo speared one hand beneath the surface. The pack reemerged in his gloved hand and he slung it over his shoulders.

Through a fogged visor, Aether watched as all but their skimmer vanished. For a moment it looked as though the vehicle would float there, perfectly fine. Why had she worried? Didn't she know they'd all been built to float?

Water drilled its way into the skimmer's every orifice, filling the outer shell, and the heavier front end tilted forward, dunking under. The round white pad bobbed for a few fleeting seconds, then rapidly sank amid a hissing fizz of tiny bubbles.

3.9

"*What good is sleep? I've never accomplished anything beneath a sheet.*"

Plodding across the barren beach, Onjr, Leeg, and Fitchsher walking ahead, Minnie's eyes sore from brackish air and sleepless night, she recalled the quote from an odd book Zisa had sent her. DIARY OF THE STERILE AND SLEEPLESS, or maybe THE INFERTILE INSOMNIAC JOURNAL. 300 digitized pages of half-depressing, half-psychedelic rambling from a barren woman in Shenzhen, ending with a failed adoption. When she'd finished it—the whole time waiting to reach whatever profound meaning Zisa had wanted her to glean from it—she sent a pic of the last page to Zisa along with "WTH?"

"Wasn't it just bokeh?!" Zisa had replied.

A) Minnie *hated* when Zisa tried to casually add into station vernacular the "new" 20-year-old Earth slang she'd just acquired from a supply pod's catalogue, as if these were normal words that everyone used on a daily basis.

B) How many actually useful things could Minnie have read/done/watched/played instead of reading this crap?

"You know, because you talk about insomnia sometimes, and because we'll never have babies."

"You're an idiot," Minnie had replied.

What an absolute bitch Minnie had been. What the hell could Aether have *possibly* seen in her? Her delusion about John and Aether conspiring against her maybe wasn't so loonish. It *seemed* like they were all such close friends, her clique—Minnie, Tom, Angela, Pablo, Qin—but was she just the station bully, and they were the ones sure to remain on her good side? Conversations outside her presence … What happened in those? And not just John and Aether. Had she ever snapped at Tom? Qin? Did Qin hate the nickname Chinstrap? Was it racist? Had Minnie's occasional Ish snubs contributed to Ish's withdrawal and isolation, essentially pushing her into her fantasy world, placing responsibility for this entire situation squarely on Minnie's shoulders? It all seemed very, very plausible, nigh conclusive. Aether and John would do *anything* to ensure crew—no, *community*—wellbeing.

Or were these thoughts more chemical demons, the initial signs of her next full-on attack? Were Fitchsher and Onjr, and Leeg even real? An intelligent, friendly Hynka nuclear family of interbreeding *Oss Khoss* and *Khoss Feej*—Greaters and Lessers—sharing with her a pleasant artificial campfire in the middle of nowhere? Pffft, sure, that all sounded perfectly legit.

She'd felt the familiar trickle of endorphins the night before, communicating with the Hynka. Her glands had recharged. It would be a little early yet, but she was primed for another episode. However, this awareness only served to validate her questionable suspicions. It was *too soon* for her thoughts to be paranoid or delusional. Her judgment was clearly sharp.

Oh, really? So was it mere lack of sleep that led to Zisa's book, leading to guilt and insecurity, doom and gloom, John and Aether? Real sharp, babe.

Minnie looked up at the Hynkas' backs, Onjr with a cautious arm floating near Leeg, ready to help her along if she faltered. Leeg, her lumpy, pregnant pouch hidden beneath a freshly sewn fur cloak.

What would be the fallout of Minnie sharing such technology with them? And did she really care? Tear some thin strips, take a sharp tooth, poke holes in the skins, stitch. Was it like handing a nuke to tribals? Please.

Now she was exchanging other survival skills. Their insistence on continuing north would lead them to certain death, but maybe her lessons would help to delay it a bit.

She glanced up and saw up ahead the cave from her map.

"There, wall, hole," her PA called out to them.

A few minutes later, Fitchsher said, "*Uh pohtz.*" He was pointing to the cave.

Minnie added pohtz:cave to the DB. Overnight, she'd grown the catalogue by more than 200 words.

She pointed to the cave, testing the new word. Fitchsher confirmed she said it correctly and lumbered on. It was fun for Fitchsher. He was very childlike, maybe around three years old, she guessed by his size.

And Onjr, a full meter taller, fingers and thumbs riddled with scars—Minnie *got* him, too. Just a surly, impatient, protective husband and father without a verbal filter: "Yeah, I'll say it—she smells like damned food, okay?" And it was true. Not only was her environment shirt specked with dry milk from her delightful nursing session with Mama, but she'd had an unsealed pocket full of bunny jerky. They'd all had the Hynka equivalent of a *good laugh* about it, later that night.

It was hard to form much of a read on Leeg, other than seeming to be in charge and in pain. She was worried for her baby's survival, while somehow certain that it would grow into a disloyal, murderous thing. Apparently, she had little faith in her parenting skills, even with such a fine lad as Fitchsher to prove her abilities.

Fixated on Onjr's attentive hand, Minnie wondered if the Greaters, as a breed, would really go extinct, and if they'd take the Lessers down with them. A village of ostensibly enlightened Hynka like this family could launch a highly advanced civilization. Then again, they exhibited intelligence and behavior unlike any Greaters or Lessers that Ish (or Minnie) had observed. They'd somehow taken a giant step ahead of their species. Onjr had also tried to explain this the night before, but the DB simply didn't have the vocabulary to extract an intelligible interpretation. He'd mentioned a place name, times (before and after the place), and indicated Fitchsher's size back then. All Minnie could extrapolate was that Onjr and Leeg remembered thinking one way, went to some "red place," and then thought another way after. It smelled of religion, but she really had no clue.

If this family actually represented some leap in Hynka evolution, the Greaters were still the prevailing force—a crushing foot upon any subversion by passive progressives of either breed. Harsh reality: nature troubles not with justice.

Inside the cave, Minnie highlighted a precarious slab in the roof. "Bad. Fall."

Leeg rested her legs in a large nook at the deepest end, leaning on a shoulder. "Stay here."

Minnie knelt down and brushed some rocks aside. A thin sheet of ice lay above sandy soil. She broke the ice and examined the soil. Saturated.

"Bad cave," Minnie said. "Water come from there. Big water." She mimed a crashing wave and water rushing in.

Fitchsher copied her wave gesture. *"Rwitz pyj. Pyyyj."*

She added pyj:wave to the DB. "Yes. Bad wave. Water close bad."

Onjr pushed a mass of smooth rocks gathered along one wall into a pile at the cave entrance, building a small wall. He looked at Minnie and hung a hand a meter above the mound. "Wall. No wave."

Minnie stepped to the outside of the pile, gently pushing the loose rocks with her boot. "Wave strong. Wall weak."

Onjr snorted and swatted the top of the heap toward Minnie. A dozen strikes against her legs; only a clap against one kneecap smarted.

"No!" Fitchsher barked at his father.

Onjr grumbled and went to Leeg.

"Onjr stop," Minnie said. "Minnie show no fire."

Hearing this threat, Fitchsher tramped to Onjr. "Nnn-nee show no fire! Onjr bad!" He shoved Onjr's back with a violent shoulder, inadvertently pushing him toward Leeg. Onjr stopped himself with a foot against the wall.

Crap, not another fight.

"Minnie show fire!" she announced as Onjr righted himself. "Show fire now. Come."

Both males stared at her with glistening eyes.

"Show fire now?" Onjr said.

"Yes. Come."

As if the conflict had never begun, Fitchsher strode toward her, and Onjr aided Leeg to her feet.

Epsy's first dysfunctional family.

With the morning sun in their eyes, they exited the cave.

An eager Fitchsher gestured to the ground between them. "Fire here?"

"No." She picked up a rock and asked what it was called. "It?"

"Khohsh."

"Rock fire no." She pointed to a band of brown soil up the cliff face. "Dirt fire no."

He understood. "Yes. Fire no."

Minnie attempted to mime blowing wind. Fitchsher didn't get it.

"Tcheesh," Onjr explained to Fitchsher.

Fitchsher jolted a little, mouth wide, and made his own blowing wind motions. "Yes! *Tcheesh! Tcheesh!*"

Minnie smiled, despite her exhaustion. Fitchsher reminded her of her ferret, Noodle. "Yes. Small wind fire yes. Big wind fire no. Here fire," she indicated the entire beach, "big hard."

"Rock no, fire no, big hard!" Onjr groused. "Where fire *yes*?"

ALERTS: Direct Connect request from Aether.

What the—?

Alert from what? Something wrong with the skimmer? A DC ... Why would it say Aeth—

Minnie looked past Fitchsher, down the beach, then turned to the ocean. Only blinding sun and glinting water. Nothing in sight ... No, *something*—an odd shape beyond the cresting waves and swells. A white arch—the top of an EV—no, a skimmer. A skimmer. A SKIMMER!

Breakers fell, swells shifted, and a jumble of silhouettes bracketed the skimmer. She zoomed in, light sensors struggling to balance the sunlight, focusing. Where ... Where was she ... Where was—

Aether.

And right there, standing tall on the skimmer, Aether wore an expression that erased any ridiculous fear of manufactured love.

Minnie's knuckles cracked in front of her. Her fingers had smashed against something hard. The helmet. Visor.

Wow. And she saw that.

Laughing, Minnie looked up and saw Aether doing the same.

Now what? What was Aether waiting for? She was on an afvrik. Threck busying themselves. Pablo, too! This was real. This was happening. What did Minnie need to do? Why no instructions? Why—

Oh jeez … the DC. Haven't accepted it.

What to say? What had she planned before? There were perfect words to be said. Aether would have perfect words. Minnie accepted the DC request, tossing out the chaotic jumble in her head without thinking.

MINNIE: No wrds
MINNIE: o.M
MINNIE: OMG

AETHER: Well hello, stranger.

She felt like her throat would seal up, her brain about ready to hang the CLOSED sign, BACK IN FOUR MONTHS—mind employees letting the heart folks know their shift's about to begin—all before she could even wrap her arms around that woman. Why the hell was Aether just standing there? She should be flying the 300 damned meters between them, jumping off the skimmer, and into her effing arms!

MINNIE: GET THE EFF OVER HERE, YOU.
MINNIE: Before I swim out there. I swear I will.

AETHER: You made some new friends…

New fr—Crap! Of course!

The world around her, the ground beneath her feet, all reappeared. Fitchsher was staring at her. Had he been talking? It didn't matter. They had to go. They'd have to figure out fire starting on their own time.

"Minnie clan here," she explained. "Clan see Greaters only. See Fitchsher, Leeg, Onjr, Greaters. Clan kill Greaters."

Onjr stiffened, his hulking body growing even larger, and he moved closer to Leeg.

"Where clan?" Fitchsher asked, perplexed. Minnie pointed. He scanned the horizon. "Water clan?"

"Clan come here?" Leeg said.

"Greaters no," Fitchsher said. "Nnn-nee clan, show clan Greaters no. Leeg Greater no more."

Onjr began tugging Fitchsher's arm.

"Come!" Onjr barked, and trod away with Leeg.

Fitchsher stumbled backward a few steps, then gawked at Minnie, unsure. He wasn't ready to leave her. No goodbyes, if he was aware of such a thing.

Onjr called back, mushing Fitchsher on.

Minnie whispered behind her visor, "Sorry."

AETHER: We've got some jumpy Threck over here. You're buddies going to scram or what? Tell me what we should do.

Handled. Now get your butt over here.

MINNIE: All clear. My camp is inland. Tons of supplies. Or should I leave them? I honestly don't care at this point.

AETHER: Where's John? Ish?

She didn't know. Of course she didn't. How would she?

MINNIE: It's just me.

Aether's body seemed to deflate. A hand went to her neck. She looked lost.

AETHER: Are you sure?

What to say? She didn't want it to be true. This shouldn't be happening over M's. Minnie couldn't go to her. They couldn't go to each other in that second.

MINNIE: Yes. I'm so sorry.
MINNIE: I have something to give you from him.

Some sort of commotion, Aether arguing with one of the Threck. Tentacles waving about. Something had gone wrong. The afvrik was hurt. One of the Threck missing. No, something to do with Aether, Pablo, Minnie. She'd said the Threck were worried about the Hynka. Could that be it? They'd seen Minnie with Hynka and interpreted some sort of alliance? Such theories seemed below the Threck.

Or not. Minnie watched with horror as Aether and Pablo were lifted into the air, walked to the edge of the afvrik, and hurled out to open water.

* * *

The tip of the skimmer vanished below. Two helmets bobbed at the surface.

Boots glued to the beach's rocks, Minnie began a new M, interrupted by one incoming.

AETHER: We're OK. Don't move. Coming to you.

Minnie held the flood of questions filling her head.

MINNIE: OK.

For a while she observed little progress until the helmets began rising and falling over growing swells as they neared the cresting surf. She scanned the terrain beneath the surface in search of rocks or anything else the pair might encounter after a violent break. There was ample clearance and their inflated suits would keep them from sinking too deep.

They climbed a high wave just before its break, disappearing behind it, and a moment later, reached their turn. The ominous shade projected over them, rising and collapsing into a rumbling wash.

Orange orbs seemed to roll atop the white lather, and then their arms appeared, right, left, right, propelling them closer, closer, to the second and third ranks of breakers.

Minnie leaned, worked her knees, longed to run into the surf, but stayed. She'd said to stay. She'd said she was coming to her.

Both found their footing, held hands for balance, slogging now through waist-deep outflow, free hands scooping, closer. Aether's eyes met Minnie's. Aether stuck out her tongue, rolled her eyes, dragged a leg forward—a grueling exhibition of the longest yard.

On the beach, finally, Pablo dropped to his knees. Aether remained on her feet, shoulders slumped, a few meters from Minnie. She unsealed her helmet and pulled it off. Minnie removed her own and let it fall to the rocks, her white weather cap remaining on her head.

"Hey," Aether said, panting.

Minnie's eyes blurred as her smiling lips trembled. "Hi." She tried to move but was stuck, as if she needed permission to go to her. She tried to ask, her mouth opening but no words escaping. She moved a hand, a tiny movement—*may I?*

Aether closed her eyes, dropped her helmet, and held out her palms, fingers curling—*c'mere.*

Minnie's legs moved like Frankenstein's monster, heels digging between clacking rocks, arms rising as she came upon her. She knew this moment already, knew exactly how her arms would wrap around Aether's back, her face would squish into Aether's chest, and she'd squeeze and collapse against a sturdy body. But she was wrong.

They collapsed into each other—two withered, boneless bodies melting together. Two overwhelmed, exhausted, depleted minds with so much to say and no energy or desire to say any of it. So they sobbed and their chests quaked and the sounds of pounding waves seemed all too fitting.

Their grips gradually eased and Minnie peered up at Aether's face. "That was from John."

Aether choked a little, nodded and blinked rapidly, lips curling and compressing, fresh tears streaming down frosty trails. Her lips were turning purple; her whole face was a bit blue.

Minnie let go, picked up Aether's helmet, and helped her put it back on. "You need to warm up."

Intense eyes glued to Minnie's, Aether wiped away the tears and lowered her visor until it was open just a crack.

"Hey, Minnie," Pablo said.

Pablo!

She felt awful. She'd forgotten he was there. "Come here, you!" She threw her arms around him and he lifted her off the ground, waving her left and right. "So good to see you … and not just 'cause you're here to save my life."

He chuckled. "Well, we'll see how much saving—ho hey-hey-hey, what's this?" Pablo set her down and tried to check beneath her cap. The gauze over her ear must have been peeking out.

She smiled, grabbed his hand, and squeezed it lovingly. "A little project for you. But later." She turned back to Aether, whose focus had shifted southward, down the beach.

"Where'd your friends go?" Aether asked.

Minnie cocked her head to the sea. "I was literally about to ask you the same thing."

Aether cast a scowl to the horizon. "Biggest hole you'll ever meet, and they put her in charge of our afvrik. She's gone and not coming back."

Minnie pointed past the surf. "What about that one?"

Aether spun round and spied the other afvrik that had been hanging out since the first one left. "Tunhkset! She stayed!"

The afvrik's handler made a gesture Minnie recognized at once. "Come now."

Lined up in one row across the bobbing creature's back, the rest of the Threck echoed their leader, "Come now."

Pablo clapped his gloves together. "Ha! She actually stayed!" He grinned, astonished, as he shook his head. He clapped once more and eyed Minnie. "Soooo … You happen to have a skimmer parked around here somewhere? I've got a pregnant girlfriend waiting back home."

Minnie blinked. "Wait, what?"

*

40

Gotta pee.

Sounds outside the tent. Distorted echoes, heavy, shuffling feet, labored breathing—deep, fast, and everywhere. Hynka! Dozens of them! Where was Minnie's MW? She couldn't remember how she'd gone to sleep. How was she back here? Where was here? The Hynka couldn't access the ice cave behind the waterfall. No, she left there … Was this her snow camp by the coast? Outside, getting louder, about to attack! She slipped her arm out of her survival bag and patted frantically around her.

"Hey, quit it," the groggy voice beside her moaned. Aether.

Rain outside, and gusty wind, blasting over and between their Threck Country encampment's porous, seaside rock walls.

"Sorry," Minnie said, and rolled to face Aether's back. She wrapped her arm over Aether's side and belly, and tucked her hand between waist and bed cushion. Aether's warmth soothed into Minnie's cheek.

Was it nighttime? The tempshelter's vinyx wall's blocked all light, and they'd sealed the roll-up windows for the storm. Her fone was off, and would remain so until Pablo needed another biostat report from her. It was the only way she could continue this stretch of regenerative sleep. Even just a glimpse of her notifications count, the time, activity recommendations, or whatever else it was probably dying to tell her, would definitely keep her up for hours. Not that she wasn't curious.

How long had they been back at the rally point encampment? Three days? Four? Minnie only recalled sliding out of this glorious bed a couple times, but she seemed to remember climbing in under the covers a dozen or more. And there were the brief outings strewn throughout the recent days: nodding off during conversations with Qin and Tom in the mess tent, falling asleep in a hammock tied between two of the EVs (ah yes, that was where she'd been sunburned), and an unexpected visit from a clan of Country Threck—or Farmers, as Aether had corrected, not Threck—who'd been told to deliver fresh food to the Syons People camp. In her head, all of it was quite murky, and her half-dreaming strolls to the toilet all seemed to overlap. She might've peed in here six times, or thirty.

Half-awake pee breaks. Speaking of…

Careful not to disturb Aether again, she recovered her hand, inched away, and stealthily made her way out of bed. Her bare feet padded one step at a time on the soft floor mat as she waved her arms out as antennae, guiding her through the pitch black to the corner lavbox. The luxurious nature of an actual sit-down release had yet to lose its glory.

Back in bed, her mind drifted back to a mix of hallucination and lucid thought. The fungi cocktail Pablo was giving her for HSPD management had its surpluses and shortages. Fortunately, when she was up and about, the most powerful effects only came in quick, passing bursts a few times a day, after a dose. Though when lying down, she experienced a constant sinking feeling, trippy auditory effects, and brutal lethargy that made getting up feel like extracting herself from a concrete tomb—but perhaps the latter had more to do with her exhaustion. Thus the need to continue this extended rest.

Aether, too, had to catch up on sleep. Over the weeks it'd taken getting to the Hynka Country coast, and then roughly the same time back, she'd only caught the sporadic hour or two of fitful rest, and had eaten so little, Pablo thought she might've done some serious damage to herself.

Now, Pablo had Qin acting like a strict mom, nursing sick kids back to health. "You really need to eat this, all right?" and "I'm not leaving this room until I see half of that plate cleaned."

Food would be nice, Minnie thought as she drifted back to sleep. *Just no more of those boiled purple roots that taste like pickled anus.*

* * *

Inundated *woodash* bulbs, like teal pumpkins with fragile, rose petal-like shells, littered the encampment area, and exhaled a constant steam flow. Combined with the misting soil, the entire cliff shelf was an unwelcome foggy sauna this morning. The team's new home, 800K northeast, offered much more temperate, human-friendly conditions, and would be ready for move-in in less than two weeks—an extraordinary six weeks early. Sadly, Tom would not be joining them. At least not for some time.

"Is it me?" Minnie asked him with a facetious pout. "Do I still smell?"

Standing beside a skimmer, Tom returned only a faint smile as his tired eyes seemed to track a nonexistent fly around Minnie's head. He tightened his pack around his shoulders and patted his suit's many pockets in search of forgotten items. Or he didn't know what to do with his hands, or how to respond.

Minnie had never been very good with *"getting real."* Tom was a simmering vat of misery and all she could think to do was distract him, try to lighten the mood, pretend this was all business as usual. While she'd always thought they were close friends, they'd really only been close *work* friends, hadn't they? There'd never been any true intimacy between them. 80% banter and jokes, 19.9% professional interaction, and then that one awkward episode in the showers that, for seven years now, neither had—or ever would—acknowledge.

"Hey," she said solemnly, and stepped up on the skimmer pad to reduce their height disparity. "Come here."

He caught where she was going and knit his brow. "You don't have to ..." He waved off the sympathy as unnecessary, and peered around in search of Aether. He'd already said his goodbyes to Qin.

Without knowing how long he'd be gone, she couldn't let this wait. "No, come here, you. This isn't just for you. I loved her, too—still love her. I ... I don't even know how to *be* with this. So, please ..." She stretched out her arms and motioned him in.

He blinked and finally looked at her eyes, his chest rising in quick little starts. She nodded, and Tom lowered his head, shuffling into her arms. Minnie slid her hands in between his pack and back, burying her face into his neck.

"She loved you so much," she babbled against him. "You were her everything. I don't know how … I mean, I can only imagine the pain in here. When I thought you were *all* gone …"

He wasn't making any sound, but she felt his whole body quaking. She thought of John—nearly mentioned him—but thought better of it. No one, not even Aether, would understand Minnie's despair over John. It was her own, and would remain so. As with Tom's love for Angela, Minnie could never truly get that, either.

Tom's grief—a violent, sentient substance—seemed to seep through his neck pores, and drilled tiny holes into Minnie's skull.

She wept, "I wish I could just cut out the hurt and take it on for you," and a small, wounded peep escaped Tom.

They stood there quietly for another minute, both bodies relaxing a little, and then a little more. Minnie found her face soaked with tears and more. She'd also drenched Tom's neck and whatever top he had on beneath his suit.

She pulled back and peered up at his face. "I snotted all over you."

"It's all right," he replied. "Mine is in your hair."

They exchanged pained smiles, and a new, connected sort of look they'd never before shared. "You better come back, dammit. I need you. You mean more to me than … than I've probably ever let on."

His eyes wandered again. "I'll be back, Minnie. I just need some time on my own. Aether thought it'd be a good idea, too." He wiped his face on his sleeve. "Here she comes."

Minnie glanced toward the kitchen tent, spotting Aether striding toward them through the steam mist like some bad ass action hero. "Holy crap, I gotta slomo that." She turned back to Tom. "You're going to live with the *farmers*. How is that 'on your own?'"

"They're, uh, not the sharpest bunch. Too much chlorine in the gene pool."

"Whoa! Chlorine in the gene pool … Did you just pull that masterpiece out of your ass?"

He smirked and shrugged. "Nah. That was Angela's."

Minnie sighed. "Hm … well."

"We ready to fly?" Aether asked as she approached. Minnie and Tom nodded. Aether set her hands on Tom's shoulders, inspecting his suit like a son going off to college. "You sure you have everything you need, honey? Comms?"

"If you prefer, I can lie this time and say I'm bringing comms."

Balancing on her boot tips, Aether kissed Tom's cheek. "Hush. All I'm saying is if we don't see or hear from you in ninety days, expect a check-in."

Minnie powered up the skimmer and Tom climbed on with her. Behind them, Aether mounted her own.

MINNIE: I'll follow you.

AETHER: I haven't been there either.

MINNIE: Mapping it is.

AETHER: After we drop Tom, right?

Oh yeah.

She looked at Tom beside her, his gloved hands wrapped around the grab bar. "You want me to drop you at a specific farm?"

"I'm hiking in. Just follow Mapping to the new site and we'll find a good spot along the way without diverting."

"That's a lot of hiking," Minnie replied.

"That's the plan."

She cranked the lift grip, sending electrostatic force blasting the surrounding steam outward, and the skimmer shot upward from the encampment much faster than her squishy senses immediately perceived. 300m up, she cut the lift. Negative *g* woozed her head more than it already was, while her guts floated up into her chest.

"Wow," Tom choked as he linked a safety cable to his suit.

"Sorry. Meds." She held the skimmer there, waiting for Aether to catch up.

"You know, I can probably just walk it from here."

The snarkster Minnie treasured was still very much alive in there.

Aether floated up beside them wearing the expression Minnie expected.

AETHER: WTH was that?

MINNIE: Some sort of anomalous ionic interaction with the steam. Let's do this!

Minnie zoomed off northeastward as she opened a new M to Qin.

MINNIE: See you in 2 days, buddy! Don't burn down the camp while we're gone!

QIN: Now you tell me.

* * *

After dropping off Tom, Minnie and Aether paired their skimmers and chatted for much of the remaining hours to the permanent settlement. The dimpled fangs of Threck Country's thin alpine mountain range streaked by below, signaling the final countdown to arrival, so Aether took the helm, allowing Minnie focus time for reviewing her scripts.

A week earlier, Dowfwoss Unhkte, head of the Thinkers, set out with one of the supply convoys from the city, and was expected to arrive at "Syons City" this afternoon. During her scarce waking hours the past few days, Minnie had been rehearsing and refining what she'd say to Unhkte, plotting out layers and layers of branching threads depending on responses. It was strange relying on Aether's Threck expertise, but her input continued to prove eye-opening and essential.

Minnie's scratchnote list titled **My Bonehead Misses and F-ups** expanded each day. She was embarrassed, angry at herself, frustrated, and—when she didn't fight it—felt more than a little responsible for the tragedies that occurred prior to her arrival. Ish might've set the disaster ball in motion, but Minnie was pretty sure it'd rolled into her own blame court shortly thereafter. "Sea Threck," political structures, key phrases and gestures, "Country Threck," the nursery, and of course, most decisive of all: Threck evolution and *kee*.

Despite her own touted best practices and her obsession with scientific self-awareness, she'd fallen into the age-old trap of confirmatory memory. "Kee *seems to be a prefix and suffix denoting age, like preteen and teenager. Looks like pretty standard elements of a rite of passage out there in the woods … Done. Facts!*" What path might her research have taken had she deepened her focus on the *keepock* circle, and the nursery, and what they did with *Sootskee* who failed to pass conditioning? Evac protocol would've emphasized staying the hell away from Sea Threck, that's for sure. But it wasn't as though Aether and Qin had much choice when they landed …

It was exhausting to think about, and she eventually dismissed her every conclusion as self-soothing, self-punishment, or impossible to predict.

Aether steered the skimmers over the final chain of foothills, and Minnie spotted to her left the snaking Threck convoy marching and rolling over a recently established road. Dowfwoss Unhkte, and Minnie's formal introduction to the Thinkers, drew nearer still—a fantasy encounter she'd never expected fulfilled.

She tapped Aether's hand, and pointed to the distant caravan. Aether looked, nodded, and then directed Minnie's eyes forward, to the road's eventual end.

"Eff me," Minnie breathed. "How …?"

Ahead, the lowland's fuchsia and teal fungle came to an end where the shimmering ocean began, speckled whitecaps stretching off and fading toward the pronounced curvature of Epsy's horizon. But Aether and Minnie perceived only the astonishing scene at the two panoramas' meeting, where immense cream-colored structures emerged from the landscape.

As Aether descended for final approach, fine details rendered across the buildings, materials, and terrain. Slowing to land in an adjacent clearing, Minnie observed the Threck laborers busy at work, blurs of tentacles scurrying every which way. Their bodies moved with incredible speed, as if time had sped up by a factor of four. Teams of Makers linked to each other, forming ladders up the high stone walls, continuing a body chain that led all the way to a rock quarry across the dirt field. Large, prepared cubes coursed effortlessly down the line and up the walls, as Threck at the top joined with a separate procession, preparing and applying mortar between each block. It was no wonder the facilities superstructures appeared nearly complete.

Aether and Minnie left the skimmers behind, and strode across the freshly leveled field. The copper-toned topsoil smelled rich and fertile, a perfect foundation for the team's future farm.

"Are you not awed by this?" Minnie asked.

"Oh, I'm awed," Aether replied, "but not surprised. Makers are chosen for their tireless, self-driven natures. Believe it or not, every one of these laborers actually enjoys their work, and they're perfectionists. If something turned out to be wrong, like a misplaced brick at the bottom, they'd say 'let's tear it down and start again,' and everyone would agree, jumping right on it. I can't necessarily say the same of some of the other groups, but the cultures definitely appear to fit the roles. The council, for example. Evidently, *gridlock* is the optimal state for any governing body in the Galaxy."

Pablo waved from atop a debris hill at the end of the largest building (no doubt the future petroleum jelly production facility), and a direct connect request appeared in Minnie's fone. She accepted, and an M instantly popped up.

PABLO: Come around this way, please. Need a quick word before you see Zisa.

As they neared the lines and general bustle of Makers and Materials workers, individual laborers zipped by the pair without a sideways glance or acknowledgement, but even in the thickest body chaos, Minnie felt not a single tentacle graze her shoulder.

"What now?" Aether said when they reached the Threck chain conveying blocks from the quarry.

"Attention, please," Minnie called out in Threck.

Eyes hid and ogled, but the well-choreographed procession of massive cubes didn't slow a bit, each piece's heft always supported by three arms at any given point.

PABLO: Sorry, just keep walking, they'll work around you. You don't have to say anything.

Minnie peered between the whipping arms, and caught sight of a beckoning Pablo a short distance away. She shared a skeptical look with Aether.

"How's that sound to you, love?" Aether motioned to the Makers. "*This* ... working *around* you."

"Kind of seems like jumping between linked train cars. Each one of those blocks must be at least one hundred kilos."

Pablo suddenly appeared just beyond the line. "Watch me!"

He proceeded forward at a swift pace, and the nearest Threck instantly alerted the area.

LIVETRANS: Going up!
LIVETRANS: All up! Up with it!
LIVETRANS: Higher! Good! Clear!

Two of the laborers spread apart, creating a wide gap for Pablo, while two other helpers left the line and joined them at their sides—all four now maintaining the flow of stone slabs, now over a living bridge. Pablo walked right under without slowing, and took Aether's hand.

"Come on," he said with a grin. "Cool, right?"

Minnie followed them under the animated tentacle arch, and watched the workers return to their normal column.

Cool, sure, but was it right? It seemed jerkish, even if the Threck offered no negative reactions.

She paused on the other side and called out to them, "Thank you!" receiving only a couple glances.

She quickstepped to catch up with Aether and Pablo, on their way to the end of the last building.

Pablo halted and turned to them both, pointing down the row of structures. "PJ production and packaging here, the one-story after is the research labs, some storage, my sick bay, and I think an attached guest quarters, but she might've moved that to the side of our personal *apartment* building, which is the other two-story you see at the end there. And …" he nudged them a few steps to the right until a fourth structure in the distance came into view, nestled in beneath a pink foliage overhang, "that is the kitchen and dining facility, which she insists on calling the 'mess hall'. Oh, and that's only half of the frame. There'll be a big pergola extending out the front with plenty of outdoor seating. She wants to be sure we can accommodate larger visitor groups."

"This is fantastic," Aether said. "I just hope their leaders don't feel that Zisa's overstepping. The original agreement was for two structures."

He laughed. "It was the *leader's* idea! The top one, Artsh. She asked Zees where food preparation would take place. Zees tells her in our living building. Artsh goes 'You can't do that. Where shall we construct a separate food facility?' And you know Zees … 'Are you sure? We really don't want to put you out …'"

"Well, fantastic," Aether said. "It looks like everyone has gone far above and beyond what I would've ever imagined."

"So where is she?" Minnie asked Pablo. "You know I haven't seen her since the station."

Pablo furrowed his brow and huddled in close to Minnie. "Right, yes, that's the thing. That's what I wanted to talk to you about before you head around to the front."

"What? What'd I do?"

"No, nothing yet!" Pablo laughed nervously. "A little request is all! Just from me to you—she didn't say a word, trust me."

Minnie glared at him. "'Blo, you better say *something* before I—"

"Yeah yeah, see, I'm just saying—*asking*, I'm just asking—that you not make fun of her at all when you see her."

Zisa's PA boomed Livetrans somewhere around the corner. *"Eetensa! Sheh shoosh paykoss!"*

Minnie shook her head, a bit hurt. "I won't, okay." She moved to follow Zisa's PA-borne Threck voice, but Pablo put up his hands.

He blurted, "You know, not even in a playful ribbing kind of way. No backhanded compliments, or a quick look at me or Aether. She'll catch it."

Minnie's mouth hung open. "You think …? Seriously, Pab, am I *that* horrible of a person?"

He screwed up his face. "Of course not! No way! It's just, she's kind of like Zisa-times-three right now with the triple dose of estrogen. And … she had this idea … Just please don't say anything, I'm begging you. Don't even acknowledge it."

Minnie shared a look with Aether (who appeared equally perplexed), and then brushed past Pablo to finally see Zisa.

"Like that look just then," Pablo called after her. "None of that!"

Minnie rounded the corner and spotted Zisa up on a scaffolding platform a dozen meters away from the production building front. Her PA called more instructions to unseen workers on the roof, while she performed all of the associated gestures—and extremely well. Zisa was the dancer/gymnast of the group, but Minnie was no less shocked to see how gracefully she twisted and posed, even drawing a leg up behind her shoulder for a tense modifier that Minnie wouldn't even half-attempt on an empty stomach.

And then Minnie spotted what had Pablo in such a panic. Zisa had on some sort of prosthetic tentacles. Blue-green material began at her shoulders, tapered down her hidden arms, and extended down another full arm-length to her ankles. When she used her arms for a gesture, the fake tentacles whipped outward and trailed her arms, as one would expect.

"Zees!" Minnie called, and Pablo murmured close behind her.

"Begging you, Min …"

Zisa snapped out of her zone, dropping her *enhanced* arms to her sides, scanned … scanned, and spotted Minnie. Her eyes widened as hidden hands flew up to cover her mouth. "Omigod!"

Minnie grinned and ran toward the platform while Zisa made her way down a wide ladder on the far side. They met at the ladder's base and embraced, high-pitched squeals from both women.

Zisa bounced up and down for a second until Minnie stopped her. "Whoa there, easybake. No snow-globing the baby!"

They stepped back from each other, Zisa's chalk blue eyes alight. "Oops, yeah … So you heard."

"I heard." Minnie smiled wide and tenderly. "So happy for you. And you thought you'd never have one of those things!"

Zisa nodded. "Exactly! Or one of those!" She pointed to Pablo as he and Aether walked up, Zisa's tentacle flapping out and swinging around to whip her elbow. Suddenly remembering the faux appendage, she stuttered, "I … I made them out of some sheets … You know how some of the plurals require—"

"Yes, I do," Minnie replied. "And you're an effing genius! Are they velcroed at the shoulders?"

Uncertain, Zisa peeled back the top of one, revealing the Velcro.

"Like I said," Minnie enthused, "brilliant."

"I know they look loonish, but it really helps with comprehension, especially from a distance and when it's too noisy."

"I bet! Now you're on the hook to make me a set. And maybe when you're feeling extra frisky, you can design a pair with actuated mini-joints that link to Livetrans. I'm sure the EVs have enough parts you can salvage."

"O-M-G, I was totally thinking about that!" Zisa peeked over Minnie's head. "Hang on a sec." She composed something in Livetrans and sent it through her PA. Apparently, the workers on the roof were about to seal off a ventilation port. She hugged Minnie once more. "Sorry, I have to get back up there. They're super fast and efficient, but get caught up in patterns. And my basic design maps make zero sense to them, so everything's gotta be verbal."

Minnie let her go, turned, and squinted at Pablo. He mouthed "Thank you," and Minnie sighed. She still had work ahead of her, undoing a decade of bad behavior. Hopefully, with time, perceptions would evolve with her.

She walked with Aether alongside the building fronts, peering into open window spaces.

"That was great back there," Aether said. "I'm sure it meant a lot to her."

"Yeah, well, it was genuine. I wasn't just blowing smoke to make her feel good, or because Pablo asked me to be nice. Believe it or not, I *actually* missed her, and I *actually* appreciated her ideas."

"I know," Aether said. "And when I applaud you, it isn't a comparison to or condemnation of past incidents. I think you're carrying a mountain of guilt. We'll work on that—together if you're willing—just try not to project your internal judgment onto others."

"Mm-hmm. I didn't see Pablo begging *you* not to abuse his woman."

"That's because I only make fun of you. The rest of you have always had that jabbing-jibing repartee. I guarantee he'll say the same thing to Qin and, eventually, Tom."

Minnie hoped this was true. Her rearview mirror was indeed a bit concave at the moment, and every moment she recalled was mortifying. Regardless, she planned to embrace the very best parts of John in her future communications, and she was sickened by the very idea of exuding a hint of negativity to any member of her tiny, surviving family.

Threck voices from the roofs called out, announcing the supply convoy's arrival at the site. Workers from the Materials group streamed from the crowds, and headed toward the road.

Aether eyed Minnie. "You ready?"

"I've been ready for this moment since …" Minnie counted silently on her fingers. "… Nope. Still not ready."

* * *

Loaded carts and marching Threck filled the clearings on either side of the road's end, with still more flowing into the site. Aether and Minnie waited near Pablo's debris pile as a passenger cart split off from the convoy, and headed toward them. Minnie spotted three of the six-or-more passengers wearing the Thinkers' signature garb.

"Which one is Unhkte?"

"Can't say yet," Aether replied. "I should be able to tell after they get out."

Minnie skimmed through her opening statement one more time. She wondered how the head of the Thinkers would react to a human fluently speaking the language without Livetrans.

"In the middle," Aether murmured. "That's Unhkte."

"And the other two?"

"Not sure." Aether stepped forward as the three Thinkers approached.

Minnie trailed a pace behind her, just as the other two with Unhkte hung back at her sides.

Aether greeted them via Livetrans. "Welcome to Syons City."

"Thank you, Aether," Unhkte replied with formal flourish. "Are you satisfied with the pace of construction?"

"More than satisfied. We wouldn't have expected this amount of progress in ten times as many days." Unhkte's eyes rotated to Minnie, and Aether stepped back. "Dowfwoss Unhkte, I'm pleased to introduce you to Minnie, a very special Syons People who is here thanks to your benevolence."

The other two Thinkers eye-hid in sync, but Unhkte only fixed her gaze on Minnie and moved closer to her. "Thanks not to benevolence," Unhkte said as she perused Minnie's neck, chin, ears, hair, and facial features. "Persistence and astuteness. It's Aether who's deserving of thanks. Peaceful greetings, Minnie."

Minnie inhaled, relaxed her limbs, and proceeded without Livetrans. "Peaceful greetings to you, Dowfwoss Unhkte. My impassioned respect and admiration for you and every Thinker is only surpassed by my eternal gratitude for your aid. Like the members of your group, I study the underlying philosoph—"

Unhkte bowed her head forward and dipped her eyes just short of an actual hide—the Threck equivalent of raising a finger and saying *"Hold that thought."*

"Your words are warm," Unhkte said, "and your phrasing remarkable—admittedly superior to my own. However, the grating tenor of your vocalizations inspires only anguish and repulsion." She turned and consulted with her colleagues. Both expressed emphatic agreement.

"The sounds make me anxious," said one.

"I wish to hear more," the other concurred, "but never again in that way."

Minnie felt she might at any second explode with either vomit or laughter, and Aether's utter stillness beside her only made it worse. Minnie refused to look at her. There was no expression Aether could be wearing that wouldn't send Minnie into snorts.

Unhkte addressed Minnie again. "Are you able to use garb to speak, as Aether and the other Syons People do?"

She'd already activated her suit's PA, and opened Livetrans. "Yes, I can. My apologies for any damage to auditory receptacles. Better?"

Enthusiastic agreement from her audience.

"Significantly," Unhkte confirmed, and then instructed her associates to continue on to their tasks. After they'd left earshot, she continued, "Please, resume your lecture. Devoid of the punishing shrieks, your introduction portends stimulating and enjoyable discourse."

"Dowfwoss," Aether said before Minnie could respond. "I, too, have tasks to perform. Is it acceptable that I leave you two to your dialog?"

MINNIE: Abandoning ship before I further shame our species?

"This is acceptable," Unhkte replied.

Aether turned to Minnie. "No rush. I'll see you in a bit."

AETHER: You'll do amazing now, my love. Jumping off before you two shame my intelligence. Winks n kisses.

Minnie and Unhkte strolled away from the hubbub while Minnie repeated her introduction, continuing all the way through her comparison of several Earth philosophers, and their ideas, to notable Threck precepts. Riveted, Unhkte shared updates to many of the theories Minnie had brought up—Thinker concepts having expanded and merged since Minnie's most recent data.

It wasn't lost on Minnie, the fact that she had to draw parallels from over 3,000 years of human philosophy to only 159 Epsy years. Less than that! The Thinkers wouldn't have been around in those early years, when Eshkowoss Peekt was raising the first generations of young Threck.

"How long have there been Thinkers?" Minnie asked.

"Formally?"

Minnie signed affirmative.

"Ninety-two."

Ninety-two years! Where will they be in another century?

Unhkte halted where leveled soil met the beach sand. "This is irregular pace from your reference point, is it not? Tom and Aether appeared concerned upon learning of our civilization's maturity."

"No, not concerned. *Surprised.* And, yes, it's been highly accelerated compared to my people's pace." Minnie nodded skyward.

"You *are* from the stars."

Oops.

Minnie floundered, "We're from … a great distance away."

"Indeed. No greater distance than the stars. I wonder … Syons People could see us from the stars, yet we study the stars for years and see only the pattern map. If it was night, could you look up and see your home right now?"

"No," Minnie said. "Our home was destroyed. It no longer exists."

"I see," Unhkte signed, and then gazed off to the construction flurry and the parked skimmers. After a quiet moment she spoke again, but with a peculiar, deliberate cadence. "We have much to learn from you."

Minnie didn't respond right away. She didn't wish to think about Epsy's human population's expiration date. The Threck council worried about Syons People eventually spreading across their land, but this seemed an unlikely future. Perhaps Zisa and Pablo's child would be joined by another Epsy-born human … from *somewhere*, and then those two would have children. But then what?

Unhkte went on, "I don't refer to your technology, if you are concerned. Threck are curious about that which we don't understand, but we are also wary of those things we did not ourselves create. No, I refer to your moderation, your *pace*."

"You think your people need to slow down?"

"Absolutely. Observe those Makers, moving like the unhindered river. They will have your facilities completed in two more days, at the most. And then they will move on to the next project—the next bend in the river—and then the next, but to what end? Every watercourse either splits, spreads, and fades away, disappearing into the soil, or it flows to its inevitable end, and merges into the ocean, no longer a river at all."

"This is fitting analogy for Syons People, too. We're this tiny creek, split off from a great river, and we will, indeed, disappear into your soil."

"Your appropriation of my analogy is much more disturbing than its intended meaning."

"Apologies. You made me think of time and the importance of pace. Perhaps Syons People can further slow our pace, extending our time here."

Humanity's clock on Epsilon C might've been ticking away, but every moment Minnie lived now felt like a bonus, extended-play extra life. And her team—her family—were only refugees here. It wasn't as though they were Earth's last survivors, and trying to reestablish the species.

Minnie's body buzzed, suddenly finding herself vividly *present* in this moment, savoring every word they shared, every thought inspired, as well as other sensory input, from the ocean's scent, to the translucency and texture of Unhkte's skin. The nagging itch behind her ear where cellcream was busy finalizing Pablo's repair job. Resounding *pings* and *tinks* from the quarry. Zisa's PA relaying instructions in the distance. Aether—somewhere nearby, safe, and apparently in love with Minnie, despite the contrary wisdom of imaginary voices. And this new friend, Unhkte, with whom she foresaw decades of inspiring conversation. She was hopeful and curious about how long such a relationship would last, and if she'd one day realize, in the middle of such a discussion, that the point had just then been reached where Unhkte and her people surpassed two million years of human evolution.

"I wonder," Unhkte said, "if some time we could speak again like this."

Minnie grinned. "I was wondering the same thing."

"I wonder if we could continue speaking right now."

"I'm free until supper," Minnie said, and glanced back at the sun. "Ten gaps, at least."

She motioned behind Unhkte to a pair of rounded-top rocks. A moment later, she sat down on one of the rocks and watched as Unhkte draped her cloak over the other, coiling her legs beneath her to match Minnie's seated height.

Unhkte faced Minnie and said, "One's time is their greatest gift to another."

Minnie replied, "Well then I thank you for this gift."

*

EPILOGUE

Magnified through a biotherm optic, a parasitic worm clings to a brain's limbic cortex, two rows of tiny barbed appendages anchoring the creature to the organ. When the host moves, the parasite writhes subtly. A horror scene.

Zooming out from the brain, outside the host creature's body cavity, sits an intelligent lifeform—a distinguished member of her society and the head of her civilization's revered assembly of philosophers—gazing with wonder at a rapidly growing construction site, a symbol of her people's incredible progress. A scene of accelerated evolution.

Floating upward to a bird's-eye view, the leader exchanges ideas with another intelligent lifeform—a distinguished member of a different society, recently rescued from a dangerous land. A scene of peace, optimism, and potential.

Zooming out again, beyond the bustling construction site, and across an ocean to another land, the view descends on a shaded patch of coastal vegetation, and a frenzied pack of massive predators ripping plants from the soil. As they claw at the entrance to their prey's burrow, a red cloud of disturbed fungus spores drifts about, sticking to the beasts' mouths, and flowing into their windpipes. Another scene of potential.

And finally, zooming out once more, past the clouds, past an orbiting debris field in the thermosphere, the planet shrinks from a globe, to a ball, to a speck, to nothing. Zooming out farther still, farther, and further.

Acknowledgements

Editing services provided by the keen eyes and intellect of Kristina Circelli from Red Road Editing. As always, these stories would be nothing without my growing list of amazing beta readers: Alyssa W, Angela P (with additional proofing), Bill H, Bill R, DeeDee B, Eric D, Jessica B, Joe S, Karen L, Laura B, Laurie J, Lori W, Pascal B, Scott K, Stacey L, Venture C, and Vicky W—thank you all! Thank you to Audrey Collins for her probably accurate suggestion of a potential future for popular music. Andreas Raninger and Matthias de Muylder for their brilliant concept art, releasing the stuff in my head, and making it all realer (yes, realer). Further thanks must be flung to Hugh Howey, John Chiu, Mary Roach, Jon Reiner, Eugene Mallove, Gregory Matloff, Kevin Fong, M.D., everyone else who took the time to answer one or more of my silly questions over the past two years, and, of course, my wife, Ana, for all she does, and all she puts up with.

Front cover art by the brilliant Andreas Raninger. Back cover art by the brilliant Matthias de Muylder.

About the Author

Michael Siemsen lives in Northern California with his wife, three kids, dog Brody, cat Atom, several fish, two chupacabrii, and one pesky demon. He continues, as we speak, to spill his guts for your entertainment.

Connect:
facebook.com/mcsiemsen
michaelsiemsen.com
twitter: @michaelsiemsen
mail@michaelsiemsen.com

Also by Michael Siemsen:

A Warm Place to Call Home (a demon's story)
The Many Lives of Samuel Beauchamp (a demon's story)
The Dig (Book 1 of the Matt Turner Series)
The Opal (Book 2 of the Matt Turner Series)
Return (Book 3 of the Matt Turner Series)

CPSIA information can be obtained
at www.ICGtesting.com
Printed in the USA
LVOW11s1024190717
541880LV00001B/90/P